THE DOOM LOOP SYSTEM

DORY HOLLANDER, Ph.D.

T·H·E

DOOM LOOP SYSTEM

SYSTEM

A Step-by-Step Guide to Career Mastery

VIKING

VIKING
Published by the Penguin Group
Viking Penguin, a division of Penguin Books USA Inc.,
375 Hudson Street, New York, New York 10014, U.S.A.
Penguin Books Ltd. 27 Wrights Lane,
London W8 5TZ, England
Penguin Books Australia Ltd, Ringwood,
Victoria, Australia
Penguin Books Canada Ltd, 10 Alcorn Avenue, Suite 300,
Toronto, Ontario, Canada M4V 3B2
Penguin Books (N.Z.) Ltd, 182–190 Wairau Road,
Auckland 10, New Zealand

Penguin Books Ltd, Registered Offices:
Harmondsworth, Middlesex, England

First published in 1991 by Viking Penguin,
a division of Penguin Books USA Inc.

1 3 5 7 9 10 8 6 4 2

LIBRARY OF CONGRESS CATALOGING IN PUBLICATION DATA
Hollander, Dory.
The doom loop system / Dory Hollander.
p.   cm.
Includes index.
ISBN 0-670-84229-X
1. Career changes.   2. Career development.   I. Title.
HF5384.H64   1991
650.14—dc20   91-50315

Printed in the United States of America
Set in Baskerville
Designed by Victoria Hartman

AUTHOR'S NOTE

As you read the examples and cases in this book, you may wonder whether they reflect real people and true situations. The answer is yes and no. The issues and the dynamics are real; the names and actual situations are not. I have made some changes and occasionally combined information from individuals who shared similar stories to maintain the privacy of those involved.

For my clients, who have been my teachers,
and for all of us who work

ACKNOWLEDGMENTS

We all need a little help. You know—a brain to pick, a shoulder to lean on, and whatever else it takes. So here goes.

First—the brains to pick. In the course of my education as a psychologist, I have benefited and learned from the work of many professionals in psychology and organizational development. Their theories, research, and ideas have contributed to my thinking and to the underpinnings of this book. Specifically the studies and writings of Daniel Levinson in adult development, David McClelland in achievement motivation, Kurt Lewin in organizational psychology, John Holland in career development, and Isabel Briggs Myers in psychological type have deepened my understanding of how we approach work, organizations, and change in our adult years.

Next—the shoulders to lean on. Here I had help from my friends. Even though I enjoyed writing this book, I wrote *The Doom Loop System* during times that made me especially sensitive to the bonds of friendship. To those friends, colleagues, and clients who kept track of my progress and me as I commuted back and forth from the village of Cambria, California, where I lived and wrote, to the heartland of St. Louis, where I work, my message is simple: your support was vital.

You know who you are, but I would like to single out a few of you for special accolades:

Janice Galka for her ability to get to the heart of things.

Richard and Bonnie Polinsky for good company and a lion's share of commiserating through two years of writing and growing pains.

Bruce Wexler, who began as my agent and outside editor and became my friend, for helping me rediscover simple English sentences and for uncommonly good sense.

Dawn Drzal, my Viking editor, who is speeding along the Doom Loop's Quadrant I to II path, for her fresh vision and faith in *The Doom Loop System*'s success.

Last—whatever else it takes. I would be remiss if I didn't acknowledge a few other key players, notably Charles C. Jett who created the concept of the Doom Loop and who first sparked my interest in the Loop in 1985 when I met him at the American Psychological Association in Los Angeles where he presented a symposium paper on the Doom Loop. I also want to thank in print: my former spouse, and friend of three decades, Jerry Blumoff, for usual and unusual dedication; my friend and colleague Fred Nader for weathering two years of Doom Loop evolution, and for sticking around until the book was done; and my good friend and fellow writer George Salamon for making me laugh even while in the throes of last-minute editing.

Have I left anyone out? Sure. Just ask Sam Blumoff and Rebecca Hollander-Blumoff. They will tell you they have stood by their mother and made it all possible. And of course they are right.

CONTENTS

THE DOOM LOOP SYSTEM

CHAPTER 1

The Doom Loop

When I first came across the Doom Loop in the summer of 1985, I was intrigued. Here in a disarmingly simple form —a half-loop plotted on a two-by-two matrix—was a powerful career management tool that resembled nothing I had seen before. Somehow this matrix created an instant mirror and self-assessment tool that encouraged people to view their past, present, and future jobs with new, sometimes startling insight.

I am an organizational psychologist and career coach. My clients tend to be bright, motivated people who are discontented with their careers. The seemingly elusive goal they seek is a more fulfilling work life. In the Doom Loop I sensed the potential for a remarkable shortcut to that end—one that also promised to be fun to use. Part of the Doom Loop's appeal was that it could be tailored to benefit nearly anyone— whether that person was just beginning a career, was suffering from a bad case of midcareer blahs, or had recently been spewed into the swelling ranks of the unemployed; whether he or she was a banker, a secretary, or a rocket scientist.

Helping people effect positive career change is my business. And the Doom Loop, despite its ominous name, had possibilities.

In the coming years I would witness similar "aha" reactions from all kinds of people—students, professionals, small-business owners, executives, entertainers, military personnel, office workers, and technicians. What these people had in common was a keen desire to find happiness in their work. Merely grasping the Doom Loop's simple concept seemed to help many of them get a better grip on what they had to do to avoid or resolve career crises, and to steer themselves toward more satisfying career paths.

What is the Doom Loop and where did it come from? To answer that question, let's go back to 1978 and the Harvard Business School.

THE GENESIS

Charles Jett is a leading career management consultant. In the spring of 1978 he was in Cambridge, conducting interviews with the latest batch of hopeful, eager Harvard MBAs, many casting longing eyes in the direction of management consulting jobs. As Charlie tells the story, after a long day of interviewing, the last candidate appeared. After a few minutes of talking to him, Charlie could see that this young man was not cut out for a consulting career, despite his aspirations. Charlie decided it would be an act of mercy to convince him that a consulting career was a disaster waiting to happen.

When the young man started talking about a matrix approach to strategic planning—an approach that was then very much in vogue—Charlie decided to fight fire with fire. He would use this same matrix approach to convince the young MBA that consulting just wasn't in the cards for him.

He began by asking the young man to list ten basic consulting skills that a consultant would need to acquire during the first few years on the job. The young man thought about what he had learned in his basic business courses that might apply to consulting, and about the consulting jobs that two of his professors had described to him. He realized he would have to interview a variety of consultants in some depth to figure out what the basic ten skills might be, but being bright and eager to please, he still took a stab at it. And his impromptu list of consulting skills turned out to be reasonably accurate. It included proposal writing, fact-finding, problem identification, interviewing, analysis, drawing conclusions, writing reports, making recommendations, and a few other skills.

Charlie then requested that the young MBA rate himself along the following lines: whether he liked or disliked those skills and whether or not he was any good at them.

After going through the list, the young MBA decided he wasn't really very good at any of the skills, primarily because he had never had any job experience that required them. Still, that didn't seem to faze him. After all, as an ambitious new MBA in search of the right fast track, he certainly wasn't afraid of hard work and learning. It did, however, make him wonder out loud at the sheer magnitude of work and learning a consulting job would entail.

When he rated the skills he "liked" and "didn't like," the new graduate said he didn't like two critical areas: writing and analysis. There were a few others he wasn't over-enthusiastic about, either. What he did like was the people contact: interviewing and making recommendations.

He and Charlie plotted his ratings of all the skills he had listed on the following matrix. They then used the following matrix to plot the ratings of all the identified skills.

	LIKE	DON'T LIKE
GOOD AT	QUADRANT II	QUADRANT III
NOT GOOD AT	QUADRANT I	QUADRANT IV

Then Charlie asked the aspiring consultant to analyze each of the four quadrants in the matrix by answering a simple question: "How would you feel if most of the skills of your job clustered here?" They started with Quadrant I.

	LIKE	DON'T LIKE
GOOD AT	Happy Satisfied QUADRANT II	Frustrated Bored QUADRANT III
NOT GOOD AT	Anxious Challenged Uptight QUADRANT I	Unhappy Miserable QUADRANT IV

Here is an approximate reconstruction of what the graduate said:

• **Quadrant I**—If he were doing something he liked that he was not yet good at, he would feel challenged, but it could be a mixed bag. He might feel pretty insecure about his performance and about hanging on to his job. On the other hand, even though he might be uptight and anxious, he decided that these feelings might not be all bad. In fact, they might motivate him to learn more quickly.

• **Quadrant II**—If he were doing something that required skills he was good at and liked, he would probably feel happy and satisfied. Why not? Wouldn't anyone?

• **Quadrant III**—If he had the skills to do the job well, but didn't like most of them, he would feel frustrated and bored. He'd had enough classes like that. A job in this quadrant was totally unappealing to him.

• **Quadrant IV**—If he found himself working at a job that he neither liked nor was good at, then he would probably be extremely unhappy and would look for an immediate change of scenery. He certainly wouldn't choose a job in this quadrant.

It was a simple and obvious exercise, permitting straightforward conclusions. But, in fact, when the MBA plotted his ratings for the ten consulting skills he had listed, he saw that most of them clustered in Quadrant IV. He thought a minute; then his eyes lit up. It was a revelation. "Okay," he said. "I get it! If I go into consulting, the odds are that I won't like most of the skills involved and I won't be particularly good at them, either. So I've been interviewing for the nightmare job without knowing it. I guess I'd better rethink my career choice, and find something that capitalizes on what I like. Something like working in the sales and marketing end of a business using people skills—right?"

Without any browbeating, the matrix had helped him see for the first time that consulting might not be the right career for him. But instead of feeling bad about it, he walked away feeling relieved, ready to try something more promising, more satisfying, that fit his own particular pattern of likes.

After the young man left, Charlie studied the matrix. He was stunned. In his many years as a consultant, he'd often tried to convince people to change careers they obviously weren't cut out for. It was no easy task. Yet the matrix had achieved that objective almost instantly. It was enough to deter a determined and strong-willed MBA from blindly making a poor choice.

How else could the matrix be used? Charlie found out when he met the president of a large Midwestern university who faced an altogether different career crisis.

DOOMED

Richard Keefer had served successfully as a university president for ten years. Though he had been enthusiastic about his job early on, he gradually found himself becoming bored and distracted. A robust man in his mid-fifties, he figured he still had enough good years left to try another career. But what would he do? Where could he go? To another school? To a different type of institution? Back to a professorial or departmental chairperson's slot? To something altogether new? His crystal ball was cloudy. Nothing really excited him.

Charlie trotted out the matrix. He wasn't sure it would work. After all, Keefer was a seasoned professional who was set in his ways. Any way you viewed it, his situation was substantially different from the young MBA's.

Richard Keefer had been elevated to the rank of full professor at thirty-five. Three years later he was appointed college dean. He became a university president in his early forties. In his first years as president, he was understandably anxious about proving himself on the job. He was challenged, sometimes even overwhelmed, by the job's ever-expanding demands. Though being a university president was his capstone—the long-range goal that represents personal career success—he didn't possess enough of the skills that were necessary to succeed in his capstone—skills like jousting with the state legislature for funds and dealing with the escalating demands of departmental fiefdoms.

But he loved the challenges and possibilities the position offered. And the prestige and the trappings that came with the job sweetened the pot. So he pushed hard and eventually acquired the skills necessary to perform effectively. He established a track record for himself by helping the school successfully weather a few serious financial storms and a particularly rending tenure dispute.

In time, Richard Keefer settled into his role. And why not? He was happy, successful, and skilled. After a number of years in the job, however, Richard began to stagnate. He began to feel inexplicably bored with the daily tasks of running a university. Little things began to irritate him, and he found himself oscillating between frustration and apathy. He was tired of grappling with cigar-smoking politicians for tax dollars and weary of going to the same old parties and fund-raisers year after year. The campus press labeled him the "old man," and on his fifty-third birthday, after ten years on the job, he felt like one.

At the annual faculty meeting a particularly outspoken critic suggested that Richard had exceeded the life cycle of his job. Things were taking a downturn. Richard complained to Charlie, "I'm doomed if I keep doing what I've been doing."

Doomed. The word would stick in Charlie's mind.

Charlie helped Richard examine his career progression through the matrix's perspective. Looking at the quadrants, there was no denying that his career as a university president had slowly progressed from Quadrant I to II to III. He had taken on the presidency in Quadrant I, liking the skills involved but still having to acquire the whole array of proficiencies required to be an expert administrator. Over time he mastered the skills demanded of a university president. Then, to his amazement and eventual chagrin, he found that performing these skills well in a stable and prestigious job often as not bored and irritated him. Though Richard intuitively knew that something was wrong, he couldn't get a handle on it. He wondered if perhaps the problem was in him.

When he saw his career progression through the matrix's windows, the light poured in. He was bored and frustrated because he had mastered nearly all the skills his job required. What he needed was the challenge of new learning: it was time for a change. The "aha" experience for Richard Keefer was that he was ensconced in Quadrant III of the matrix.

To help Richard make the right change, Charlie asked him about the skills he used in his job that he liked—skills that could return him to Quadrant I or II of the matrix. Richard was thoughtful. He considered the various skills required in a typical week's work. A pattern emerged. His Quadrant I and II skills involved dealing with academics, mingling with important people, working toward culturally significant goals, and providing an educational experience. His Quadrant IV skills involved dealing with faculty grievances, university politics, and classroom teaching.

Given his likes and dislikes and the skills he possessed, Charlie suggested that Richard might search for a job as head of a cultural institution. Such a job would recycle the university president into Quadrant I, providing him with renewed energy and fresh challenges.

The following fall, Richard Keefer accepted an offer to

head a prestigious historical society. He called Charlie after a year on the job and exulted, "I'm back in Quadrant I and I love it!"

THE LOOP

Charlie was impressed. Thinking about Richard Keefer's progression through the matrix's quadrants, it occurred to him that a pattern actually showed up over time—a pattern that might apply not only to Keefer's career, but to anyone's.

	LIKE	DON'T LIKE
GOOD AT	**Satisfied** t_2 QUADRANT II	QUADRANT III
NOT GOOD AT	t_1 **Anxious** QUADRANT I	QUADRANT IV

For example, suppose an individual starts working at time "t-1." This person is in a position she likes, but she still has a lot to learn. At "t-1" the concentration of required job skills (plotted as points on the matrix) is primarily in Quadrant I. Now suppose that several months or even a year later, this person takes a second measurement. She rates the skills of her job according to whether or not she likes them and whether or not she is good at them. She finds that some things have changed. Now, at time "t-2," the concentration of points has moved upward and slightly to the right, into Quadrant II.

This movement takes place because the person has the ability and motivation to learn (upward matrix movement) and has gained greater mastery. But other movement takes place because daily repetition of the same skill knocks some of the fun and challenge out of the job (movement to the right). Still, the bottom line is that this person has become more competent over time and feels genuinely happy and satisfied with her work.

Now, suppose more time passes, and this person takes another measurement at time "t-3." Now the concentration of her job skills (plotted as points) has moved farther to the right and has ceased moving upward. What's happened? In Quadrant III this person has reached the top of her learning curve, mastering all the requisite skills. Yet this is the very same job that once caused excitement and satisfaction. Boredom and frustration have set in, not because the skills are inherently dull, but because they've been repeated ad nauseam. Unchanging job content, paired with decreased challenge, will guarantee nearly anyone's eventual arrival in Quadrant III.

	LIKE	DON'T LIKE
GOOD AT	Satisfied t_2 QUADRANT II	Frustrated/Bored t_3 QUADRANT III
NOT GOOD AT	t_1 Anxious QUADRANT I	QUADRANT IV

Unfortunately, the process doesn't stop there. Staying in any job too long can ensure downward movement into Quadrant IV. Here an individual loses interest in the job, failing to keep up with changes in the field, new technologies, and competitors' advances. Motivation flags; performance plateaus. At the "t-4" measurement, the person not only doesn't like what she is doing, but her skills have actually diminished through neglect and lassitude. She has unwittingly tumbled into Quadrant IV.

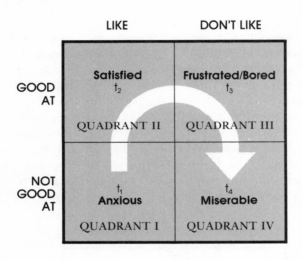

As you can see, this progression through the quadrants forms a half-loop. Anyone who stays in the same job long enough, repeating the same old skills day in and day out, is *doomed* to ride the loop. If you're not learning new skills, the excitement and challenge will eventually vanish along with your enthusiasm. If you have the capacity to learn—and the learning stops between "t-2" and "t-3"—you'll ride the downside of the Doom Loop into Quadrants III and IV.

Almost everyone experiences the Doom Loop in one job or another at some time in his or her career. It's not that people intentionally choose this outcome or want to be doomed in their work. Quite the contrary. Most of us long to be happy and satisfied in our livelihoods. But it's been drummed into our heads that career advances depend on our experience, longevity, and staying power. When economic conditions tighten, fear and job insecurity worsen this tendency. We develop a recession mentality. We think security rather than challenge and growth. We fear that changing jobs, even hated ones, will leave us stranded on the curb, put us in serious career jeopardy, or label us "job hoppers." So instead we keep our noses to the grindstone, failing to look up and see what else is out there after we've mastered a job's skills. We feel secure but bored. We wish we enjoyed our work more, but have made an uneasy peace with what we have chosen to call reality. The learning stops, career crises develop, and we make poor career decisions.

Perhaps we need a new framework for thinking about our careers that works in every economic climate and that puts us in greater charge of our own career outcomes.

LEARNING HOW TO USE THE LOOP

In 1986, Charlie Jett asked me to help develop and expand the concept of the Doom Loop. The result was the creation of a series of career management strategies and tactics that revolved around the Loop. These strategies and tactics applied in one aspect or another to virtually every career situation we had encountered—from identifying the ideal first job to planning the ideal career capstone position, from managing a traumatic life crisis like being fired to evaluating an enticing midcareer opportunity.

The uninterrupted progression of the Doom Loop shows one all too common career outcome among many possible ones. We tackled the problem of how people could halt or reverse this process and avoid plateauing in Quadrant III and bottoming out in Quadrant IV. We found that the first step was simply being aware that Doom Loops happen. Once people saw the matrix and plotted their own career course through the quadrants, many of their long-held myths and assumptions about careers began to fade. Seeing their own career progression through the perspective of the matrix allowed them to stop blaming themselves for feeling unhappy in their lackluster jobs and to take a fresh, upbeat approach in their next round of career decision-making.

With Charlie's encouragement and my own interest in helping people become better career managers, I continued to develop the Loop. In my work with bright, competent people who are unhappy, bored, or derailed in their careers and who want something better for themselves, it made sense to explore how the Doom Loop might provide insight and the impetus for positive change.

I realized that people in the thick of numbing career decisions could use the Doom Loop as a shortcut to clearing away some of their confusion and seeing how a particular career move fits the bigger picture. Perhaps the idea of the Doom Loop would jolt people in the midst of serious career crises into making better sense of what was happening to them and reversing the trend line.

I distilled from the Doom Loop a few basic operating principles:

- Liking or not liking the skills of a job can make or break our career satisfaction—no matter how prestigious or remunerative that job may be.
- Ongoing learning and challenge in a job are the life and breadth of sustained career interest.
- Goals that fit our individual preferences, personalities, and ideals will motivate us and accelerate our competence.
- Competence in a job is rarely sufficient to ensure or maintain work satisfaction.
- We can expect to change and develop over time, and we need to plan for this by seeking and designing jobs that keep pace with who we are.
- No matter what else is going on in the world, we are still in charge of the way our own career paths develop and change.
- Careers, like family and personal life, are a critical arena where our identity and self-esteem are put to the test.

Because our careers are important to who we are and who we become, successful career management involves much more than choosing an occupation and moving up its ranks;

it involves the construction of a meaningful life against an ever-changing backdrop.

When I compared these premises with what I knew about adult development and career decision-making, I found a match. Using the Doom Loop reinforced the importance of staying excited about work and learning. People would find it hard to consider the progression of the Loop without factoring in the need to keep adapting to change.

Though I was encouraged by people's initial reactions, I realized I had to use the Doom Loop more extensively. Could a half-loop and a matrix really help empower people to change their approach to work? I decided to gather case data by applying the Doom Loop to various career situations and exploring what it revealed from career and psychological standpoints.

In the following years, I incorporated the Doom Loop into my work with more than five hundred clients of different ages facing different career dilemmas—as well as in seminars with thousands of participants. They were company presidents, accountants, lawyers, engineers, artists, teachers, sales clerks, waiters, architects . . . you name it. But whether they were recent graduates, downsized top executives, seasoned professionals, or homemakers returning to the labor force, they shared the desire to find satisfying work. I added the Doom Loop to my little black box, along with traditional career coaching and psychological profiling, and tracked what happened. In addition, I used Doom Loop principles with hundreds of executives, managers, and business owners to help them rethink how to motivate and develop their employees.

The results were fascinating. The Doom Loop pushed people to look at challenging Quadrant I options they hadn't considered before. Using Doom Loop principles, many set bold new courses for negotiating troubled career waters. The Loop gave them a new language and framework for understanding their careers. Most people immediately identified with the message of the Loop. They understood the journey into Quadrant III all too well. Time and time again, the Loop produced new insight. As soon as they grasped its concept, many clients would announce, "That's me in Quadrant III."

It was a freeing "aha" experience. Suddenly people grasped a hidden reality behind their career choices. They saw that sticking with a job, whether or not they liked it, along with reluctance to apply for jobs where they weren't already experts, had inadvertently sent them over the top of the Loop. The lesson of the Loop was helping people peel away another layer of illusion.

One Quadrant III marketing executive told me, "For the first time I can actually understand what happened to me. I can stop feeling like a dumb failure for not loving this great-paying job I feel buried in. I can stop trying to prove myself; I can move on with my life. What a relief! There's nothing wrong with me. Why didn't someone show me this years ago?"

The Doom Loop reassures. It has a logic that helps free people from guilt over not liking their dull jobs. But that's not all. People like the way the Loop helps them rethink their past, present, and future career choices.

It gives them a new way to frame what has happened to them and what they need to do next. The Doom Loop is so simple that they can draw it on a napkin and explain it to a friend or coworker over a cup of coffee. Word spread as they used it to explain their situation to their spouses, their friends at work, and their bosses.

With wonderfully rich input from my clients, students, and colleagues, and through presentations to various business, trade, and professional associations, I expanded the Doom Loop's applications. I developed inventories, checklists, diagnostic exercises, skill assessment profiles, workbooks, and other methods that helped people and people managers pay better attention to individual preferences and adapt the principles of the Doom Loop to their own career and company needs.

THE FINISHED PRODUCT

I'm not sure any product is ever truly finished, but gradually it did come together. The Doom Loop meshed with much of what organizational psychologists and good managers already know about enhancing motivation, productivity, and satisfaction in the workplace.

The Loop can play an instructive role in helping people understand how to self-direct and redirect their own careers, to choose energizing, ideal future jobs—"career capstones"— that will set a course for new professional growth.

It works as a diagnostic tool for pinpointing where people are at any given time in their career journeys. By helping people become more conscious of what they're doing, the Loop sparks insight and new decisions that lead them out of the career doldrums and empower them to change.

It also functions as a lens for viewing and analyzing specific job options, helping people select positions that push them to keep developing and to turn down or leave jobs that don't.

In short, the Doom Loop seamlessly joins preference with performance. This is no trivial feat. As a psychologist and career coach, I've watched a single-minded obsession with competence trap people in stifling jobs and divert them from promising careers. I get tired of hearing bright, talented people ask, "Am I any good at this?" without considering whether or not they enjoy the skills involved, or whether the work is worth pursuing over the long haul. As one unhappy Quadrant III computer analyst told me, "This is my operating system: if you're not good at something, don't try it, don't want it, don't do it." No wonder he felt stuck.

In fact, the tyranny of competence is so pervasive that many professionals lose perspective. Even when they are abjectly unhappy in their careers, they continue to believe that they should like anything they are good at. This shortsighted attitude prematurely pushes these intelligent, achieving people into Quadrant III, where they chafe and languish, afraid to let go of their expertise and take the risks necessary to find the exciting career path they deserve. As one young physician put it, "My specialty? Being unhappy at what I'm good at."

Typically this is how it happens. If Pat is terrific with numbers, standard career wisdom requires that Pat consider something mathematical. So well-meaning advisers funnel young Pat into an accounting track. Never mind that Pat can't stand the routine skills required to succeed in this job. Eventually the plan backfires. Ignoring preferences plunges most people into a motivational backwater after the first few years. Pat learns the hard way that competence alone doesn't produce satisfaction. She begins to feel trapped in a career she doesn't like. Eventually her irrepressible creative problem-solving begins to get her into regulatory hot water. She needs to change to a career where her creativity will be an asset rather than a liability.

The Doom Loop emphasizes the importance of climbing a steep learning curve firmly grounded in what you enjoy. Your preferences, passions, and predilections become important predictors of how satisfied you will feel in your work. The Loop forces you to identify the skills you actually enjoy performing so that you can plug them into a career management strategy that gives you plenty of stretch space. Because preference is a powerful wellspring of motivation, working hard to improve skills you enjoy but haven't yet mastered invigorates. When you're mastering skills you enjoy, your job expresses your personal as well as your professional identity.

Of course, competence is important, especially from an employer's viewpoint. But managers need to remember that competence without a strong underlay of personal preference is as likely to produce mediocrity as excellence. The Doom Loop helps put competence in perspective to create a more balanced and personally fulfilling approach to work life.

The Doom Loop shows you that it's okay—even desirable —to recycle into Quadrant I, the learner's quadrant; that Quadrant II, the high-competence, high-satisfaction quadrant, is a place to climb to time and time again, rather than a place to land, roost, and slumber. I've seen the Doom Loop's principles catalyze talented but lethargic professionals into leaving their boring Quadrant III jobs for exciting new ones. For the first time in years these people were following their own needs and feelings, not someone else's.

As you read on, you will find the return to Quadrant I to be a continuing source of career renewal. Whenever you face a career crisis or seek change, you will be well advised to consider your Quadrant I options.

In the following chapters, I'll show you how to use the Doom Loop as a decision-making tool and as part of a larger career management strategy. The next three chapters lay out the nuts and bolts of using the Doom Loop, so you'll want to read them carefully. First, we'll look at choosing a career capstone, so that you'll know where you're heading. Then I'll show you how to develop your personal operating plan—your target mosaic. With a capstone and a target mosaic in place, you'll be ready to learn how to apply the principles of the Doom Loop to making career decisions that put you in the driver's seat. We'll also use the Doom Loop as the framework for analyzing and overcoming six common career crises you may face at various points in your work life. No matter what your job is, no matter the stage of your career or the particular crisis you are weathering, being aware of the Doom Loop can change the way you think about your career options and help you assess the risks involved in building new work skills. Once you get the hang of it, you can use the principles of the Loop to combine your quest for greater work satisfaction with greater career success.

All I ask is that in the pages ahead you consider this career management approach with an open mind. If you've been waiting for other people to discover your worth and take over the care and management of your career, this book offers you an altogether different option. You don't have to wait. You don't even have to stay in a job until it gets so bad you can't stand it. You can redesign your career at will. Any time— even today. Even when the economy takes a downturn or gets hit with a major recession, you can still apply the principles of the Doom Loop to tinker with your job description and combat work stagnation and discontent. You deserve that. Besides, when times get tough, people who keep developing their skills and stay motivated by their work will have the competitive edge.

Sure, career change is much riskier than staying put in the same old job. Identifying what you want and achieving it take effort and determination. But taking the risk also offers you a chance to take charge, to express who you are in the workplace, and to develop yourself according to your own agenda.

Some of the ideas presented in the chapters ahead may rattle a few of your assumptions. They will challenge pervasive but out-of-date myths about career advancement and management that are no longer working for you or anybody else in today's rapidly changing world. Remember that what isn't out of date may just be wrong—an unfortunate amalgam of half-truths and wishful thinking that will land you and keep you in Quadrant III or worse.

Besides, no one really stays put in a job anyway. Even if you don't leave or get escorted out, you will experience subjective movement over time—generally from being more challenged and satisfied to being less challenged and less satisfied. What would happen if you used the Doom Loop to stop that process and to put your own career progress and satisfaction on a well-tended front burner?

Of course, the Doom Loop is no panacea. It is just a simple model that brings together a few good ideas that open the way to new insight. How you use that insight is still up to you. But if you are ready to try something new, it could give you just the thrust you need to plan small, manageable changes that will get your career moving in the right direction.

CHAPTER 2

Capstone Power

If you could have any job, what would it be?

It would be your capstone.

Without a capstone, your Doom Loop strategy and tactics will lack direction. You'll be shooting in the dark. It's possible to master the skills involved in a series of high-growth jobs and even wind up liking them without getting where you really want to go. The Doom Loop can be a great map. But without a destination, it won't do you much good.

WHAT'S A CAPSTONE, ANYWAY?

A capstone is a targeted career success position that you're not likely to reach for another five to eight years from the time you choose it. But it's not the end goal of your career. It's one of a whole series of success positions that powers your career strategy at the same time that it empowers you. It determines what happens next in your career. Reaching a capstone is an important career benchmark—the proof that your vision, careful planning, effort, tactical savvy, and purposeful skill-building are all working.

People sometimes confuse choosing a capstone with choosing a profession or an occupation. Think of it this way: a capstone is a specific job within a profession or an occupation. That's why it makes sense to know whether you want to enter business, medicine, history, law, social work, or whatever field you choose before selecting a capstone. But keep in mind that in choosing a capstone you will be asking yourself many tough questions that could lead to major revisions in your career direction.

What jobs qualify as capstones? A capstone can be any job or position, so long as it represents success to you. Capstones are very personal. They should capture your excitement and passion about something. Don't worry about what your husband, wife, mother, father, current boss, or mentor wants for you. Your capstone doesn't belong to any of them; it belongs to you. When you reach your capstone, you, and only you, are the one who needs to be happy to be there.

Any career position you can describe with a job title and a corresponding set of skills will qualify as a capstone for someone. It doesn't have to be the top position in a field, like CEO of a company or managing partner of a law firm, although it can be. Capstones can range from a senior vice president of pension and institutional services in a bank to a pit boss at a casino—from a human resources specialist to a religious radio announcer. But whatever your capstone turns out to be, it should be as specific and concrete as you can make it.

For example, it's not enough to say, "I really want to succeed in advertising." That represents a vague wish that's too hard to translate into clear-cut action. You just invite yourself to get stuck. Instead, invest your time and energy conceiving of and locating the job title—creative director, account manager, vice president of marketing—that describes exactly what you want to do in the advertising industry. Only by being nit-pickingly specific about the title of the job you want can you generate an achievable plan of action that's right for you.

But there's more to it than this. Any success position won't do. You can't expect to construct a capstone from the outside in. The Doom Loop's strategy and good career management dictate that your capstone be tailored to fit your own personality, values, interests, and abilities. To choose the right capstone you must be willing to risk some soul-searching, some self-study. You must become intimately acquainted with who you are and what you are genuinely interested in. Yet even this is just the starting point. A well-chosen capstone combines old-shoe comfort with long-distance challenge. It extends well beyond fitting the person you are now to fitting the person you hope to become.

That's because, by definition, a capstone is a position you are not currently qualified to hold, and that you will not be qualified to hold for some time—perhaps five to eight years or more from the time you choose it. People often ask me, "Why wait so long? Why not choose a capstone that's right around the corner?" Even though it's natural to want that big-bang career success today or tomorrow, it's a mistake to let your impatience tether you to a bunch of quick-fix, short-term capstones that fail to challenge you. You'll run a serious risk of underselling yourself, locking onto a self-limiting future, and wasting your precious lifetime. Besides, a capstone isn't something that just happens to you while you passively sit back and wait it out. You are the star player. Expect the pathway to any well-chosen capstone to be every bit as engaging and challenging as the capstone itself.

See the capstone as a "stretch" position that demands your continuing professional development. It sets the direction for a plan of action based on learning new skills critical to your success. Because you are the major stakeholder in your continuing career success, you will be highly invested in managing every stage of your journey toward your capstone. If the capstone you choose perfectly fits your current skills, then you've missed the whole point of a capstone.

Remember: a capstone should provide you with long-term learning objectives. If it doesn't—if you've already mastered most or all of the capstone's skills—you've fooled yourself into mistaking a dead end for a shortcut. You'll have too little to learn and you'll slide into the boredom and frustration of Quadrants III and IV long before you reach one.

GOING ALONG WITHOUT A CAPSTONE

Lots of people cruise through their careers without a capstone. Why not you? Despite what you've read up to this point, you may persist in thinking that you don't need a capstone to succeed in your career. Instead, you may elect to trust a ragtag assortment of beliefs and truisms. For example, you assume that solid work performance, dependability, and achievement will guarantee satisfying career advancement. You say, "My parents (or aunt or older brother) didn't have capstones and they did just fine."

Perhaps then. But not now. In a time of recession, downsizing, large-scale white-collar layoffs, flattening organizational charts, and massive federal and trade deficits, hard work and achievement, along with a dash or two of hope, are no longer enough. The odds aren't in your favor.

Why choose a well-traveled road to disappointment? Relying on hard work or loyalty to the company when golden boots, handshakes, and parachutes have replaced traditional gold watches is extremely hazardous to your career health. Even if your hard work singles you out from among the seventy-eight million striving baby boomers and their up-and-coming offspring, do you really want to turn your career management over to the organization—to disinterested strangers whose choices for you will be dictated by their own needs and self-interest rather than yours?

Or perhaps you believe the way to be recognized is by being employed by the "right" company—a *Fortune* 500 giant or a choice blue-chip firm.

Look around you. Even the best, most employee-centered companies have become high-risk victims of buyouts, acquisitions, restructurings, cost-cutting, and economic downturns. When these things happen, all you're left with is the skills you've acquired along the way. Those skills are your real money in the bank. In a tough job market, if those skills aren't based on what you need to qualify for your next capstone, your career dreams are likely to go unfulfilled.

Career management without a capstone is often career management by default. Ask yourself which strategies or assumptions you are using to guide your career management process instead of a capstone. Do any of these sound familiar?

- The company is responsible for my career development.
- Hard work pays off.

- My seniority and experience here are my career insurance.
- Staying power is what it really takes to come out on top.
- Proving my competence is what counts.
- When things go wrong, work harder.
- If I do my job well, no one will bother me.
- If I work hard enough, someone will notice.
- Having a mentor will protect me.
- If I play it right, this job will last forever.

Compare your own assumptions and strategies with this list of common career myths. If you are allowing any of these outdated ideas to guide your career strategy, you're probably heading into unnecessary turbulence. If you're not satisfied with your old assumptions and answers, let them go. Make a commitment to taking care of yourself in your career. No one else can be trusted to do it for you.

THINKING ABOUT WHO YOU ARE AND WHAT YOU WANT

Choosing a capstone requires you to know yourself and the world of work. The challenge is to get the right fit between who you are and what you do for a living. The principle is simple: the more precise the fit, the more satisfying your work life. This means continually tracking your natural preferences, needs, values, interests, and abilities and calibrating the fit.

A good capstone lets you express your values, your mission, and your current *raison d'être* through your work. It offers you opportunities to satisfy the most compelling needs that motivate you—for example, your need to achieve, to feel part of something, to take care of others, to feel secure, to wield power.

Choosing a capstone is a lot like choosing an occupation. But there are differences. It is vital to select an occupation before choosing a capstone because the selection of an occupation tailored to your interests will present you with the wide range of possible capstones to fulfill your needs. There are all kinds of positions you can hold, roles you can assume, skills you can acquire. Remember: the key is to make choices based on what you like and who you are. The more you know about yourself, the better. And the more you value yourself, the better. I think it helps to have a good career coach to guide you through the decision-making process, although many people make good decisions without one.

Begin thinking about your next capstone by focusing on yourself. The trick is to be relentless in the pursuit of information about yourself. Be a dedicated sleuth. Keep a daily log or journal of your likes and dislikes and observations about yourself. Be a keen observer of your own reactions, feelings, and aspirations. But whatever you do, keep in mind that the bottom line is to find and evaluate as much data about yourself as possible. The sole purpose of all this is to help you make better, more informed decisions—not to judge your own merit or lack thereof.

Take time to ask revealing questions about yourself and answer honestly. It's just between you and you. Remember, the only dangerous question is the one you fail to ask yourself. Use the following questions to catalyze your thinking:

- What activities and skills do I genuinely enjoy?
- When I have spare time, what do I do for fun?
- What kinds of tasks, work, or activities get me so involved that I lose track of time?
- What knowledge, skills, and activities do I naturally gravitate toward?
- What knowledge, skills, and activities do I avoid like the plague?
- What five or six words capture the essence of how I approach problems?
- What makes me feel outstanding when I do it well?
- If I were to look back at myself from some time in the future, what would I say I have done to date that has been most worthwhile?
- Which of my accomplishments add to my sense of personal worth?

- What places, people, things, and information am I most curious about or interested in?
- What subjects, skills, and activities do I have an aptitude for or do well in?
- What is my greatest weakness?

Your answers provide enormously rich information about you. Consider the following scenario.

In answering this list of questions, you learn that what you enjoy most is spending time talking to people. In fact, you seek out situations where you can be friendly and helpful. You love feeling connected to people. Although you hate to admit it, you realize that money is far less important to you than making a difference to someone. Helping people triggers your personal sense of accomplishment. Fun is doing something adventurous with people you like. Your interests scatter all over the board, but there's one unifying pattern: they gravitate toward any new situation or problem that poses a challenge. In terms of your aptitudes, perhaps, you were above average in school. But where you really glowed was as a leader—you were president of your class. Your weakness is that you have never done well at humdrum tasks, even when your success depended on it. You put off until tomorrow your expense charting, report filing, and other routine chores. Sometimes, it has been ruefully noted that tomorrow never came.

What capstones will fit this profile?

Based on your responses, you can eliminate a certain genre of capstones: partner in an accounting firm, director of research, investment analyst, nuclear power plant technician. Given your preferences and abilities, you need to avoid detail-oriented, technically intensive, deadline-driven jobs. You're better suited to capstone positions that involve direct people contact and helping relationships—capstones in service and customer relations, for example. An ideal capstone might be working with the public in some problem-solving capacity that allows you to tackle a series of new projects where people in temporary crisis need and appreciate help. A few capstones that meet these specifications include hotel manager, hospital social worker, and consumer affairs director.

Once you begin thinking this way, it's easy to come up with a few potential capstones, especially when you further narrow your options by focusing on your chosen profession. If you have trouble coming up with a capstone on your own, ask someone you trust to sit down with you and brainstorm as many capstones as possible.

Next, figure out the requirements of any capstone (or capstones) you are considering. This will require effort and energy. You'll need to read, observe, and think of questions to ask people who already hold this capstone. Consider the following issues in your quest for knowledge about your capstone:

- the special training, education, or credentials associated with this capstone
- the qualifying "starter pack" of skills, knowledge, and abilities
- the survival skills a person will need to hang onto this position through thick and thin
- the skills most frequently repeated in daily performance of the job
- the "success" skills needed to excel in the position
- the "experience trail" or "feeder" positions leading to the capstone
- the pace and demands of the position
- the organizational cultures and politics likely to be associated with the position
- the life-style associated with the position
- the likelihood of your attaining the capstone, given personal abilities (*e.g.*, personality and motivation) and family and marketplace factors

Now, look at the way the information you've generated about yourself either aligns or fails to align with the information you've generated about your capstone.

If the fit is a good one, this capstone falls into your personal comfort zone, the area of activities, interests, and skills that are in harmony with your natural preferences, interests, values, and life-style. When a capstone lies in your comfort zone, you've selected a promising capstone worth further investigation. The skills, the focus of the work, the environment will feel right to you. But don't confuse comfort with complacency. Pay close attention to whether this capstone offers sufficient challenge to hold your interest.

Suppose the fit is poor? Then this capstone is outside your comfort zone. You'll probably chafe just thinking about all you have to do to snare this "prize." If so, don't worry. At this stage it's no more than a paper loss. Go back to the drawing board and rethink this capstone, or come up with some other possibilities.

The rule to learn from all this is:

Any job that requires you to develop skills and perform tasks that go against the grain of your nature creates trouble—no matter how well you're actually able to do the job.

So refuse to settle on something that doesn't fit who you are just to end your indecision. The pressures to do this are especially strong when your family is anxiously waiting in the wings for life and economic security to begin again. But your career satisfaction counts, too. So commit yourself to spending time identifying, analyzing, and evaluating your own preferences, needs, values, interests, and abilities. Find two or three trusted people who have different and broader career knowledge than you possess right now. Ask them to help you generate all kinds of capstone possibilities. Break out of stale thinking. Generate innovative ideas that challenge and transform your tired old models. Give yourself license to get excited about capstones you've never considered before. Be playful. At this point, you're just thinking about new possibilities; you're not committing to them. Stay open to any capstone positions that seem to fit, however preposterous they might seem at the moment. Look at what these choices show you about what interests you and why. You might find it a worthwhile investment to hire a psychologist to assess your personality and career interests and relate this information to your capstone choices.

All in all, there's no single right way to think about selecting a capstone. But there are plenty of wrong ways—like discounting your own needs so that you force yourself into a convenient or trendy capstone. Or closing down and settling on the first feasible capstone that pays top dollar.

Look for what energizes you and keeps you feeling lively. Prioritize the personal. You don't want to end up as a bystander in your own life. You will make far fewer errors requiring mop-up if you:

- trust your own intuition
- attend to and catalog what you really enjoy
- factor fun into your capstone skill package
- leave plenty of room for learning new skills
- merge your personal life mission wherever possible with your career capstone
- become aware of which of your needs aren't fulfilled by your capstone
- avoid comparing yourself with people you see as successful

HOW AND WHEN TO SELECT A CAPSTONE

How? Carefully. When? Periodically. Selecting a capstone is an art that you'll have plenty of time to practice and perfect. Every experience counts. So the richer your life and work experience, the more options you'll have to choose from.

Don't look at your capstone as a straitjacket. You're never locked into a career capstone unless you choose to be. It's just a helpful guide for setting your course of action. Naturally, you'll feel differently about your capstone choices at different stages of your career. But no matter what your stage of career or life, you'll find many acceptable capstones. In fact, the selection and reassessment of your capstone should be a recurring theme throughout your career.

Capstones aren't forever. Selecting the right capstone isn't an end-of-the-line, one-time event. Your ambitions and needs will change over time. The capstone you choose in 1992 might fit you perfectly then, but three or more years down the road things may start to look different. The best-kept secret of career life is that hardly anything—knowledge, technology, personnel, organizational climate—stays the same. You yourself are evolving, too. And it's up to you to track this evolution and make it part of your career plan.

Over time, you can expect to alternate between periods of feeling stable and settled in your career path and feeling uncertain and insecure. This natural fluctuation, as shown in the research on adult development by Daniel Levinson and others, helps you know when and how to reset your course.

During the stable periods, which may last a decade or more, you'll probably opt to stick with your chosen capstone. If things are going reasonably well and you feel good about your choices, it's normal to put your energy into building on what you have. You can expect to be more of a doer and a builder than a critic.

During unstable, transitional times, you'll question your capstone and much else that you've worked hard to build. Nothing feels quite right—not your job, your values, or even your life. This can spur serious soul-searching. You may find yourself confronting tough questions like:

- What do I really want in my career and in my life?
- Is this all there is for me?
- Do I have to settle for this?
- What kinds of trade-offs am I really willing to make?

During these periods, exploring other capstones seems logical. The challenge is to learn from what isn't working for you and to use this learning to create something better. Look at it as an opportunity to realign your work with the ongoing changes in your personal and professional life. Only by calibrating and recalibrating will you attain the best fit. This is an ideal time to risk change: to rebalance your fast-track career with your family life, to go after a new degree, to get serious about developing your earning power, or to seek work more in tune with your beliefs and values.

Periodically reevaluating your capstone is not cause for alarm. It doesn't imply that you're hopelessly shallow or fickle. To change is normal. It's evidence that you are still breathing. You alone are the best judge of what changes to make and what's worth risking. Hitting the capstone reset button is one way to keep in step with yourself.

If you've just graduated or entered the work force, you're likely to be knowledge-rich and experience-poor. This makes it all the more difficult to assess fully your own potential and your range of feasible choices. So it makes good sense to go out and gather data before choosing a capstone. This takes time. Plan on trying out a rich assortment of different jobs and organizational cultures, on acquiring an inventory of basic, all-purpose work skills, and on monitoring carefully how you feel about working in different settings. These few early years you spend in data-gathering have an enormous payoff in making you more capable of choosing better capstones.

Suppose you've already made it into your thirties, forties, or even fifties without having chosen a capstone. Don't despair—it's not too late. In fact, your accumulated knowledge and experience might give you the tools to choose a better capstone than the one you would have chosen ten years (and four jobs) ago. You are armed with real data about what you like and don't like, about what's worth doing, about organizational cultures that feel comfortable or don't. Now you have to make sense of all this and choose a capstone that matches your data.

Whether you're in a stable or unstable period, whether you're a young college graduate or middle-aged, selecting a capstone is de rigueur. As I see it, there are few good reasons for not selecting one. You can always change your mind. You're never too old or too young, too experienced or inexperienced to make new choices.

But how do you do it? There's no magic formula, no single

right way. Some people know immediately what their capstones are; others struggle to find something that genuinely
interests them and is worth pursuing.

Consider these ten steps as a summary and a guide to the
process:

TEN STEPS TO SELECTING A CAPSTONE

---

1. **Take stock of yourself.** Think about each job
   you've held and the daily tasks it required. If
   you're just starting out and haven't held any jobs,
   think of projects, activities, and coursework in
   which you've participated. What were the actual
   skills that you needed to perform these tasks
   successfully? Whether you were paid or not
   doesn't count; only your skills count. Create a
   general skill profile for yourself by core-dump-
   ing all the job-related skills you have acquired
   over the years: empty your memory banks,
   dumping out every skill you possess regardless
   of its merit or significance. Like an old desk
   drawer, your memory may yield many forgotten
   treasures. Don't stop there. Now add the non-
   job-related skills you've picked up through your
   life experience.

2. **Take time to find out what makes your pulse
   race.** Decide what you like. Figure out what genuinely interests you. Look your list over and decide which skills you really enjoy, regardless of
   your present level of competence. Decide what
   activities have been fun at work and outside
   work. What is there about these activities that
   makes them fun? Sort out the skills you use in
   these activities. Write them down in a separate
   list. Add any skills and activities you naturally
   gravitate toward when you have time to yourself.

What you discover will be critical to choosing a satisfying capstone, so take your time.

3. **Play detective: find the themes and patterns.**
See what pattern of preferences, needs, values, and abilities emerges. What feels most comfortable? What are you highly motivated to do? What is really worth doing? In what areas could you develop outstanding expertise? Add your natural preferences, strengths, and key values to your skill list. Add whatever else is important that you believe is still missing. Now make sense of your sleuthing. What does this pattern of preferences, needs, values, and abilities suggest to you? Write a sentence or two about it. What does your sentence tell you about who you are and what is important to you?

4. **Transform your list into a generic job description.** Treat this distillation of preferred skills, strengths, values, and abilities like a hypothetical, content-free job description—a generic job wish list. Here's one person's wish list: lots of people contact, problem-solving, leadership and people management, a chance to apply ideas to practical situations, some creative writing, computer graphic skills, lots more emphasis on start-up than maintenance, ability to delegate details, lots of travel, new work environments, starting one new project after another, minimal supervision, weekends for self. Use this list to go capstone shopping.

5. **Think about some matching job titles.** Ask yourself what kinds of jobs might fit this general description. You may not have enough experience to do this well on your own. Get help. Take time to talk to people whose work experience differs from your own. Show people your list.

Brainstorm job titles with them. Stay playful as you consider positions and projects that require some or all of these skills, strengths, values, and abilities.

6. **Tap your intuition.** Be creative. Come up with a few "what if" and "if only" capstone possibilities that supplement or even run counter to your evolving list. Don't censor yourself. Not yet. You are still gathering important, not-so-obvious information. What contributions do you want to make through your work life that are not yet represented in your list of capstones?

7. **Research these capstones.** Fan your curiosity. Get out there and talk to people who hold capstones you are interested in. Find out what they do, how they got there, how they like it. Go fishing for information. Ask them to help you think about related or nonrelated positions that might fit your skill and preference profile.

8. **Play devil's advocate.** Identify all the barriers that might get in the way of your reaching a particular capstone. Remember that barriers can be external—like industry obsolescence or a shaky economy—or they can be peculiar to you—like fear of failure, a desire to please someone, or lack of confidence. Don't be afraid of identifying a barrier. It's what you don't know that can hurt you. And there's still plenty of time to check it out.

9. **Problem-solve.** You've found the problems; now it's up to you to solve them. Figure out how to get around each of the barriers on your list. If you get stuck, find someone with more experience in that area to help you. Now is the time to ask tough questions—before you invest

your time and effort. Questions such as: What is the subjective cost to you of reaching this capstone, given these barriers? What are your objective chances for success if you go for it? If you sincerely believe you can't surmount the challenges these barriers pose, think of related capstones that don't pose the same problems for you.

10. **Select a capstone.** For every person there are a number of good capstones. Choose the one that gives you the best fit, that feels most intuitively comfortable, and that is a realistic possibility. Remember that a capstone is not a profession. If you want to be in a profession, the best strategy is to choose a field or discipline and earn your educational credentials before choosing a capstone.

Sounds straightforward enough, right? On the surface, it is. But remember, selecting a capstone is more an art than a science, so it takes practice. You're not dealing with a static picture. You're making choices based on future expectations as well as present realities. There are no hard-and-fast rules. So concentrate only on what works best for you. Take it as a given that you will make errors. That goes with the territory. And part of the art of capstone selection is avoiding certain predictable errors that are extraordinarily easy to make.

A "HOW NOT TO" PRIMER:
FIVE TYPES OF CAPSTONE ERRORS

There are at least five common capstone errors you should watch out for. Let's examine each:

- the "But I'm so good at it" Error
- the "I am my degree" Error

- the "I just want to please them" Error
- the "I follow my heart" Error
- the "I wannabe an expert" Error

The "But I'm So Good at It" Error:
Choosing a capstone based only on how well you do something

When it comes to careers, people tend to assign a much higher priority to their performance than to their preferences. Taking a short-term perspective, this makes sense: you choose a field you're good in so that you can get a job and hang onto it. Besides, being good at something ought to boost your confidence and ability to forge ahead.

Taking a longer-term perspective, however, this common strategy can be remarkably self-destructive. No matter how good you are at a job, you can wind up feeling miserable and unmotivated if it doesn't provide enough personal satisfaction to sustain your interest.

Anyone reassessing a career direction can make the "But I'm so good at it" error. But some people are more prone to it than others. You're a prime candidate if your self-worth hinges on achieving "get it right the first time" perfect performance, and if the thought of making errors sends you shivering back under the sheets. The "But I'm so good at it" error is also likely to be made early in a career or upon reentry into the work force after a hiatus. This is when you feel compelled to make major career decisions based on shaky confidence and too little data.

Since you don't have a current baseline of paid work experience or have one that's outmoded, the only things that stand out are your obvious aptitudes and abilities. Ironically, the more outstanding these talents and skills, the more you are in jeopardy of being propelled by well-meaning family, friends, and teachers into careers that tap these specific abilities. This is fine if you also happen to like what you're good at. But that's not necessarily the case. I, for one, am good at a number of tasks—like editing—that also cause me to break out in hives. That's an attention-grabbing clue that tells me that editing, even though I'm good at it, is not for me. I have heard scores of unhappy people who have made this particular error protest, "But if I'm good at it, I like it." What they really like, however, may be the praise and the promotions, which keep their discontent under wraps for a while. Somewhere down the line, however, kudos and nice job titles prove insufficient compensation, and they begin to feel boxed in by their personally unsatisfying jobs. When you seize on being good at something as a compelling reason to enter a field you don't like, chances are you're heading straight for career trouble.

Consider the case of Rebecca Pollard, a twenty-eight-year-old math and science whiz. She'd always done well in these subjects, so when her high school counselor advised her to pursue engineering—a field that had recently opened up for women with her talents—she took him at his word. She majored in electrical engineering in college. But after three years as an electrical engineer, Rebecca was short-circuiting. She hated getting up in the morning and going to work. Still, her natural ability earned her excellent ratings. Finding herself unexpectedly trapped by her own competence, Rebecca wondered, "What's wrong with me?"

Luckily, she sought the help of a career counselor. In the course of their work together, Rebecca realized that what she liked best was totally absent from her job. She liked communicating with people, being the center of attention, confronting and influencing others. Based on an analysis of Rebecca's preferences, personality, and interests, the counselor helped her select the new capstone of labor negotiation lawyer—a capstone with skills Rebecca thought she'd go after and enjoy.

The story illustrates the first general rule in capstone selection on the following page:

CAPSTONE RULE I: Separate your fondness for the skills involved in any capstone from the question of whether or not you are good at them. Then, in making your decision, pay as much attention to your preferences for these skills as to your ability to perform them.

If you have average or above-average intelligence and the ability to learn, eventually you'll acquire proficiency in the skills you need to perform most jobs. Of course, there are exceptions; some people will never master the skills necessary to become a nuclear physicist or a portrait painter. It's important to acknowledge those personal limitations that cannot be overcome. On the other hand, if you don't like the particular tasks needed for a given capstone, you'll lack the motivation to overcome the inevitable daily hassles and built-in roadblocks that accompany any serious effort to achieve. Ultimately, you'll begin to question if what you're striving for is worthwhile. You're likely to drop out or burn out. If you must do things you don't like day in and day out, it's natural to become bored and frustrated, even in work you do well. To find a capstone that will sustain your interest, motivation, and commitment over the long haul, be sure to attend closely to what you like to do.

The "I Am My Degree" Error:
Confusing a profession or an occupation with a capstone

Possessing a professional identity should not be confused with having a capstone. I see this as the second most common error people make. Sometimes it takes people a decade or more to realize what's happened. Getting a law degree and passing the bar exam may make you a lawyer, but neither will automatically determine your capstone or specify the path to take to become a Supreme Court justice.

It's simply not enough to obtain the right degree or pass

the right exam. Planning shouldn't stop there; your credentials are merely career foreplay. Just because you've exited from the sacred groves as a lawyer, doctor, accountant, or MBA doesn't mean you can expect to glide through the next decades of your career on automatic pilot.

Sure, you've earned a certain status, a sense of entitlement. You're a member of the club. But watch out! No matter what your credentials, you are not your degree. A strong professional or occupational identity may foster a false sense of security that deters you from planning beyond it. Within your own field, you are competing with top people with credentials similar to yours. And although your professional credentials make you a qualified contender for many entry-level jobs, they will rarely provide you with the specific skills you will need to succeed in a particular job, much less a career capstone. To get ahead, you must plan on acquiring skills no one ever told you about in graduate school.

This brings us to the second capstone selection rule:

CAPSTONE RULE II: A profession or an occupation is no more than a baseline for career start-up—and you should never confuse either one with having a capstone.

Think about it this way. Your professional or occupational identity is a launch point for your career. In managing your career, you will have to identify and target a series of capstones that will fit your changing career needs. No matter what your profession, it helps to know the full range of capstone possibilities before choosing. A physician needs to determine the right capstone within his or her profession—a director of an HMO, a medical school faculty position, an independent practitioner, a medical lobbyist, a director of a research team. Each capstone carries a different set of implications in terms of the post-degree skills you will have to learn. A professional without a capstone will flounder just like anyone else without a capstone—but with higher status and earnings. Just keep in mind that professional identity alone won't automatically lead you to the next level and beyond; a capstone will.

The "I Just Want to Please Them" Error:
Choosing a capstone based on family tradition, a mentor's agenda, or someone else's dream

Have you ever noticed how occupations run in families? John will take over the family business; Susan will be a doctor like her father; Ted will be a writer like his mother.

Capstones run in families, too. The family-directed capstone might be the easy route to the top—John's rise to president in the family business is a fait accompli. Susan will have a hard time turning down the inside track to private-practice obstetrics. But if John doesn't like the family business, it's the wrong capstone for him. And if Susan longs to do medical research she will be unhappy in private practice.

It may feel as if someone is making you an offer you truly cannot refuse. You will let people down or break their hearts. This is tough. But don't choose a capstone based on what your family wants or expects of you unless that's truly what you want, too. If you choose an occupation or a capstone to please your family or a boss or a mentor, you could end up trapped in someone else's dream.

Be careful to avoid another family-generated error: choosing a negative capstone. Three generations of a family have been ministers. The son is also expected to be a minister, and, indeed, he goes through the seminary and is assigned to a church. He hates it and rebels, looking for a totally different kind of work. Eventually he becomes a car dealer. The problem? Although there's nothing wrong with selling cars, he doesn't like selling cars any more than he liked being a minister; nonetheless it's a way to assert his independence from the family and make a personal statement.

When you respond to family pressures with rebellious noncompliance, you often spin your wheels and dig yourself into a new rut. You can spend whole decades of your life in unsatisfying jobs that confirm your independent identity by violating the family imperative. The trick is to choose a capstone based on what you want, rather than on what your family doesn't want. To do otherwise is to give away your career satisfaction.

Don't think the "I just want to please them" error is limited to young people just starting out. A capstone imperative can come from a husband or a wife, a mentor, or company management. One career imperative (*e.g.,* "People in this family always become . . .") is merely substituted for another (*e.g.,* "The company knows what's best for you"). What these imperatives have in common is failing to prize what you as an individual enjoy and value.

Yet the fact that someone is sure about what you should be doing can be very appealing, especially when you're feeling uncertain and indecisive. Because you're lured by other people's certainty, you assume that they have better judgment than you or know what is best for you. The hope is that if you listen to them you can avoid angst and get on with your career program. Unfortunately, this may turn out to be one of those hard-to-rectify "buy now, pay later" trade-offs. So before committing this type of error, carefully consider this capstone rule:

CAPSTONE RULE III: Refuse to commit yourself to a family- or mentor-directed capstone. No matter how seductive that may be, you should first explore other options, experience the crisis of capstone indecision, and identify your own dream.

Most crises of indecision beg to be resolved through immediate action. But if you can just slow down your natural tendency to reach a slam-bam conclusion, the stress of indecision will give you a chance to reflect and search your soul.

The mere fact that you are questioning your choices increases your chances of finding better-fitting, more creative options.

Don't try to resolve a career crisis—like a first-job decision or being fired—by running for the immediate shelter of a family or mentor-dictated career path. Instead, stay open. Sure it's going to be uncomfortable. But accept the fact that periodic indecision goes with the territory of selecting and reselecting the right capstones.

Have faith that the best answers reside in you—not in them. Take time to decide what really makes your pulse race, then find a capstone that will keep it racing.

The "I Follow My Heart" Error:
Choosing jobs based solely on likes and dislikes,
rather than on a capstone

You've heard it before. Just do what you like; good things will follow. Don't fret about having career goals or capstones. All's well that ends well. Right?

Spontaneous, free-spirited types and bright, multitalented people are at high risk for making this error. It's especially easy for them to follow their hearts and forget entirely about planning. They have interests as unique as their fingerprints and do them all well. There are all those interesting forks in the road, and they aim to go down as many as they can. These curious and aspiring Renaissance men and women may excel in many unrelated jobs and acquire a disparate group of skills in the process.

Unfortunately, these skills may not fit any feasible capstone.

Mindy Lange made this error. Bright, energetic, and ambitious, Mindy began a career as a social worker. After far too many years of peanut-butter-and-jelly dinners, she decided she wanted to make a ton of money. Since she liked finance, she easily made a challenging shift to a job as an investment broker. At first it was fun, but she disliked the office politics at the brokerage house and decided to pursue something artistic. She landed a position with a film production studio, taking a second job as a waitress to bring in additional income.

Mindy was a terrific waitress and soon quit her other job to pile up money. But her self-esteem suffered. To bolster it and prove herself academically, she entered a Ph.D. program in sociology.

Now, at thirty-eight, Mindy is having serious second thoughts about sociology. For her, the very idea of a capstone is difficult to accept. Working toward any long-term goal feels like a claustrophobic nightmare. She wants the success that achieving a capstone brings, but equates commitment to a career capstone with losing her spontaneity and feeling trapped.

Mindy's at the hub of a skill profile that extends in as many directions as the spokes of a wheel. But it's Mindy's career that is spinning in circles.

Based on her current scattered skills, all Mindy can hope for is a low- to midlevel position. A recruiter or interviewer would see her as a job jumper with superficial skills. Even her friends think she's a dilettante. Mindy would do better if she considered this capstone selection rule:

CAPSTONE RULE IV: No matter how rich and varied your preferences, link them to a feasible capstone.

People like Mindy need a capstone with a wide variety of skills—ones that satisfy the desire for continuing change and flexibility. Mindy needs to integrate her skills in a way that gives method to her job-change madness, that shows that these changes aren't merely impulsive moves but part of a well-planned design. At this point in her career, Mindy needs to identify the key skills she has acquired in her diverse work experiences and link them to a capstone directly related to her graduate studies. This will be a challenging task. She has fifteen years of helter-skelter skill-building to sort and integrate into a plan—all well after the fact. Still, she has a lot going for her. She has acquired solid sales, customer service, people, and research skills. What she likes best is figuring out why groups of people behave the way they do. An analysis of her work experience shows that finance, trend analysis, and media research head her list of likes. This pattern makes consumer behavior, marketing, and advertising research fertile fields for finding capstones. These are all high-change, project-oriented areas where Mindy is least likely to get bored and most likely to find similar free-spirited types. If she can link one of these areas to her graduate degree, she may be able to commit to a course of deliberately planned action without feeling too hemmed in.

With a capstone as a guide, bright, multitalented individuals like Mindy, who enjoy exploring new skills and jobs, can follow their hearts right to their capstones. They can build impressive résumés that hitch their skills to the right capstone and permit prospective employers to see them as stable, talented job candidates.

The "I Wannabe an Expert" Error:
Rushing out to get the technical skills that make you an expert at your capstone without first mastering the generic skills

Once you've decided on a capstone, it's natural to want to reach it as fast as you can, so that you can distinguish yourself from all the other "wannabes." A common strategy is to go for the high-tech, expert skills that transform you overnight from a novice to an expert via technical competence. Who knows? Maybe having all those impressive technical skills will grant you early entry into coveted job slots.

At first blush this makes good sense. Who ever heard of a computer analyst who couldn't program a computer or an economist who couldn't forecast? Yet acquiring technical skills too early or at the expense of generic skills can be a costly strategic error.

Suppose for a moment that your capstone is a chief financial officer. You do your homework. You go to the library and read all the occupational reference books that detail what a CFO does. Then you go out and interview a few CFOs, along with a headhunter who recruits them. By the time you finish you easily have ten pages of helpful notes on skills a CFO position demands. You also learn that companies generally seek CFOs who are either treasury-oriented or control-oriented. So you naturally target these skills first, because you think they will get you where you want to be fastest:

TREASURY AND CONTROL SKILLS FOR THE CFO POSITION

TREASURY SKILLS	
Banking relations	Credit analysis
Loan structuring policies/ procedures	Cash management
Putting deals together	Capital budgeting
Foreign exchange	Forecasting
Interacting with legal system	
CONTROL SKILLS	
Data processing administration and usage	Monitoring company profitability
Computer-based forecasting/ analysis	Management information systems

You are acquiring the skills that make your capstone unique—the technical skills. These are the cutting-edge skills that require special training, education, or experience. When most people think of an expert, they imagine someone who holds a specific set of unique technical skills.

But no matter where you are in your career, you are making a rookie's error. There's another area you will need to attend to: acquiring the generic skills—the building-block skills— that cut across many different capstones and the positions that feed into those capstones. They provide a time-honored experience trail to your capstone. Different jobs will require different combinations of generic skills. You can learn what they are by talking to people who hold any particular capstone. In the next chapter I'll show you how to develop the kinds of skill lists you will need for detailed planning. On the next pages are samples of generic skills for the CFO position that I have developed in my work with individuals and corporations.

It's all too easy to overlook these generic skills when you're pushing hard to gain expert status. But when you take a good look at generic skills, they're so basic that it's hard to think of any capstones where they don't play a substantial role. If you don't master these multipurpose generic skills, you'll handicap yourself. You could even miss your targeted capstone altogether.

One good strategy is to move toward your capstone, acquiring generic skills first and technical skills later, moving from the bottom up as shown below:

THE CAPSTONE SKILL HIERARCHY

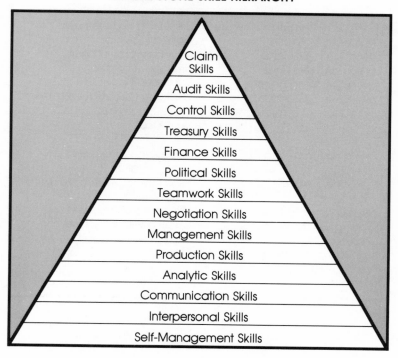

Claim Skills

Audit Skills

Control Skills

Treasury Skills

Finance Skills

Political Skills

Teamwork Skills

Negotiation Skills

Management Skills

Production Skills

Analytic Skills

Communication Skills

Interpersonal Skills

Self-Management Skills

GENERIC SKILLS FOR THE CFO POSITION

COMMUNICATION SKILLS

Oral communication skills

Written communication skills
Microcomputer skills
Group communication skills
One-on-one communication
 skills
Skills for conducting meetings
Interviewing skills

Networking up the
 organizational chart
Networking down the
 organizational chart
Giving and getting feedback
Record keeping

Public communication skills
Stand-up presentation skills

MANAGEMENT SKILLS

Directing people
Planning activitives

Delegating tasks
Demonstrating accountability
Gathering data
Coordinating actions
Organizing meetings
Recruiting/hiring people
Evaluating performance

Setting priorities and goals
Supervising activities of
 subordinates
Reporting to supervisors
Identifying key problems
Problem-solving
Developing personnel
Time management
Firing people
Providing career development

INTERPERSONAL SKILLS

Providing leadership

Persuading external
 community
Negotiating conflicts
Coping with problem
 employees
Showing professional
 judgment
Mentoring/training

Persuading other members of
 organization
Functioning as effective team
 player
Using negative feedback
Dealing with personnel
 problems
Providing guidance and
 counseling
Motivating others

GENERIC SKILLS FOR THE CFO POSITION (*cont.*)

FINANCIAL SKILLS	
Keeping general ledger	Performing basic accounting skills
Conducting inventory functions	Performing payroll functions
Cost accounting	Forecasting
Preparing budget	Allocating and controlling budget
Preparing financial statement	Consulting with financial analysts
Monitoring expense controls	Monitoring grants/financial agreements

POLITICAL SKILLS	
Positioning accomplishments	Identifying organizational norms
Using informal communication networks	Aligning personal and organizational needs
Maneuvering in troubled political waters	Identifying actions that the organization rewards
Coping with difficult coworkers	Staying alert to environmental maneuvers

ANALYTIC SKILLS	
Identifying problems	Reaching data-based conclusions
Gathering appropriate information	Reasoning logically
Recognizing relevant patterns and themes	Recognizing assumptions
Separating the essential from the nonessential	Developing cogent arguments
Generating/testing hypotheses	Evaluating arguments
Generating logical solutions	Solving the selected problem

Generic skills form the broad base of any capstone skill hierarchy. These all-purpose skills stabilize your rise up the career ladder by grounding you in the fundamental requirements of many different capstone choices. The beauty of this approach is that even if you change your mind en route to a particular capstone—say you decide to be a fund-raiser or a corporate-turnaround consultant instead of a CFO—these generic skills will carry you to many others. They maximize your career maneuverability and give you a natural buffer against high-tech obsolescence.

In contrast, if the only skills you had were technical skills, you would lack general know-how as well as broad-based adaptability. Any job that demanded more than technical expertise could throw you out of kilter. And your hard-won technical skills would not be easily transferable. This is a serious liability, especially in grim economic times when industry-wide layoffs cause the skies to rain technical experts. It won't be your technical skills but your relevant all-purpose skills that will give you the edge in flattened organizations that demand greater flexibility and more roles from fewer and fewer workers.

Besides, most complex, higher-level positions require considerably more than technical skills. Technical industries commonly report a shocking lack of basic interpersonal and management skills among their experts. If you tried to balance the triangle on the preceding page on its apex, the skill hierarchy would need to be propped up by external forces like a mentor, luck, inside information, a successful image, and so on. This strategy is just as precarious to your career success as it looks—which brings us to the fifth rule for choosing a capstone:

CAPSTONE RULE V: Acquire all-purpose, generic skills first. Then acquire the technical skills for your particular capstone. Sometimes you'll have to get them simultaneously. In that case, strike a balance between them.

This approach gives you the most resilience and flexibility in managing your career in unpredictable times. The rule is most applicable when you are making a major shift in your career direction—near the beginning of a career, for example, or while reentering the work force. These are times when it's important to take jobs that allow you to master important, transferable building-block skills. Proficiency in interpersonal, self-management, communication, analytic, team, political, and production skills creates the *savoir faire* and adaptability to succeed.

TRUST YOUR INTUITION

Have you ever noticed that when careers go awry, people tend to obsessively play back every small detail leading up to the trauma? Then something seems to click, and they wind up saying, "I knew something was wrong from the very start," or, "I should have listened to my gut."

Too often, we listen to anything and everything but our own intuition. When choosing jobs, we compare salaries, perks, job titles, bosses, work loads, and so on. When choosing capstones, we gravitate to the same hard facts and figures. We revere what's coolly rational and quantifiable. My experience is that the more rational, scientific, or technical the training, the more vulnerable a person is to the tyranny of impersonal logic.

Why tyranny? Because choosing a capstone is an intensely personal decision, and logic, while important, fails to account for all the factors that sustain satisfaction. You are going to put your life effort into your work. To a great extent, how you feel about your career will affect how you feel about yourself. No one but you is really qualified to tell you what your capstone should be.

Your best strategy is to trust your own intuition. Whether or not you're excited about a capstone, whether or not you will enjoy learning and performing the skills required to succeed in it, whether or not it feels worth striving for—these are the factors that count most.

To tap into your intuitive knowledge, ask yourself some probing questions: What would you love to do if you had absolutely no constraints? Or: When you come to the end of your career, what would you like to have contributed or accomplished? Or ask yourself: If you had complete freedom, what would be the most fun for you to do for a living?

Your answers, however farfetched, tap into a storehouse of important personal data about what really matters to you. Your next step is to look beyond each answer, translating and refining it, to see the underlying needs and values your capstone must satisfy.

Here is an example of how this works. John Licata was an investment banker. Happily married, with two children, he was successful by most middle-class standards: big house, expensive car, a purebred black Labrador, and a good-sized expense account. But he wasn't sure where his career was going. He had reached his first capstone in banking, and he felt curiously flat. He complained, "I just don't seem to have any more wind in my sails. I feel like a beached whale."

John subjected himself to some intuitive questions. If he had no constraints, he maintained, he "certainly wouldn't stay in banking." When he asked himself what he would do that would be the most fun for him, he didn't hesitate: "I'd be a zookeeper."

The problem was that John was not prepared to take the steps necessary to pursue a zookeeper capstone. Still, he analyzed the reasons that being a zookeeper appealed to him. He realized he loved taking care of animals; he liked puttering around; he enjoyed physical labor; he hated wearing business suits; and he had never liked the urban banking milieu. What he hated most about banking was the environment, not the tasks and skills required by the job.

Through this self-assessment, John came up with an alternative capstone: being a bank president in a small town where ranching and raising livestock would be possible. He began a job search. John's wife wasn't as thrilled with the prospect of rural life as John and the kids were, but after some lively discussions they agreed to try it out—so long as they could find a locale within an hour's drive of a large university. John temporarily stepped down in rank to take a job as an assistant branch administrator with a growing financial institution in a rural area that met both his and his wife's specifications. He bought some land where he could ranch and raise livestock. He solved his capstone dilemma by tapping into what seemed an absurd initial response to the probing questions he had asked himself. Yet his answers contained the intuitive information he needed to make the right choice.

IS A CAPSTONE A PIPE DREAM?

How realistic is all this? Can a middle-aged attorney set a capstone of symphony conductor? Can a construction worker select a capstone of professor of neuroscience?

It depends. We all realize there are limits to our ability to reach our capstones or any goal in life. Our limits are imposed by who our parents happen to be, when and where we were born, our financial and physical health, our inherent talents and abilities, our personalities and beliefs, and an array of other circumstances like technical obsolescence, the economy, war, and natural disaster. If the attorney who longs to be a symphony conductor has no musical talent and is the sole support of her family, then she will have little chance of reaching her capstone. Unfortunately and painfully, reality can transform some capstones into pipe dreams.

Fortunately, if we do our research and choose reflectively, most of our capstones are dreams that can be turned into realities. If there is one thing I have learned as a psychologist and career coach, it is that most of us, myself included, underestimate our capacity for achievement. Too often we are well versed in the hundred and one compelling reasons we can't change. We don't have to rely on fate or external conditions to stop us; we impose our own limits on ourselves. We haven't a clue as to how good we really are. This makes it easier to keep on doing whatever we are used to, even though we are unhappy with our lot.

No one will change this for us. It's up to us to get enough information about what our capacity is and about what is required to succeed in a given capstone to make informed choices. Though a particular construction worker might not be able to become a professor of neuroscience, his or her interest in this lofty capstone speaks to a high level of aspiration and a strong drive to achieve. And with commitment, it may be possible to define and achieve some other ambitious and appealing capstone—computer systems analyst, entrepreneur, physical therapist—that fits his or her unique abilities as well as the difficult constraints of reality.

Not all things are possible, but many are. Though not all people have equal capstone choices, all people do have choices. We have the right to decide to what extent we want to manage or be managed by our circumstances. The secret is in knowing yourself, being a good chooser, and having the hard-nosed resilience to stick it out. None of this is easy. Yet I've seen people overcome substantial barriers that family, coworkers, and friends believed were insurmountable.

So in the pages ahead you won't find me warning you much about your limits. I trust you know them all too intimately. When you are choosing a capstone, my advice is to be wary of that inner voice that whispers, "Who are you kidding? You'll never be a psychologist or an accountant, or a CEO." Listen to what that voice is saying, then assess whether it is telling the truth about the facts or merely betraying your own self-doubt. Check it out with a career professional or a person in the field you are considering—someone with no vested interest in either your success or your failure. Your future deserves a second or even a third opinion. Whatever you do, don't dismiss a capstone as too difficult or too preposterous until you've done your homework and carefully analyzed its feasibility. Approach each barrier to your capstone as just another problem to be solved.

Your career happiness is worth that effort.

CHAPTER 3

On the Road to Capstone

When you choose a capstone, you are making a powerful commitment to an idea, a dream. Now you have to make an equally powerful commitment to a course of action. But how do you do that? Where do you start? How do you keep from feeling overwhelmed?

Even though Sam has a capstone, to be a best-selling novelist, he's unlikely to reach it if he's neither learning his craft nor getting the experience he needs to qualify him as a fiction writer. Hoping and yearning will neither get him into print nor pay his mortgage. If you want to own a health spa in Santa Fe, but you keep working as a cash manager in a Detroit bank, you're not doing a very good job of managing your journey to your capstone. You've failed to commit yourself to the kind of skill-building that will get you there.

Finding the right capstone is a major step. It's also a tremendous relief. You realize that if you pull it off, career satisfaction is out there waiting for you. But reaching your capstone requires more than knowing your destination. It requires a detailed, step-by-step itinerary that specifies your next moves in conjunction with Doom Loop principles.

First of all, shelve your old misconceptions about dressing for success, basking in a mentor's glow, rising to the top via a prestigious company, or climbing what's left of the corporate ladder. And don't wait around for someone else to offer you a career opportunity you can't refuse.

Get ready to change your mind about how to reach your career capstone.

With just a little effort you can discover and use readily available information about yourself and your capstone to design a personalized step-by-step operating plan. This plan puts you in charge of your journey to your capstone. It's called your target mosaic and it tells which skills you must learn to become a contender for your capstone. Once you know this, you can set a course of action that enables you to acquire the right skills, knowledge, and credentials at a pace that's right for you.

At this stage, getting accurate information is central to career management success. So even if you prefer to wing the details, don't do it this time. Make obtaining the precise information you need to construct your target mosaic a top priority.

No matter what your capstone, you will begin by focusing on these two critical sets of information:

- everything you can discover about your capstone
- everything you can assess about your current skills and competencies

In the pages ahead you'll find a basic primer on how to profile your capstone and your skill competencies. Although this process of constructing a target mosaic tailored to your capstone is straightforward enough, keep in mind that you are both the architect and the one living on the construction site. So take time to think about what will keep you happy and satisfied as you skill-build your way to your capstone.

THE JOURNEY TO CAPSTONE

Although we may know our next capstone, we don't necessarily know the best path to it. So respect your personal style and plan wisely. Map a simple point-by-point navigational system with many built-in markers or checkpoints along the way. Then pay attention. These markers will tell you whether you're on or off course, and by how much. That way you can correct your course or abandon ship.

No matter where you are in your career, this applies to the many journeys you'll be making to your next capstones.

To make your next capstone more than a tantalizing dream, you'll need to carefully design an operating plan. To do that, get on a first-name basis with:

- **your capstone profile**—that describes the skills and credentials that anyone would need to hold this specific capstone
- **your career mosaic**—that catalogs all the skills you have already acquired through various paid and unpaid work experience
- **your target mosaic**—that pinpoints the skills you still need to acquire to attain and succeed in your capstone

After all, your career success depends on them.

YOUR CAPSTONE PROFILE

A capstone profile is a list of the skills any successful contender would need to qualify for any capstone, including yours. It also tells you which of those skills are most critical to your success, in what kinds of environments you will find this capstone, whether there is anything else you need to know about this capstone to succeed in it, and whether there are any back doors or shortcuts to it.

To choose the right capstone you focused your attention on what you enjoy doing and what's important to you. Your preferences were critical to your choice. Now, to reach that chosen capstone, you must shift your attention to your competence, to the actual skills your capstone demands.

Why? Because it is your skills, not your preferences, that will qualify you for the job.

Any capstone you can imagine, any job you may hold, can be broken down into a descriptive set of required tasks. For example, as a self-employed comedian, George has to do a lot more than mouth funny one-liners. He has to get bookings, keep an audience amused, manage an entrepreneurial business. In her work as a secretary, Alice has to manage office correspondence and schedules, keep the bosses' calendars, maintain supplies, handle public relations between the office and other parts of the organization.

But the tasks that compose any job description tell only part of the story. Tasks require a complex combination of specific skills, knowledge, and abilities. To qualify for any capstone, a person has to acquire most of the skills needed to perform the tasks it involves, as well as a necessary knowledge base and appropriate credentials.

In thinking about jobs, it helps to distinguish between tasks and skills. Tasks are impersonal and descriptive: they describe the job. Skills are personal and prescriptive: they dictate what you must do to perform each task successfully. Consider the skills George and Alice actually need to do their jobs. George must have solid marketing and public relations skills to get bookings as a comedian. But that's not all. George must continually improve his written and oral communication skills and his stand-up presentation skills merely to stay competitive. And he needs a well-developed sense of timing to keep his audiences amused. For her job, Alice needs an altogether different set of skills. She needs sound organizational, word processing, and written communication skills to manage office correspondence. She needs excellent auditing, record keeping, and bookkeeping skills to retain her authority over maintaining supplies. And Alice's skills at phone answering, conflict resolution, and interpersonal relations have become legendary.

When you leave a job, the tasks stay behind with that job. But the skills are portable competencies that travel well. If you list only the tasks of a job on your résumé, you are failing to state which skills you are bringing with you. You are leaving it for the reader to extrapolate. Aside from the question of whether or not you want to put such career-shaping responsibility into someone else's hands, there's a more important issue.

Using a skill-based approach shows others and yourself that

you are a free agent who can learn new skills anywhere—no matter what your job title or the size or prestige of your company. This increases your power as a career manager. Focusing on the specific skills a job requires shows exactly what it takes for *anyone* to do that job. When that particular job happens to be your capstone, these skills define your capstone profile. And once you have a skill-based capstone profile, you can compare your skills against it to determine whether or not you are qualified to hold this capstone.

Let's suppose you're not qualified. From the Doom Loop's skill-building perspective, that is no more than a temporary judgment. True, it may knock you out of the running for the time being. But with direct analysis you can determine which skills you must learn to overcome this obstacle and become qualified. Then you can develop a personalized target mosaic.

So if you are really serious about reaching your capstone, your first order of business after choosing it is to discover precisely what skills, knowledge, and credentials anyone holding it must possess. Then you must target those you lack.

No matter what the capstone is, anyone who has mastered these specified skills and knowledge can look and, with practice, act the part of someone who holds it.

Constructing an Insider's Capstone Profile

When you first consider a capstone, you're an outsider. You're like a kid pressed up against a store-window Christmas display longing for what's inside. You see what you want, but you're not sure if or how you can get it.

Being an outsider puts you at risk for choosing an important career success position based on an outsider's perceptions—hearsay, impressions, and myths—and for using these perceptions to plot your pathway.

This is a mistake.

When I was growing up, I read many movie magazines, which led me to think I wanted to become an actress. So at nineteen, with my capstone of film acting in mind, I set off for Hollywood. I wore a strapless dress and spike-heeled shoes

in the best tradition of the early sixties and wobbled my way
to the corner of Hollywood and Vine, where I patiently stood
and waited for hours and hours to be discovered. After all,
that was how the movie magazines said it happened. Of
course, I was one disappointed cookie. My feet hurt and my
career dreams were dashed. Too bad. I had an outsider's view
of how to reach my capstone that led nowhere.

Don't make the Hollywood and Vine mistake in researching
your capstone. Wishful thinking, inaccurate information,
well-meaning advice from people who know less than you do,
cultural myths, and patently false hopes will get you nowhere.
Your job is to get an insider's view of what your capstone is
about—from how to get noticed and break into the targeted
field or organization to knowing the skills and knowledge
required to do the job.

How do you do this? The best place to start is with quick
and easy basic research.

Learning the Lingo: Basic Research

Getting an insider's track to your capstone is a lot easier
than most people think. First, get an overview of your capstone. Then learn the lingo—the language associated with
your capstone and the ideas of people who hold it.

Your lowest-risk, first-stop option is a two-hour visit to the
reference section of the library, where you'll find assorted
career reference books like the *Dictionary of Occupational Titles*
(D.O.T.). Use them like a dictionary—as a source of quick
factual information.

Depending on the book you choose, look up your capstone
position by occupation or title and jot down the tasks it requires. Most of the books will describe the tasks required by
the job rather than the skills required to succeed, so you'll
have to translate the tasks into skills yourself.

Even though we are now focusing on competencies rather
than preferences, pay attention to how you feel as you read
these descriptions. Which skills do you feel excited about
learning? Which put you to sleep? These insights can help
you plan the right strategy.

By collecting background data on your capstone, you're

building a useful knowledge base that will impress others when you conduct capstone profile interviews with people in the field. You will be letting people know you've done your homework and merit being taken seriously.

Interviewing Insiders: The Capstone Profile Interview

Career reference books in the library are the equivalent of tourists' guidebooks to foreign cities: they give you a good overview of your career capstone, but fail to provide the rich firsthand experience of being there.

The capstone profile interview changes this. It provides you with a native's perspective. Here's where you'll get the real insider's guide to your capstone—the best shortcuts, the hidden booby traps, the pick of the local spots. Interviewing people who already hold your capstone is the shortest, least risky way to get this information, whether you're a rookie or a seasoned veteran making a career switch. Contact three or four people who currently hold your capstone. Tell them who you are, that you are interested in eventually holding a job like theirs, and that you'd like to talk with them. Ask them for their help. If your capstone is unusual or specific to another region, locate two or three people anywhere in the country who currently hold it. Talk with them about what they do and what it takes to succeed in the position.

How do you find insiders who already hold your targeted capstone? All kinds of ways. Network. Talk to friends, neighbors, and family. Mine their contacts and resources. Even casual acquaintances are often delighted to provide leads. Ask them if they know anyone who holds a similar position to your capstone or who works in the industry or profession. Even if these people are not the ones you need, they can usually lead you to the right people. Don't be afraid to head for the top. Surprisingly, people at the top of the profession are often more generous with their time than those still struggling in the trenches. Go where the action is. Show up at national and local meetings. Call the appropriate national professional or trade association for your capstone and ask for names of people who hold your capstone. Don't be embarrassed to call someone who is well known or widely published. One responsibility of the professional is to aid and mentor people entering the field. Besides, they can always say no or refer you to someone else.

When you interview these people, be matter-of-fact and to the point. Don't cast yourself in an outsider's role. Think of them as future colleagues who will be glad to help you. Perhaps you'll have the opportunity to return the favor later. Tell them you're considering a career change, that you're interested in doing what they do somewhere down the line, that you'd like to talk with them about what their work is like and how they arrived in this position.

Here are some specific questions you'll want to ask to get an insider's perspective on your capstone:

- Which skills are most critical up front to be seen as qualified for this job?
- What routine skills will I need to keep up my performance in this post?
- What skills are most frequently used in this job?
- Which skills are most critical to success in this job?
- What is the best way for someone to go about acquiring these skills?
- What does a person in this job have to do to be recognized in this organization? In general?
- What's required for someone to look the part in this job?
- How does what you actually do differ from your job description?
- What experiences or jobs do you recommend as being especially good "feeder slots" for this position?
- How did you come to hold this position?
- What shortcuts to this job can you recommend?
- What are some of the common mistakes people breaking into this field make?
- What should I watch out for or avoid?
- What is your best advice to me as a newcomer who hopes to become a qualified candidate for this job?

You may be amazed by how willing people are to help you. Although not everyone you contact will grant you an interview, many will. When you make it clear that you're not seeking a job interview but are simply seeking information about the job they hold, people usually respond positively. Often one or more of the people you interview will take a personal interest in your career plans, offering to help you network, or keeping you posted on new opportunities. This gives you instant insider access to your capstone. But even if that doesn't happen, you'll still gather information invaluable to constructing your target mosaic.

Mining Other Sources of Insider Information

Where else can you gather accurate information about your capstone? Two other sources can prove quite useful:

• Formal job descriptions posted or filed in personnel departments of companies provide clues but rarely insider information. Keep in mind that the person who holds your capstone might tell an altogether different story.

• Headhunters can be good sources of information if you can find the right ones and if they will talk to you. Because they are often close to the power brokers who make hiring decisions, they can give you an insider's perspective that's hard to come by elsewhere. They can tell you which skills and "specs" companies are looking for. So ask them about trends in hiring, the culture of organizations, and other factors that may affect your planning.

Generating Your Capstone Profile

The information you have collected has powerful implications. Now you have to convert it into something more manageable. To create your capstone profile, use this process:

Step I: Create a capstone profile information bank. Assemble all the information about your capstone in one place. Consolidate your notes from the library, networking, capstone profile interviews, job descriptions, and talks with headhunters. You will keep adding to this as you collect more information. Write down all your randomly associated thoughts, impressions, "he said/she said" information, tips and shortcuts, fears and reservations. Get some distance. Look for patterns you couldn't see when you were nose to nose with your information sources.

Step II: Create a list of capstone-relevant skills. Sift out the specific skills that define your capstone profile. Include the skills that are:

- the minimum you need to be considered for the job
- the ones you actually need to perform the job
- the ones you must perform most frequently or daily
- the ones most critical to being seen as successful

Step III: Divide this skill list into three sublists. Make a list of the skills that people agree are the bare-bones minimum needed to get a foot in the door. Then make two other skills lists: basic and specialized skills. The basic skills (communication, interpersonal, production, and so on) should generally be acquired first. The more technical or specialized skills can often be acquired later.

You now have a capstone profile. If your information is reasonably accurate, your capstone profile will tell you those skills anyone would need to become a qualified contender for your capstone. This capstone profile is at the core of your Doom Loop strategy—to seek only jobs, assignments, and educational experiences that help qualify you for your career capstone.

But before you use this capstone profile to guide your journey, you must define the two critical reference points that specify all the stops, starts, and turns ahead. They are:

* where you are now
* where you hope to finish

While the skills in your capstone profile define your destination, the ones you hold right now define your point of departure. To determine what you must do next, you will have to assess where you are now, and which skills you've already acquired through your work and life experience. These skills make up your career mosaic.

UNDERSTANDING YOUR CAREER MOSAIC

Your career mosaic is centered on you, not your capstone. It tells a personal story about what you have already learned.

Your career mosaic is a unique inventory of your competencies—a compendium of all the skills you've managed to acquire in life so far. Because we are all learners, the skills we use in and out of the workplace are continually evolving. Everyone who has ever worked anywhere has a career mosaic in progress. So do you. By cataloging your own career mosaic at any given point, you can get a personalized readout of the skills you've already mastered. Your career mosaic will reflect your predilections and aversions, your strengths and weaknesses, your assets and liabilities. For better or worse, it will capture your current range and level of skills.

Try seeing these skills as part of an unfinished mosaic, to be designed and redesigned as you go along. Each new skill you add is like a small, well-crafted tile that fits nicely into the larger design. But, given Doom Loop dynamics, that design is rarely static. It will keep changing over time and under the influence of your emerging career capstones.

How to Construct Your Career Mosaic

Knowing that your career mosaic is always evolving is important. But you'll need to know more than that. You'll need the relevant facts face up, in front of you. Plan to devote a few hours to finding out what your career mosaic looks like.

A lot of people want to skip over this step and bag a quick-fix success job. They see delineating their career mosaic as a trivial task or a tedious detour. It's neither. Your most important asset in planning your career at this stage is charting in nitpicking detail which skills you have and which you don't.

Follow this step-by-step approach for constructing your career mosaic.

> **Step I: "Core-dump" your skills.** Empty your memory banks. Gloss over nothing. Write down all the skills you can think of—essential or trivial—that you have acquired in paid or unpaid work up to this point. When you come up for air the second time, you're probably still not halfway finished. Take time to focus on different periods of your life, different jobs, different interests. All your life experience counts. Consider what you had to do most often on a job, what you enjoyed doing, what you despised. All skills should be included, regardless of how you feel about them. At this point, the question isn't even how well you can perform the particular skill—just whether or not you can do it. This list merely describes; it does not evaluate. For example, Allen worked as a night auditor in a fourth-rate hotel when he was in college. Even though he's no accounting wizard, he lists bookkeeping and cashier skills in his career mosaic. If your competence in a skill is passable, it's okay to put that skill in your mosaic. Include general skills like dealing with difficult people, keeping orderly records, and meeting deadlines, as well as any esoteric blue-chip skills you've acquired, like managing individual client investment portfolios, tracking airplanes on radar, or restoring damaged sixteenth-century paintings.
>
> **Step II: Mine your successes.** Thinking back to your last few jobs (and important experiences outside the

workplace), recall a time when you solved a problem or performed in a way that made you feel supremely competent. Recall what happened in glowing detail: What did you do? How did you feel? At the top of a page, write the heading "Success Skills." List the skills you used to achieve your successes. Be prepared for surprises. For example, although Cynthia has been an elementary school teacher for twenty years, her success experiences are not centered in the classroom. They revolve around organizing two conferences on gifted children for her school district. Under success skills she listed designing brochures, managing public relations, planning conferences, and networking. If she hadn't focused on her success experiences, she might have failed to include these important and satisfying skills.

Step III: Consider your failures. Look at the situations in which you felt oddly uneasy or incompetent, or in which you experienced failure. Sure, no one likes to think about these situations, but they happen to everyone. And they're packed with information about skills you may need to develop further or ones you need to avoid. List these skills on a separate page under "Improvement Skills." Here's an example. In Lee's work as a hospital social worker, he must review the departmental budget with auditors. Although no one knows it, Lee feels very uneasy about this process. What Lee knows and keeps hidden is that he neither understands nor feels comfortable with financial matters. So under improvement skills he lists budget writing, money management, bookkeeping, and financial planning skills. Even though finance is a small part of his job, the inadequacy he feels is not correspondingly small. Grouping these skills together makes it easy for Lee to see that he has to improve or avoid these skills as he moves toward his next capstones.

Step IV: Develop a skill competence list. This is tricky because most of us aren't very objective about ourselves. Some are overoptimistic; most of us underrate our skills. Keep your own biases in mind as you review your competence in the skills you have listed. Reorganize your skills into two groups that reflect your current mastery level. The first group contains the skills in which you have "can do" competence. You either can or cannot ride a bicycle. If you can do it, the skill in question belongs in the "can do" group. The second group contains the skills in which you've managed to attain a fair degree of mastery (not to be confused with perfection). Suppose you bike regularly and last year pedaled your way along the Tex-Mex border just for the fun of it. For you, biking is a skill that goes beyond "can do." You'll place it in the mastery group.

Depending on where you are in your career and the richness of your experience, your career mosaic could fill several pages or several dozen. Since the design of your mosaic is a continuing process, dating your last entries will help you remember when you stopped. Periodically update this mosaic by adding new skills you are learning and by reevaluating your level of skill mastery.

What Your Career Mosaic Tells You

Let's suppose your career mosaic is safely tucked away somewhere. How will it keep you from making mistakes and help you reach your capstone?

For starters, having a career mosaic in progress keeps your finger on the pulse of your skill development, which helps you gain access to what you know, to how much you've already learned, and to all you've had to overcome to get to where you are now.

Your career mosaic helps you convert your past work history from a disparate assortment of unrelated job titles and tasks to a cogent, personalized set of skills that describe your competencies. This skill-centered focus is at the heart of developing a successful Doom Loop career strategy based on preferences and performance.

Your career mosaic also serves as an important diagnostic tool. Remember the generic, all-purpose skills we talked about in the last chapter? These are the skills basic to nearly any job or capstone that also boost your adaptability across different organizations and situations.

Assess your career mosaic to see whether you have acquired a reasonable distribution of all-purpose skills in such categories as:

- self-management skills
- communication skills
- interpersonal skills
- analytic skills

Since most people think in terms of specific job skills rather than these skill "headlines," it may be hard for you to tell at a glance which categories your skills fall into. Scan the skills you've listed and think about which ones relate to each other. Let's say you have skills in hiring and firing, training new employees, supervising a department, organizing and implementing direct-mail marketing, assigning tasks, and evaluating performance. All these skills—except for direct-mail marketing—fall under a management headline. Direct-mail marketing falls under a marketing headline.

To tell an accurate story with these skills, you'll need to think through which skills fall into common categories, and why. Although this takes practice, using your common sense, you'll get the hang of it soon enough. The best way to find out how skills naturally cluster together in work situations is to interview people who use the skills that interest you.

Once you begin analyzing the skills in your career mosaic according to their similarities, you will get a broader view of your competencies. You'll see where they fall relative to various headline skills like management, finance, organizational, and customer service skills. With this information handy, you'll be able to see which basic skill headlines you have or lack. You'll be able to see what's missing and which categories are too sparsely populated.

If you lack a group of building-block skills, you're likely to be career disadvantaged no matter what your current capstone. So if you find any gaping holes in your skill groupings, it pays to add these missing basic skill groups to your target mosaic even when they are not critical to your next capstone.

Look at your career mosaic as a personal history that traces revealing patterns in your career evolution. For example, do your skills accentuate people more than things or information? How happy are you with any patterns you identify? This information can help you decide what kinds of jobs to take next.

YOUR TARGET MOSAIC

Your target mosaic is the bridge to your capstone. It is the set of skills—the career "tiles" next in line to be added to your career mosaic. Once you know what these tiles are, you can seek the jobs, training, experience, and environments that allow you to develop them.

The target mosaic pinpoints what you still must learn to qualify for your capstone. It describes in illuminating detail the skills that will transform you from an unqualified "wannabe" into a highly qualified "gonnabe."

How do you know which tiles to add? Easy. By carefully defining your capstone profile and your career mosaic and by discovering which skills in your capstone profile are not in your career mosaic.

Here are six simple steps you can use to define your target mosaic.

Step I: Review the two lists you've already made: your capstone profile and your career mosaic. Remember, your capstone profile details the skills and knowledge anyone needs to reach a particular capstone. Your career mosaic lays out your current base of skills and knowledge.

Step II: Compare your capstone profile and your career mosaic lists skill by skill. There are only three possible results. Any given skill listed will be:

- in your career mosaic but not your capstone profile—so let it go
- in both lists—so you're all set
- in your capstone profile but not your career mosaic—so you've got work to do

Obviously it is this last category that interests us most.

Step III: Cross off skills in your career mosaic that do not appear in your capstone profile.

Step IV: List any skills that appear in both your career mosaic and your capstone profile. There are usually a few. But before you set any of these skills aside, carefully consider your competence in them. For each, ask yourself whether it's one of those "can do" skills or a "mastery" skill in which you have achieved experience and reasonable comfort. If you current mastery of any skill is sufficient to be considered for entry to your capstone, shelve it for now. It requires no immediate attention. But if your competence in a given skill isn't up to par, that skill goes on your target mosaic list.

Step V: Pay close attention to skills in your capstone profile that aren't in your career mosaic. Write these skills down and hang onto them. Along with the skills you have but need to improve, they form the core of your target mosaic. These remaining skills prescribe exactly what you need to learn next in order to qualify for your capstone. If you've chosen a sufficiently challenging capstone, you'll have quite a few skills to learn. If you come up with none or very few, your capstone profile and your career mosaic are a near-perfect match. Your target mosaic reveals that you've chosen a low-challenge, right-around-the-corner capstone. If you've been working steadily toward your capstone over time, this could be positive evidence that you're getting close. But if this is a new capstone, the Doom Loop predicts that you're courting career jeopardy. True, you won't have to achieve much to qualify for such a capstone, but you won't find much challenge, either. If this is the case, you may want to rethink your capstone.

Step VI: Write down all the skills in your target mosaic in a separate notebook or computer file, and keep a copy where you can easily get to it. This is your personalized career "to do" list. As you attain mastery in various skills on this list, you'll want to check these skills off. At any given time, your target mosaic should tell you the specific skills you still must learn to reach your capstone.

Now that you have your target mosaic, you are ready to design a career strategy that leads you directly to your capstone.

Your Target Mosaic Strategy

Get ready to change your mind about how best to manage your career. Your target mosaic is an alternative career management strategy that gives you a competitive decision-making edge. It may go against the grain of your old assumptions about fancy job titles, length of stay in a job, upward mobility, and other career advice you've been given.

Use it to help you select wisely the kinds of jobs, projects, and environments that develop the capstone profile you are aiming for. If you are tired of grazing the classifieds in hope of a "career opportunity" or being managed by other people's agendas, follow these strategies:

- In your next career decision, choose job opportunities or projects that permit you to learn the skills in your target mosaic.
- Remember that the skills a given job permits you to acquire are far more important than the particulars of the job itself—place, title, status, or grade level.
- Stay in any organization or department only as long as working there contributes to the acquisition of your targeted skills.
- Regard lateral moves and even downward moves that give you needed skills as more desirable than upward moves that do not.
- Should you elect to stay in a job that isn't contributing relevant skills to your career mosaic, it's up to you to expand and enrich this position, taking on new tasks and responsibilities in line with your capstone profile.
- Add targeted skills to your career mosaic through special projects and task forces, work teams, community and board activities, continuing education, and training to avoid dead-ending or plateauing in your career.

If you adopt these approaches, expect your career mosaic to undergo many positive transformations. Your success in skill-building will depend on your own ability to seize and create opportunity. This, in turn, will bring you face to face with potential jobs, projects, and work environments for acquiring the skills in your target mosaic.

To the uninitiated or the conventional, your approach may appear eclectic. But so long as you're deliberately using your target mosaic—rather than fate or a company or a mentor—as a guide to your capstone, you're on the right path. And, whatever happens, your work life will be interesting.

SOME TARGET MOSAIC ADVICE

The principle of using your target mosaic to acquire skills for your capstone is simple enough. However, the process of actually acquiring these skills requires careful analysis and planning.

For example, Andy seeks any new job that gives him the opportunity to develop any skill that is still on his target mosaic. When it comes to skill-building, Andy's like an opportunistic virus seeking a host. He doesn't mind job hopping as long as he's bagging another target mosaic skill. In times of massive cutbacks and unemployment, Andy's approach can serve as a reasonable and effective survival strategy. But in calmer times, his approach is long on energy, short on strategy.

A better operating plan as you move toward your capstone is to make thoughtful decisions based on the experiences that will give you the greatest adaptability and satisfaction. As you make skill-building decisions, remember these six principles:

- Don't paint yourself into an expert's corner.
- Piggyback new skills on old skills.
- Roll related skills into one work experience.
- Use old skills to break into new environments.
- Compress the time needed to learn less-preferred skills.
- Choose learning-driven work environments.

Don't Paint Yourself into an Expert's Corner

Why lock yourself into a highly specialized technical job too early in the game? Resist the temptation of trying to become an instant expert. Build generic, all-purpose skills first. This maximizes your protection against unforeseen changes in your industry and in technology. When organizations restructure and decentralize, management often asks employees to do work far beyond their original jobs. When this happens, an engineer who can write and manage has an edge over one who can't.

Developing a broad generic skill base also has a high payoff should you change your mind about a particular capstone, since it's easier to transfer these all-purpose skills to other capstones. Reanalyze your target mosaic in terms of the generic and specific skills it requires. Then develop a plan for acquiring both that gives priority to generic skills. If you aspire to a position as a corporate vice president MIS, get interpersonal, production, communication, management, finance, sales, and political skills under your belt before you become the reigning monarch of silicon chips. You won't be sorry.

Piggyback New Skills on Old Skills

By definition, your target mosaic contains skills you don't possess yet. But in choosing the jobs, experiences, and workplaces that will give you the opportunity to learn them, why start from square one?

Economize your efforts. Take assignments and jobs that build on your current skills and knowledge. Use your tried-and-true job skills as an entry card into jobs that use old skills and teach a few new ones.

Sally used her eight years of nursing to land a job as an editorial assistant with a medical textbook publisher. While still a far cry from her capstone of documentary film producing, this job gave Sally the opportunity to piggyback targeted new skills in writing, documentation, distribution, and publishing on older nursing skills that made her an instant asset to the company. Piggybacking new skills on old skills is a strategy that achieves positive results.

Roll Related Skills into One Work Experience

Why not preserve your energy and accelerate your progress by killing two birds with one stone? Analyze your target mosaic to find skills that pair together. Try grouping skills using the basic headlines (interpersonal, production, management, and so on) discussed earlier, or broader skill categories like people, things, or information. Ask yourself which kinds of jobs or projects might combine two or more of these skills.

Chuck's target mosaic showed that he lacked mastery in the management and people skills he needed to qualify for his capstone of hospital administrator. His solution was to take a job in a small medical supply firm that gave him management responsibility as well as human relations and people skills in the sales end of the firm. Marianne combined learning several different skills related to her capstone of vice president of communications for a financial institution. She used a shadow-box approach, taking a job that gave her experience in public relations for a local business college and, at the same time, enrolling in an evening course that helped her develop her business writing skills. Then Marianne took it one step further. She paired her paid work with community volunteer work, writing a column on finance for older adults. Marianne shortened her learning time by focusing on simultaneous skill-building in a series of related target mosaic skills.

Use Old Skills to Break into New Environments

You're a claims adjuster who wants to be a buyer in the retail fashion industry. You know what your target mosaic looks like, and the bridge between you and your capstone looms before you like the Great Wall of China. You fear it's going to be a long and costly journey.

The answer? When you're long on ambition and short on time, get smart, not discouraged. There are few miracles on the road to your capstone—only good and not so good strategies. If you don't have contacts who can sneak you through the back door and you can't manage a transformational transition by going back to school for an image-changing credential, rethink your strategy. Try plugging your old familiar career mosaic skills into a job in the targeted new industry or organization.

The advantages of this approach are that it can be done relatively easily and that it frees you to concentrate on learning the new environment and work lingo. What you avoid is the harsh struggle to learn new skills and a new culture simultaneously. Instead, you will be learning the operations of the new industry, as well as the subtler norms, values, and politics of the new setting.

So if you're a claims adjuster who wants to become a buyer in the retail clothing industry, consider working in the claims department of a corporate retail chain. It's a low-risk transition that familiarizes you with the inner workings of the new industry. This knowledge gives you a competitive advantage when you go for that lateral move that puts you closer to your capstone. And the information you gather in an environment relevant to your capstone will provide you with valuable insider's shortcuts and insights.

Compress the Time Needed to Learn Less-Preferred Skills

Why suffer longer than necessary? Even the best of all possible capstones will require learning some skills you're not going to like. Learn those skills as quickly as possible. Begin by identifying these target mosaic skills you can't stand. Then look for brief seminars, college courses, apprenticeships, or internships that teach them. People who have been working for decades often overlook these options. If you need to learn a skill you dislike—say, statistics—for your personnel manager capstone, why slug it out in a long-term job in finance or wage and salary compensation when you can take a neatly packaged one-semester college course instead? Remember, quality of life counts.

Choose Learning-Driven Work Environments

Not all workplaces are created equal. Some encourage growth and development; some encourage stagnation and stasis. Knowing what your target mosaic looks like gives you an advantage, since you know what to learn. But in some work cultures you'll have to fight for the opportunity to learn, to be a rookie, and to make mistakes. In these cultures, errors will stick with you, and your penchant for new skill-building will cause resentment. So, if you're committed to acquiring the skills in your target mosaic, why not choose a learning-driven work culture?

How do you recognize one? If you're interviewing with a company, ask relevant questions. Does the company have a team-based culture that rewards employees for developing skills outside their job descriptions? In the next decades many organizations will pay their employees bonuses for developing greater adaptability and skill diversity. Does management encourage employees to participate in multidepartmental task forces and projects that build skills and foster new approaches? What is the company's tuition reimbursement policy? Are people who gain new expertise or degrees promoted or left languishing in the old job?

A learning-driven work culture will accelerate your skill-building program, the foundation of your journey toward capstone.

CREATING A JOB SKILL PROFILE

Using your target mosaic as a guide, you can go job shopping for positions that allow you to develop the skills you need for your capstone. But how do you know which jobs to take? First, find out which skills a job requires. Which are on your target mosaic? Which are in your capstone profile?

If a job fails to offer you sufficient opportunity for target mosaic skill-building, it's nothing more than an attractive nuisance. It will take you on the wrong journey.

Say no, and keep hunting. If a job offers the skills in your target mosaic, assess it carefully. The next chapter, on Doom Loop dynamics, will give you more detailed information on how to do this in a way that will keep you happy and satisfied in Quadrant I of your Loop.

NEGOTIATE BEFORE YOU SIGN THE CONTRACT

They made you an offer you can't refuse. But before you accept any offer, negotiate for the right to learn certain skills, to participate in certain projects, and to work with certain people. This will be taken as further evidence that you have the right stuff, that you're this company's kind of person. This is the time to tinker with the skill profile of the tendered job and stretch its skill-building potential. See to what extent the company will let you do this. After you've become the old kid on the block, you may not be accorded as much consideration.

BE A GOOD CHOOSER

No matter where you are in your career, choosing the right path to your capstone is vital. Take on jobs and projects that are compatible with your personal preferences and that you can tolerate long enough to achieve mastery of your targeted skills. Since job titles won't tell the whole story, it will be up to you to decode the skill opportunities in each position.

In the next chapter, we'll look at how the Doom Loop can help you keep a realistic, upbeat perspective as you move through the various feeder jobs and assignments that lead to your capstone. Unlike the target mosaic, the Doom Loop, with its four quadrants, is constructed from the skills within a specific job you are considering taking or leaving. We'll explore how the Doom Loop can help you make intelligent career choices that provide greater challenge, satisfaction, and competence on the road to your capstone.

CHAPTER 4

How to Succeed at Doom Looping

Why the "Doom" in Doom Loop? Why not something more upbeat?

Because "doom" is an appropriately ominous term, ringing like a loud alarm clock, awakening you to present and future dangers of sleepwalking through your career. Knowledge of the Doom Loop puts you in a better position to avoid "doom" in your work life. By alerting you to what's likely to go wrong and showing you how to avert it, the principles of the Doom Loop can dramatically alter your career management strategies.

You can enlist the principles discussed in this chapter to keep yourself happy, satisfied, and challenged in the jobs you will take en route to your capstone. Forget about having to settle for an indigestible daily fare of career frustration and boredom. You can do much better. But how?

You've already set your direction with your capstone and pinpointed the specific skills you need to acquire with your target mosaic. But you'll need even more.

You'll need to keep creating and re-creating challenge and excitement in your work, and to make smart job choices at critical junctures. Once you decide to manage your career rather than let it manage you, you'll be faced with all kinds of course-setting decisions.

This is where a decision-making model like the Doom Loop comes in handy. It acts as a check against making spur-of-the-moment, knee-jerk career decisions that you'll regret. Most people are too close to the action to make wise tactical decisions about their own careers. And so are many of their career advisers.

The result? Career myopia. Sometimes it's hard to see the forest for the trees. It's natural to get caught up in the daily grind—the job itself, the organizational culture, the rumors, the politics. This makes it easy for smart people to arrive at wrong conclusions. When they feel dissatisfied, they blame themselves or whatever or whoever else happens to be in closest proximity. Or they close down, slipping defensively into denial and ignoring the common early warning signs of career doom, hoping things will magically right themselves. Too often people conclude that a fatter paycheck will nip their career problem in the bud.

But even when things are going well, a complacent "it won't get any better than this" attitude is a major liability. It just keeps you from planning. And "planning," for some people, has a more unpleasant ring to it than "doom." They confuse planning with worrying, and hit the procrastination button to keep their anxiety at bay. But whether or not you plan for it, things change.

The problem comes from misdiagnosing what is happening. Rather than interpreting career discontent (or success) as part of a larger, more predictable career picture, we view whatever happens as intensely personal and idiosyncratic. We feel ashamed, inadequate, and upset. In failing to see the larger scheme of things, we unintentionally set ourselves up for hasty decisions that cure the wrong malady and cause hurt for years to come.

The Doom Loop can help you see that bigger career picture by providing a framework for looking at what happens to people in their careers over time. You can use the principles of the Doom Loop to help escape feeling doomed in your career.

DOOMED BY ONE'S OWN HAND

It happens every day. Bright, talented people regularly doom themselves in their careers. It's certainly not intentional. Consider the following examples:

ANNA BARLOW: a successful entertainment production executive. Without knowing it, Anna has been building a target mosaic for more than ten years. She is in her mid-thirties and is just where she has always wanted to be. No one is any better than Anna. Just ask Anna or her legions of satisfied clients. Yet inexplicably, Anna feels bored by her job. She blames herself and wonders how she can possibly feel this way after all she has put into it, after all she has sacrificed to get here. All she can do is try to tough it out. But Anna is doomed.

BOB BERGER: a young lawyer, five years out of law school, recently hired as a lobbyist for a brewery, what Bob knows about the beer industry could fit inside a bottle. Outside of a summer job as a congressional intern, he has no experience as a lobbyist. But he's excited about his work, and the brewery executives really like him. Still, Bob feels edgy about his competence. His enormous performance anxiety drives him to work long hours researching the industry and networking with key legislators. His wife wants him to go to work for her father's law firm, where the work is more routine and he won't have to fly by the seat of his pants. Reluctantly, Bob accepts his father-in-law's offer, and is doomed.

LINDA SONNENSCHEIN: a forty-five-year-old top-of-the-line executive secretary. In her heart, Linda knows she would be much happier designing offices than working in them. But when she tells her friends about her career aspirations she always sighs, adding that leaving her job would impose too many harsh financial burdens. In reality, Linda is afraid of becoming a novice at this point in her career. When she is offered another executive secretarial job involving duties nearly identical to those of her present one, but at twice the pay, she doesn't hesitate. She grabs the offer. Her friends are delighted for her, and Linda is doomed.

JACK CARBONI: an award-winning veteran sales-person. Here is a man who loves his work and is good at it. His company recently offered him a job as a sales manager. Jack has a capstone: someday he'd like to own a sales incentive company. So he turns the company's offer down. His reasoning: Why should he take this offer? He figures it means in-creased responsibility with lower income. It's a lot safer just to wait another five years until the economy shifts upward, or wait until his earnings wear thin and then leave. But when Jack turns the offer down, he dooms himself in a job he loves.

What do these bright, conscientious people have in common? Each has made a detrimental career choice that could have been prevented with even a cursory understanding of the mechanics of the Doom Loop. Yet, as their dissatisfactions play out, none of them will even realize that they've been doomed by their own hand.

If they did realize it, how could they make better career choices? How can you make better choices?

DECISIONS AND THE DOOM LOOP

No matter what stage of your work life you're in, you'll make scores of decisions that will shape your future. Many will revolve around when to leave your present job and which new ones to take or target. If you're like most people, you decide to take a new job because of push factors (you realize you're unhappy with your current position) rather than pull factors (what a new job offers you). Here are some sit-uations that can push people to get their résumés out on the street:

- Your boss infuriates you by underutilizing your abilities and attributing your successes to favored players.
- The vice president you report to makes Attila the Hun look like a four-star humanitarian.

⌄ • You feel patronized by oversupervision and long for more autonomy.
⌄• The politics in your work environment consume your energy and are driving you batty.
⌄ • Your accomplishments are unsung, unappreciated, and taken for granted.
⌄• You're not being paid enough for what you do.
• You spend most of the day wondering, "Is this all there is?"
• You squander each day watching the second hand on the clock.
• You've been passed over for a promotion you thought had your name on it.
• You've been fired and have to land a new position quickly to make the mortgage payments.

These situations make you highly vulnerable to action—any action. Change is full of promise; your current situation is not. Your discontent creates work-stopping wanderlust. You scan the available options and grab the best-looking one.

When you make important career choices in a reactive way, you're likely to create as many problems as you solve. Or you may find yourself traveling down a brand-new fork of the same old career path. Like a love affair you jump into on the rebound, the miraculous new job often turns out to be an immensely promising, ultimately disappointing quick fix.

You may be drawn to new jobs not only as a reaction against your old one, but because you're lured by a glamorous location, a substantial salary increase, perks, status, company reputation, and so on. These are tantalizing bait. But unless you're extraordinarily lucky, none will move you closer to your capstone.

The principle of the Doom Loop will. It takes into account that you'll regularly change jobs and assignments, seeking new career opportunities consistent with your capstone. It will help you decide:

• the best time to take a new job or assignment
• when it's time to leave the job you're in

- given your career and target mosaic, the kind of job to take next
- the kinds of jobs to turn down

Regardless of your situation and the pressures you're under, you can enlist the Doom Loop to chart your career trajectory more objectively and make choices that better fit your needs. The Doom Loop provides a clear standard for assessing whether or not the position or project in question is worth pursuing.

THE BASICS OF DOOM LOOPING

When you think about taking any job, you are likely to ask yourself two basic questions:

- Will I be any good at this job?
- Will I like this job?

The first question relates to performance. If you are like most people, being competent in your work is a major consideration. You want to be good at what you do for a living. It's more than a matter of pride; it's a matter of self-worth. It affects how you feel about yourself. But if a job involves skills you've never used, predicting your competence can be tough. However, if you have some experience with the skills involved, you will be able to rate your performance more accurately. Although there's room for differences of opinion among observers or between supervisors' evaluations, a person's level of competence can be objectively verified—more or less.

The second question is far more subjective. It concerns your own preference. Preference taps into your attitudes and feelings about what you do at work. Your liking for a job is an instant attitudinal shorthand for a whole array of complex factors. How much do the tasks of the job let you express your values, interests, and sense of yourself? Are some parts of the job pure fun or challenge? Do the job's skills play to your needs and motivations? Do you get so involved that you lose track of time? How do you feel at the end of a typical day on the job? How did you feel at the beginning?

Start by asking yourself these two simple questions—whether or not you like and are good at your current job. Give your instinctive, unexpurgated reaction to each. Be totally honest with yourself; you don't have to tell your answers to anyone else.

Now ask yourself these same two questions again, only this time be specific.

Identify each of the sets of skills you use to do your job—just as you did when researching your capstone and developing a target mosaic. Write down the skills you use most frequently to get things accomplished. Think of a time when you scored a success on the job. Which skills came into play then? Think of a time when you dropped the ball with dire consequences. Which skills tripped you up? Write all these skills down. Then look over the list and add any skills you've left off that your job requires occasionally.

Now, for each specific skill, rate your own preference and performance. Some people find they have a hard time liking skills they are not good at. If they are not proficient at something, they avoid it. It's not that they dislike the skill; what they dislike is their lack of expertise. If this describes you, get around this confusion by asking—one skill at a time—"Would I like it if I were good at it?" Take a yes answer as evidence of liking.

What you come out with will look something like this:

RATING PREFERENCE AND PERFORMANCE FOR YOUR CURRENT JOB SKILLS

| | PREFERENCE | | PERFORMANCE | |
	LIKE	DON'T LIKE	GOOD AT	NOT GOOD AT
Skills	•	•	•	•
	•	•	•	•
	•	•	•	•
	•	•	•	•
	•	•	•	•

I developed the skill list that follows while working with a personnel supervisor who was considering a career change. To identify the skills in her job, she first logged the skills she used most frequently in a week. That log gave us plenty of raw material for figuring out the basic headline skills and filling in the more detailed ones that comprise each skill cluster. She also looked at the kinds of skills that had helped her successfully negotiate some sticky situations, as well as those that made her want to wave an instant job change wand, such as organizing meetings. We checked her company's job description, too, just to make sure we hadn't overlooked anything obvious. On the next pages is a partial list of her skill analysis for the job of supervisor of personnel services.

SKILL ANALYSIS FOR SUPERVISOR OF PERSONNEL SERVICES

MANAGEMENT SKILLS				
Like	Don't Like	Good At	Not Good At	Skills Used in Current Job
———	———	———	———	Directing people
———	———	———	———	Setting priorities and goals
———	———	———	———	Planning activities
———	———	———	———	Supervising activities of subordinates
———	———	———	———	Delegating tasks
———	———	———	———	Reporting to supervisors
———	———	———	———	Demonstrating accountability
———	———	———	———	Identifying key problems
———	———	———	———	Gathering data
———	———	———	———	Solving problems
———	———	———	———	Coordinating actions
———	———	———	———	Developing personnel
———	———	———	———	Organizing meetings
———	———	———	———	Time management
———	———	———	———	Hiring/recruiting people
———	———	———	———	Firing people
———	———	———	———	Evaluating performance

				PERSONNEL SKILLS

Like	Don't Like	Good At	Not Good At	Skills Used in Current Job
_____	_____	_____	_____	Human relations skills
_____	_____	_____	_____	Communication skills
_____	_____	_____	_____	Administering personnel policies
_____	_____	_____	_____	Performing personnel services
_____	_____	_____	_____	Maintaining personnel records
_____	_____	_____	_____	Assembling pension information
_____	_____	_____	_____	Handling transfers/hires/ terminations
_____	_____	_____	_____	Maintaining payroll, medical, tax records
_____	_____	_____	_____	Interacting with legal system
_____	_____	_____	_____	Coordinating personnel-related programs
_____	_____	_____	_____	Negotiating
_____	_____	_____	_____	Dealing with irate employees
_____	_____	_____	_____	Handling confidential matters

APPLYING THE PREFERENCE/PERFORMANCE MATRIX

The next step involves using preferences and performance to construct a two-by-two matrix as shown on the next page. The matrix shows four possible skill-based ways of evaluating jobs.

As you may recall from the first chapter, each quadrant carries certain implications.

	LIKE	DON'T LIKE
GOOD AT	QUADRANT II	QUADRANT III
NOT GOOD AT	QUADRANT I	QUADRANT IV

If, for example, your job skills fall mostly into Quadrant I, you like the required skills well enough, but aren't particularly good at them. You're a rookie faced with the task of proving that you have whatever it takes to do the job. Until you do that, you'll be living with your own doubts and sense of inadequacy. Therefore, even though you're likely to feel challenged, it's normal to feel anxious or insecure. Some people get so uncomfortable about their lack of expertise that they make a career out of avoiding Quadrant I jobs and tasks. This is a big mistake.

If your skills fall predominantly into Quadrant II, you enjoy the skills required for your job and are competent in them, too. When you think about the last Quadrant II job you held, you probably remember feeling happy, satisfied, and lucky to hold the position. A Quadrant II job is a hard job to leave.

If your skills cluster in Quadrant III, even though you're good at most of the skills of the job, you don't enjoy doing them. You're likely to feel bored and frustrated—even trapped—in a job where you've worked hard to develop your mastery and expertise. People in Quadrant III jobs often blame themselves for not being happier with their lot. It seems unfair: if they're so good at what they do, why aren't they more content?

Should you find your skills clumped in Quadrant IV, you neither like the skills of your job nor are good at them. You feel you have "the job from Hell," and for you that's true. The thought of going to work each morning causes you to break out in a cold sweat. If this quadrant captures your situation, you're likely to feel depressed and hopeless and yearn for faraway places.

Which quadrant fits your current job? You can pinpoint the quadrant that best describes your current position in two different ways: tapping intuition and matrix mapping. Let's begin with intuition.

TAPPING YOUR INTUITION

The feelings and attitudes common to each quadrant of this matrix have been distilled from the descriptions of more than two hundred fifty people who have worked with the Doom Loop. Some of them are noted on the chart on the following page.

When you think about your current or last position, which feelings are closest to your own? Which quadrant captures most of them? Which is the runner-up? Even though this approach gives you a broad-stroke, impressionistic view of the quadrants, do you feel relatively certain of your judgment?

To get a firmer handle on your feelings about your job, complete the Doom Loop Quadrant Finder on pp. 90–91. It describes some typical attitudes, behaviors, and feelings that people in each quadrant of the matrix are likely to hold.

After you rate your level of agreement with these twenty statements, use your score to locate yourself on the Performance/Preference Matrix. Your highest quadrant score indicates that your feelings and attitudes resemble those of people who have actually rated their skills and landed in that particular quadrant. But remember, the Doom Loop Quadrant Finder doesn't rate your actual competence in the particular skills required by your job. It simply uses your feelings

FEELINGS AND ATTITUDES OF PEOPLE IN EACH QUADRANT

	Like	Don't Like
Good At	**Quadrant II** Satisfied Committed Challenged Involved Attentive Focused on the here and now Excited Confident Striving Energized through work Glad to be here In control	**Quadrant III** Vaguely dissatisfied Panicky/in crisis Bored/frustrated Lacking self-discipline Careless/distracted Questioning self/past Secure Disappointed Passively coping Meeting needs outside work Mechanized/dusty Out of control
Not Good At	**Quadrant I** Motivated Insecure Pressured Eager Challenged Excited Fearful of failing Connected Nervous Worried Overwhelmed	**Quadrant IV** Lethargic Desperate Hopeless Angry Trapped Disillusioned Feeling like a failure Alone Depressed Worried Bored

and attitudes as indicators to sort you into a particular quadrant. For example, if your highest score on the Quadrant Finder is in Quadrant I, it means that your feelings and attitudes about your job resemble those of people whose ratings of their own skills for a given job fall in Quadrant I. But your score on the Quadrant Finder doesn't show that you actually like most of the skills of your current job without being good at them.

In other words, this is an intuitive analysis of your job based on your feelings. For many people, this type of analysis is all the confirmation they need. They feel sure that the quadrant in which they've placed themselves is right. When they think about their skill preferences and actual performance, the pattern fits their intuitive analysis closely enough for them to feel comfortable moving on to the next step. But other people don't feel they can rely on their intuition—they're more comfortable with the more precise skill analysis of matrix mapping.

DOOM LOOP QUADRANT FINDER

1. First, relax and picture yourself in the midst of an ordinary work day. Then look at each of the following statements and ask yourself how well it describes your typical attitudes, behavior, or feelings.
2. Now assess your agreement or disagreement with each statement:

    1. Highly disagree
    2. Disagree somewhat
    3. Neither agree nor disagree
    4. Agree somewhat
    5. Highly agree

_2_ 1. I am confronted with so many new tasks at work that I worry about failing.
_5_ 2. I feel lucky to hold a job that allows me to accomplish what I really enjoy.
_1_ 3. I am not as attentive to details as I used to be.
_4_ 4. Often, I feel overstimulated at work and have a hard time coming down.
_4_ 5. I exert a good deal of control over the quality and quantity of my work.
_1_ 6. Many mornings I think that I would rather be almost anywhere other than at work.

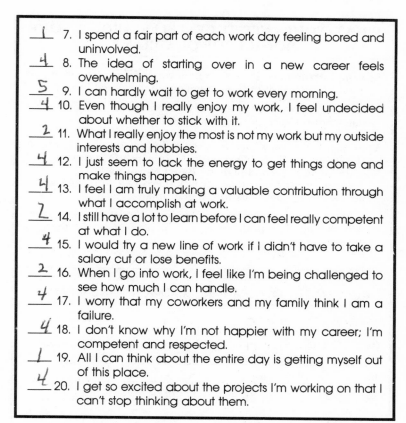

__1__ 7. I spend a fair part of each work day feeling bored and uninvolved.

__4__ 8. The idea of starting over in a new career feels overwhelming.

__5__ 9. I can hardly wait to get to work every morning.

__4__ 10. Even though I really enjoy my work, I feel undecided about whether to stick with it.

__2__ 11. What I really enjoy the most is not my work but my outside interests and hobbies.

__4__ 12. I just seem to lack the energy to get things done and make things happen.

__4__ 13. I feel I am truly making a valuable contribution through what I accomplish at work.

__2__ 14. I still have a lot to learn before I can feel really competent at what I do.

__4__ 15. I would try a new line of work if I didn't have to take a salary cut or lose benefits.

__2__ 16. When I go into work, I feel like I'm being challenged to see how much I can handle.

__4__ 17. I worry that my coworkers and my family think I am a failure.

__4__ 18. I don't know why I'm not happier with my career; I'm competent and respected.

__1__ 19. All I can think about the entire day is getting myself out of this place.

__4__ 20. I get so excited about the projects I'm working on that I can't stop thinking about them.

WHAT YOUR ATTITUDE TELLS ABOUT YOUR DOOM LOOP QUADRANT

Scoring Instructions: Place the rating you gave each statement on the list to the right of the statement number listed below.

After you have done this, total the ratings you assigned each statement for each of the four columns.

Your Score: You now have your scores for Quadrant I, Quadrant II, Quadrant III, and Quadrant IV. In which Quadrant do you score highest? Second highest? Based on your attitudes to your work (not your competence or lack thereof), you feel most like people in the quadrants with higher totals.

Compare your scores on the Quadrant Finder to your actual skill ratings for preference and performance. Is there a difference?

QUADRANT I	QUADRANT II	QUADRANT III	QUADRANT IV
1 2	2 5	3 1	6 1
4 4	5 4	7 1	8 4
10 2	9 5	11 2	12 4
14 2	13 4	15 2	17 4
16 2	20 4	18 2	19 1
14	22	12	14
Total	Total	Total	Total

Write your total scores for each quadrant in the DOOM LOOP MATRIX on the next page.

DOOM LOOP MATRIX

	LIKE	DON'T LIKE
GOOD AT	22 QUADRANT II	12 QUADRANT III
NOT GOOD AT	14 QUADRANT I	14 QUADRANT IV

Do your scores correspond to your intuitive sense of where you are located on your Doom Loop?

MATRIX MAPPING

Matrix mapping is a simple exercise that yields useful information. All you do is plot the job skills you've rated in the appropriate quadrants of the Performance/Preference Matrix. What you get after you have entered your ratings for each skill will look something like this:

SAMPLE MATRIX MAPPING FOR THE SKILLS OF A JOB

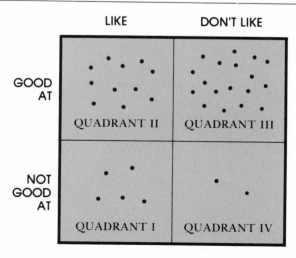

Because you are the one who is doing the rating, the actual distribution of skills, as shown by the number of skills in each quadrant, will cogently reflect your own personal evaluation. For example, in the matrix I've drawn here the majority of skills fall into Quadrant III, so we can safely predict that this person is likely to be experiencing relatively low job satisfaction and motivation. But since some skills also cluster in Quadrants I and II, this person encounters enough occasional challenge to cloud his or her decision to leave.

The way your skills shake out in the quadrants of the matrix tells a story about how you feel or will soon feel about the job you are evaluating. It also tells which skills you should seek and which you should avoid in planning your next career move.

WHEN MATRIX MAPPING AND INTUITION CLASH

Suppose you take both approaches to finding your Doom Loop quadrant, only to discover that your intuitive analysis lands you in one quadrant while your matrix mapping lands you in another.

For example, say your matrix mapping places most of your job skills in Quadrant II. You like what you're doing and feel competent in the skills of your job. But using your intuition or the Doom Loop Quadrant Finder as a guide plunks you squarely into Quadrant III! This shows that you feel trapped and discouraged about this job, even though your matrix mapping suggests that you should feel challenged and content.

What's wrong here? If your skill assessment is honest and accurate, your problem is not with the skills required by this job. It's with something else—like the work setting, the organizational culture, the personalities, or the office politics. If this is the case, consider changing departments or companies, not careers. The skills required by the job may be okay, but the fit isn't. You've got a diamond in the wrong setting. Find out what's causing you to feel discontent. Perhaps your own coping skills need fine-tuning. If so, seek feedback. Focus on adding vital interpersonal or political skills to your target mosaic. The trick is to identify the right problem before rushing out to fix something that might not be broken. Before you act, read the crises and politics chapters (Chapters 5 through 11) in this book to help you better analyze what's happening.

WHICH QUADRANT IS BEST?

For most people, there's no contest. Quadrant II is the winner. This makes sense. After all, Quadrant II represents a kind of career nirvana—a job where you like the skills and are great at performing them. Add a dash or two of recognition and a liberal sprinkling of pay and benefits, and who could ask for anything more?

But believe it or not, there's a problem in taking Quadrant II jobs. In fact, there are two problems. One is called time; the other is called learning.

So far we've been looking at a cross section of how the skills of your current job are distributed in the Doom Loop quadrants at a particular moment. But it's clear that nothing stays the same: not you, not your work situation. The passage of time will affect where your skills cluster in the matrix. Suppose you were to rate your preference and performance for your current job skills two or more years down the road. If the tasks and skills of your job remained the same, would your skills still fall in the same quadrants? Or would your liking for the job and your ability to perform it well change in predictable ways?

Time and learning are at the core of Doom Loop dynamics. As you'll recall from the first chapter, time and learning conspire to doom you when the skills of your job remain relatively stable over a period of years. In many instances, you'll have arrived in Quadrant II from Quadrant I, where you liked most of the skills of the job but lacked sufficient experience to be good at them. In Quadrant I, when you have no proven track record, you're likely to be motivated to master the skills you enjoy performing. And you'd better be—your survival in a Quadrant I job depends on it. If you have average or above-average intelligence and the ability to learn, you'll develop greater competence over time, eventually moving into Quadrant II. Otherwise you'll be out on the street looking for a new job.

Even though you started in Quadrant I, you've managed to land feet first in a coveted Quadrant II position. You're good at what you do and you like doing it. You are experiencing the inevitable effects of the learning curve and moving up its slope, gathering expertise in the skills required to succeed.

It would be nice if everyone's career journey could end with Quadrant II bliss. The problem is that even though you're happy and satisfied in Quadrant II, time and learning will continue to produce progressive changes in your performance and preference. If you fail to seek fresh challenges and new skills to master, or if your organization pigeonholes you, you run the risk of slipping right over the top of your own learning curve and sliding into Quadrant III.

How does this happen? If there's no new learning, you'll grow bored. The blush fades from the rose. Tedium replaces challenge. It's as inevitable as it is disheartening. People who repeat the same tasks day in and day out begin to lose interest in their performance, no matter how good they are at those tasks. They begin to feel flat and stagnant, even as they achieve more success. The work you used to love becomes old hat. The symptoms of Quadrant III malaise become harder and harder to ignore: it takes longer to get out of bed in the morning; you become a water cooler junkie; you have fantasies of heading west or heading anywhere. In the grip of Quadrant III you're likely to feel both trapped and guilty. You used to be driven by challenge, but now it's security that counts. Change frightens you. But if you stay in this job much longer your performance will wane.

And the story isn't over yet. Unless you do something to halt this slide, you'll drop into the dreaded Quadrant IV. Lack of learning combined with the passage of time in any job tends to wear people down. They lose interest in their jobs, failing to keep up on new developments in their fields and missing important deadlines. Their desks become top-heavy, sagging under massive heaps of untended, half-finished projects. Major assignments slip through the cracks and disappear. People in Quadrant IV dream about being somewhere else and being someone else. Their focus subtly shifts from striving toward success to avoiding failure.

In Quadrant IV you understand the "doom" in Doom Loop from firsthand experience. You're no longer good at what you do, and you don't like it much anyway—none of which makes you feel any better.

You experience Doom Loop dynamics firsthand as you move through the entire cycle from Quadrant I to Quadrant IV. The challenge that caused trepidation in Quadrant I has been transformed over time into a dull routine. In Quadrant II, you felt lucky to have this job; in Quadrant III you blanched at the prospect of another dreary day of applying your expertise in the same old way. In Quadrant IV you've lost your energy and motivation to perform your job well or at all.

If this pattern describes your career path, don't blame yourself. Like most people, you probably assumed that work competence conquers all, that being an expert is what counts. Whether you thought about it or not, you probably assigned a low priority to doing what you liked in the workplace. You opted for the tried and true, the familiar—not the new or strange. But when you stopped learning, you also stopped liking.

Even though you had never heard of a Doom Loop, you flipped right over the top of one. Lack of awareness of the Doom Loop won't keep you out of it—it will merely put you at a career disadvantage. When you don't recognize the journey you're on, you inadvertently risk taking a free fall down the backside of the learning curve. Welcome to the Doom Loop.

Now that you know about the Doom Loop, it could be time for you to reverse this cycle.

USING THE DOOM LOOP
QUADRANTS TO CHART YOUR COURSE

As the manager of your own career, expect to face many confusing decisions. To avoid grabbing ultimately unsatisfying Quadrant III or IV job offers, keep in mind that:

- No position, in and of itself, will fall exclusively or permanently in Quadrant I, II, III, or IV. The same job will fall in different quadrants, depending on who evaluates its skills and when. At different times the same person will place the same job in different quadrants. Change is the only career constant. You're not static, the job is not static, and time is not static.
- Just because a job falls in Quadrant I or II doesn't mean it's worth taking; it also has to fit your target mosaic and move you toward your capstone. Remember that your personal values and life-style count.

By bearing all this in mind when using the Doom Loop, you'll avoid many common career errors.

CHOOSING: THE DOOM LOOP'S
QUADRANTS CLOSE UP

Progress through the Doom Loop's quadrants can be subtle. If you've never heard of a Doom Loop, you might fail to protect yourself from an eventual slide into Quadrant III.

Instead, you might take this line of reasoning. After struggling to prove yourself in a Quadrant I job, you figure you'll take a time-out. You'll relax awhile and just enjoy your work. You deserve it. You've climbed the hill; you've mastered the challenge. Now it's your turn to sit on top and take in the view from Quadrant II. But if you rest too long or get too comfortable, you cease learning and discontent sets in. You try to compensate by working even harder at your job. Or you try to assuage your discontent by going after a higher salary, a bigger office, or more perks. Or you might change jobs, choosing a more grandiose version of your current position—one that merely guarantees your early arrival into Quadrant III or IV. Unfortunately, none of this helps.

The help you need is of a different type:

Doom Loop Tactic I: Take only those jobs and seek only those assignments that fit your target mosaic and have a high concentration of Quadrant I and II skills.

When you choose your jobs this way, you will avoid the ones that fall on the unfriendly right side of your matrix in Quadrants III and IV.

Let's take a closer look at each quadrant and how to make the Doom Loop work for you.

Quadrant I Plums

Once you know the Doom Loop it seems obvious: Quadrant I jobs—those high-challenge, high-preference positions—are the choicest plums in the job market, if:

- you can position yourself to land one
- the job you land helps you develop target skills that move you closer to qualifying for your capstone

Quadrant I jobs maximize your motivation to learn because they are compatible with your personal preferences and needs. In fact, acquiring many of the skills in a well-matched Quadrant I position is just plain fun! You are near the bottom of your own learning curve, mastering these skills because you want to. It's true that Quadrant I jobs can be risky: the more challenge you face, the more vulnerable you are to failure. But there's no shame in being a novice or in needing help. It's an exciting opportunity to stretch your skills and knowledge. Your lack of top-notch competence in Quadrant I skills may cause you anxiety, but you can use this anxiety to spur greater effort and performance. As long as the stress isn't overwhelming, Quadrant I jobs put you on fast forward to your capstone.

As a rule, then:

Quadrant I jobs are preferable to Quadrant II jobs.

Many seasoned professionals have trouble with this idea, even when they're disenchanted with their present positions. They dislike moves to Quadrant I because they often entail a reduction in status and pay. Experts who have already earned their stripes may balk at returning to a "novice" position even when the opportunity sounds exciting and right.

Recent graduates and career switchers, on the other hand, gravitate to Quadrant I jobs. Unlike veteran professionals who have made a substantial investment in developing expertise in well-circumscribed areas, these groups have a much easier time accepting the implications of Quadrant I. Of course, they have less choice. If they are to develop they have to start in either Quadrant I or IV, and I has a lot more appeal. Then, too, some personalities are more naturally amenable to Quadrant I choices. Entrepreneurial types, self-confident risk-takers and those who thrive on start-up, challenge, and high stimulation fall into this category.

No matter who you are or where you are in your career, adopting the following mind-sets will help make your transition into a Quadrant I plum easier:

- feeling confident you have the ability to learn something new
- communicating your enthusiasm
- tempering fear of making mistakes with motivation to learn and succeed

- being willing to take the risk of becoming an on-the-job learner
- convincing an employer that what you lack in skill mastery you will make up for in motivation and the commitment to learn quickly

Here's what makes it difficult for people to take the Quadrant I plunge:

- a fear of failure that prevents you from trying anything new
- a relentless perfectionism that won't let you make mistakes
- out-of-control anxiety that causes you to mistake Quadrant I challenge for Quadrant IV misery
- self-esteem that requires you to be recognized as the expert
- not regarding your own preferences as relevant
- a belief that no one will hire you unless you are a finished and perfect product

Remember the four doomed individuals I introduced earlier in this chapter? All of them were full-fledged Quadrant I avoiders. Here's why:

ANNA BARLOW: This top-of-the-line entertainment executive was trapped midcareer in Quadrant III and heading south on the Doom Loop. But she couldn't face giving up the self-made status for which she had sacrificed so much. Her strong needs for uninterrupted praise and power got in the way of change and doomed her to a predictably unpleasant slide into Quadrant IV.

BOB BERGER: This young lawyer turned brewery lobbyist was enjoying the fruits and angst of Quadrant I and managing to work his way toward Quadrant II when his wife interceded with her father's job offer. Acceding to family pressures and valuing standard legal expertise over the excitement and occasional terror of learning something new, Bob forsook Quadrant I for a stodgy Quadrant III position. He ignored his own intuition and preference, and so doomed himself.

LINDA SONNENSCHEIN: This executive secretary made a Quadrant III to Quadrant III job transfer rather than risk becoming a Quadrant I novice in office design. She took a job that bored her silly, hoping that a substantially bigger paycheck and a more prestigious work environment would bolster her outlook on a career she had long outgrown. These surface rewards, however, were no substitute for challenge.

JACK CARBONI: This award-winning salesperson was basking in the career glow of Quadrant II when he was offered a Quadrant I position that perfectly fit his target mosaic. When he turned it down, he made the mistake of assuming that his Quadrant II bliss would last until an economic upturn or until he was ready for it to change. He made the classic Quadrant II error: he failed to see and respond to the larger picture, and thereby unwittingly doomed himself.

How could these people have stayed out of doom's way? The answer is simple: by choosing jobs requiring more Quadrant I skills that express new parts of themselves and that match the target mosaic they need to reach their capstones.

Evaluating a Quadrant I Job Opportunity

Suppose you've been offered the chance to do something new—something that stretches your abilities. You're excited about the prospect of change, but you're anxious about failure and learning the ropes all over again. If you're coming from a Quadrant II or III position, you have to trade in your expert status and perhaps accept a pay cut. This Quadrant I dilemma confronts nearly everyone who has invested time and energy to attain a certain level of achievement. It pits the excitement of new learning and challenge against our natural desire for worry-free security and comfort. And it's a tough choice.

If your skill analysis shows that you'll be learning new Quadrant I skills that fit your target mosaic, this a fine career opportunity. Grab it. Though you may be uncomfortably close to the bottom of your learning curve, this is actually where you want to be—developing critical competencies that exponentially advance your career in the direction of your capstone.

A TYPICAL QUADRANT I JOB OPPORTUNITY

	LIKE	DON'T LIKE
GOOD AT	QUADRANT II	QUADRANT III
NOT GOOD AT	QUADRANT I	QUADRANT IV

Are there exceptions? Sure. Stress goes with any new learning. So as Quadrant I positions pressure you to prove yourself, your anxiety can mount. If you're already under a lot of stress or experiencing a serious life crisis, you may want to sit out this Quadrant I career opportunity and wait for a sunnier day. Or, after investigating your options, you may decide to decline a Quadrant I offer because you can't afford the pay cut or because you'll be too far removed from key decision-makers. But before you say no, diplomatically discuss your reservations with the top people involved and see what, if anything, is negotiable. Sometimes what appears to be a barrier turns out to be one of your own making—one that stems from your own fear of being a rookie again.

It helps to face up to your own nervousness about taking a Quadrant I slot. To make the transition into Quadrant I easier, look for jobs that give you a security net—like a few Quadrant II skill clusters you've already mastered or a familiar industry or company where you feel comfortable. Look for an organizational culture that mirrors your own style and values. If this isn't possible, see what conditions you can build in or negotiate to reduce stress. Remember that even without familiar props, you will have the advantage of riding the crest of your own motivation and enthusiasm toward your capstone. The Quadrant I job that fits your target mosaic will keep you feeling energized.

But without understanding the principle of the Doom Loop, it's easy to turn down Quadrant I jobs. By putting higher priority on fancy titles, salary, and prestigious companies than on learning new skills and striving toward our capstones, taking a Quadrant I job seems to be a step backward.

Taking Quadrant I opportunities that are related to your target mosaic should be the norm. The tactic is simple:

Doom Loop Tactic II: Seek out Quadrant I jobs that fit your target mosaic.

If they have a thread or two of the familiar, all the better. But even if they don't, they are prime career advancement opportunities.

Quadrant II Lust

Everyone lusts after Quadrant II jobs. And who can blame them? People who have Quadrant II jobs feel wonderful. They say fantastic things—like they "can't wait for the alarm clock to ring in the morning." And, what's more, they mean them! People who aren't in Quadrant II dream about what it would be like to have such jobs. For many less fortunate folks, the Quadrant II job represents an Atlantis of the work world—a romantic myth they've read or heard about but have no hope of ever experiencing themselves.

The problem is that even when the reality of the Quadrant II job lives up to its promise, in real life nothing is forever. Not even the ideal Quadrant II job has an indefinite shelf life. Just as Quadrant I leads to Quadrant II over time, so Quadrant II leads to Quadrant III.

It's hard to keep all this firmly in mind when you're smitten with a Quadrant II job. We all know how easy it is to be blinded by love. Like newlyweds, people in Quadrant II—especially early career entries—think their honeymoon in Quadrant II portends a permanent state of "happily ever after."

It doesn't.

Quadrant II tenants make their first mistake by drifting into a laissez-faire complacency. They're so content to be where they are that they often can't conceive of wanting anything more. They assume they've finally arrived, that they can relax a bit and rest on their laurels. They fail to aggressively seek the challenges that will keep them motivated and striving.

For these people, the secret is:

- to lace Quadrant II jobs with plenty of Quadrant I skills
- to stay doggedly alert to new Quadrant I opportunities beyond their current job

No doubt, it's never easy to leave paradise. But it's far better to leave and return to a new Quadrant I than to be rudely awakened by the grim reality of a Quadrant III crisis.

Evaluating a Quadrant II Job Opportunity

The Quadrant II job opportunity looks too good to be true: you're offered a job consisting of skills you enjoy and have achieved competence in. Pay and other factors look good. Is there a catch? Depending on the particulars, taking this job opportunity could be an excellent choice.

A TYPICAL QUADRANT II JOB OPPORTUNITY

	LIKE	DON'T LIKE
GOOD AT	QUADRANT II	QUADRANT III
NOT GOOD AT	QUADRANT I	QUADRANT IV

Still, why not dig in, take your time, and investigate? Before you accept this job, analyze the skills it requires and matrix map them. Ask yourself some calculated questions. If you're coming from a Quadrant I job, does taking this job offer grant you any clear advantage, given your target mosaic? Do the new skills fit your capstone profile?

Next, decide exactly where in Quadrant II the skills of the job actually cluster. If they are close to the border of Quadrant

I and II, this could be the ideal job offer, combining comfort with new learning. But if the skills collect at the border of Quadrants II and III, you would be wise to exercise due caution. You could be taking a top-of-the-Loop job masquerading as a Quadrant II opportunity.

Consider this tactic:

Doom Loop Tactic III: Stretch Quadrant II jobs in the direction of Quadrant I by being on the lookout for new Quadrant I projects, team activities, and skills that broaden your job description and move you closer to your capstone.

In any Quadrant II job, make time and learning work for, not against you by adding Quadrant I skills calibrated to your target mosaic. No matter how good a Quadrant II job feels, it is not your final destination. So keep your eyes on your capstone.

Quadrant III's Velvet Handcuffs

When you're good at what you do but you don't enjoy it, you've entered the motivational flatlands of Quadrant III.

How did you get there? People manage to find their own pathways. Some stay too long in the same job and become Quadrant III barnacles clinging desperately to the known. Others unwittingly reenter Quadrant III while futilely trying to escape a similar position. Like Linda Sonnenschein, the executive secretary, they inadvertently boomerang into Quadrant III while pursuing a higher salary or some other panacea. Then there are those who actually begin their careers in Quadrant III and stay put—people who so fear the risk of being found imperfect that they refuse to experiment with something they're not already skilled at.

People choose Quadrant III positions for a surprising number of reasons, including:

- falling in love with their expert status
- being afraid to start over
- clinging to die-hard perfectionism
- failing to track their own rise and toppling over the top of the Loop
- being seduced and shackled by attractive salary and benefits
- being unwilling to chance risk
- hitching their self-esteem to pleasing others
- not seeing their own personal preferences as worthwhile
- not really expecting work to be enjoyable

People in Quadrant III often feel underused and underchallenged—on the verge of being prematurely "retired in place." What they crave most is being involved and in the thick of things again.

Why not just leave? Because Quadrant III jobs bind people to the status quo with velvet handcuffs. As long as they remain perfectly motionless—locked in the daily grind—they scarcely feel the pinch of the cuffs. It's business as usual. Besides, so many people are wearing the same velvet cuffs that it's easy to think, "This is just the way work is."

Ironically, people stuck in Quadrant III may not even recognize that they're trapped until they begin seeking alternatives. Then the struggle to break loose can be harrowing. It unleashes tremendous anxiety about whether or not they have what it takes to start over and compete in today's world. Rationalizations and self-doubt take over:

- "I have a good salary, perks, benefits; I'm respected and valued by others in the company."
- "I know the ropes; why should I give up my status? For what?"
- "What proof do I have that I'll like anything else any better?"
- "Suppose I fail?"
- "I can't compete with young kids just coming out of school."

- "How will I explain my urge to give it all up to my family, my friends?"

The cuffs tighten.

If you stay in a lackluster job too long, the sheer boredom of it could eventually push you over the cliff. The result? You do something you'll later regret. For instance, you finally react to the excruciating boredom by making a sudden, totally uncontemplated job change. You make a move that places you in a job as irrelevant to your capstone as your present one. Or you use chancy default tactics like relying on a mentor or grabbing at high-status, low-development jobs. Sometimes even a poor decision can unshackle you, but sometimes it just drives you into a deeper rut.

When enough money and benefits are attached to their Quadrant III jobs, people are more likely to find themselves stymied, torn between staying put and moving on. Anxiety soars as they attempt to leave and try something new; boredom and discontent mount as they seek the shelter of their familiar routines. Ultimately, many settle into life in Quadrant III and whatever that brings—often free passage to Quadrant IV, where the most exciting part of the job is the retirement benefits package.

Evaluating a Quadrant III Job "Opportunity"

You're poking through the newspaper's classified section, feeling bored with your current job and lethargic about your career, when you spot an ideal Quadrant III job listing. You know you're good at what you do and the advertised job perfectly matches your expertise. You have what it takes to get hired and you need a change to break out of your career doldrums. You apply, do well in the interview, and are offered the job. It's a safe, logical career move.

Should you take it?

Of course not. That would be a serious tactical error. There simply aren't enough challenging skills in Quadrant III positions to keep you developing. After the hoopla dies down, you'll be wondering why you feel so bad when you're so good at your new job.

A TYPICAL QUADRANT III JOB "OPPORTUNITY"

	LIKE	DON'T LIKE
GOOD AT	QUADRANT II	QUADRANT III
NOT GOOD AT	QUADRANT I	QUADRANT IV

Watch out. Expert status alone won't sustain satisfaction. Remember, the Doom Loop predicts that over time, if the tasks of the job remain basically the same, the Quadrant III job opportunity will produce Quadrant IV ennui. The only real question is when.

Consider the best possible scenario. You accept the job and perform so well that you're lavished with praise. At first, you feel pride in your work and get a real lift from being appreciated. Eventually, however, the praise lessens. When the applause dies down, there's not enough intrinsic satisfaction in the skills of the job itself to prevent your slide down the Loop. And if you didn't like the job much in Quadrant III, you're not going to like it any better when you hit Quadrant IV.

When faced with a Quadrant III opportunity, use this tactic:

> **Doom Loop Tactic IV: Exercise extreme caution in accepting Quadrant III job offers.**

Slow down; analyze and matrix map the skills required. Compare the results with a matrix map of your current job skills. If they are similar, consider staying put and actively seeking a Quadrant I or II job opportunity.

A Special Case: Evaluating a "Top-of-the-Doom-Loop" Job

What if you are offered a "top-of-the-Loop" job—one with skills that cluster right between Quadrants II and III?

These jobs are very difficult to turn down, even when you know better.

You're likely to find yourself in this situation if you're being pursued by smooth-talking executive recruiters who are masters at stroking your ego. You are among the best and the brightest, the perfect candidate for a top job. The top-of-the-Loop job offer seems like your dream come true. It's the once-in-a-lifetime career opportunity you've been waiting for.

Caveat emptor! Taking a job at the top of the Doom Loop differs only in degree from taking a Quadrant III offer. Even though the job won't immediately place you on the downslope of the Loop, it will put you at the top of the hill, where you can gather momentum for the short ride down. If this job doesn't offer substantial new skills that you like but aren't yet good at (or an opportunity to build such Quadrant I skills into the job description) the slide down is a sure thing. The top-of-the-Loop job can be deceiving—maybe it dangles one or two glittering skills before you. But after you've mastered these skills in a few months, what then?

A TYPICAL TOP-OF-THE-LOOP JOB OPPORTUNITY

	LIKE	DON'T LIKE
GOOD AT	QUADRANT II	QUADRANT III
NOT GOOD AT	QUADRANT I	QUADRANT IV

Job hopping is an occupational hazard for people at the top of the Loop. They sense something is wrong but aren't sure what. To fix the problem, they burn through a series of related jobs, often ones for which they're overqualified. Improved work environments, titles, and salaries give them a false sense of career progress. Even though job hoppers add a string of impressive items to their résumé, they fail to add anything notable to their target mosaic.

When faced with a top-of-the-Loop opportunity, try this tactic:

Doom Loop Tactic V: Treat top-of-the-Loop jobs like Quadrant III offers; turn them down in favor of Quadrant I and II offers.

Are there exceptions? Yes—when the job provides some hard-to-obtain skills you need for your capstone or offers you a unique opportunity or foot in the door. But in either case, don't stay too long!

Bottoming Out in Quadrant IV

You might think you can spot a Quadrant IV job as soon as it appears. If you're like most people, visions of poor pay, dingy offices, and mind-numbing assignments dance in your head.

But in reality, Quadrant IV jobs look no worse than jobs in any other quadrant. Sometimes they even look better. They may come with fancy titles and all the trappings of success. They can be high-status positions like bank president, law partner, sales director, acquisitions editor, and so on.

A position only becomes a rock-bottom Quadrant IV job when the particular person who holds it both dislikes the work involved and isn't doing very well at it.

If this describes you, no matter what your job, you're probably miserable. No matter how well you've done in the past, your disenchantment and lack of motivation sabotage your present performance. It may feel as if the whole world is judging your performance and finding it lacking. Under these conditions, you can expect your self-esteem and confidence to plummet. In a society that equates work with worth, you've fallen off the track into the tumbleweeds.

Who takes Quadrant IV jobs? People with no career strategy are candidates. It's easy to see how they might end up in Quadrant IV by ignoring their own interests and preferences, and by overlooking the interaction of time and learning via the Doom Loop. So are people who have been fired recently or have been unemployed for lengthy periods. In the last two instances, any job offer seems preferable to the continuing uncertainty of remaining jobless. The path of least resistance is looking for work similar to what you've done in the past. But if you follow that course, and fail to develop a new capstone, you're likely to end up with the "old wine, new bottle" Quadrant IV job.

Then again, for some people the tumble into Quadrant IV isn't accidental at all. They actually choose their Quadrant IV jobs deliberately.

When asked to explain how they could have made such a blunder, these people often tell stories with revealing themes like these:

- They feel this is the only kind of job they deserve.
- They are addicted or habituated to misery.
- They see themselves as victims with little recourse.
- They don't believe they have other options.
- They can't muster the energy to effect change.
- This is the way it is: their parents were miserable in their jobs, too.
- They are preoccupied with a serious health or family problem.
- They hate the work, but all their friends are here.
- They don't see their work as being a principal source of satisfaction in life.

Of course, not everyone who chooses Quadrant IV fits these patterns. Some Quadrant IV choosers are relentlessly hard-driven, task-focused achievers who habitually ignore their own preferences in choosing jobs. They are the challenge junkies, who are attracted to Quadrant IV because it seems to provide them with the most strenuous career workout. It never occurs to them to question whether or not they like the skills involved. Their routine is to master disliked Quadrant IV skills and struggle up the backside of the Loop into Quadrant III. For many of these high achievers, their own preferences are an absolute nonissue. What matters most is against-all-odds mastery. But even for top achievers who insist on remaining oblivious to what they actually like doing, Quadrant I skills can boost their performance.

Evaluating a Quadrant IV Job "Opportunity"

You're offered a job and when you Doom Loop it, the skills cluster like this:

You're face to face with a high-paying Quadrant IV position that offers excellent advancement opportunities in a good

A QUADRANT IV JOB "OPPORTUNITY"

	LIKE	DON'T LIKE
GOOD AT	QUADRANT II	QUADRANT III
NOT GOOD AT	QUADRANT I	QUADRANT IV

location, and that is fairly similar to your current job. Unfortunately, no matter how you slice it, you don't particularly like your present job, and your performance ratings have been dropping each year. Still, this other company wants you, and it feels awfully good to be wanted. You're flattered by the offer.

Should you accept the position?

Obviously not. It's just another instance of the "new" old job. Refuse to be enticed by its seductive surface attractions. After the excitement of the new workplace and bigger paycheck wear thin, you'll be the one mired in Quadrant IV, feeling rotten.

In the vast majority of cases, you will be well advised to shun Quadrant IV jobs. There are many less painful ways to self-destruct than intentionally setting up housekeeping in Quadrant IV.

To avoid this predicament, look for Quadrant I jobs. Or, at the very least, look for jobs with skills more evenly distributed among the quadrants. When faced with a Quadrant IV career opportunity, keep this career tactic in mind:

Doom Loop Tactic VI: Routinely turn down Quadrant IV job opportunities. Jobs that concentrate skills in Quadrant IV are jobs to flee, not grab.

Yet there are exceptions. Sometimes, a brief stay in a Quadrant IV job is just what's required to reach your capstone. You need a specific cluster of hard-to-get skills to qualify for your capstone, and the only way you can obtain them is the Quadrant IV job. Sure, it's much better to obtain missing skills via brief seminars or training programs. But when these options aren't available to you, the trick is to make your stay in the Quadrant IV job as brief as it is productive.

PUTTING IT ALL TOGETHER

If you take the advice in this chapter, you'll choose job opportunities that keep you on the upslope of the Doom Loop, continually seeking projects, experiences, and jobs that expand your skill base and transport you along a well-traveled corridor between Quadrants I and II. Each move you make —and there may be plenty of them—should also bring you closer and closer to your next capstone. You'll rarely find yourself in Quadrants III and IV unless you have a very good reason for being there. Your target mosaic, along with continuing skill analysis and matrix mapping, will show you which jobs to take, what to do when the learning stops, and when to leave a job.

Graphically, what you will be doing looks like this:

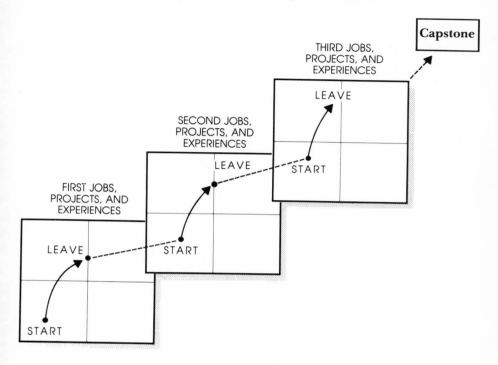

Capstone Strategy and Doom Loop Tactics

Armed with information on capstones, target mosaics, and Doom Loop analysis, you're ready to practice Doom Looping yourself into more favorable career situations and out of less favorable ones.

But that doesn't mean you won't encounter a few crises along the way—crises like first-job decisions, early career disappointment, unexpected opportunities, losing your job, dealing with midcareer discontent, and even being doomed upon reaching your capstone! During the intense pressure of a crisis, it's easy to make career-threatening mistakes.

The following chapters will show you how to weather these crises and emerge from them with a stronger sense of who you are and a sharper understanding of where you are going in your career.

CHAPTER 5

■

First-Job Crisis

Ah, take the Cash, and let the Credit go,
Nor heed the rumble of a distant drum!
—*The Rubáiyát of Omar Khayyám*

I just want to get a job that gives me enough money
to move out of my parents' house. Then I'll decide
what I want to do.
—New university graduate

I don't want to be one of those people who works
in a job I hate for thirty years and winds up feeling
bitter, like I haven't accomplished anything in life.
—Psychology graduate student

How the hell am I supposed to know what I like
when I haven't done anything except go to school
for nineteen years?
—Student seeking career coaching

My mistake when I first graduated was looking for
a job—not a career.
—Regional sales rep

If you're like a lot of people, finding your first real job is the
worst job of your life. If you're a recent graduate, you're
leaving your comfortable student status behind you and beginning at the bottom all over again.

You don't know what to expect. How could you? You've never done it before. But it seems as if nearly everyone has more of an inside track to the world of work than you do. And what little you do know about that world you may not like. So there's a certain trepidation about marching out into the adult world and finding your way. You want it—or do you? It's exciting, risky, and overwhelming.

Then there's the pressure. Yesterday you worried about sleeping through your midterm; today you worry about making a living. What are you supposed to be doing and how are you supposed to find out? You're not even sure what to wear to an interview—should you ever get one—much less which job to interview for. And your family, who never even sent you a care package at school, now provides round-the-clock coverage of your career distress to assorted friends and neighbors. Even without all the publicity, you're deathly afraid of making the wrong choice, looking foolish. But it's now or never. Perhaps you've already delayed this moment once or twice with an extended stint in graduate school or a course of study abroad. Or perhaps you have devoted the past few years to staying home to raise a baby.

Depending on your background, you begin your job search with your degree or coursework, possibly a brief exposure to the working world through summer jobs or an internship, a vague knowledge of your abilities, and an even vaguer sense of what you really want to do.

That's what you bring with you. What you're up against are hordes of recent graduates, an astonishing mass of unemployed senior professionals (doesn't anyone have a job anymore?), far too few interesting entry-level jobs to go around, intense financial and parental pressures to grab something quickly, and an overpowering sense of confusion about the type of job that's right for you. It's enough to send anybody back under the covers.

Given this scenario, most people react. They throw cool reason to the wind and hustle to find something, anything, that pays and will look halfway decent on their résumé.

Why shouldn't you?

Because of the Doom Loop. If you blindly plunge forward,

you could wind up in a Quadrant III or IV job, and that's the last place you want to start your career!

But there's hope. There are many ways to avoid the frustration and boredom of Quadrant III and IV jobs. By the end of this chapter, you should be ready to tackle this crisis with a job that you will enjoy and that will give you the experience you need to become a better career manager.

HOW PEOPLE CHOOSE FIRST JOBS

There's a lot of agreement about how you should choose your first job. In fact, people everywhere seem to concur. Try asking friends, relatives, or a professional career counselor what you should do with your life. Chances are they will respond with, "Do what you're good at." And when you actually apply for jobs, you can always count on job interviewers to ask the standard, "Tell us about your strengths."

The deck is stacked. The assumption is that being good at something or having a certain set of strengths should determine your career direction and success. If you're good in English, be a journalist. If you're good in chemistry, be a chemist.

On the surface, this is logical. But it's a poor assumption for several reasons. To figure out what you're good at takes considerable work experience and analysis. And as a newcomer to the world of work, that's exactly what you lack. Even if you are a business school or law school graduate, your analysis of your performance is derived from evaluations of your exams, class participation, or term papers. This hardly takes into account your motivation to achieve outside school or how relevant your coursework has been to real workplace issues. You have no feedback to help you determine how talented you will actually be as a product manager or as a corporate attorney. Basing your career decisions on past performance at this stage of the game will just take you on a voyage into the unknown.

But even if these classroom judgments were perfectly accurate, using competence alone to choose your first job invites you to sidestep the obvious. To succeed in any job you need to enjoy your work. That's why tracking your natural preferences is important. By choosing jobs that follow your preferences you make your work life natural and comfortable, not a chore.

At first, considering what you genuinely like to do might seem irrelevant. You've probably been led to believe that work is serious stuff—what grown-ups do. Play is for kids—it's fun and what you really enjoy—so you don't factor it into your job choice. Besides, your first job is a rite of passage into the adult world and you truly want to be taken seriously. So you discount your natural preferences and try to fit yourself into the rigors of work life.

If this is your view, you're in danger of sliding into Quadrant III or IV in the first inning. Because you're still a rookie at many things, you're actually more in danger of pulling a Quadrant IV (not good at, don't like) than a Quadrant III (good at, don't like) job on your first trip out. Of course, you'll be able to move "up" to Quadrant III as you become more skilled. But that's as far as you'll get.

Do you remember the college courses you did well in even though you spent your class time counting the days until the semester was over? Those were your Quadrant III courses. You don't want to duplicate that painful experience when you enter the real world of work. To avoid this possibility, make preferences a priority in your job search.

If you like your first job—even if you're not particularly good at it—your enthusiasm for your work will be a source of energy and commitment that you can use to overcome the myriad daily hassles of organizational and professional life. You'll have the motivation to learn, to move from Quadrant I to Quadrant II.

AVOIDING THE COMMON MISTAKES

As easy as it is to say, "I'm going to find a first job I really like," it's tough to put that ideal into practice.

Perhaps you've been biding your time in school or in the

military. Perhaps you've spent the past five years at home raising the kids. You're itching to begin your professional career. You may have financial headaches. You may want to move away from your parents' house and be able to afford the good things adulthood promises.

You're not thinking about what you like or even what you're good at. You worry about convincing any employer to hire you—even for boring jobs where you know you can hold your own. What, you wonder, will anyone think you are qualified to do? Then there are other issues. You want to be independent and have your own life and your own identity. The first job is often a means toward that end. You interview for a job with one thought in mind—"I've got to get my own apartment soon!" You're very tempted to take the cash and let the credit go, by placing a higher value on a convenient job or a top-dollar offer than on your professional growth and development. The future seems very far off, and the present is very compelling. So you use a series of risky, often random "buy now, pay later" job search tactics.

As a result, you're a likely candidate for committing the following familiar mistakes:

- **Cruising the Classifieds**—The promise of all those quarter-inch squares of tiny black type proclaiming instant career opportunities is awfully seductive. If you send out your résumé to enough of those box numbers, something good is bound to happen, right? Never mind that those tiny boxes also carry the words "three years of experience required" and you have none, that the work is routine, or that everything you are currently qualified for is either menial or Quadrant III work you've been doing since eighth grade. For the price of a postage stamp, you're invited to try your luck. It's a tactic all your friends and neighbors are pursuing, so why not you? Easy. Because you need to focus on what you want rather than responding to someone else's shopping list. To do otherwise is to make a quick trip to the gloomy side of the Doom Loop.

- **Taking a More Personal Approach**—Your friends and relatives have all kinds of job search suggestions for you. Have you ever noticed how they all seem to have a better idea about how you should be spending the next decade of your life than you have? The family business beckons. A friend tells you there's an opening at the company where he's just landed a job. The problem: you're turning your decision-making over to people who have little or no understanding of what job is best for you. It's your job and your life, not theirs.

- **Working the Alma Mater**—Your college placement office has a listing of jobs, many offered by fellow alumni. This is your "in," you think. Unfortunately, it's nothing more than a narrower version of the classified ads where you will be competing with current, past, and future graduates for a handful of relevant jobs you may not want. Why allow these jobs to direct your future? (There are exceptions, however—particularly placement centers that offer phone numbers of alumni in various fields who are willing to talk with you about their work for the price of a phone call or a trip to their office.) Again, you need your own game plan.

- **Giving In to Sheer Convenience**—You see a "Now Hiring" sign in the window of a store a block away. Or your mom says she's just bought a car from a dealership in the neighborhood that's looking for salespeople. You'll save money on gas and can eat lunch at home. And you will finally join the ranks of the gainfully employed. If you choose this route, you're choosing a job, not a career. You're putting your career in the hands of fate. Stop. Ask yourself, "Whose life is it, anyway?" And ask how you will feel if you are still performing a variation on this theme ten years from now.

If you've considered or implemented any of the above tactics, you're probably in the midst of your first-job crisis. You have some important tasks to master that will significantly influence your future career path. You are faced with:

- choosing the cornerstone job on which you will build your future
- identifying and prioritizing what you truly enjoy
- learning how to manage your own career
- absorbing what you need from the first job experience
- deciding when and how to move on

By deliberately dealing with these issues, you're more likely to reach your career objectives faster and easier.

If you don't, you could have a serious job crisis on your hands.

HOW DO YOU KNOW WHEN YOU'RE IN A FIRST-JOB CRISIS?

What's normal and what's a crisis? It's hard to tell when you have no established baseline of experience for knowing what normal is. But first jobs do provide rich opportunities for crises to develop. Since most of us get little or no training in managing our careers, we need at least a few years of seasoning before we're ready to decide what we truly want to be when we grow up. Whenever we burst into a future for which we are wholly unprepared, we're likely to feel out of control and upset. This is the stuff crises are made of.

When we look closely at the first-job crisis, it actually turns out to be a series of at least three overlapping crises that affect how a fledgling career will progress. These crises focus on:

- choosing your first job
- proving yourself in your first job
- leaving your first job

The secret of getting through each of them is to realize that it's normal and natural to have all kinds of feelings about these crises. Confusion and uncertainty go with the territory of striking out on your own. But you still have to assert yourself and manage the situation, or the crisis will escalate. Recognizing what is happening and putting each of these crises in perspective are the first steps in figuring out how to get relief.

CHOOSING YOUR FIRST JOB

Choosing your first job can be agonizing. How are you supposed to know what to choose? And even if you do know, how do you go about finding it? Look at the comments of first-jobbers in the checklist below. They reflect the stress of beginning a career with few clues as to how to proceed. Compare their comments to your own feelings to determine whether this crisis has you in its grip.

CHOOSING YOUR FIRST JOB: CRISIS CHECKLIST

1. ____ I'm clueless; I have no idea what to do with my life.
2. ____ Everything seems like a gamble; I want the sure thing.
3. ____ How am I supposed to know what's out there or what to do first?
4. ____ I feel totally overwhelmed (paralyzed, stuck).
5. ____ Everything I want I'm not qualified for and everything I'm qualified for I don't want.
6. ____ I have no idea how to organize a job search (write a résumé, a cover letter, et cetera).
7. ____ I am embarrassed (feel too awkward) to ask for an informational interview.
8. ____ I really sweat it—I blow my interviews.
9. ____ I'm afraid that if I choose the wrong job I'll ruin my career.
10. ____ I can't imagine liking anything I'm not already good at.

The remedy? Accept that beginning a career requires forethought. Even though you don't know what you want to do for life or even for the next six months, you will still need a game plan. Relax a little. You still have plenty of time to decide on an occupational niche if you don't already have one. Even though everyone acts as if you should already know your vocational destiny, it's still way too early to lock onto a cap-stone. Try thinking small. Even a little structure will go a long way toward easing your way into the world of careers and will make starting out a less scary business. Be reassured; there's no evidence that excessive worry magically creates instant so-lutions. So take your time, be generous with yourself, and give yourself a chance to figure things out.

Think about it this way. Sure you're overwhelmed. Since you've never done this before, you don't know the ropes. How could it be otherwise? Of course it's intimidating. You're a blank slate when it comes to résumés, cover letters, network-ing, and interviewing. But these basic skills are easy to learn, and you'll get a lot of mileage from them once you do.

Trade in your anxiety for a few highly focused, purposeful activities. Back up and do a few simple things: read some books on the nuts and bolts of searching for a first job, hire a career coach. Talk to a few people you respect who are five to ten years your senior and are working in fields that interest you. Find out how these people tackled choosing their first jobs and ask them to give you their best advice based on their experience. Find, even hire, someone savvy to help you write an attractive résumé that shows prospective employers that you are an eager and dependable person who is willing to learn. Don't try to go it alone. It's simply too hard to capture your own strengths on paper when you're feeling so uncertain about your skills and about being accepted. Instead, let some-one else package your virtues. You can always tone down your résumé and cover letters later. While none of these things will guarantee you a terrific first job, they will make the process considerably less forbidding.

Next, don't confuse being inexperienced with being inad-equate. Besides being plain wrong, this will add to your sense of powerlessness and will spill over onto your self-presentation. Remember that most employers are hiring you for your potential, not your expertise. That's why companies have training programs. In fact, many employers prefer to hire new graduates because they get a chance to train them their own way. Try presenting your lack of experience, combined with a high ability to learn, as a training asset rather than as a liability. Talk about yourself as a good problem-solver, a self-starter. Stress your analytic abilities and communication skills. And while you're at it, don't forget to present yourself as an enthusiastic Quadrant I learner.

Once you get to the interview, be yourself. Don't try to come off as more experienced than you are, or as the slick, know-it-all expert you think the interviewer is expecting. Be positive and friendly. The interviewer is scrutinizing you as much for fit with the organizational culture and its people as for skills and knowledge. Besides, interviewers hire people they like, not necessarily those who are most qualified. If you can convince the interviewer that you're a personable, high-potential Quadrant I learner, you've probably got a foot in the door. The rest is up to the employer.

Finally, practice telling yourself that making the wrong first-job choice won't end the world. No matter what happens, bombing in your first job will not permanently maim your chances for a fast-track glamour career or any other career path you might want. Finding out what doesn't work for you is a legitimate part of your mission in your first few jobs. Don't let black-and-white thinking trap you. Catastrophizing about hypothetical future events just inhibits you from taking creative action and from exploring what appeals to you. During your first-job search you should be collecting all kinds of data about your choices. As we'll discuss later, a first-job mistake can easily be corrected, so long as you recognize the mistake and make up your mind to leave as soon as possible. Employers will respect you for knowing that a job wasn't for you, and for leaving to seek your niche. Even if the worst happens and you are fired, that's no blight on your record, either. For now, just take it on faith that lots of successful professionals were fired from their first job or quit in disgust. I'm one of them.

CAREERS 101: A STRATEGY
FOR GETTING STARTED

The best way to get started is to recast the entire first-job experience in terms of what you are most familiar with—the student role. I know this runs counter to your instincts. You want to be taken seriously, to be treated as a professional, to be independent. In fact, the last thing you want is to see yourself as an inexperienced student again.

But try looking at it this way: your first few jobs are really high-intensity, post-degree internships, not a test of your career competence. They offer a splendid opportunity: you're getting paid to learn, to make mistakes. Here's your chance to learn what they didn't teach you at the university. Consider it a real-world "Careers 101."

Your ideal course of study should put you on a steep learning curve for hard-core generic career skills that are useful for any capstone. It should expose you to all kinds of technical skills, work environments, and organizational cultures. Contrary to popular opinion, your first few jobs are not there for you to settle into and prove yourself. Instead, use this time to:

- learn the ropes of the world of work
- sample and develop basic generic skills (communication, interpersonal, political, analytic, production, management, and the like)
- learn basic self-management skills
- identify your own reactions to work life; your strengths and weaknesses
- develop skills for managing both adversity and success

If you're going to grade yourself, evaluate how much you are learning about the workplace, not your work performance. Your mission is to soak up all the information you can, to get feedback on how your interpersonal style affects others, and to develop a repertoire of marketable skills. It's the ideal educational system: personalized learning for learning's sake.

You determine the length of each course (job). The idea is to stay until you've mastered the course material; then you're ready to enroll in the next course. The beauty of seeing your first few jobs as an extension of your education is that jobs offering high-growth opportunity become less risky to take and, eventually, less risky to leave. You're also learning the art of the graceful exit.

LOWERING FIRST-JOB ANXIETY

"Are you still looking for a job?" asks your Stanford law school graduate friend, who's just landed a $75,000-a-year starting salary.

"Your mother and I are sure you won't let us down," your father tells you as you embark on your first job interview.

Yes, there's reason to be anxious. Everyone gets a little nervous about the uncertainty of beginnings and endings. Starting out in your career has elements of both. It is a significant life event with major impact. For better or for worse, there is a sense that real life is about to begin. As one of my college professors used to tell me, "The dress rehearsal is over." You feel as if the whole world is keeping tabs on your career decisions—or lack thereof.

This leads to fierce anxiety about making the wrong choices. And once you get through the recruiting, interviews, and salary negotiations and find yourself in your office—if you're lucky enough to have snared one—the anxiety doesn't necessarily abate. Instead, as the new kid on the block, you are confronted with brand-new stressors related to proving yourself.

It's important to confront, understand, and respect your anxiety. Ignoring it doesn't make it go away. It just goes underground for a time, where it gathers strength to break out in less controlled ways.

You can look at anxiety as a friend or as an enemy. It's your friend when it tells you about yourself and motivates you.

Anxiety can instill legitimate caution that keeps you from getting in way over your head. Fear can keep you alert so that you avoid unnecessary error. But high anxiety is an enemy when it paralyzes. It can hurt your job search and your job performance. You sweat through interviews like an escaped convict. You take the first job that's offered, convinced that no one will ever offer you another one. After you start the job, you feel like an impostor who doesn't belong there. Fear of failure can transform even the best and the brightest into risk-avoiding slow learners.

What can you do to lower your anxiety? Relax. Take stock of what you're telling yourself. If you're agonizing over every mistake, stop it. Tell yourself something else, like "I'm still learning" or "I'll do better next time." You're a graduate student in Careers 101, remember? People expect you to make mistakes. Remind your boss and coworkers that you need help, that you'd appreciate their advice. Almost everyone will respond. They were once enrolled in the same course you're taking, and they'd like nothing better than to help you pass.

Put things in perspective: a first job choice isn't a make-or-break career decision. If the job isn't the right one, so what? It's like the shopping period at school when you're allowed to pick up or drop courses without penalties. Cut yourself some slack and let your anxiety drop to reasonable levels.

PROVING YOURSELF IN YOUR FIRST JOB

Okay. We're ready to deal with the real event. You've landed that first job and you want to show the world—and yourself —that you've got the right stuff. You throw yourself into mastering your job. Sometimes this turns out just fine; sometimes it doesn't. How do you know when proving yourself in your first job is precipitating a crisis? For starters, look at how you feel. If, with the wisdom of hindsight, you yearn for the happier days of idle unemployment that you shunned only months before, there's a good chance your discontent is reaching crisis proportions. If worrying about your performance keeps you up at night or interferes with your social life, you've progressed well beyond garden-variety first-job stress. Compare your on-the-job reactions with the following statements made by people in this crisis:

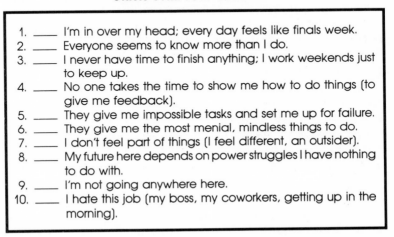

PROVING YOURSELF IN YOUR FIRST JOB:
CRISIS SYMPTOM CHECKLIST

1. ____ I'm in over my head; every day feels like finals week.
2. ____ Everyone seems to know more than I do.
3. ____ I never have time to finish anything; I work weekends just to keep up.
4. ____ No one takes the time to show me how to do things (to give me feedback).
5. ____ They give me impossible tasks and set me up for failure.
6. ____ They give me the most menial, mindless things to do.
7. ____ I don't feel part of things (I feel different, an outsider).
8. ____ My future here depends on power struggles I have nothing to do with.
9. ____ I'm not going anywhere here.
10. ____ I hate this job (my boss, my coworkers, getting up in the morning).

What's wrong? You're not perfect; neither are they. Each symptom on this list will help you identify a solvable problem. The first five items on the list deal with overload: too much work and not enough time or expertise to do it all. Take time out and think about what is causing this problem. Is the learning curve you are on too steep for the amount of backup and support they give you? Perhaps you need more training through in-house programs or outside seminars to accelerate your skill acquisition. If so, ask for it. Take advantage of every skill-building opportunity that presents itself. Don't wait for someone in authority to point the way. There may be no one looking out for you—except you.

A common, but deadly, first-job mistake is taking on too much, wanting to please too many masters and not using the magic word "no." If this sounds familiar, you may have discovered a shortcut to Quadrant IV via the turbulent route of high anxiety paired with below-par performance. Protect yourself by setting limits on the scope of your projects. Retain your sense of self on and off the job. Don't be afraid to tell your supervisors or coworkers you're overloaded. Delegate. Take your ego off the hook by reassuring yourself that delegation is an important management skill.

Allow people to help you. Remind them that you're still a novice. Get comfortable with your lack of knowledge: accept it as a natural state. There's no rule that says you have to be perfect. You'd be surprised at how eager people are to help first-jobbers. Try playing Bambi periodically. I know this may go against the grain of proving yourself to the world, but paradoxically, when you act less competent, people help you and you learn faster. They also buy a stake in your success. Later, these same people are most likely to be your ardent supporters. Networking on the job will help you learn who can help you with what. And while you're looking, why not find a mentor? Why spin your wheels when a veteran out there already has the answers?

Item 6 on the list poses the opposite problem: your learning curve is too long and too flat to hold your interest. You are willing to do whatever it takes to soar to the top, to perform the heroics that will win you recognition. But instead you find yourself in stagnant organizational backwaters, underutilized and in perpetual pursuit of the trivial. You are pining for "real responsibility" and feeling desperate about being ignored. Steel yourself. This is more often the norm than not. Many first jobs require that you prove yourself by persevering, not excelling. You are faced with a never-ending stream of mundane tasks—typing, filing, and assorted forms of gruntwork no one else claims. Don't take this personally—at least, not for starters. Management often views newcomers as raw material to be shaped and tested over time. If you are different in some way—a woman or a minority member, for example—this testing may intensify. But you are being exposed to the business, and if the exposure takes, eventually you will be given more substantive work. Your cleverness is not the point here. Your willingness to put up with monotonous daily fare is. In fact, this entire frustrating, demeaning gestation period may actually be a rite of passage that establishes you as one of the gang. The important questions are whether or not entering this industry or organization is important enough to you to endure all this, and whether or not you are being discriminated against relative to other newcomers.

When you long for the challenge of writing a term paper again or cleaning the garage, you know it's time for a change. If you're bored to tears, assess and test the situation. Ask the powers that be for more challenging work or design a new project yourself. Before you do any of this, however, carefully read the chapter on politics. That chapter will also help you analyze what to do if you checked any of the last four items on the list. Remember, there may be other factors at play as well. You may be encountering race or gender discrimination. Sometimes the problem is just "bad chemistry" between you and a key supervisor. Occasionally, people in organizations may even go so far as to subtly haze newcomers, setting them up for failure or embarrassment. If this is the case, set some clear limits on what is and is not acceptable. No one has to accept being victimized by a dysfunctional or unfair work group. You have other choices. Stay alert and get advice from someone you trust about what is happening. See if you can find a former employee who is willing to talk to you about how to establish yourself in this environment or consult with someone on the outside who is familiar with the place.

If discontent and ennui are still the order of the day, you may have already progressed to the third first-job crisis.

LEAVING YOUR FIRST JOB

The third crisis involves leaving your first job. You don't need another six months to know that you've landed the nightmare job. You don't like the work, the people, or the place. You feel trapped and afraid to leave. Often, first-jobbers are like kids on a first date—they don't know when to call it a night. You hold onto that first job with all your might, afraid that if you quit, other potential employers will view you as fickle, disloyal, or both. Or maybe you're following a time-

honored family tradition of dying in the job with your boots
on. See whether any of the statements below capture your
feelings:

LEAVING YOUR FIRST JOB: CRISIS CHECKLIST

1. _____ I watch the clock all day.
2. _____ I can't stand this place (these people, this product).
3. _____ I can't get interested enough to learn the work.
4. _____ I don't feel my work is appreciated (recognized, taken seriously).
5. _____ I'm not going to leave; I'll wait for them to fire me.
6. _____ The politics of this place are killing me.
7. _____ If I quit now, who else will hire me?
8. _____ I want to change jobs, but I don't know what to do next.
9. _____ I'm afraid to be unemployed again.
10. _____ What will I tell my family (my husband, wife, friends, boss)?

If these statements sound entirely too familiar, don't be
afraid to leave. It's past time. Even though there are no hard-
and-fast rules for when to move on, inertia should never be
your reason for staying put.

There are only two reasons for sticking with your entry-
level job:

- because you're acquiring building-block skills
- because you like what you're doing

As soon as you've learned all you can or start disliking what
you're doing, get going. Don't allow yourself any excuses for
sticking it out. There are a million of them: you can't quit because your boss depends on you; they can't replace you; you
feel guilty about leaving all the friends you've made; no one
else there has left; people (employers, friends, parents) will
call you a quitter; your coworkers won't like you, and so on.

Whatever you do, don't stay because everyone tells you how
good you are. If you do, you are making a pact with a Quadrant III future.

Keep the Doom Loop in mind. Don't wait until you go over
the top to move on. Leaving a job is often your very best

career move. But don't let them take your decision away from you. You are in charge of your career from your very first day in your very first job. And you—no one else—should be responsible for leaving a job.

DON'T HITCH YOUR CAPSTONE TO THE JOB

In Careers 101, the last thing you want to sign up for is the "forever option." It's way too early. You loved your first bike, but aren't you glad you moved on to four wheels? Careers 101 is Quadrant I's basic training. It implies learning and movement.

It's highly unlikely that the capstone you choose now will be the capstone you'll want ten years from now. Let's say you've just landed a job in an ad agency as an assistant account executive. You say to yourself, "My capstone is to be vice president of management and finance with the agency. I'm going to start acquiring all the management and financial skills I need to qualify for that capstone."

If you're like most beginners, your capstone will evolve with experience. You might find that you like the creative side of the business much better than the account side. Or you might learn that you prefer to be on the client side. Resist pressure to settle in too fast and hitch your capstone to the first job experiences you've had.

Follow this rule:

Don't set your first capstone in concrete before two or three years of high-intensity learning in Careers 101.

FOCUS YOUR LEARNING

Focus your learning in three key areas: your job, yourself, and the fit between you and the organization. Most people have no trouble focusing on the job. It's basic survival to learn all you can about the required tasks and skills, the norms, the people, the work environment, and the particulars of the company.

It's easier to forget to track your own reactions to the world of work. Try using your own "heat of battle" reactions to learn what you want and like. Ask yourself leading questions: what drives you crazy? What makes your pulse race? Where do you feel truly deficient? How do people see you? Use your answers to these questions to plan, to get feedback, and to grow.

Don't overlook learning about the fit between you and your work culture. Every organization is like a little country that has its own way of doing things, its own customs and unwritten rules. No two work cultures are exactly alike. Some are rigidly formal and paternalistic. Expect dress codes and proper formats for everything. Others are warmer, freewheeling places where you do your own thing with only minimal supervision. Some of these cultures will match your own way of seeing and doing things; some won't. Your task is to figure out to what extent your current work culture is a match or a mismatch with your own style and values. If you're having trouble understanding the organizational environment and your role in it, find a mentor; get help. Determine what the problem is. No matter how good you are, the fit between your own style and the organization's culture will have major impact on your success. If you and the organizational culture are mismatched, use this as an opportunity to develop your own "spec list" for getting a better organizational fit next time.

SET A TIME LIMIT ON YOUR STAY

Whether you love or hate your first job, don't make it your final resting place. If you've chosen well, there's real danger in getting too comfortable. After all, you like the work; they like you; you like them. You're in Quadrant II. So why rock the boat?

Remember Doom Loop dynamics. Why risk trading Quadrant I and Quadrant II satisfaction for Quadrant III stagnation? This is always risky, but it's particularly chancy when you have no baseline comparison and when you've imprinted on one job experience.

Suppose you get a promotion? Analyze the situation carefully. Does this promotion put you back in Quadrant I and offer you new and relevant skill-building related to a potential target mosaic? If it does, you might want to extend your stay for a while. But if the promotion is in title only—more of a reward for your hard work than a developmental opportunity—my advice is to accept it and get your résumé circulating.

It helps if you decide in advance to review your decision to stay or leave on a certain date. At the end of two years, or when you have learned all the basic building-block skills this job offers, move on to the next course in your career apprenticeship program. Then give yourself another two years before settling anywhere.

FOCUS ON ACQUIRING THE RIGHT SKILL MIX

Watch out for the fallacy of early technical competence! This is a first-job precursor of the "I wannabe an expert" capstone error discussed in Chapter 2. Many new graduates believe it's important to specialize. They respond to the first-job crisis by building their high-tech expertise as fast as they can. The idea is this: the more technical knowledge they have, the more "professional" and marketable they will be.

But in their quest for technical knowledge they paint themselves into a corner. They may choose the wrong capstone, or outgrow the one they have chosen, and in this process waste valuable years accumulating skills with too little versatility. Even if they choose well, their early capstones will probably change, leaving them with a wardrobe of skills that aren't adaptable to new work climates. This shortsightedness can lead to a bad case of midcareer blues down the road.

Counteract the trend toward high-tech specialization by concentrating on basic, generic skills that balance out your career mosaic and allow you to move in the direction of nearly any future capstone. In your first few years of working, sign up for jobs that are more akin to a liberal arts than a technical education. Specifically, look for jobs that offer the chance to acquire the following generic skills:

• **Communication Skills**—speaking and writing skills that involve taking complex ideas from your own head and getting them into someone else's. To accomplish this, you must realize that other people have different ways of framing the world than you do. Once you understand that we each speak our own language, it's easy to see that the challenge of successful communication is sizing up the situation and performing on-the-spot translation.

• **Interpersonal Skills**—"people" skills that permit you to deal effectively with others whose ideas, values, and personality traits differ from your own.

• **Production Skills**—action skills that allow you to take an idea from its inception to the development of a product or service that is then introduced into the marketplace.

• **Political Skills**—organizational awareness skills that enable you to learn the ropes, positioning your needs and accomplishments for rewards by the system while protecting your own back.

• **Analytic Problem-Solving Skills**—intuitive and analytic skills that permit you to objectively gather and sift information, identify problems, see patterns, brainstorm alternatives, test solutions, and implement actions.

• **Conflict Negotiation Skills**—problem-resolution skills that promote consensus among people with different vested interests and with differing, often hidden, agendas.

• **Teamwork Skills**—an amalgam of people, communication, and problem-solving skills that pulls all the players together to work as a well-functioning, integrated unit with agreed-upon goals and outcomes.

These are the basics that go into any skill profile. But there are other skills just as important that most people don't think about acquiring. If you take your work life seriously, don't overlook these less obvious career survival skills:

• **Self-Management Skills**—You may not hear many people talking about these skills, but their absence or presence can make or break your career, so the earlier you get the hang of them the better. Mastery will give you an edge in making the most of yourself. They include skills in self-assessment, self-esteem building, self-motivation, goal setting, time management, mood stabilization, crisis management, support seeking, and balancing-act skills. They require you to use your strengths consciously and manage your weaknesses. If people see you as moody or as having a chip on your shoulder, your career progress will stall. Just remember: most organizations value predictability, not irascibility.

• **Organization-Specific Skills**—These are skills your organization's leadership values; they may be industry-specific or more general, like stand-up presentation skills, joke-telling skills, social skills. Since they vary from organization to organization, the key is to recognize them early and add an appropriate mix of them to your career mosaic.

• **Career Management Skills**—These are skills that you won't want to flaunt in your organization but you will want to acquire quickly. These skills allow you to market and position yourself well beyond your current job to a broader audience or move toward a longer-range goal. They include networking, interviewing, image management, résumé editing, and general job search skills.

Jobs that allow you to add the right mix of skills to your career mosaic are good first-job choices.

IS THERE AN IDEAL QUADRANT FOR FIRST JOBS?

Let's say you find a job that will allow you to gather many of the skills described in the previous section. But then you remember the Doom Loop and you wonder what quadrant this job will place you in. Since you are not yet good at many of the skills of the job, the odds are you will be in either Quadrant I or Quadrant IV, the two "not-good-at" quadrants.

	LIKE	DON'T LIKE
GOOD AT	QUADRANT II	QUADRANT III
NOT GOOD AT	*First Job* QUADRANT I	*First Job* QUADRANT IV

Either quadrant can help you, in that each provides opportunities to learn generic skills, acquire experience, and test preferences. The main appeal of Quadrant IV jobs is often seductive convenience, high salary, or status. You might be tempted to make this trade-off—sacrificing what you like in exchange for the dollars and prestige.

If you make this choice, watch out! These Quadrant IV jobs present difficult challenges. Any first job is inherently stressful. But when you find you don't enjoy the skills you're forced to learn, this normal stress flares and intensifies. Early job burnout is one predictable outcome.

In a Quadrant I job, however, enjoying what you're doing makes all the difference. It gives you the fortitude and energy you need to overcome the daily hassles of first jobs, and it confers the stress-buffering resilience you'll need for all those "I should have known better" mistakes.

But even Quadrant I first jobs are difficult for some personalities. Perfectionists—those people who can't bear making errors—often find even the most ideal Quadrant I first jobs inherently stressful. If this describes you, you might find it hard to remember that you are in a coveted Quadrant I—not a dreaded Quadrant IV job. Take it on faith that the stress would be as bad or worse in a Quadrant IV job, but the outcome would be far less favorable. Once the trauma of being a novice has passed, all that the Quadrant IV experience will have offered you is a trial by fire into Quadrant III humdrum.

Not liking what you're doing makes you much more vulnerable to all manner of crises.

For example, here's a quick sampling of what Quadrant IV first-jobbers said:

> There's nothing I like to do here. I have no reason to get out of bed in the morning. It hurts and I'm disgusted with it.
>
> —New sales manager

> I have spent my whole first year as an engineer running computer models, asking myself, 'Is this all there is?'
>
> —New mechanical engineer

> I'm a basket case over this job. It rubs me the wrong way. I have to kiss ass; do administrative detail; deal with unintelligent people. I can take criticism if it's honest, but I dislike criticism of my personality.
>
> —New public relations liaison

Compare those comments to what these Quadrant I first-jobbers say:

> I can't believe they are paying me to learn to do all this! I go home and bore my roommate to death talking about my day.
>
> —New financial analyst

> There's something going on here all the time and that suits me. I can't believe it when it's time to go home.
>
> —New public defender

> I love the responsibility, the variety, the commotion. I like getting people excited about what we're doing. I've taken the basic duties of this job and gone even further.
>
> —New special events promoter

Before accepting your first job, determine the skills to be learned and think long and hard about whether they are skills you'll enjoy. If so, you have a Quadrant I job that will get your career off and running.

"WHAT NEXT" TACTICS

You've been in your Quadrant I job for some time. You've learned the organizational ropes—the norms, politics, and people. If you still like the skills involved and find your work meaningful, you've made it to Quadrant II. There isn't a cloud in the sky.

But don't get complacent. The weather will change. Remember the Doom Loop's potential momentum. It could carry you over the top of the Loop into Quadrant III unless you do something to halt the ride. So help head this off by taking action:

* List all the skills required by this job.
* Pinpoint the skills left for you to learn.
* Write down exactly what you have learned already.
* Recall positive incidents in which you felt proud of yourself and excited about your contribution, when you were totally involved in your work.
* Pay attention to your emerging patterns of likes and dislikes.

Now implement the following tactics to make this job part of your larger career management scheme:

Barnacle Prevention Tactics: Once you know your way around and have your anxiety under wraps, set and mark time lines in your calendar for beginning your next job search and moving on. Think in terms of nine-month to one-year (not five-year) segments. The rookie's most common mistake is staying too long!

Cornerstone Tactics: Stop fooling around. Turn your attention to intentionally acquiring the remaining generic building-block skills that develop and fill out your career mosaic. You are laying the foundation for your future.

Tinker Tactics: Tinker with your job description to include more Quadrant I responsibilities involving skills and tasks you like. A little creative job enrichment can stretch your tenure in a Quadrant II position. Network. Poke around and get yourself involved in new Quadrant I assignments and short-term projects.

Antiburnout Tactics: Look beyond the here and now. Create opportunities on and off your job for successes that energize and empower you. Seek a sponsor in the organization who can arrange for you to meet and be noticed by local rainmakers and open other doors of opportunity for you. Begin to build stronger support systems for yourself, both inside and outside your workplace. Build a balanced life with fun, friends, and family. Don't let the job engulf your life and identity.

Don't stop here. No matter how blissful you feel in your Quadrant II job, recognize that things will change. You'll need all the tactics at your command to prevent the slip into Quadrant III. Try these external-to-the-job tactics that stress and stretch your adaptability:

Toehold Tactics: Don't become too inbred. Being an established member of the clan isolates you and makes you vulnerable when organizations restructure or cut back. Gain a toehold in other parts of your organization by participating in work- and non-work-related task forces, networks, or recreational events. Tap into the broader professional, business, or local community as well. Gain visibility in the world outside your immediate job. Create new contacts by joining clubs, associations, and political groups. Try serving on committees, giving local talks, and writing for newsletters.

Mosaic Tactics: Even if you don't have a capstone, you can still concentrate on building your career mosaic. Determine which of the generic building-block skills you lack that aren't provided by your job. Look for jobs that will let you gain these skills in your current organization, on the outside, and in community service. Interview for these positions. Focus on growth opportunities.

Exploration Tactics: Regard every life situation as a learning opportunity. Informally interview people about their work, their satisfaction, and how you might do in their areas. This is strictly information-gathering; no action is required yet.

Search Tactics: Use your analysis of your current career mosaic to write an updated résumé. Circulate it to key industry or professional figures for advice on what experience and skills you'll need to advance. Target generic skills over technical ones. Even though you probably haven't determined your career capstone, establish a few likely directions and actively investigate them.

Catalytic Tactics: Recent college graduates who are impatient with the long, slow career climb ahead might want to shift gears after two years and go back to school for an advanced degree. Some of the fastest-growing career opportunities are in areas requiring graduate study. But be discriminating. Don't sign up for any old advanced degree. If you are not sure of your eventual destination, consider broad, short-commitment degree programs that boost your earning power and give you maximum flexibility— like the MBA, the MA in international studies, or the JD, among others. Carefully investigate your options and once you decide on an area, aim high. Try for a degree from the finest university for which you qualify. A degree from a top school will dramatically enhance your earning potential and create more opportunities and mobility than one from a more convenient but less respected institution.

Whatever you do, don't get too comfortable. It's way too early in your career to settle into a "till death us do part" job. Develop a sixth sense about the right time to exit. Be prepared to leave perfectly good jobs that you have outgrown and take less comfortable but more challenging Quadrant I jobs.

SOME LAST CAREER-ENTRY ADVICE

There is more to a first job than simply landing one. You are at the beginning of a life-shaping journey that can lead to many different futures, many different selves. The Doom Loop is a simple reminder that you are much more than your current competencies. You are a whole person with likes and dislikes, needs and values, interests and potential for growth. The holistic premise behind the Doom Loop—that preference and performance deserve equal emphasis—has many implications for your future.

Staying Balanced

If you're like most achievers—ambitious, determined to succeed, dreaming of reaching your capstone—then you could be vulnerable to one-track ideas about how to get ahead. For example, you might fall into the trap of valuing your career above all else, putting your energy into climbing the ladder as quickly, even as ruthlessly, as possible. Do yourself a favor: don't. Driving, single-minded ambition can take you up fast and down even faster. No matter how important proving yourself seems right now, it's just as important to build a satisfying life outside work. Building that life will take time and energy, and you will have to decide where to expend each. Many of us at later stages of our careers will be glad to tell you that all work and no play is a dull and dangerous long-term strategy.

Being Self-Managed

A better approach is to see your career entry as marking your passage into a new era of self-managed living and learning. If you're leaving a student role you're saying good-bye to a world where other people looked after your interests and took primary responsibility for your well-being. If you're leaving a basically homemaking or parenting role, you're entering a world where it's important to put your own needs—not someone else's—on the front burner. Chances are, your co-workers, colleagues, and supervisors—no matter how nice— will be looking after their own well-being, not yours. Eventually most people get the message: if you're not taking care of yourself and tending to your own career progress, who is going to? In the world of careers, happy endings depend on your own ability to take charge, seize the day, plan, and adapt. Early in my own career, I used to ask myself three basic questions every morning:

- Am I going to make something happen today?
- Am I going to let something happen today?
- Am I going to prevent something from happening today?

These questions put responsibility for what happened right where it belonged—on me. Is there a downside to this heightened sense of self-responsibility and strong ego investment in your career path? Sure. You may be tempted to allow your sense of self to be so dominated by your professional work role that you put the rest of your life on hold. In the heat of battle, it's easy to lose track of what's important. Ten years from now, or whenever you next come up for air, you may dejectedly wonder what happened to all your other interests, friendships, and social life.

To counterbalance the demands of work life, get into the habit of spending time examining what you're giving priority to. Ask yourself:

- What would it take to achieve a better balance among my work, personal, and family life?
- In what ways am I a good self-manager of my life outside of work? A poor one?
- Am I building a strong and varied outside support network?
- Am I developing the kind of intimacy and personal relationships I need and want?

Creating a Future Vision

To achieve balance think about who you are and who you want to become. Create a vision of your future success for yourself. Take some time and imagine where you'd want to be in ten years if you had no constraints. Travel beyond immediate barriers (job, finances, et cetera) and picture yourself in a totally satisfying life-style. Don't isolate your work from the rest of your life. Imagine yourself on the job and off. Think about family, friends, what you do for fun, where and how you live. Think about your job from your perspective, not your employer's. Certainly you have to give the organization something in exchange for your salary. But you don't have to be locked into your employer's perception of who you should be. What do you crave most from the job: recognition for your work, high achievement, being liked, job security? Can your current job satisfy those needs? Where else can you satisfy them?

Respecting the Past

Watch out for common career traps that keep you from developing yourself. For example, to what extent are you responding to your company as you would to your family? Many times, people unknowingly re-create past family dynamics in the workplace—even when they have intellectually distanced themselves from their own families. They see the boss as being unappreciative of their efforts—just as Mom or Dad was. Or they believe they'll get universal praise—just as they did at home. When the workplace becomes a surrogate family, it's easy to work yourself to death to get your boss's or someone else's approval or love—or even to provoke anger. You may be replaying old dramas and unresolved issues with your parents and siblings. This eats up your energy. It can even keep you from leaving a distressing work situation. If this sounds familiar, be aware of the trap. Once you recognize what you're doing, it's easier to take steps to adjust your thinking or get outside help.

Observing the Context of Your Job

Another trap is getting so caught up in the tasks of the job that you forget to take note of your organization. Ask yourself what the culture is like. Assess the "chemistry." Do you feel you fit in? Can you be yourself, or do you feel you have to act like someone else? When you feel comfortable with an organization, learning is less stressful and more satisfying. You can show different aspects of yourself and be accepted. Look for work cultures that allow you to make a rookie's mistakes without penalty.

And don't make the mistake of downplaying the politics of the organization. Politics can be as important to your success as competence and solid career management. The sooner you're able to understand the politics, the faster you'll become an integral part of the work team. If you ignore politics you run the risk of having your projects and progress sabotaged. It pays to know which people you can trust. If you're like most beginners, you'll equate liking someone with trusting him or her. They're not synonymous. Start out liking as many coworkers as possible and trusting as few as possible. Trust takes time.

Using the Doom Loop

In the midst of this complex balancing act, use the Doom Loop to track your progress. Regularly plot your location. As long as you're moving between Quadrants I and II, you're doing fine. Don't worry if you move "backward"—from II to I. As a beginner, you've still got a great deal to learn, and the more time you incubate in Quadrant I the better.

If, however, you find yourself in Quadrant III or IV, your internal career alarm system should start buzzing. Follow the tactics I have suggested here to return yourself to the growth side of the Loop.

Above all, don't panic. Although you may be facing your first job crisis, it won't be your last. Job crises are inevitable. Rather than looking at them as obstacles, view them as stepping-stones. They force you to confront your career choices. They make you examine your likes and dislikes about a job and the skills you've acquired or failed to acquire. A crisis is a natural event in the course of a career. It allows you to step back and analyze where you've been and where you're going and to correct your course.

Use the Doom Loop and the advice offered in this chapter to better understand and analyze this first-job crisis, to achieve balance, and to keep yourself alert for the next career crisis waiting around the bend.

CHAPTER 6

First-Career Disappointment

> The idea of making things better always appealed to me, but I have trouble thinking 'I'm an engineer'—you know, the details, the boredom, the stereotype. I'm not a robot—I have dreams!
>
> —Dissatisfied mechanical engineer

> I just want to live on a farm in Appalachia and rock on the front porch all day—never have to worry again about whether something *I did* is going to kill someone. But my family! They would never forgive me for bagging it all.
>
> —Disaffected young physician

> I hate finance! Every day I alternate between watching the minute hand drag itself around the clock and wanting to hit the expressways where I can scream my guts out in the privacy of my car. Does everyone do that?
>
> —Midcareer auditor

You've chosen your career path with high hopes and good faith. You've jumped through enough of the right hoops to land on the threshold of occupational success. You're about to step into career paradise, ready to enjoy the Quadrant II fruits of your labors. You plan to stay for the millennium. Then, to your chagrin you find paradise isn't quite what it was cracked up to be.

When this happens, most of us feel shocked and cheated.

We paid our dues; it wasn't supposed to be like this. But when we moan and complain, no one offers us much sympathy. Our friends label us malcontents. We ourselves don't understand what is happening, so we feel alone and panic-stricken.

First-career disappointment, however, is a common and predictable career crisis. Once you understand it, you can deal with it.

Take a look at the following checklist to see whether you identify with any of these symptoms of first-career disappointment:

SYMPTOMS OF FIRST-CAREER DISAPPOINTMENT

1. _____ I just can't marshal the interest and enthusiasm I need to succeed here.
2. _____ When you get down to it, what I do here makes no difference at all.
3. _____ I don't fit; I have no future here.
4. _____ I feel like an utter and complete failure.
5. _____ I never dreamed this job (occupation, profession) would be like this.
6. _____ The more my performance drops, the worse I feel about myself.
7. _____ This job is the pits, but I am at a total loss about what to do next.
8. _____ Maybe I should go back to school, get married (divorced), start a family, buy a farm.
9. _____ I'm losing faith that there is a right job out there for me
10. _____ I've been soul-searching for two years and I still don't have any answers.

If you can make any of these statements, it may be time to stop floundering and to start understanding your first-career disappointment. Now is the time for turning this crisis around.

TRAPPED IN PARADISE

How does it happen? Is this another instance of the best-laid plans going awry? Is it a capstone problem? Consider the following scenario. You make an occupational choice—sales, management, law—that draws universal approval. Your friends and family give it rave reviews. Relieved, you take the next step. You land the desired job. Now you're ready for life to begin in earnest.

All you want is a chance to prove yourself, to give it your best shot. And you do just that. In the beginning, you're so busy learning the ropes of your trade and making your mark that you shrug off the early warning signs. Career discontent is inconceivable. This makes you susceptible to denial. You refuse to believe this is happening!

Denial helps insofar as it holds your anxiety in check. But the downside of this is that you ignore the obvious symptoms—that knot in the pit of your stomach in the morning when you leave for work, the urge to take a long winter's nap right after your morning coffee break, the aversion you've developed to sitting at your desk. If you can't ignore them, you downplay them. Or you try to talk yourself out of your slump—the economy will get better, the takeover won't go through, the place will loosen up, your boss will seek psychotherapy. You work even harder and attribute your secret doubts to stress, overwork, a personality conflict. You take up running, racquetball, needlepoint. But it's all just a matter of time.

You're like a gardener who inadvertently plants seeds in the wrong soil or climate. No matter how hard you work, the crop will turn out badly. You're so involved in tending your garden that you fail to realize just how exhausted and frustrated you really are. Eventually you wonder what's wrong with you.

By the time you land in this crisis, no matter where you started out, you'll probably be in Quadrant III or IV. As the kudos slack off and daily life grinds on, there's no more denying it: there's trouble in paradise, and nothing short of moving out and on will cure you.

But the cost! The humiliation! What will people think of you? And what will you do now?

PRECOCIOUS FIRST-CAREER DISAPPOINTMENT

Usually first-career disappointments occur a few years into the job. Sometimes, however, they happen shortly after you walk through the door. Among the first-career-disappointed, these precocious few are the lucky ones; they don't have to be struck by a bolt of lightning to realize that who they are and what they are doing for a living don't match. As one new accountant put it: "I feel like I'm allergic to my work. My throat closes up when I get to my desk."

In my early days as a psychologist, I suffered migraines every time I saw a patient. No matter how competent I was, being a psychotherapist clearly wasn't good for my health. My only possible progress would be from a Quadrant IV learner to a Quadrant III expert. My body had made a visceral judgment on the suitability of my initial career choice that commanded my attention. I heeded it and chose a new specialty in psychology that didn't make me sick.

Responding to how you feel in this crisis is often difficult. Most people tend to want to tough it out. Never mind the storm clouds gathering on the horizon! The Quadrant IV medical intern is urged by family and friends to see it through, despite her intense dislike of the job ("You've invested so much and you're so close, don't quit now!"). The Quadrant III chemist who hates the lab's isolation and longs to work with people is told, "You're making great money; there are people who would kill to have your job."

In fact, friends, relatives, and strangers will throw a number of familiar refrains your way, just as you decide to call it quits:

- "Stick with it; give it a chance."
- "Things usually have a way of working out. Just buckle down and do your job."
- "Don't be a quitter; you have too much at stake."
- "You expect too much."
- "Wise up. A lot of people don't like their jobs. At least you've got one."

To a certain extent, this advice makes sense. You do have a lot at stake. Suppose you make a critical decision to leave your chosen niche based on too few data points, a temporary industry setback, or unrealistic expectations? Maybe you expect to be an instant expert. If this is your first serious job, you certainly ought to first give yourself a chance to adapt. If you're among the precociously career-disappointed, try the following:

- Tinker with your job description to make it more satisfying.
- Try transferring to another department.
- Change companies to see whether a particular corporate culture is a contributing factor.
- Identify and learn two or three new Quadrant I skills.

In other words, don't overgeneralize from too little information and jump to the conclusion that you're in the wrong line of work. You might be like the person who gets sick after eating a meal; not everything you were served made you ill, just one thing. So before you radically change your career direction, find out what you're allergic to, eliminate it, and move on. On the other hand, you might find that you're allergic to the majority of tasks the job requires. If so, a more radical career change is required. Knowing when to stay and when to cut your losses is an important career management skill.

THE GILDED POPE SYNDROME

Envision the legions of gilded popes laid out in permanent display in the vast catacombs of St. Peter's Basilica in Rome. Each has earned the right to remain there forever, encased in the regalia of exalted status.

Some people believe the occupation you choose early in life has a similar permanence. Having donned your occupational robes—particularly if they're high-status, coveted professional robes—you risk being typecast forever.

Once a corporate mogul, always a corporate mogul. It's easy to confuse the job with the person and to ignore or discount the individuality of the person who inhabits those robes, regardless of the fit. You will be expected to wear those same robes in silent, pained dignity until you die. Career satisfaction becomes a moot point when the gilded pope syndrome takes over.

Do you really want to be a gilded pope? Remember, it's your career and your life we're talking about, not the lives of all those other people who advise you not to be a quitter. Does the prospect of being permanently entombed in Quadrant III or IV bother you?

Confront your first-career disappointment and avoid premature burial. Begin by applying a little Doom Loop methodology. An honest assessment of your skills and preferences will allow you to distinguish between genuine career disappointment (when you're in Quadrant III or IV and don't like most of the skills your job requires) and normal discomfort as you try to find your career niche. You don't have to be a gilded pope unless you truly want to be.

LATER FIRST-CAREER DISAPPOINTMENT

When career disappointment comes later—even a decade or so after you begin working—the odds are good that there is a true mismatch between you and your career choice, or that there has been a major change in your industry or corporate culture, or that you have outgrown a limited career path. Unlike an early first-career disappointment, this one is hard to ignore. Unfortunately, it's also easy to resist. You've invested such an enormous amount of time and energy in your work that it's hard to admit you've made a mistake. If you change, you risk trading off your hard-earned margin of expertise for some yet unknown gamble. So you question your own emotions—How unhappy are you, really?—and tell yourself it's not that bad. Perhaps you've acquired family or financial responsibilities that prevent you from dealing head-on with your unhappiness. You're wary of your options.

Don't be. This crisis is an opportunity for discovery and for constructive career change.

THE ENEMY IS US

First-career disappointments often are caused by us, not our environments. The enemy lies within.

That means you can change jobs, workplaces, or occupations without effect, because you're not changing yourself. You cling to an old mind-set because it's comfortable. It makes a complicated, unfriendly world simple and familiar. It lessens your anxiety. And it goes where you go. You may not even realize how you're limiting your own options. When this happens you're operating out of your blind spot, unwittingly constructing a disappointing world that you name "reality."

From a psychological perspective, you're trapped in a Recurring Universal Theme—a RUT. Instead of responding to the real events of your current life, you're making decisions based on past experience and involuntary, often family-based learning.

RUTs let us take the path of least resistance. They permit us to repackage old beliefs in new protective camouflage that keeps alive the old familial wisdom we heard growing up, in messages like:

- "Everyone in town tries to push the Lamberts around."
- "Your brother Tom is the achiever (the smart one, the athlete)."
- "No one in this family works for the government (the phone company, the university)."
- "If you can't do it well, don't make a fool of yourself."

If you can identify a RUT as the source of a first-career disappointment, you'll know that the problem is internal rather than external. And you'll have to root out the RUT.

Here are five common RUTs: the Prima Donna, the Perfectionist, the Pleaser, the Plodder, and the Victim. No one likes being called any of these names. As you read through the next few pages, your first impulse may be to say, "That's not me." And of course it's not the "total" you.

But one or more of these themes may capture a part of your personality, or describe your tendency to behave in a particular way under particular circumstances. For instance, you may not be a Pleaser every hour of the workday, but you still exhibit predictable Pleaser traits under certain circumstances. Depending on what these circumstances are, that can be enough to lead to disappointment.

Consider which of the following RUTs might apply to you, then review the remedies for ideas on new ways of dealing with the crisis of first-career disappointment.

Prima Donnas

Prima Donnas love being the center of attention. They thrive on praise. They dislike ordinary backstage routines in which their work goes unappreciated. If they go without encouragement for too long, they will find a way to draw attention to themselves, even going so far as to "stage" a problem that puts them back in the spotlight.

In Quadrant I and II jobs, Prima Donnas frequently wear down the people around them with their continual dramatizations of the ordinary and their gargantuan requests for feedback. If the feedback they do get is less than superlative, Prima Donnas have been known to sulk for weeks. Their desire for constant center-stage presence sets them up for disappointment, since typical work environments are short on praise and long on criticism. Too bad, since Prima Donnas often have a great deal to offer, but they need much more than a laid-back "business as usual" work environment to do it. In my experience, Prima Donnas are as likely to gravitate toward Quadrant I as any of the other three quadrants. But because of their need for close to intravenous reassurance, early career disappointment tends to be the rule for Prima Donnas. This often drives them into Quadrant IV in record time.

If this sounds like you, here are some options to help overcome your first-career disappointment:

- Realize that everyone is egocentric. Consequently, people are likely to be far too preoccupied with themselves to give their undivided attention to your performance.
- Make yourself responsible for dispensing your own kudos. Figure out what you'd like to hear from others, then pat yourself on the back several times daily.
- Turn the situation around by giving what you want to get: praise others in appropriate situations, especially with the kind of praise you'd like to receive. More than likely, you'll receive praise back. But if not, avoid taking it personally. Remember, some people don't know how or when to give praise.
- Understand the benefits of negative feedback. If you can keep an open mind, you may garner nuggets of valuable data on how to improve your performance.
- Choose Quadrant I and II work that is intrinsically satisfying and absorbing. Even if no one else notices, meaningful and enjoyable work is a good substitute for encouragement from others.
- Choose fields that reward the kinds of visible performance on which you thrive: advertising, sales, theater, trial law, and so on.
- Choose companies recognized for rewarding achievers, ones with employee incentive programs, above-average salaries, bonuses, perks. Before signing on, take a good, hard look at what the organizational culture is like.
- Develop Quadrant I and II hobbies and activities outside work to satisfy your need for approval. Consider getting involved in community theater, heading fund-raising drives, running for local office.

Perfectionists

They hate to make mistakes. To Perfectionists, mistakes connote failure, inadequacy, criticism, rejection, and loss of esteem. Quadrant I jobs send Perfectionists into a tizzy; there's just too much room for uncontrollable error. As a result, many Perfectionists choose low-risk, low-fail Quadrant III occupations and jobs. In fact, Perfectionists temporarily defy the Doom Loop's trajectory by feeling absolutely comfortable in jobs they're good at but don't particularly like.

Because they're control addicts—people who are psychologically addicted to maintaining as much control as they can—they have no trouble trading off the satisfaction of doing something they like for well-choreographed routines. They can stay in a Quadrant III job much longer than most before taking the inevitable plunge into Quadrant IV. But when they reach Quadrant IV, they're like everyone else: frustrated, bored, and miserable.

Career disappointment often comes to Perfectionists after a prolonged period of being underutilized in a Quadrant III job. Because they fear making mistakes, they find hundreds of excuses for avoiding challenging, skill-building jobs in Quadrant I. They long for the perfect Quadrant II job, but the high-anxiety learning required to get there holds them paralyzed in place. Voilà, the ingredients for disappointment!

If you're a Perfectionist, here are some remedies to consider:

- Be aware of your need for perfection and see it for what it is: old, obsolete learning that is holding back your career development.
- Listen to what you say to yourself when you make a mistake. If you're unforgiving, realize that this probably incorporates some old message you got when growing up. Even if you are not ready to kick the habit, recognize when you're being too hard on yourself.
- Break your goals down into small, trivial steps. Borrow a little bit of the Prima Donna personality. Tackle one step at a time and congratulate yourself after each small success. Try laughing at yourself now and then.
- Allow yourself to experience small failures in noncritical performance areas. Talk about your mistakes with friends. Watch their reactions. Do they seem to think less of you? Do you?
- Draw up a comprehensive balance sheet of perfection's payoffs and liabilities. See what you think.

• Find occupations and jobs you enjoy where your tendency toward perfectionism is viewed as an asset: accounting, research, copyediting, typography, aviation, police work, pharmacology, the nuclear power industry.

Pleasers

Pleasers have a bad habit—they pay more attention to what other people want than to what they need and desire. In fact, they have a special gift for this, which makes it easy for Pleasers to choose a job or capstone based on someone else's dreams.

As a result, when the fanfare dies down, Pleasers are likely to experience the odd sensation of slugging it out in Quadrant II of someone else's Doom Loop.

Obviously, career disappointment hits Pleasers hard.

After all, if you choose your occupation for Dad's sake—think how proud he will be to say, "Let me introduce my son (or daughter) the doctor"—you'll find yourself pasted into a trompe l'oeil Quadrant IV that looks deceptively idyllic to the rest of the world. But you know better. It's Dad, not you, who is happy and satisfied with your career.

The disappointed Pleasers who consult me about this problem often seem to be suffering from amnesia. They ask, "How did I get here? Who am I?" And these turn out to be critical, if basic, questions. Without the answers, Pleasers will have a difficult time moving to Quadrant II. But by making critical life decisions based on someone else's agenda, Pleasers are saying, "Who I am and what I do don't count—unless I am making someone else happy." This tendency to discount the self rarely ends with the act of career choice. It plays itself out in the workplace, family life, and other arenas. All this makes Pleasers great short-term employees, good friends, and terrific relatives. At least until they burn out from trying so hard.

But the struggle to maintain their satisfied and happy demeanor in Quadrant III or in view of a fast-breaking Quadrant IV gradually wears Pleasers down. As long as they are successfully pleasing others, Pleasers receive sufficient positive reinforcement to sustain themselves in the short run. But they can only hold down their growing career disappointment for only so long before it begins to surface, along with pent-up resentment and anger. When it does, they start to wake up in the morning asking, "Is this all there is?" They may realize they don't have enough intrinsic interest in their work to sustain committed job performance over the long haul.

Still, confronting first-career disappointment is difficult for Pleasers. They are capable of identifying what they don't like, because they're experts at scanning, critiquing, and reacting to external events. But they have a good deal of trouble valuing their own needs enough to identify what they do like.

Another problem is that Pleasers must struggle with two issues: their own personal career disappointment and dealing with the people their original career choice was meant to please. When Pleasers try to change careers, they suffer from a sense of having let others down. For Pleasers holding high-status professional slots like physician or lawyer, or for Pleasers whose achievements are the first of their kind in the family (like "my daughter the engineer), the break can be wrenching. That's why when Pleasers change careers, they often fail to make real changes. Although a new position may seem different, it's often actually more of the same. For example, a lawyer who longs to teach preschool children finds himself teaching law at a university. His friends and family believe this is a radical change, but once again the Pleaser has pleased them, not himself.

Old habits die hard, and when it comes to articulating their own preferences and dreams, Pleasers are often in Quadrant IV. This means they neither are good at following their own vision nor feel comfortable enough meeting their own needs to enjoy making their dreams come to life. Even midcareer Pleasers changing jobs tend to repeat these same patterns, this time pleasing a spouse or even a professional career consultant instead of a parent.

If you're a Pleaser, try these remedies to move yourself off center:

• Practice seeing your own needs as important. Tell yourself that you are a deserving person. If you accept this, decide what you would do differently. Begin right now by changing just one small, even trivial, thing. Like all long journeys, you must begin this one with the first step. Give yourself the time you need. Get the right professional help. Join a support group. See pleasing as an addiction that keeps you from functioning at capacity.

• Fine-tune your awareness of your own needs by keeping a regular log of your attitudes, feelings, needs, likes, and dislikes. Try seeing yourself as an interesting and complex person. Allow yourself to be fascinating and fascinated.

• Determine what you don't like about your work life. Take it further: What is abhorrent about your job? Look for patterns. What do they tell you about yourself?

• Identify the person you've been trying to please with your career choices and behavior and consider how successful you've been. What else could you do to please this person? Continue thinking about this question until you see the method in your madness or begin to laugh at the absurdity of it—whichever comes first.

• Resolve to construct your own life based on what is pleasing and meaningful to you—not anyone else. Experiment. Try new things; broaden your options. Get professional help and talk it through. Remember that your career is just one aspect of who you are.

• Consider occupations that will allow you to use your well-developed Quadrant II ability to read people and please them. Explore careers in fields like health care, social work, the ministry, counseling, teaching, customer relations, advertising, consulting, and special events planning.

Plodders

We all know them. They subscribe to the theory that hard work pays off. Plodders believe that anything is possible if only they put in enough hours. Fueling their strivings is a tenacious belief that anyone can get to the top with effort and ability.

Though anyone can be a Plodder, this group generally contains a large number of "first-timers" in particular professions and/or the labor force: minorities and women; the first in the family to have an MBA; those making the leap from blue- to white-collar work. Without access to role models or mentors, these people rely mainly on their own efforts for advancement. They revere self-sufficiency. There's nothing wrong with hard work, of course. But if you make it your guiding career management principle, it can backfire and lead to disappointment.

Plodders are victims of myths about hard work and success. They believe in these myths with all their hearts. For a time these myths meshed with their experience: they got parental encouragement for "trying hard" and recognition from teachers for prodigious productivity; their hard work in school paid off with high marks. So quite naturally they expect more of the same in the workplace. And they do what they've always done to get approval—they work harder.

At first, this work ethic keeps Plodders contentedly exhausted in any quadrant of the Doom Loop. As long as they're fed projects that keep them hustling, they're happy. But Plodders make a false assumption: that hard work is the single most important factor in getting ahead.

Plodders, therefore, experience an intense and shocking disappointment when they realize that other factors count as much as or more than hard work: factors like cronyism, office politics, seniority, social grace, talent. Stunned and disillusioned, they come to suspect that the American dream—anyone can get to the top through hard work—actually masks a hidden standard of corporate mediocrity.

It takes a while for this to sink in, but Plodders finally get it. The more successful they are in meeting deadlines, the more work is loaded on them. They develop a reputation for being drudges. They have committed a career management faux pas: they sweat and they show it.

Plodders are initially too preoccupied with putting in a full day's work to assess what is happening or to plan ahead. Eventually, though, they begin to chafe under the heavy work load and lack of appreciation. Cut off from the organizational mainstream, they lose sight of Quadrant I growth opportunities. After a while, they're trapped in a dismal Quadrant III morass of their own making.

Making matters worse, Plodders are labeled by coworkers as "rate busters" who set unrealistically high standards for others. They're objects of scorn and ridicule. Their productivity is taken for granted, not acclaimed.

One disappointed Plodder worked so long and so hard that she eliminated the need for her own job! Her company, with typical hypocrisy, rewarded her by simultaneously praising her performance and firing her. Her Herculean performance threatened the mediocre status quo, and she was forced out.

First-career disappointment often hits Plodders when they're on the cusp of Quadrant III burnout or when they realize they're doing the work of two or three people without commensurate recognition, pay, or enjoyment, and that their dronelike status in the organization is taken for granted, an unescapable and uncelebrated tradition. They feel betrayed and misled. They think, "I should have been out there schmoozing and scheming, not plodding."

Take heart, Plodders! You can plan your escape from Quadrant III with these tactics:

• Take a sheet of paper and jot down every platitude about the American work ethic you can think of ("The early bird gets the worm" and "Idle hands are the devil's playground" will get you going). Which platitudes best describe your attitude toward work? Which ones are patent myths, and which ones pushed you into Quadrant III? Decide to discard those myths.

• Observe and respect the influence of organizational norms. Observe the unwritten rules in your workplace: How hard do people really work? What is their style? Do they work alone or in groups? Do people have mentors? Does your style match or clash with the norms? If you were a Rockette, would you be in step with the rest of the chorus line? If you can't adapt to the norms, look for an organization or team of independent professionals whose style matches your own, or who will appreciate someone like you.

• Analyze your job and figure out which are your Quadrant

III tasks and assignments. Set goals and tight deadlines for each of these Quadrant III tasks for one week. Break the mold: do the minimum required to complete the tasks. Aim for absolute mediocrity. Brazenly ask others for feedback about the quality of your work. Did anyone notice you performed less well?

• Select one or two projects requiring Quadrant I skills and concentrate your energy on them. Intentionally skew your workaholism in the direction of new skills leading to your capstone.

• Find a mentor or at least a brain to pick among your colleagues. Get coaching and feedback. Discover what you need to succeed in this work environment. Learn where your problem lies: style, excessive effort, not fitting in, failure to recognize and respond to politics. If you find it hard to change your work habits, move on to a better-fitting job, workplace, or occupation.

• Look for a new job where Plodders are rewarded—for instance, positions in small, understaffed companies where high output is essential; executive staff positions in professional and trade associations; work in fields such as medicine, nursing, software analysis, accounting; work in service professions.

• Choose a new capstone where your workaholism has high Quadrant I and II payoffs—for instance, entrepreneurial endeavors such as small-business ownership and professional private practice. You can doggedly pursue hard work and new skills to your heart's content. These areas permit you the luxury of being a Plodder—without ridicule.

• Go for balance and hit the priority reset button. Is your single-minded devotion to hard work making you any richer, happier, smarter? Consider redirecting some of your energy into family life, volunteer activities, hobbies, and sports.

Victims

Anyone can be a victim of circumstance or the machinations of others. But this career disappointment category involves people who are victims of themselves. They experience first-career disappointment primarily because they are determined to see themselves as Victims no matter what the facts of the situation actually suggest.

Victims are "turnaround" experts. Time after time, they turn win-win situations into disappointing lose-lose ones. But their own part in this magical transformation is often hidden from them. All they know is that they are unhappy and disappointed in their work life, the universe, and everything— and that it's not their fault.

Whomever they blame, the finger rarely points in their own direction.

They can recite a well-rehearsed litany of "they done me wrong." And there may be just enough truth in these charges to give them credibility.

From a practical standpoint, a Victim's first-career disappointment is indistinguishable from that of someone who has truly been wronged. Victims act as if they've been given hopeless assignments that would make Sisyphus's rock-rolling project a piece of cake. Listen to their stories. They tell you that they get no help from coworkers or appreciation from their bosses. They are extraordinarily creative and believable in explaining how and why the world is against them through no fault of their own.

But listen long enough and engage in a little cross-examination about the facts of the case and you'll find that the Victim doth protest too much.

Why would anyone act in such a self-defeating way? Because Victims fear giving up the sympathy and attention their status brings. Psychologists label this hidden payoff "secondary gain," and habitual Victims thrive on it.

Perhaps a long time ago, Victims learned that the way to get Mommy's, Daddy's, or Teacher's attention was to act helpless, dependent, or like an underdog. This learning pattern enables Victims to exaggerate the dog-eat-dog aspects of work life and turn themselves into the designated prey.

But as opportunity after opportunity passes Victims by, they cease to relish their status; they become depressed and disappointed. The Victim is caught between desperately craving recognition and cleverly avoiding the responsibility required to get it.

Quadrant I and IV jobs are fertile fields for the Victim. Because these are learning quadrants, there is abundant opportunity to err and receive criticism. Since Victims in first jobs don't yet know the ropes, it's easy for them to distort even the best-intentioned feedback into malicious persecution.

When coworkers and supervisors finally realize the game Victims are playing, they often elect not to play. Then, without recourse to either feedback or sympathy, Victims grow more isolated and powerless. They move directly from Quadrant I to Quadrant IV: disappointed in themselves and others, finding nothing to like in their jobs.

If you put Victims in a Quadrant II job, they'll shoot themselves in the foot. Then they'll look around to see whose gun is smoking. One way or another, they'll find a method of truncating their stay and moving into another quadrant. What's scary here is that Victims really don't know how this happens. This makes them powerless to prevent it.

More so than other "types," Victims have enormous difficulty admitting who they are. If this section describes your behavior, it may be hard for you to recognize it. You might need a career counselor or a psychologist to help you move toward this self-realization. Once you acknowledge your Victim mentality, however, a number of tactics can assist you in dealing with your disappointment:

• Look at your career disappointment under a microscope. Which quadrant were you in? What have you done to shoot yourself in the foot? Write down the ways you explained the situation to yourself and others. Do you sound like anyone else in your family? Do you attribute this turn of events to bad luck or conditions beyond your control? What was your role in what transpired? Do you hold yourself blameless? What do you wish had happened?

• Ask yourself what would happen if you had to stand on your own without blaming anyone else. Write down what you fear most.

• Give up expecting others to change. Tackle changing yourself; it's easier. Since you're the one who's unhappy, you're the one with the most to gain from changing. Recognize that you have control only over your behavior, not anyone else's.

• Practice non-Victim talk. When things go wrong, tell yourself what you have to do to right the situation. Stop blaming anyone else, even if you're still convinced somebody besides you was responsible.

• Take a Quadrant I job or project and take responsibility for small failures. Find a friend or a mentor to talk about those failures and see how it feels.

• Consider jobs and occupations that capitalize on your ability to analyze who is at fault: investigatory work, loss management, insurance work, auditing, arbitration, regulatory enforcement, Social Security administration, quality control, law, engineering, customer relations.

OCCUPATIONAL HAZARDS

The source of your first-career disappointment might not be in you. It might be in your occupation. This could be the result of an early career selection error that took years to manifest itself.

Three categories of professions that often attract people for all the wrong reasons and that often are associated with first-career disappointments are glamour professions, secure professions, and boring professions.

The Glamour Professions

These high-profile, glitzy jobs grab you early, when you're still gulping down hot chocolate in front of the TV after school. You love Marcus Welby as a teenager and decide then and there that you want to be a doctor. When you tell your parents, running the last episode through your mind, they rejoice: "My son/daughter the doctor!" You could have said lawyer, actor, astronaut. You're a hero just for uttering the words. So far as the family is concerned, it's a done deal. The romance of these professions is irresistible.

Unfortunately, close up, most glamour professions are anything but glamorous. Instead of solving mysteries like Perry Mason or experiencing the warm humanity of "L.A. Law," you find yourself researching obscure property law in a dimly lit, dusty law library in the middle of nowhere, working with law partners about as interesting as the telephone directory. Instead of sweeping the top award categories for most creative commercial of the year in front of a national television audience of millions, you find yourself forgotten, between two other hunched-over artists similarly warehoused in a "creative" sweatshop, where you alternately sleep and cry in the rest room stalls—as time permits between a never-ending barrage of deadlines.

You expected a career filled with Quadrant I and II skills, but instead find yourself in Quadrants III and IV of the Doom Loop. The gap between your expectations and reality leads to terrible disappointment.

Which glamour capstone hooks you is irrelevant. The problem is that you fell in love with a myth. Possible glamour fields include politics, writing, futures trading, acting, modeling, journalism, advertising, publishing, and public relations. If you've wandered into one of these with stars in your eyes and been cruelly disappointed, recognize where the fault lies.

The glamour makeover has failed. You're still the same person you used to be, minus the hope of transformation, and facing three-plus decades slugging it out in a slot you don't like.

What should you do?

If you were led down the primrose path by a glamour profession, take defensive countermeasures. Don't let yourself be seduced and abandoned by future glamour jobs. Think of yourself as someone who has a weakness for surface charms —status, appearance, life-style, money—that distorts your good judgment. Attraction, in and of itself, is not enough. If you don't carefully consider an occupation's more pragmatic daily components, you could end up deceived and disillusioned again.

At a time in our society when so many people are afraid of

commitment in relationships, searching for the right job rather than the right mate can be a convenient substitution. We simply take the cultural dictate to find someone to be in love with who will meet all our needs, and apply it to choosing our life's work. But there are all manner of right jobs. And no job can be expected to fulfill all your needs, just as no person can. If you're seeking a career to fill a void in your life or to give you a reason for waking up in the morning, you're probably looking for love in all the wrong places. In both relationships and careers, being in love hardly guarantees infinite bliss. If you don't care much for the actual skills the job requires, being in a glamour profession like medicine, media, or law is small compensation for the painful daily reality. Your love will fade.

To counter this trend, I have found this rule helpful:

"Like lasts." Choose to fall "in like" with the skills and tasks required by a job or profession.

Avoid falling in love with the status or image that a profession or job signifies to you. If you're attracted to a glamour capstone, talk to people who have that job. Perform a skill analysis of the professional niche you're considering and rate each skill on whether you like it or not. Look for high interest and passion for the skills and values this capstone demands. Then rate each skill again, this time on whether you're good at it or not. Construct a matrix map by plotting these skills on your Doom Loop grid.

If the majority fall in Quadrants I and II, great! It's safe for you to follow your heart's desire. If, however, they cluster in Quadrants III and IV, beware! You will want to investigate this occupation or capstone further before tying the knot. It could be a case of love at first sight that doesn't deserve your commitment.

The Secure Professions

The promise of security is a powerful lure. Perhaps your parents taught you to make security your number-one priority. You joined the corporation because it virtually guaranteed you a job for life. Or you chose an occupation like nursing, data processing, or accounting where you thought you'd always be able to find a job.

Unfortunately, you've discovered that secure jobs don't always foster continued learning, challenge, creativity, and personal growth. Once you learned the ropes, you went over the top of your Doom Loop faster than you could daydream about collecting your pension check. Stuck in a routine Quadrant III job and surrounded by "don't rock the boat" types, you feel bored and frustrated.

Or perhaps you are disappointed to learn that no job today is secure—not in an age of recession, downsizing, and hostile takeovers. Trading career excitement for career security might have been acceptable, but being stuck in a job that's both insecure and dull is not. You've opted for the worst of all possible worlds. Now first-career disappointment pushes you to look at personal and professional change—and change was what you wanted to avoid.

If your first-career disappointment is linked to being stuck in a secure profession, you'll want to counter your drive toward high-security positions with managed, planned risk. This will help you get more comfortable with uncertainty and change.

First, decide which skills and talents you want to develop. Pay attention to the parts of yourself that have been stifled in your current job. Then scan for career opportunities that move you from where you are now toward achieving these changes. No action is required at this point, so there's nothing to be anxious about.

Begin by thinking small. Manageable change is nearly always small-scale change. Ask yourself what a reasonable career risk might be. Is it taking a course you're interested in, or beginning a degree program leading to new career directions? Taking on new work roles? Rewriting your résumé?

The key is to find a level of change that stretches your comfort zone only slightly. Then, concentrate on adding as many Quadrant I skills as you can to your portfolio. The rule here is to:

Get free. Redefine security as being a free agent in your own career, so that you won't have to depend on unstable institutions and people. Then make continuing learning the number-one objective of all jobs leading to your next capstone.

Get comfortable with the idea that change is the only constant you can count on.

The Boring Professions

These are harder to define than the glamour and secure professions, since what's boring to one person might not be boring to the next. In fact, what's boring depends on many factors, including which quadrant of the Doom Loop you're in relative to any job or occupation. A position that doesn't change over time will become boring, because as professional mastery increases, challenge decreases. So within a given profession, any stable job can, and probably will, become boring over time. Rather than provide a subjective list of boring occupations, let's look at what makes any occupation boring.

Actually, there are two key factors: competence and availability. Either you or someone else decides you're good at something. And since you have to work, people ask, "Why not do something you're already good at?" These are transformational words. They instantly transform your job experience into a potential Quadrant III ordeal. That's the competence factor.

Now let's look at availability. You're good at organizing, so you become a paralegal or a secretary. You're good at languages so you become an interpreter.

There are thousands of high-structure, low-variety jobs out there. You're tempted to take them not only because you have the skills to do them well, but because, like Mount Everest, they're there.

You start these boring jobs in Quadrant II (if you like the skills required) or Quadrant III (if you don't like them). If you're bright, once the newness of the job wears off you enter a prolonged period of what I call "dustout": the severe stress of having your talents and skills ignored and underutilized in the workplace. Sometimes there's a brief second honeymoon when you get praise, a promotion, or a raise. But eventually, you slide down into Quadrant IV.

You join the ranks of the first-career-disappointed by failing to demand continuing challenge and growth in your job. Most people fail to realize that demanding and receiving growth and challenge are what their first series of jobs is about.

What's the remedy if your disappointment is the result of a boring profession? Take a long, hard look at what you really like to do and go after a job that satisfies those likes. Realize that self-knowledge is your most important weapon in fending off brain-deadening jobs. Don't be content with taking the path of least resistance—the job that's offered or the one that doesn't require much effort. Fight any "out to pasture" tendency you might be harboring by gearing up for a real job search. Take courses that broaden your credentials; decide to retool for a brand-new career path. The scariest time is right before you make the commitment to a new course of action. Once you make the decision and get started, you'll feel wonderful about yourself.

To avoid future disappointments because of boredom, the rule is:

> **Create a vision of success for yourself that integrates what you enjoy doing with jobs that stretch your competencies. Once you're energized by this vision, take action, one step at a time.**

And remember to use your experiences to be a better chooser—next time.

USING THE DOOM LOOP TO AVOID THE BLUES

What if you've experienced first-career disappointment but the preceding categories don't seem to apply to you? What if the disappointment seems to be a result of a combination of factors? Or what if it stems from the lack of "fit" between you and your work environment?

Can the Doom Loop help you understand what's happening? Try viewing your disappointment through the Doom Loop's dispassionate lens to learn more about the causes and cures of this crisis. Let's look at first disappointment from five general perspectives.

The No or Wrong Capstone Blues

Even if you have a Quadrant I or II job, without a capstone you're likely to be disappointed, particularly if you're in a fast-track corporate environment. Because you don't have your eye on one of those coveted middle-management positions, you're going to appear merely aimless in a culture where a watchful management expects everyone to be highly competitive, ambitious, and goal-focused.

For example, the company wants you to work sixty-five-hour weeks. Perhaps management is priming you for the capstone of its choosing. But you want to spend more time learning all kinds of non-capstone-related skills. Or perhaps your priorities are outside work, giving time to causes, recreation, or your family. The result: you are dismissed as a serious contender. You receive negative performance reviews, no promotion, mediocre raises and bonuses. You're shelved. And, of course, you're disappointed.

The remedy here is to take the time necessary to formulate a capstone that fits who you are. Next, find an organizational culture where your work pace fits, where the priorities match. It's important to begin with your needs first, then look for an organization that fits you. Don't find an organization first, then try to fit yourself to it. Keep in mind this simple rule:

> **No matter what your capstone, when your style matches their style you increase your comfort zone and reduce the risk of career disappointment.**

The Quadrant I Blues

When you encounter first-career disappointment in Quadrant I, lack of adequate coaching can be the culprit. Quadrant I jobs can be overwhelming. There's an enormous amount to learn and you're not quite sure how to master it.

Since you're a novice, much of the battle is in ferreting out what you need to learn—and much may be hidden. Since there's no step-by-step manual, Quadrant I jobs usually require intensive coaching for optimum performance. Don't let pride stand in your way. Otherwise your efforts may be diverted into damage control and mop-up.

The rule for Quadrant I jobs is:

> **Hitch your performance to a coach, mentor, or adviser who will facilitate the learning process and keep you on course.**

But sometimes your tenure in a Quadrant I job may yield a different type of disappointment. You're treading water as fast as you can, but you still can't stay afloat. Perhaps you're receiving a great deal of negative feedback and you feel it's reasonably accurate. It looks as if you're not going to make it into Quadrant II in this particular occupation or job.

Your first-career disappointment centers on realizing your own limits. You're in over your head and you have to swim back to safer waters. You're slipping under the Doom Loop from Quadrant I to Quadrant IV. "Good at" has become a lost cause, and you no longer like the skills you perform. Your confidence is ebbing.

What to do? Assess and take advantage of your strengths. Are you using them every day? If not, push on. Why stay in a job that requires you to lead from your weaknesses? Talk with a seasoned veteran in your field or a professional career coach. Find out if poor early performance is the norm for your job. Analyze your past training for dropped stitches— find out if you've missed something that is causing you to fail. Try intensive one-on-one supervision or taking courses to get you up to speed. Take steps to lower your anxiety since high anxiety is an enemy of learning. Confront your limits relative to the demands being made on you. If the Quadrant I learning curve you're climbing is too steep, take a time-out or slow it down. You might have to decrease the grade to a negotiable level. There is no shame in making a realistic assessment. But there will be shame if you continue on a track that leads you to failure.

Use this principle to guide you:

Some Quadrant I positions push your limits more than others. You have a choice. Choose a middle route where you experience moderate rather than debilitating challenge and have a strong liking for the skills involved.

The secret to career success is in finding the niche where your talents, capabilities, and contributions fit. You can be proficient in many Quadrant I skill combinations, but some will just be too difficult. There's no shame in cutting yourself loose from a no-win situation and finding a more suitable Quadrant I position.

The Quadrant II Blues

Can you get Quadrant II blues? Unfortunately, the answer is yes. Even if you like and are good at your job, disappointment can spring from what I call the contextual issues —organizational culture, personalities, values and ethical concerns, office politics—rather than from the job itself.

Again, fit is the problem. You may be a cooperative and trusting type, internally motivated to do well, who is plunked down into a culture that is competitive, distrusting, and punitive. You suggest new ideas and someone else takes credit for them. You expect to be applauded when you do well, but you receive feedback only when you err. The only way you know you're doing well is when no one talks to you.

You are in the unique position of loving a job that's killing you. It's a match made in hell. What should you do about it? It could be that you're the right person in the right job in the wrong place. If that's the case, stick to your knitting, but take it elsewhere.

Before you dump your Quadrant II plum of a job, review the factors that create Quadrant II mismatches:

• **Organizational Culture**—When a culture doesn't match who you are, you feel like Alice in Wonderland. Your world becomes predictably unpredictable.

• **Personality Clashes**—You can't tolerate someone you work with, usually your immediate supervisor. The two of you are out of sync. You say red, she says black. The mere sound of her voice or sight of her face makes you cringe. It's no longer a matter of right and wrong, it's war and sport. And it's your future that is most likely to be on the firing line.

- **Values and Ethical Dilemmas**—The company decides to market a product with serious safety problems; your boss is sexist; you're asked to cover for a misuse of funds. If you stand up for what you believe in or blow the whistle you'll be censured. You're legitimately disappointed.

- **Office Politics**—This is a major source of Quadrant II distress. You learn that it's not how hard you work, but who you know and how you position yourself that count. If you're sufficiently idealistic, you refuse to play political games. Of course, those who do play politics move ahead, and you're left behind. Either you accept politics as a Quadrant IV skill you must learn or you find a job (good luck!) where politics isn't a major factor.

- **Mergers, Takeovers, Restructuring**—Downsizing is a dirty word spoken with increasing frequency. Downsizing turns Quadrant II heaven into hell. Even if you don't lose your job, you lose just about everything else: coworkers, bosses, esprit de corps, stability, a sense of the company's direction. You're a survivor, but you no longer feel like you're in control. And you're not. The rules of the game have changed and no one's saying what they are. You're at the mercy of outside forces. It may be time to press on to a new Quadrant I position. Heed the advice given to Lot's wife: "Don't look back."

What next? Identify which of these Quadrant II spoilers are causing you angst. Make a point of not confusing these contextual factors with being unhappy with your occupation, your position, or the work itself. Separate the contextual factors from the skills your job requires; recognize that you like the latter and dislike the former. Remember that contextual factors vary from organization to organization, from department to department, from trench to trench.

You have a lot of choices. It's up to you to determine the right fit. Decide what you are willing to compromise on and what is sacred.

Then go out and learn what other environments are like. Read. Network with people in your field. Ask questions about the culture, the personalities, and the politics. Shop around until you find an environment that feels comfortable. When you locate a culture that will appreciate you, let key people in on the secret. Tell them what you want.

The Quadrant III Blues

It's easy to be disappointed in Quadrant III. Disappointment here is often due to lack of challenges, underutilization of talent, and plain old dislike of the day-to-day skills required to maintain operations.

The first-career-disappointed in Quadrant III fall into three groups.

If you're an upwardly mobile fast-tracker and your climb to the top has been blocked, you're likely to feel angry and frustrated in your Quadrant III slot. Your Doom Loop preferences have been secondary to your climb. When you cross into Quadrant III positions you're usually on your way somewhere else. But for one reason or another—downsizing, recession, personnel changes, age, sex, race—this time you got stuck. This astounding absence of movement confounds the fast-tracker locked in Quadrant III.

Don't remain motionless! Find another organization that will encourage your desire to climb quickly. Without movement, you're bound to be disappointed in Quadrant III.

Or you might be disappointed in Quadrant III for another reason. If you've paid your dues and you are approaching your capstone without an accompanying sense of fulfillment, you might poke around in Quadrant III and see why you're bored and dissatisfied. The problem may be a serious mismatch between the real and the ideal.

Learn from this mismatch. It's a warning that you're on the wrong track. You may want to investigate new capstones and alternative paths that will lead you to greater satisfaction.

Finally, you might be the type of person who never liked your job to begin with—but assumed that things would get better. They haven't. And they probably won't. New competition is coming up the pipeline, you're older, and your performance reviews are backing into Quadrant IV. The remedy is to review your preferences, find a capstone that fits, and recycle into Quadrant I and II activities. Now is the time to take action.

The Quadrant IV Blues

Disappointment in Quadrant IV is often directed at yourself. How could you have let yourself get into this jam? You feel like a failure.

If this is your first serious career effort, you've probably been a poor chooser. You've made an important decision without knowing enough about your strengths and what the world of careers offered.

Call it bad luck, call it a bad fit, call it being unprepared for managing your own career. But whatever you call it, stop blaming yourself. This will only deflect your energies even further from constructive change.

Regard your Quadrant IV disappointment as the learning opportunity of a lifetime. Identify and challenge your assumptions about yourself and what is possible. There's a satisfying career out there waiting for you, as long as you make an effort to find it. The trick is to start your search now.

FIRST-CAREER DISAPPOINTMENTS
AND THE DOOM LOOP

First-career disappointments are powerful teachers. They challenge our assumptions about who we are and who we want to become; they force us to question how and why we make the choices we do and what we are and are not willing to compromise on to reach our goals. They push us up against people and systems with more clout than we have. They frustrate us at the same time that they enable us to learn our limitations and our strengths.

First-career disappointments are crises, and crises have enormous power: power not only to trouble us but also to help us learn who we really are. Self-knowledge is critical, an integral part of the Doom Loop strategy. The crisis of first-career disappointment provides a time to reflect, explore, and learn before committing to a new capstone or pathway.

Use the Doom Loop skill analysis to clarify your first-career disappointment. Draw a matrix map. Rate and plot the skills of your last positions in the four quadrants. Analyze the results.

Was it the skills required by the job itself or the personal and contextual issues that created your crisis?

If the problem was a result of Quadrant III and IV skill groups, rethink your capstone or reconsider your occupational choice. Compare your present occupation and other potential occupations with your personal preferences, values, personality traits, and motivations. Remember, it's your satisfaction and no one else's that counts here.

If your Doom Loop analysis puts your job skills in Quadrants I and II, it's probably not the work itself that has caused your disappointment. Concentrate on contextual issues as well as on an assessment of your attitudes, beliefs, and assumptions. Decide which new skills you must develop to be more adaptable and to thrive in various organizational cultures.

Look upon this crisis as a positive event rather than as a failure. It invites you to explore possibilities that years or even months ago you wouldn't have considered. This crisis issues you a challenge to overcome your disappointment and get your career back on track.

CHAPTER 7

Fired

Fire—v.t.: **11.** to discharge or shoot (a gun, bullet, etc.) . . . **16.** to dismiss (an employee) from a job.
—*The Random House Dictionary*

You can't eat the orange and throw the peel away—a man is not a piece of fruit!
—Willy Loman in Arthur Miller's
Death of a Salesman

Eighty percent of my self-worth was my job.
—"Early retirement" loss prevention manager

When I met with my boss two weeks ago he said there was a problem. I didn't even know there was one. Then today he said I was fired. All of a sudden I feel like I've lost control of my life.
—Fired advertising executive

Fired! For any employee that word feels like a bullet aimed straight at the heart. It shatters our stability and plays havoc with our identities. It wounds our self-esteem and destroys our sense of being part of a friendly and predictable world. No matter what the circumstances, it hurts.

While few people still expect cradle-to-grave corporate coddling, time-honored myths like "the company will take care of me" and "hard work pays off" persist. These myths leave us unprepared for the changing realities of the American workplace. In today's corporate world, being fired has become a predictable, grand-scale daily event. It may or may not have anything to do with your performance. And it isn't something that will only happen to the other person; if you work long enough you can probably count on it happening to you.

Cutbacks and downsizing are taking place everywhere. To downsize means, of course, to make smaller, which is precisely how the downsized executive feels. The outplacement industry—an industry that provides halfway houses and "aftercare" for those who get the ax and that facilitates breaking the news to fired employees—now grosses $1 billion annually, and the number of outplacement firms has tripled since 1980. No career position is sacred. The resulting insecurity has been compared to waiting in the trenches for the inevitable bullet with your name on it.

After being fired, you'll enter an emotional whirlpool. Financial, social, familial, and personal pressures will swirl around you and sweep you away from making wise career decisions. You'll struggle to make rational sense of what's happened, recounting each detail of the firing as if understanding could free you of the horror.

As you scramble to begin your job search, you'll run a gauntlet of closed doors and unreturned phone calls. You'll get turned down for jobs you thought you had. You'll be fending off persistent, sometimes accusatory questions from friends and family about your job search, and you'll juggle mounting bills. You can expect to experience a full range of uncomfortable and conflicting feelings, like the ones listed on the following page.

Given all this, who can think clearly about his or her career? Most people haven't maintained their job search skills or kept their résumés current. They've bet the ranch on the status quo, not on change. But the average terminated manager can look forward to a minimum of six to eight months of search activity before finding a job, and in a recession-wracked economy it often takes significantly longer. Many senior executives remain jobless for a year or more. And even the most

HOW PEOPLE SAY THEY FEEL AFTER BEING FIRED

Disbelieving	Panicked	Angry
Shocked	Anxious	Distraught
Bewildered	Grief-stricken	Frantic
Betrayed	Numb	Resigned
Depressed	Disillusioned	Nauseated
Empty	Withdrawn	Upset
Hopeless	Free	Violent
Insecure	Unworthy	Rejected
Incompetent	Desperate	Relieved
Listless	Ashamed	Fearful

enthusiastic job seekers lose their optimism as the months drag on. Unrelenting rejection is a powerful antidote to self-confidence.

No wonder that when a job is offered your first impulse is to seize it. It's easy to fall for any stable job when your security is threatened. Yet in many instances the first job offered is the first job you should turn down. At best it will do nothing to accelerate your career trajectory; at worst it will send you into a nosedive.

Your reaction to being fired and the career tactics you should pursue next will vary according to the Doom Loop quadrant you were last in. For instance, if you were fired from a Quadrant I job, you'll probably have to fight your natural urge to scramble for a play-it-safe Quadrant III position. But first, to give you a sense of the gestalt of this sudden career crisis, I'll present two case studies to show you how even the best and brightest executives can lose sight of career strategy and tactics when the ax descends. One case deals with the decisions of one executive prior to being fired. It shows how knowledge of the Doom Loop might have led to a different outcome. The other case illustrates how using the Doom Loop after termination paved the way to a new career.

THE CASE OF THE GOLDEN GIRL

Like it or not, the experience of being fired gives you critical new data about yourself. In the unsettling wake of your termination you can use the Doom Loop to help evaluate whether or not your capstone is still viable, and what you've learned from this experience about your own skills and needs. Consider the case of Gretchen Cavanaugh.

As a lending executive with a large financial institution, Gretchen Cavanaugh was on the fast track. In three years she had moved through a series of starter positions with ease. She was tagged a "golden girl" in a company that could boast of few top managers who were women. Under the guidance of various mentors, Gretchen learned the lending business, receiving superior performance reviews and salary hikes in each of four jobs within the organization.

At twenty-seven, Gretchen had everything going for her. Then she moved into her fifth position, a promotion to management. Her boss, Martha Medden, quickly became her nemesis.

Martha called Gretchen in after six months on the job and told her that her performance was unsatisfactory and that she should meet with Personnel.

Gretchen came to see me for a career consultation. Distraught over her trouble with Martha, she was in shock. A pink slip was around the corner. But she couldn't accept that inevitability. Instead, she agonized over her fall from grace. How could she have lost her golden-girl status? She had only continued to do the things she had been highly rewarded for before. But instead of praise and recognition, this time she was criticized and given warning. She called her former mentor, but his advice to work harder and make fewer mistakes was too little too late. Anger mounting, she went over her review again and again, wishing she could be exonerated and Martha could be fired.

A few weeks later, Gretchen was fired.

If Gretchen had been aware of the Doom Loop, she would have had a better chance of predicting this outcome and might have avoided it. A skill analysis would have shown her that her career mosaic was missing some crucial pieces; though she had developed technical mastery in basic lending operations skills, she still lacked an entire group of generic skills critical to her success in this Quadrant I position: people skills, communication skills, management skills, and political skills.

Under the protection of mentors, Gretchen had flourished. She had developed and moved from Quadrant I to II as a financial lending and collections supervisor. But when she was promoted to a higher managerial position involving many interpersonal skills—under an unsympathetic boss who was clearly not a mentor—Gretchen was lost. And she lacked the career management tools to realize that she had entered a job requiring new Quadrant I skills (people, communication, and management) and—also new for Gretchen—the Quadrant IV skill of office politics.

After her first week on the job Gretchen instinctively knew she was in trouble. There were a lot of little things that added up: Martha would glance at her watch every time Gretchen came into her office; Gretchen wasn't copied in on memos; Martha failed to introduce her to a visiting regional director. But Gretchen denied her instincts; she had no formal method for confirming them. She wondered if she was being over-sensitive. Without a mentor to coach her, she failed to understand that Martha resented her meteoric, mentor-boosted rise and saw Gretchen as a threat to her own power base. Martha's strategy was to isolate Gretchen from important decision-makers and information and then to let nature take its course. Instead of going to Martha and others for help, Gretchen took the bait. She isolated herself. She responded by putting her effort into working harder and longer at what had always produced rewards in the past. Ultimately she learned that this was like beating her head harder and longer against a brick wall.

Gretchen was playing by the same rules she had always played by. But with this promotion the rules of the game had changed. She needed additional skills to succeed in this position, and, for the first time, she needed to develop those skills without a mentor's guidance. Unfortunately she was so busy frantically reviewing loans and bank paper that she didn't even notice Martha's calculated refusal to help her.

The moral of the story here is *not* that you should avoid Quadrant I jobs. Rather, it is that you need to assess the skills required by a new position, then determine in which of your own quadrants those skills fall. The rule that Gretchen needed—but didn't know she needed—was:

Don't take a Quadrant I job unless you know that's what it is, your boss knows that's what it is, and you've assessed the potential risks and have developed a plan for dealing with them.

If Gretchen had realized she was in a Quadrant I job, she could have shifted her focus away from her tried-and-true Quadrant II statistical and financial analysis skills onto critical Quadrant I people and management skills. She could have delegated some of the technical analysis, thereby developing the skills of her subordinates and establishing herself as a caring manager. This would also have freed her to focus more on getting to know the people she was supervising and gaining some insight from them on how best to manage the relationship with Martha. Putting this new promotion in the framework of the Doom Loop would have given Gretchen the career data she needed to build a qualified skill profile for this job —without the aid of a mentor.

It also would have pointed her in the direction of her weakest skill subset—political skills. Under the strong aegis of mentors, Gretchen had never needed to develop these crucial survival skills. Her mentors had always made sure she was included in the pre-meeting meetings, was visible at the right times in the right places, and so on. Gretchen had never before experienced what it was like to be a competent but disempowered outsider. And she had no idea how to overcome the disadvantage. For Gretchen political skills fell into Quadrant

IV. If she'd performed a Doom Loop Quadrant Analysis of this position, Gretchen would have seen the problem graphically and would have been able to pinpoint the most likely sources of calamity. She could have used this as an opportunity to learn how to forge the political alliances she needed to protect herself from the Marthas who exist in every corporation.

Using Doom Loop diagnostics to decipher her situation, Gretchen could have generated a number of reasonable career alternatives. She could have seen that without immediate training or additional coaching, she lacked the requisite managerial and communication skills to handle her new position. Unfortunately, without Martha's support, she could not learn them fast enough to succeed in this particular situation. After that first week on the job, if she couldn't change Martha's attitude, she could immediately have requested a transfer to a position under a more supportive boss. She might have decided not to accept the new position at this point in her career. Martha was clearly not the right supervisor for a high-profile fast-tracker like Gretchen in need of coaching and guided skill-building. Recognizing the new job as a Quadrant I position that could make or break her rise to the next level of middle management, Gretchen might have elected to do some preliminary training and wait another six months.

In any case, by using the Doom Loop to analyze her situation, Gretchen probably could have turned the situation around and averted being fired.

THE CASE OF THE FED HEAD

Steven Black was the high-powered head of a federal agency. He had earned his stripes early in his career through a combination of hard work and brilliant timing. Although he had lost his own race for political office in a tough battle with the local machine, he had won praise as a young assistant district attorney and had paid his dues by raising money and organizing his own supporters to work for the national party during a close election. Over the years, he had built an impressive track record in law enforcement and politics. And as a senior government official, he had successfully managed millions of dollars and thousands of people. He was recognized as a leader.

Then a new administration took over and he was told to pack his bags.

Steven had done well financially but was by no means rich. Without a steady paycheck and with a family to support, he realized he had to take a serious approach to rebuilding his career and his assets. But he didn't feel genuinely anxious about the future until his last day on Capitol Hill. Then the pressure began to mount.

He responded to that pressure by looking at a logical career path, one taken by many others who had held similar governmental positions: the world of big business. It made sense. Steven had cultivated numerous powerful corporate friends, and his law enforcement skills and status made him an attractive candidate for a position as a security chief with a *Fortune* 500 company. A former bank chairman he knew arranged a few interviews with CEOs for Steven. And to no one's surprise, they wanted him.

There was only one problem: Steven wasn't so sure that he wanted them. Opportunity was clearly knocking, but he couldn't get excited about it. He felt trapped without understanding why. He had no doubt that a security chief's position was the next logical step. Yet it was a conundrum: the jobs that Steven was qualified for failed to turn him on.

What new skills did Steven have to learn as a corporate security head? Nothing more than the ins and outs of being in a new organization with new routines for doing old familiar things. Sure, he would have to learn a whole new way of behaving that would fit the corporate culture. And for the short term that might hold him. But he was a fast learner, and for the long term, these skills weren't sufficiently challenging. This job wouldn't allow him to build enough new skills, capitalize on his extensive contacts, or offer him a platform from which to achieve his personal and professional definitions of success. Within a year or so he would feel buried in his logical job choice. Despite the seductive appeal of this top-of-the-Loop big-bucks position, Steven's intuition was on target. Who would get excited about boredom, frustration, and limited growth?

Everything about his skills and what he liked to do pointed to an entrepreneurial career as the next move. Steven liked to operate independently, loved diversity, enjoyed coming up with innovative solutions to difficult problems, had developed considerable expertise, and had a network of well-placed contacts. Given his experience, why not become a consultant?

But when Steven contemplated an entrepreneurial career, he balked. The prospect made him nervous. He protested that he had never worked as a consultant before. How could he just become one—especially at a time when his family was counting on him for a regular paycheck? His lack of know-how as an entrepreneur also unraveled him. He had been at the top of his field too long to feel comfortable about starting a new career as a wet-behind-the-ears consultant.

And although he wasn't excited about joining a corporation, he admitted it was hard to resist the financial security, the perks, and the prestige. "Besides," he argued, "I'd be taking a job I know I could do well, right off the bat."

Even though Steven's thinking was clearly driven by the need for security, he could still admit that he was intrigued with the idea of going out on his own. Finally, it was the Doom Loop that sold Steven on the idea. He saw how this career choice would put him in Quadrant I. After assessing his current skills and developing a capstone profile for the position of entrepreneurial consultant, it became clear that early doom was not the forecast. Although he didn't have actual experience working as a consultant, his credentials in his field were impeccable. He had a solid knowledge base, was a good communicator and writer, and had an excellent assortment of skills critical for success in this capstone. And he liked using these skills.

But this didn't necessarily mean he could consult. Would he enjoy sifting through reams of data, developing concrete findings, drawing conclusions, and making pragmatic recommendations? It was in the discussion of his target mosaic —the various skills he didn't have but would have to acquire—that his interest began to soar. He felt more excited than anxious about learning them.

After a few weeks of contemplating his options and discussing the risks with his wife Cynthia, Steven decided to start a consulting business.

Steven's first four years as a consultant have been going well—he's picked up some good clients and is earning a respectable income. His ten years of running a federal agency paid off in contacts and skills. He's not out of the woods yet; he admits he has a lot to learn, especially about marketing and selling his services. But he's experiencing the excitement of Quadrant I challenge. He has enthusiasm for his projects and his future. One thing he's sure of: he wouldn't trade his consulting job for a corporate security position no matter how many dollars they threw at him.

Using the Doom Loop to assess his career options was a key factor in helping Steven Black avoid the tempting lure of the "post-fired" Quadrant III job.

STRATEGIES FOR *BEFORE* THE TRIGGER IS PULLED

In today's uncertain job market no one is safe from being fired. But who plans to be fired? That sounds like a downbeat contradiction. Despite the strong statistical probability of being fired (about 50 percent for the managerial class), understandably few people are willing to plan for the event.

That can put you at a disadvantage. Studies in stress management tell us that unanticipated, unplanned life events—even the good ones, like winning the lottery or gaining sudden fame—are upsetting. Suddenly, we're caught without a game plan, without options. We feel out of control. And uncertainty breeds anxiety.

Unfortunately, high anxiety is also a natural enemy of good judgment. So to get back to good judgment, you'll need to tone down your anxiety. One of the best natural antidotes for anxiety is being well prepared for the event causing it.

I realize that telling a fast-tracker to have a ready-made

plan for being fired is like telling a new entrepreneur to concentrate on bankruptcy planning. Do it anyway; you won't be
sorry.

"Pre-Firing" Planning

The first step in planning your "pre-firing" strategy is to
let go of the assumption that it won't happen to you. Keep
in mind these principles:

- No job is really as safe and secure as you wish it were.
- Over time all jobs eventually lose their Quadrant II
  appeal.
- Endings happen—they fire you, you fire them, you retire
  in place.
- Dealing with endings always precedes new beginnings.
- Being fired evokes powerful negative feelings.
- Talking to a neutral third party from time to time helps.
- Having alternatives dictates choices, so develop a few
  good alternatives well in advance of needing them.
- Having a ready-to-use "Plan B" reduces anxiety.
- No matter what is happening, think long term.

The Right Advance Moves

Even if you never actually face the crisis of being fired,
practicing a few precautionary moves will help you avoid making reactive, shortsighted decisions. Being fired is no reason
to stow away your capstone. To the contrary. Your capstone
is a career life raft that can keep you from reaching for the
first bit of career flotsam that drifts by on its way downstream.
Your goal is not to take the first job offer. Rather it is to:

- Resist pressure to take any reasonable job offer. Say no
  to tempting Quadrant III and Quadrant IV job offers;
  exorcise short-term "buy now, pay later" thinking.
- Deliberately search out those Quadrant I and II offers
  that fit your target mosaic.

To make these strategies work, have your tactics in place well in advance of the speeding bullet. Here are a few specific suggestions:

Step I: Create a vision. Stay in touch with your own needs. People grow and change. You are more than this job. Refuse to let a particular place or a single set of people define your identity or limit your ambition. Let yourself daydream about your next job and your next capstone. Athletes gain the competitive edge by visualizing and mentally rehearsing future successes. You can, too. Think concretely. What will your next office look like? What will you be doing? What is success like there? What will you feel like? What stands in the way? First do the broad-brush outline, then fill in the fine details. Be creative.

Step II: Identify alternatives. Remember: any alternatives you can identify now will provide ready options for you later, when you need them. It's easier to generate viable alternatives when you're not under siege. So keep an updated list of job alternatives that match your target mosaic in your desk drawer—at home. Develop a contingency plan, too. Stay alert to new opportunities, no matter how much you love this job. Don't let job myopia or misguided company loyalty blind you to viable opportunities on the outside. You'll regret it later.

Step III: Network now. Consider networking an indispensable generic skill. Make time to network with key people on the outside who can open doors for you later. Hobnob with people who are doing what you want to do next. Be casual. Chat with them about what they do, about interesting opportunities in their organizations. Develop long-term alliances. If you're fired, these people could throw you a lifeline.

Step IV: Keep a "triple-track master mosaic." Design a multipurpose skill and experience data base for yourself that:

• lists your capstone profile
• tracks your evolving career mosaic
• monitors your current location on your target mosaic

Use this master mosaic to design a hard-hitting résumé and the kinds of cover letters that broadcast your skills to the outside world. Each time you master a new skill, make revisions. Turn this list around and view it as a skill shopping list that reminds you which skills you need to pick up to finish your target mosaic. Keep a master checklist for your capstone profile and periodically cross off the skills you've developed. Use the remaining skills to guide your next job decision.

Step V: Expand your circle of friends. Develop friendships with people who have absolutely nothing to do with your work. This tactic may sound irrelevant, but it's not. The stronger your identity with work, the more you'll feel like a lone ranger after you're fired. You'll become an instant outsider. No matter how well-intentioned your work friends are, life gets uncomfortable for everyone after a firing. They may feel guilty because they've survived a cutback and you haven't, or it may be uncomfortable for them to associate with you because of office politics. Having other supportive friends without split loyalties diffuses the impact of loss. It helps to have a support group that doesn't fade with your old job. Remember the adage, "Don't put all your eggs in one basket." There's a reason for it.

> **Step VI: Locate your Doom Loop quadrant.** Times change. And so will your position on the Doom Loop. It's easy to get so caught up in daily events that you lose track of where you are. While you've had your nose to the grindstone, what's been happening? Have you slipped over the top of the Loop into Quadrant III? Even if your job is secure, is it time to start looking around? What you do next will be influenced by the quadrant you are in when you resign or are fired, as well as by where you are in building your target mosaic.

What if you've already lost your job? Don't wait around for a new job before you implement these pre-firing tactics. Put them into action right away. And read on.

STRATEGIES FOR *AFTER* THE TRIGGER IS PULLED

How could they dismiss you? Your thoughts and feelings tumble around like laundry in the extra-dry cycle.

It's hard to walk away from the experience whistling. You aren't ready to let go. If you're like most people, you want to plead your case before the jury. You want to assign blame. You want justice. You obsess and ruminate.

Take time to deal with these feelings. Do whatever it takes. Talk to friends, colleagues, and professional counselors about what happened. Use outplacement services. Join a support group. The bottom line is to feel good about yourself again. Venting your emotions is a necessary step in letting go of this crisis and moving on. Your first priority is taking care of you.

Then take a hard, objective look at what really took place. Realize that your viewpoint, like everyone else's, will be biased. More than likely, the other side sees things differently from the way you do. They'll all have their own stories. What would your boss say about the reasons for your dismissal? Regain some perspective on the events that led up to the firing. Don't discount the context, the intangibles—like organizational climate, poor fit with the company, personal ambition, bad chemistry, personality clashes, gut feelings.

And don't run away from the facts of the situation just because they don't please you. Knowing what went wrong gives you more control and ability to change.

Use the Doom Loop to pinpoint the sources of trouble in terms of your skill development and your career management strategies. Part of the problem may be related to your Doom Loop quadrant.

Determine which quadrant you were in when you were fired. Analyze the skills required by your former job. If some skill groups were the troublemakers, which quadrants were they in? The answers you come up with could determine your next moves. This postmortem requires that you become sufficiently detached from your feelings to take a good look at your former job and your personal Doom Loop trajectory.

Skill Analysis for the Job You're Leaving

A skill analysis focuses your attention on specific skills you've added to your career mosaic through this job and on the mix of job skills that were critical and those that were incidental to your success—or lack thereof.

Let's start with the skills you added to your career mosaic. What skills are you leaving this job with that you didn't have when you started? Assuming you've gained some skills, you can take some consolation in knowing all wasn't in vain. How much closer have you moved to your capstone because of this job?

Cross these recently mastered capstone-related skills off your target mosaic. When looking for your next job, why take a position that duplicates them? Focus on the remaining skills in your target mosaic and contemplate other positions that will help you obtain them.

You might also want to use the following time-saving strategy:

> Use "down time" while unemployed and conducting your job search to pick up selected targeted skills

through seminars, apprenticeships, and unpaid community service or other kinds of volunteer work.

Take a few minutes to analyze your mix of critical and noncritical job skills. To make the right job move after being fired, you need to consider the skill mix your former job offered. Since some skills are much more critical to success in a given workplace than others, how you ranked and valued the skills required by your last job could give you insight into what went wrong. When your employer values one set of skills and you value another, problems result.

To get a handle on the skill mix, "core-dump" all the skills required to get the job done onto a piece of paper. No skill is too unimportant or too seldom used to be listed. Next, divide these skills into two columns: the ones that were critical to success and the ones that weren't.

Take an especially hard look at the skills that led to high rewards—the skills crucial to success—whether or not they ever turn up in a job description. To keep visual track of what you're doing, write these "critical to success" skills in red ink and those "less critical to success" in black ink.

POST-FIRING JOB ANALYSIS

Skills Critical to Success (red ink)	Skills Less Critical to Success (black ink)
_____	_____
_____	_____
_____	_____
_____	_____

Concentrate on the red-ink skills. Which ones did you acquire after being hired? Which ones did you fail to learn? Which ones tripped you up?

The purpose of this exercise is to help you separate performance and motivation problems from problems of fit with the organization. For instance, mastering many black-ink skills might not mean as much to the organization as mastering just a few red-ink skills, since the latter are what the organization values. Even if you performed well on the black-ink skills, you may have been seen as "not having what it takes."

Figure out what quadrant you're in for the red-ink and for the black-ink skills. If the former fall in Quadrant I or IV, your competencies may have qualified you only for the less valued black-ink skills of the job's profile. Making the distinction between these red-ink and black-ink skills can be quite tricky because what the company says it rewards and what it actually rewards may be two different beasts. The greater the discrepancy, the more likely you are to have been caught unaware.

What if you were in Quadrant I for both red-ink and black-ink skills when you took the job, but mastered mostly black-ink skills on the job? If so, you moved up the learning curve into Quadrant II, but the skills you mastered were the wrong ones for success in this particular job.

If you plan to stay in this line of work or find a job in a similar type of organization, follow this rule:

First identify and acquire the Quadrant I red-ink skills that are critical to your success.

Pick the brain of a mentor or someone politically astute about the organization who can identify these skills for you early in the job.

Consider the Doom Loop quadrant analysis of Gretchen Cavanaugh, the fired golden girl, when she lost her last position. Gretchen's "critical to success" red-ink skills are in italics.

Note how the red-ink skills in italics were the troublemakers for Gretchen. She made a double mistake. She left a series of good Quadrant II positions for what she erroneously believed

	LIKE	DON'T LIKE
GOOD AT	*Self-presentation* Finance Lending Production QUADRANT II	Accounting Organization *Customer relations* Personnel QUADRANT III
NOT GOOD AT	*Management* *Interpersonal* *Self-management* *Communication* Marketing QUADRANT I	*Leadership* *Politics* *Seeking support* Training Job search QUADRANT IV

was an even better Quadrant II position. Her first mistake was not understanding that her transfer moved her into Quadrant I with its emphasis on new skill development. Her second mistake was failing to differentiate between rewarded red-ink and nonrewarded black-ink skills. By concentrating on learning the more comfortable, but less critical black-ink skills, Gretchen took the easy route.

If Gretchen had been able to identify the quadrant of the Doom Loop she was in when she was fired, she would have had a better chance of understanding what had happened to her. Lacking that understanding, it was easy for her to believe she'd been fired because she'd lost her mentor, which was only a small part of the story.

Of course, people are fired for many reasons besides failing to master certain critical skill sets. Amazingly, incompetence is rarely the major reason. So don't assume your mastery of primary skills will make you fireproof. Always consider the broader context. Stay alert to changes in the organizational climate, a reporting structure that isolates you from the mainstream, political alliances, bad chemistry with power brokers, or a poor fit between you and the job.

What Doom Looping Your Last Job Tells You

Okay, you've been fired. In your what-next decisions it helps to identify the quadrant you were in when you were fired and to understand:

- why people in this quadrant tend to be fired
- the impact of being fired in this quadrant
- the post-firing tactics available to you in this quadrant

Getting a handle on this information lets you put the event in perspective so that you can map out your next job move and avoid certain common pitfalls associated with being fired in each of the quadrants.

FIRED IN QUADRANT I: NIPPED IN THE BUD

You didn't even have a chance to become good at the skills you liked. You never made it into Quadrant II. Even if you are pursuing a Doom Loop strategy, Quadrant I is risky business—you are error-prone by definition.

When you were hired, ideally both you and the company understood that you weren't an expert. Both of you took a chance, and unfortunately it didn't work out.

Under the worst of circumstances, you and your employer had altogether different expectations about your performance. If so, you blame each other. The company found you lacking, and you feel like a failure. The real problem, of course, is someone's failure to recognize your Quadrant I status.

Why People Are Fired in Quadrant I

In a Quadrant I position, you could be the least skillful player on the team. If the team doesn't do well and cuts have to be made, you're the obvious candidate. The firing rule in an organizational purge or a downturning econom' to be "Last in, first out." And you're out.

But that's not the only reason you're likely to be fired. There are a host of others:

- The job's skill requirements were too different from what you expected.
- You couldn't learn what was needed fast enough to get the job done.
- You burned out and lost enthusiasm before you became competent.
- You insisted on doing things your way despite contrary feedback.
- Your drive for perfection got in the way of your learning.
- Your performance anxiety was so high it stopped you in your tracks.
- Your employer didn't realize that you were starting in Quadrant I.
- There was inadequate supervision and training or a lack of mentoring.

This last point is a common cause of failure in Quadrant I. Anyone in a Quadrant I job benefits from being shown the ropes. But this is especially true if you're insecure or lack confidence. Challenge can easily turn into anxiety, and anxiety paralyzes. As a result, you fall by the wayside and fail to learn the rules and informal norms that govern good job performance.

But different personalities react differently. If you're a self-starter who learns quickly and enjoys a high level of autonomy, then lack of direct supervision often turns out to be a bonus rather than a hindrance to your career success.

The Impact of Being Fired in Quadrant I

If you're like most people fired in Quadrant I, you blame yourself. You took a chance that didn't pan out. You're starting to feel gun-shy. Next time around, you think, you won't go for the big gamble; you'll grab something more secure. You want higher ground, a sure thing. The last thing you want is another position with a steep learning curve. As one young Quadrant I law clerk put it, "I felt so bad about being fired right out of law school that I went back to waitressing for six months. I was always good at that, and I just wanted to feel I was good at something for a while." She was expressing the four common reactions to being fired in Quadrant I:

- Your absolute worst fears about your own inadequacies are confirmed.
- You long for the comfort of well-established Quadrant III competence in your next job.
- You discount your preferences in favor of tried-and-true performance.
- You act to soothe your wounded self-esteem.

Quadrant I Post-Firing Tactics

Don't dig yourself into a foxhole. It's a mistake to bury yourself in a Quadrant III job. You're just dodging your own growth. Maybe you were too ambitious or unrealistic about your last job.

Look at your next job move in terms of what constitutes a moderate but acceptable level of risk for Quadrant I skills related to your capstone. The best challenges are the manageable ones that give you a reasonable expectation of success.

Do your homework. Determine what Quadrant I skills you'll be learning in a job before accepting the offer. Learn what will be expected of you and what support you'll receive. In the interview process, ask about the feedback you'll get— feedback can help you correct mistakes before they become fatal. Accelerate your skill development by taking relevant seminars or classes before you take the job or soon after you've started it. Make a personal commitment to long-term learning.

Prioritize for your success. If you can't find a mentor or a coach inside the organization, spend some bucks to hire an outside consultant for yourself. Go to professional meetings in your field and locate someone who is familiar with your organization and your capstone and who is willing to coach you. No matter how talented, how bright, or how hardworking you are, you will need coaching—whether your organization provides it or not.

Take the edge off your need to be an expert by seeing yourself as a learner, not a pro. Remember to communicate how much you're learning to your employer, and to praise your mentor for providing you with know-how.

Even if you have been "nipped in the bud," take courage. Hit the reset button and tackle a new Quadrant I job.

FIRED IN QUADRANT II:
EXILED FROM THE PROMISED LAND

You've arrived. You have a dream job. You love what you're doing and you're doing it well. Going to work is fun. You're thrilled to be there. When other people complain about work, you gloat. You hope the job will last forever.

It won't. Being fired is always tough, but it's never tougher than when you're in Quadrant II euphoria.

Even worse, you probably didn't do much career planning in this quadrant. Why should you have? You were enjoying yourself too much to look ahead beyond a short-term promotion. With good performance reviews and raises around the corner, why risk the wrath of the gods by searching for something else? Because you didn't have a plan, being fired is even more traumatic. And because you were enjoying yourself too much to see the end coming, shock is your primary reaction, along with denial and confusion. This goes with the territory of being fired in Quadrant II, and you have to work through these feelings before you can move forward.

Why People Are Fired in Quadrant II

How does someone manage to get fired in this quadrant? You're cooking with both burners—performance and preferences. You're doing a great job. Unfortunately, just as incompetence is rarely the reason for a dismissal, excellence rarely protects you from it.

It's business, not personal. The number-crunchers in the rafters decide to eliminate your position as a cost-saving maneuver. They don't care that you're the best performer in the company.

But sometimes it's very personal. Sometimes you eliminate yourself by ignoring the political aspects of your job and company. Your productivity or high profile threatens your co-workers and your boss, and they sabotage you.

The following three factors bring the ax down on Quadrant II heads:

- **External factors**—recession-based cutbacks, downsizing and mergers, industry obsolescence, favoritism, loss of a mentor, relocation.
- **Superior performance and productivity**—your high level of performance threatens others; you're labeled the professional equivalent of a rate buster; you streamline work procedures only to eliminate your own job.
- **Carelessness**—you fail to play the political game; you act unethically or indiscreetly; you disregard the norms of the organization; you fail to be a team player.

Although these factors can result in your being fired in any quadrant, you're particularly vulnerable to them in Quadrant II. You become so absorbed in your work and in achieving success that you're caught unaware. You become a sitting duck for political attacks, territorial power plays and other people's agendas. The result is dangerous to your tenure in the Eden of Quadrant II.

The Impact of Being Fired in Quadrant II

The impact of being fired in this quadrant depends on the reason for it.

A corporate restructuring or wholesale selling off of a division tends to result in relatively less trauma than being singled out for firing. You're likely to benefit from community sympathy, access to outplacement, a ready support network, and lots of company. You were the right person in the wrong place. Circumstances were beyond your control. This helps you take your job loss less personally and present yourself to prospective employers with greater credibility than you might in other circumstances.

If you've been fired because you didn't pay enough attention to such things as politics, other people's egos, and cultural norms, you may react with shock to your termination. You may also blame yourself.

Much of the impact depends on how you felt in Quadrant II. If you felt at home, then getting the boot means you're orphaned. You loved where you were, and you can't believe you're not there anymore. You feel isolated and betrayed. It's like losing your first love. It signifies the end of a dream. You ask yourself why it had to end like this.

If, however, you felt like an imposter, someone who never really belonged in Quadrant II, being fired allows your worst fears to surface. You are suspicious of the benign reasons they gave for your dismissal. Your reaction may be: I deserved to be fired, they found me out! You're ashamed and humiliated because you tried to pass yourself off as a manager, supervisor, or a whatever.

You figure you don't have the right stuff and you want to change industries, cities, or even careers.

Quadrant II Post-Firing Tactics

First analyze what happened and get to the root of why you were fired. Consider whether you didn't pay sufficient attention to:

- other people's egos
- organizational fit and politics
- conforming to established procedures
- large-scale economic or industry-specific developments

If these were the problems, add personal, political, and culture-reading skills to your target mosaic. Talk to people who have mastered these skills and get their best advice. Try volunteering for professional and community groups: they provide handy human laboratories for successfully tackling these skills without excessive risk. But whatever you do, don't wait for on-the-job training to learn these basic Quadrant I survival skills. It's important to learn them in time for your next job if you don't want history to repeat itself.

And, don't settle for a Quadrant III job. You may be tempted to use one as a buffer against another career disappointment. But why let one bad ending make you a Quadrant II outcast? Remind yourself of how good you felt in Quadrant II and that there will be many more such jobs in your future. You've loved once, and you will love again.

Regard what happened as a rich source of learning that will strengthen your ability to hold your own next time.

Avail yourself of the tactics discussed earlier: keep your résumé in limited-edition circulation, hire a career coach to keep you on your toes, let headhunters know who you are and what you want, keep networking in business and professional organizations. Above all else, avoid complacency.

Remember, you have to reach the promised land to be thrown out of it.

FIRED IN QUADRANT III: RESCUED IN THE NICK OF TIME

You're still competent, but the thrill is gone. You've been operating on automatic pilot. You've lost your passion and wonder how much longer it will be until others notice. You're good at what you do, you're making decent money, and many people would be happy to trade places with you. Why, then, are you feeling so lousy about work? The question lingers.

Then you're fired.

People react unpredictably to being fired in this quadrant. You may feel relieved and excited about being released to pursue the next phase of your career. Or the lethargy you experienced in Quadrant III might change to panic.

For many Quadrant III dwellers, salary was the only thing that kept them going. Once they've been fired, they've lost that consolation. More than anything else, they've lost their security. With a mixture of guilt, pessimism, and anticipation, they scramble to get that security back.

Why People Are Fired in Quadrant III

Performance problems usually aren't the cause of termination in Quadrant III. Instead, attitude plays a major role. People in Quadrant III communicate their boredom through body language, a disengaged style, and a host of other cues. Whether those in management pick up on these cues consciously or subliminally, they view their Quadrant III charges as lacking the enthusiasm, leadership, and commitment to teamwork that make them key players.

Bosses notice that Quadrant III people have lost their creativity. They don't seem to have their heart in their work. Rather than coming up with innovative solutions to problems, they fall back on shopworn solutions. They cease to be idea people, instead relying on what they know to get by. Their ambivalence about their work and their general lack of involvement and inspiration show.

It adds up. The whole often becomes greater than the sum of the parts when it comes to firing someone in Quadrant III. Your employer realizes you feel trapped. When the brass starts searching for deadwood to chop, their instinct tells them that you're ready to fall off the tree anyway.

When you're fired in Quadrant III, one or more of the following events may have led to your demise:

- You decide there'll be "no more faking it": you confess to coworkers or a boss that you can't stand them, your job, or the place.
- Boredom begets boredom: morale among your charges takes a nosedive.

- Your escape-artist tactics isolate you: you stop lunching with the group and get locked out of the communication network.
- Problems arise with your reputation: your coworkers see you as unavailable, uncooperative, or worse.
- You're identified with old-guard rigidity: management classifies you as a remnant, not what the company needs now.
- The company changes direction: management shelves you far from the action.
- Management consultants have a problem with you: they peg you as a marginal contributor and recommend passing you over for training and promotion.
- You become a casualty of strategic planning: your boss wants new blood and fresh ideas—not yours.

These are just contributing causes—not bona fide reasons for firing in and of themselves. But firing decisions are subjective, and the sum of the parts begins to add up. Your name goes on someone's hit list, just waiting to be crossed off. In many instances, the reason given for your firing will be that bland euphemism "cost-cutting." Then everyone saves face. But the real reasons usually center on your attitude.

The Impact of Being Fired in Quadrant III

Being fired takes a critical choice away from you and gives it to someone else—someone who doesn't have to pick up the pieces of your life. If you've been with your organization for a long time or are close to retirement, your Quadrant III firing could leave you feeling bitter. You've given the best years of your working life to the company in exchange for a "golden boot."

You may resist trying something new after being fired in this quadrant. Your dismissal may catalyze a life crisis, during which you subject anything and everything to serious questioning and reevaluation.

Other people look at a Quadrant III termination as more

of a blessing in disguise or an act of grace. They had realized they were heading nowhere except down but were unable to rescue themselves. Although being fired is still a shock, it's a shock of recognition—they recognize that they've been miserable and see this as a chance for a fresh start.

Here's a sampling of comments from people fired in Quadrant III:

- "When he fired me I wanted to punch my boss right in the mouth. But when I thought more about it, I wanted to punch myself for not beating him to it."
- "I abused myself by staying so long in that teaching job, but I didn't know how to start over. What else would I be good at? I guess I wanted someone to tell me."
- "I had unbelievable contempt for those people, the place, the work, you name it. But no one could say I wasn't doing quality work. And I still can't believe they fired me."
- "My compass is spinning. At age fifty-four, I finally realize I'm free to become whoever I was meant to be. This is a gift—an unsettling opportunity."

Over and over again, people fired in Quadrant III wonder how they could have remained at their jobs so long. The bottom line is that they are often more outraged with themselves than with management.

Quadrant III Post-Firing Tactics

The first tactic is to be intentional, not reactive, in what you do next. Pay special attention to your likes and dislikes. Don't be afraid to do some serious soul-searching. Remember, you were ensconced in the "don't like" half of the Doom Loop. Finding new skills you like will move you toward Quadrants I and II. Consider shifting your emphasis—for instance, from working with people to working with ideas or things. If your work has been routine, look for something more creative. Analyze what needs motivate you. Think about how your next job might meet those needs.

The second tactic involves giving yourself the time to evaluate numerous options. You're going to feel pressure—economic and emotional—to take another Quadrant III job, especially if it comes with good pay and perks. Don't grab it on the rebound or you'll end up back in Quadrant III.

Third, adopt an open attitude. Be open to whatever sparks your interest and captures your imagination. Look for new information that gets you unstuck. Network with people in targeted businesses and ask them to brainstorm job possibilities. Don't reject a lateral or downward move if it fits your interests and preferences. Consider new directions, retooling. Try it out by enrolling part-time in classes. Develop a new hobby with career potential. Be willing to cut your losses and take a risk. Consider an entrepreneurial venture. But regard a look-alike Quadrant III job as a kiss of death, not a career opportunity.

Fourth, look at your capstone to see whether it's still attainable. Is it still worth your efforts? If your capstone seems unattractive—if it's no longer where you want to go—find a new one. If your capstone is still in line with your values and the person you want to be, search for a position that will take you in the right direction. If your capstone feels threadbare, reread the chapter on choosing a capstone (Chapter 2), and consider yourself rescued in the nick of time.

FIRED IN QUADRANT IV: SAVED BY THE MAGIC BULLET

Quadrant IV can creep up on you. No rites of passage herald your arrival, and you may be the last one to realize you're there. Know the quadrant by the symptoms: nothing seems to get done on time, your performance slips, you walk around doing trivial tasks, you idle away the hours with office politics or gossip, complaining about people and procedures.

A mentor or boss may work diligently to get you reinvolved.

Eventually, you're in Quadrant IV. Ultimately, you're out the door.

Why People Are Fired in Quadrant IV

Usually the question isn't why, but what took so long. Amazingly, companies put up with Quadrant IV people for months, years, even decades. Perhaps you were once a sterling employee, and your boss tolerates your current Quadrant IV status, decreasing your work load and isolating you from decision-making.

But this lack of challenge doesn't help. Boredom escalates. Quadrant IV employees sink deeper into their sense of failure and depression. As one fired Quadrant IV employee put it, "I was dumb, fat, and unhappy. They knew it; I knew it; my family knew it. I hated that job, but no one would do anything about it."

The firing often takes place when a new boss takes over and sweeps his or her division clean of unproductive people.

But if you're hired directly into a Quadrant IV post rather than cycling through the other quadrants, the firing process comes much more quickly. You have no past accomplishments to buy you time and respect. As soon as they can replace you, you're gone.

The Impact of Being Fired in Quadrant IV

Even though you hated your job, you don't feel good about being terminated. You take the dismissal as a confirmation of your low self-worth. It's easy to forget how much you disliked your position by concentrating instead on the rejection.

What are you supposed to do now? Your energy is far too low for you to promote yourself and conduct a job search. You're not even sure you have anything worthwhile to offer a new employer. You may look for part-time work or take a lower-status, lower-stress position. You may even join the ranks of the permanently unemployed.

Quadrant IV Post-Firing Tactics

Become a seeker. Get in touch with who you are now. Before you land another job, you'll need to focus on your own needs, interests, and values. Ask for feedback from people you trust. If your Quadrant IV tenure was lengthy, identify the reasons you stayed so long. Take the following steps:

- Get professional help: career coaching, counseling, psychotherapy.
- Attend seminars on stress management, self-esteem, communication, and other topics that help you feel better about yourself.
- Join a support group for people between jobs.
- Develop new interests and competencies that promise to be fun.
- Go back to school, even if it's just part-time.
- Become more active in professional and volunteer groups.

This is a good time to try new activities. Your immediate job is to restore your energy and enthusiasm, not to dovetail into another Quadrant IV job. Follow the tactics for people fired in Quadrant I and III jobs when you've found a direction you want to pursue. Until then, find solace in the fact that you've escaped Quadrant IV, even if it wasn't of your own volition.

REASSESSING YOUR CAPSTONE AND CAPSTONE STRATEGY

In the traumatic post-firing period, it's easy to neglect your capstone. Don't!

Use down time to update and reassess both your career mosaic and your target mosaic.

Get your mind off events you can't change. Look at the bigger picture instead. Write out a complete capstone profile, and list the skills you still need for your target mosaic. Focus your attention on finding activities, paid or unpaid, that build these skills.

Decide on a series of stepping-stone jobs that will take you in the direction of your capstone.

Check your intuitive responses to a whole series of questions. Has anything important changed as a result of this last job experience? Despite the bad ending, are you still enthusiastic about your line of work? Have you become embittered or alienated? What about the field or industry you're in? Is it holding its own or is it another victim of the economy?

What quadrant did the skills of your last job fall into? Did you crash into an unanticipated wall of Quadrant III and IV projects? If so, is this due to some change in you or in the organization? Perhaps you just misjudged what this career path would be like.

Before beginning a full-blown job search, you need to answer these questions: What do you think about your capstone now? Does it feel right? If not, analyze your capstone position in terms of the Doom Loop quadrants. If the skills required to make you a qualified candidate are in Quadrants III and IV, a new capstone might be in order. Just because you wanted to be a marketing director in the past doesn't mean you should want to be one in the future. When a capstone ceases to challenge you—even on paper—it's time for a change.

What if the skills for your capstone are right where they are supposed to be, in Quadrants I and II, but you still don't feel good about your capstone? It may be that being fired is the culprit. The experience of being fired can produce a nameless, overwhelming anxiety that colors your view of everything, including your capstone. Accept the fact that you'll be anxious for a while and postpone making any major career decisions until you feel more settled. Think of yourself as being in a recovery period. You'll need support, but it will pass and you'll get better.

Or you might be having a different type of problem with your capstone when the skills of the capstone fall into Quadrants I and II, but the capstone itself still turns you off. It could be that your feelings about the capstone transcend the particular skills that comprise it. For instance, at this stage of your life your capstone could strike you as trivial. It comes down to values. When you're fired, your security and sense of well-being fall away. You naturally begin to question the meaning of things. In this process your values may change so that what used to seem worthwhile now leaves you cold. If so, see this post-firing period as an opportunity to find a new capstone more in line with who you are.

DOOM LOOP ALL JOB OFFERS

Sooner or later, you'll receive a job offer. Having been fired, you will be tempted to go for the quick fix: the classic top-of-the-Loop or Quadrant III mismatch. Resist the temptation. If you take it, it's likely that Quadrant IV will be right around the corner.

To fight off a particular job offer, imagine yourself in the daily routine of this job and how you'll feel slugging it out a few years down the road. Then jot down the words that come to mind.

If your response remains positive, weigh the payoffs carefully. Understand that no matter how great the material rewards may be, you're inviting serious career risk. If your response in this exercise is negative, then turn down the offer.

Ideally, the next job you take after being fired will place you in Quadrant I or II. These are the jobs that will give you room to develop your personal career mosaic. Some of the skills should also fit your target mosaic. If you can find this type of job, the trauma of being fired will quickly pass.

Whatever job offer you receive, Doom Loop it with this three-step process:

- Break down the job by the skills required to succeed.
- Rate each skill cluster for your level of preference and performance.
- Plot the results on the Doom Loop matrix.

Subject every offer to Doom Looping and to thoughtful analysis of how you're likely to feel in that position over time. This will help you avoid the predictable traps that catch the majority of people who have been fired. Even better, the Doom Loop will help you find a post-firing job that will return you to a satisfying career track. Congratulate yourself on weathering the stormy career crisis of being fired.

■

CHAPTER 8

Unexpected Opportunity

This new company is offering me a better territory,
product line, and commission. Frankly, I don't see
how I can turn it down . . . except I was hoping to
get out of sales.
                    —Midcareer optical sales rep

Sure, it's a great opportunity. But I've already been
around the block a couple of times. What do I have
to prove to anyone?
                    —Recruited senior vice president

It's a chance to work in Japan! I know it has nothing
to do with anything I've dreamed I'd do. But it's a
once-in-a-lifetime opportunity.
                    —Recent law school graduate

When the opportunity comes, you might be right where
you want to be, warm and snug in a terrific Quadrant II job.
Or maybe you're in Quadrant I, busily gathering the skills
you need to progress to your capstone. Perhaps you're a top-
of-the-Loop expert.

But no matter how well your career is going, you aren't
prepared for this manna from heaven that changes your
world. Because you're not prepared, and because unexpected

opportunities frequently lead to errors in judgment, you're suddenly up against a career crisis.

BOUNTY FROM THE BLUE

Think of it as an offer you will find hard to refuse. It may come from a headhunter, a client, a friend, a colleague, or a total stranger. It might even come from your own company, following a training program, a reorganization, or a personnel shift.

When the opportunity presents itself, you feel surprised and honored. You've been singled out as worthy of praise and special treatment. Why not go for it?

Whether or not you accept this job offer, the mere fact of the offer changes everything. Someone has thrown a pebble in your pond with a far-reaching ripple effect. After the offer, your future looks different. You have undergone an instant psychological makeover. The possibilities multiply. Mentally, you pack your bags and rewrite your bio. The unexpected career opportunity demands that you take it and yourself seriously.

And therein lies the crisis. It's principal hallmarks are that it catches you by surprise and often forces you to choose between two attractive alternatives.

You're in an altogether different position from someone who receives a job offer he or she has been seeking. The unexpected opportunity is like winning the lottery—and we've all read stories about people who couldn't handle the sudden prosperity. You haven't had sufficient time to prepare for the change in circumstances that goes with the new territory.

Psychological research shows that the events that have the greatest negative impact are the ones we least expect or that are ill-timed, that either come too early or too late according to our own inner standards. Therefore, for any unexpected opportunity you must carefully weigh the risks and rewards as well as understand your feelings about it and all it signifies to you. The unexpected opportunity pits your need to be secure in your job against the exciting allure of risky possibilities. These unsought-after choices can have a profound impact on your career strategy, your personal relationships, and your future.

The unexpected career crisis is guaranteed to exacerbate the complex career decisions you already face. For instance, if you're a top-of-the-Loop executive, the opportunity may throw you into a Quadrant III glamour job, one that derails you from reaching your career capstone. Or, if you're a member of a dual-career relationship, this career opportunity may force you to take into account two different, often incompatible sets of career needs. Eventually, this seemingly happy career crisis can turn starkly traumatic.

What to do? For starters, prepare yourself to expect the unexpected knock on your door. This can come at any point in your career, and when it does, you can avert tactical career errors by using the Doom Loop and your target mosaic to analyze what that irresistible job offer will really do for you. Remember, not all attractive offers will promote your career growth or job satisfaction. Let's look at some useful ways to analyze your next unexpected opportunity in order to make decisions that fit your strategy.

FIRST REACTIONS, SECOND THOUGHTS

It's a thrill to be recruited. Someone wants you, and you didn't have to do a thing to sell yourself: no job search, demeaning interviews, or ego-deflating rejections. A single call has made your day. Everyone's fantasy has come true for you, and you feel great about the opportunity and yourself. Your worth has been affirmed and you're flattered.

That's fine. But take time out to consider your opportunity. This could be a major life decision, so don't sign on the dotted line just yet! First, gather information. Talk to people about what the job involves and look at how the offer fits in with your capstone, your target mosaic, your Doom Loop quadrants, and your life-style. Acknowledge that you're tempted to take it right off the bat. It is tough for anyone to resist a bigger paycheck, a more prestigious position or organization, or a refreshing change of scenery.

But no matter how attractive the inducements, allow yourself second thoughts. Don't let your ego force you into seizing the opportunity before you have all the facts.

Remember that when the novelty of the unexpected offer fades, reality will set in. Have you ever noticed how everything looks different in the bright light of morning? Expect doubts to surface about your ability to handle the proffered job. You might even wonder how good a job it really is if they recruited you rather than someone else for it.

Take an aggressive stance by subjecting your glorious, unexpected opportunity to rigorous analysis before signing on. See this for what it is: a major life decision that will shape who you are and your future opportunities. Remember, it's you, not those who recruit you, who will be enmeshed—for better or worse—in the new work culture. Avoid buyer's remorse. Start with a few basic considerations.

AN OPPORTUNITY FOR REASSESSMENT

When an opportunity presents itself, you're put in a reactive rather than a proactive position. You were on your way to Hawaii, but now you're going to end up in Saskatchawan. That might not be bad, but is it really what you want or what you would have chosen if left to your own devices? Is it a new twist in the road or a temporary detour that will lead you back to your capstone? And are you sufficiently adaptable to thrive in Saskatchawan?

These are not trivial questions. They are critical to constructing the kind of life you want for yourself and to keeping yourself on course. Like every career crisis, this one encourages you to determine what's important to you and to reexamine your commitment to your next career capstone. The trick is to keep yourself and your own needs front and center while staying open to interesting new, but off-course, possibilities.

When analyzing a career opportunity, you'll want to ask

two sets of Doom Loop questions. The first set deals with your capstone strategy. The second set deals with your own position in the Doom Loop quadrants.

A CHANCE TO CHALLENGE YOUR CAPSTONE

Unsolicited career opportunities serve an unintended but important function: they force you to challenge the career strategy you've already constructed. They create confusion, uncertainty, and indecision. And believe it or not, in the total scheme of things, that's good. An unexpected career opportunity is the siren song that tantalizes you with possibilities you never dreamed of.

It should challenge you to look beyond the expected promotion as the only acceptable next step.

It should get you thinking about taking a risk that leads to a more fulfilling career path.

It should rekindle your excitement about your career.

It should alert you to the fact that you may be bored with your capstone and that it's time to consider new career directions.

Or it should help you reaffirm or update your present capstone.

You can do this by asking the right questions, taking time to assess how you feel about your current capstone, considering what's involved in accepting this unplanned change, and doing your best to anticipate and avoid the pitfalls that go with the territory of unexpected opportunities.

Even if you haven't decided on a capstone and are still playing the field, the unexpected career opportunity could be a turning point that helps you clarify your vision and find your eventual direction.

CAPSTONE COMPATIBILITY

If you have set a reasonable capstone for yourself and are working toward achieving it when the unexpected opportunity presents itself, the first question to ask is: "Is this unexpected career opportunity compatible with my career capstone?"

If the answer is yes, the rest is easy. Talk to people and find out whether this new position involves any Quadrant I skills that fit your target mosaic. If so, talk to people about the opportunity in more depth. Learn about the daily tasks of the position. Then sit down and list the complete skill profile for this position as you understand it, rating each skill for your own preference and performance. Doom Loop the skills of the job to see which quadrants they fall into. Use this exercise as a quick test to ensure that you're not inadvertently choosing a Quadrant III opportunity.

If the skills fall into Quadrants I and II, great. From a strategic viewpoint, you're set. But before you grab the offer, ask yourself: "Am I really excited and enthusiastic about this job?"

If so, you're on the right track. If not, no matter how good it looks from other perspectives, it may not be right for you. Pay attention to how you feel. If you feel positive, it's time to move ahead and examine the *caveat emptor* factors discussed later in this chapter.

But suppose this unexpected career opportunity leads you away from your capstone? This is a very real possibility. After all, the people who are providing you with these opportunities aren't privy to or even interested in your long-range career plans. I know it's hard to keep this in mind when you are being courted so seductively. Headhunters or corporate executives might seem to have your best interests at heart, but in reality they're operating directly from their own needs. That helpful headhunter will be a distant speck on the horizon when you're out there dueling dragons six months from now. No matter how friendly and caring these bearers of gifts seem, they represent the seller, not you. So don't forget it. And don't let their needs make your decision for you.

Does this mean that when an opportunity is inconsistent with your career capstone you should turn it down?

Speaking strictly as a Doom Loop purist, the answer is yes. Although your decision is usually complicated by many other factors (you need the $25,000 salary increase, you suspect you'll be fired if you stay in your present position, and so on), the general Doom Loop rule is still:

Say no to career opportunities that are inconsistent with your capstone, involve little Quadrant I learning, and add nothing to your target mosaic.

What good is a salary increase if you end up hating your job or getting fired before the year is out? In some instances it may be better to be unemployed and searching for a job compatible with your capstone than to be employed in a position that leads nowhere you really want to go. If you don't take the job in question, make an effort to learn from the unexpected opportunity. Use it to break out of your mindset about your current job and capstone. Ask yourself why this new opportunity appeals to you, how you can incorporate these inducements into your current job and capstone. Perhaps it's time to reassess your overall career strategy.

Before making your decision about the offered job, remember that unsolicited opportunities can be black holes in your career field. They can draw you away from your capstone, swallow up years of your time and effort, and leave you exhausted, wondering why on earth you ever gave in to their treacherous pull.

But not every unexpected opportunity means danger. Lest you think they'll all leave you lost in space, here are some exceptions to the previously stated rule.

ONCE-IN-A-LIFETIME OPPORTUNITIES

Your company wants you to set up business relations with a newly liberated Eastern-bloc nation. You're tapped to run your favorite senator's reelection campaign. You're offered a job that doubles your salary.

When you're called, it's hard to say no. These jobs are special opportunities. At their most dramatic, they represent one-shot, historic moments that can't be duplicated. Opportunities like these can propel you into a different league. Not only do they increase your knowledge, contacts, and salary, but they may also allow you to fulfill a personal, cherished goal (often philosophical rather than career-oriented). They may involve Quadrant II and III skills and represent substantial detours from your capstone, but their unique aspects overwhelm the negatives of the Doom Loop analysis.

But if you embrace such an opportunity, be aware of the risks. Even if your organization has agreed to take you back after you complete such an assignment, you will probably have lost your political network, contacts, and hard-won place in the informal organizational hierarchy. You'll return to the organization different but not necessarily better. In fact, you may not fit in anymore. The old gang may close ranks. And you may have lost your momentum toward your capstone.

Still, the risks may be worth it. They may, in fact, lead to a new and better capstone or a new and better life. But before accepting a once-in-a-lifetime opportunity, take precautions. Talk it over with two or three trusted neutral observers—what do they think you should do? They may alert you to the fact that the opportunity isn't that special. Or they may confirm your feeling that if you passed it up, you'd always wonder "what if . . . ?"

DISCONTENT BEFORE CAPSTONE

This is a type of capstone burnout that I'll discuss more thoroughly in the next chapter. When an unexpected opportunity beckons, it sometimes jolts you into realizing that you're running on automatic pilot, that your current course, although right in line with your capstone, is still wrong for you.

You realize you're in a rut of your own making. Because

you aren't excited about your job or your present capstone, any opportunity that takes you in a different direction looks good. When you're feeling trapped in yesterday's dreams, it's time to take stock of yourself and reassess your vision of what's possible.

Only rarely does the urge to run away from a bland, uninteresting capstone justify seizing an unexpected opportunity. It all depends on what new capstone you're running to and why. See the unexpected career opportunity as a catalyst for doing some serious questioning, thinking, and exploring—before making your choice.

Try thinking about the new opportunity in terms of where it will take you. Is there a capstone at the end of that journey that fits your performance and preference requirements? And does it take into account your evolving values and yearning for personal and professional transformation?

DOOM LOOPING THE UNEXPECTED OPPORTUNITY

The Doom Loop can help you analyze the pros and cons of this unexpected opportunity. To assess your opportunity, you'll need to plot the following:

- your own quadrant position for your current job
- your projected quadrant for the new position

Assuming the opportunity is compatible with your capstone, you will then analyze the move from a tactical perspective.

You know the system: begin by listing the skills involved in your current job, rating them according to whether or not you like them and whether or not you're good at them. Place these skills in the appropriate quadrants of the Doom Loop matrix. Then identify the quadrant where your skills currently reside.

Repeat this procedure for the skills required by the unexpected job offer. Since you already have the offer, you don't have to worry about the skills they say you need to qualify for the job. Instead, concentrate on the skills you will need actually to perform the job—the daily maintenance skills, the high-frequency skills, and the power skills you'll need to achieve success in the position.

Do your homework beforehand. Don't rely on what your headhunter tells you about those skills (or on what any other person tells you who isn't in a position to know what those skills actually are). Conduct your own skill-gathering investigation. Go to the library. Research and read. Talk to people who hold similar positions in other organizations. Find out about the job's shelf life. Check the Dun & Bradstreet ratings on the company (if it's other than your own). See what the local business, professional, or trade journals have had to say about this organization. Look at broader economic, cultural, and marketing trends, and speculate on whether you'll be entering a growth industry. Even in an economic downturn, some industries are more recession-proof than others.

Be honest. Accept the fact that you are profoundly flattered by the offer. But understand that having our egos stroked makes us more vulnerable to overlooking or distorting data we don't like. So put your guard up a bit. Don't respond like a wallflower desperate for a date, grabbing the first eligible person who comes your way. There will be other opportunities. Keep reminding yourself of how good you are—after all, that's why they want you—of all you have to offer, and of your need to stay objective.

After your investigation, Doom Loop the skills required by the new position and locate your quadrant.

You're now ready to explore the pluses and minuses of shifting from one Doom Loop quadrant to another.

What Your Quadrant Location Tells You

Because of the intense pressure to take an unexpected opportunity, you need to step back and compare what you have now with what you may have if you change jobs.

It's not as easy as it sounds. The new job offer will distort your perspective, playing havoc with your objectivity. Because of the "grass is always greener" syndrome and the personal boost you get from the new job offer, it's natural to favor the opportunity over your current situation.

This is where the Doom Loop quadrants can be invaluable. Make yourself familiar with all the pluses and minuses this opportunity offers you relative to what you already have. Determine the quadrant your current job is in and read on.

When You're in a Quadrant I Job

You're right where you should be. So beware of strangers bearing unsolicited job offers. What more can they offer you that will offset the attendant risks? In this quadrant, you're on the upside of the learning curve, gaining competence in valuable skills that fit your pattern of likes and values. Sure you have your share of performance anxiety, but that's to be expected.

If an unexpected opportunity arises early in your career, your lack of experience or desire for "higher ground" may render you susceptible to making poor tactical decisions. It makes no sense to trade your Quadrant I job for a position in Quadrant III or IV. Even another Quadrant I position or one in Quadrant II doesn't necessarily offer a better situation. Every unexpected opportunity is a personal exercise in highly directed investigatory work and enlightened decision-making.

How often does someone in Quadrant I actually face an unexpected career opportunity? Despite what you may think, Quadrant I novices are frequently recruited. Perhaps your old company, in a rare moment of need, recognizes your worth, or a recruiter exhumes your name from an old file. Even though they may be offering you a Quadrant III or IV opportunity, you're nonetheless gratified by this affirming event.

But is it worth leaving your present job? If you're encountering more failures than successes in your Quadrant I learner's mode, you may be tempted to end the wear and tear on your self-esteem and slip into something a little more comfortable. Resist. Unless some cataclysmic change has occurred in you or your industry, the response to a Quadrant III or

IV opportunity should be an unequivocal no! You have nothing to gain but a temporary elevation in self-worth and salary, followed by the lasting setback of a humdrum Quadrant III or IV job. The rule here is simple:

Shun shifts from Quadrant I to Quadrant III or IV of your Doom Loop. *Caveat emptor* **is your correct stance.**

Or you might be recruited from your current Quadrant I position to another one: a mobile coworker or boss wants you as part of a new team; you're a highly visible, sought-after fast-tracker; you've acquired some technical skill in high demand. This is a much harder call. You may have a valid career opportunity. If so, consider this rule:

Make only those lateral Quadrant I trade-offs that put you in significantly better-fitting occupational niches or organizational contexts than your current job, and those that allow you to develop some hard-to-obtain skill on your target mosaic.

Doom Loop the skills of the new offer to see whether they will help you develop targeted Quadrant I skills any faster or better. Even though you're comparing one group of Quadrant I skills with another, the specific skills of the job will be different. Does this projected new mix of skills stretch your competencies in ways that relate to your capstone? If the answer is yes, the offer is a good one.

Next, check out contextual factors. Even though these may not be patently obvious, they are critically important to how you will feel about your work. Compare everything you can learn about the context of the new situation with your current situation. Anything important to you is grist for the mill. Use the following checklist as a guide to rate how contextual factors for your current job and new offer fit your needs:

RATING CONTEXTUAL FACTORS

| CURRENT JOB | | NEW OFFER | | CONTEXTUAL |
Fits	Doesn't Fit	Fits	Doesn't Fit	FACTOR
_____	_____	_____	_____	• Corporate culture
_____	_____	_____	_____	• Company ethics
_____	_____	_____	_____	• Office politics
_____	_____	_____	_____	• Opportunities for advancement
_____	_____	_____	_____	• Actual content of work projects
_____	_____	_____	_____	• Status and stability of organization
_____	_____	_____	_____	• Economic growth trends for industry
_____	_____	_____	_____	• High-end earning potential
_____	_____	_____	_____	• Quality of work life
_____	_____	_____	_____	• Opportunities for being mentored
_____	_____	_____	_____	• Compatibility of coworkers, peers

First rank these factors in order of their importance to you. Then make a list of the factors that closely fit your own needs for each position. Look at how you ranked the factors in each group. If you rate the factors for the new offer substantially higher than you do the ones for your current position and if the new Quadrant I skill package advances you faster, the opportunity is probably worth taking.

Your company might want to move you from a line to a staff position, or laterally into a slot that requires different functional skills. Assuming you want to stay in your current field or with your company, they're giving you a great opportunity.

What if you receive an offer that will move you from Quadrant I to Quadrant II? Simply determine whether this is the right Quadrant II position, using the criteria checks (including the fit with your target mosaic) we've discussed.

When You're in a Quadrant II Job

You're on top of the world, so why bother looking for something new? You don't have to. Just sit back and wait for your phone to ring. You're going to receive offers you can't believe in this quadrant. You feel like a prize heifer at the state fair. But given the high satisfaction of Quadrant II jobs, you're also less likely to be tempted by all this flattery or by a real opportunity.

Therein lies the dilemma. Someone tosses you an opportunity most people would die for, and you don't even return the call. Total job immersion has replaced sensible career management. If this describes your attitude, recognize that our inherent resistance to change can intensify in Quadrant II. Career myopia and staying at a job too long are common shortcomings of those who dwell in this quadrant. It's also easy to entangle your positive feelings about your professional growth with your feelings of gratitude and loyalty to the company. If these are your feelings, confront them. You may be painting yourself into a corner. Taking unexpected opportunities is not necessarily disloyal—it's enlightened self-interest. After all, your company will not consider loyalty if an industry downturn forces it to eliminate your job.

Acting on your own behalf is the essence of taking care of yourself in your career.

No matter how happy you are, keep your mind open to whatever else is out there. Remember, no matter how good it seems now, Quadrant II is not forever. And you're in your best negotiating position when you're happily and productively employed.

You have a clear advantage. If you're currently in a Quadrant II job, you don't have to grab any opportunity handed to you. You can browse through the unexpected opportunities that arise, applying this decision rule:

Take seriously any new Quadrant I or II opportunities, even those similar to your current position, if they allow you to trade up, get a better fit, or integrate relevant Quadrant I learning.

On the other hand, politely refuse Quadrant III and IV offers. Certainly you'll want to get to know the people who make those offers—they can be important resources in your professional network who will come in handy later on.

For now, recognize that you'll be tapped from time to time for fast-track opportunities, despite the fact that in the leaner, flatter organizations of the 1990s, the chances for upward mobility will be fewer than in the "go-go" 1980s. Though these opportunities aren't numerous, you're a likely candidate for them when you're in a highly visible Quadrant II position.

Put these upwardly mobile career offers in the context of your Doom Loop strategy. Prioritize new skill development, stimulation, and job satisfaction.

Consider such trading-up opportunities as:

- a chance to climb to the next rung of the career ladder
- more responsibility
- better salary, benefits, perks
- experience in new corporate cultures
- access to a new mentor or expert in your field
- a better company
- greater exposure to skills in your target mosaic
- more in-depth or hands-on experience

But always make sure that these opportunities go hand in hand with the opportunity to develop skills relevant to your target mosaic in Quadrant I and II of your Doom Loop. And beware of trading up for a job that takes you away from the skills and tasks you enjoy in your current Quadrant II position.

The right unexpected opportunities allow you to sample new corporate cultures, better suit your personality and values, explore other parts of your industry to learn what else interests you, and relocate yourself in a more desirable geographic spot.

The wrong ones take you away from the skills and tasks you enjoy in your current Quadrant II position and away from your capstone.

When You're in a Top-of-the-Loop Job

When you're riding the top of the Loop—between Quadrants II and III—you're a prime target for internal and external recruiters. Not only are you an established expert, but recruiters recognize you're ripe for a job change even before you do. You may be on the cusp of dissatisfaction, but its sources aren't yet clear to you.

This puts you at an immediate disadvantage. You may assume the problem is with the job, which makes you particularly responsive to a headhunter's temptations. As a top-of-the-Looper, you're earning the kind of money that makes you a highly attractive candidate for headhunters who will pocket up to a third of the salary for any position they fill. In return, they'll deposit jobs on your doorstep that will make your jaw drop.

A match made in heaven? Hardly! Tactically, the last thing you want to do is exchange one top-of-the-Loop job for another. If you do, Quadrants III and IV are the next stops on your career itinerary. And, of course, you don't want to let anyone talk you into a Quadrant III or IV position, no matter how wonderful the salary.

Even armed with this knowledge, expect to be tempted by offers of higher salaries and other amenities. When someone offers you a prime top-of-the-Loop or Quadrant III job, however, analyze the opportunity for Quadrant I growth and development.

Use this rule:

Seek offers that are consistent with your capstone and your target mosaic, that incorporate and emphasize Quadrant I learning, and that build on and expand your experience.

Lateral career moves that involve learning new functional skills are definitely worth considering. Lateral quadrant moves, however, should be avoided, especially if they keep you at the top of the Loop or push you into Quadrant III or IV.

If you find a new top-of-the-Loop job offer irresistible despite the blazing red flags, work with the recruiter or your future employer to see how much flexibility you have in rewriting job duties to include new Quadrant I skill development weighted toward your preferences and target mosaic. If they want you badly enough, they will accommodate your needs. You, not they, are still in charge of your career strategy. Don't let them help you forget this.

When You're in a Quadrant III Job

You're in a position similar to that of someone at the top of the Loop, only you're more acutely aware of your job discontent. This makes you very receptive to offers, most of which are likely to be Quadrant III or IV jobs. These job offers are made in good faith—based on your superb past performance in Quadrant II. Unfortunately, your past performance is no longer a wholly accurate predictor of how well you'll perform in the new position. Since you are no longer a Quadrant II go-getter, you'll probably sink into Quadrant IV if you accept one of these offers. You'll be like a typecast actor tired of playing the same old monotonous roles in a series of look-alike movies.

If this seems like a dismal forecast, understand that you can avoid it. How? Stave it off with this rule:

Look for the unexpected opportunity offering major Quadrant I and II components that are likely to rekindle your old enthusiasm and desire to learn, while broadening your career mosaic.

Say no to opportunities that merely give you more of what you already have. Consider lateral moves, line to staff moves, and even downward moves. As long as they foster skill acquisition, greater learning, and increased job satisfaction, they're fine. If you feel you can't stay another day in the job without going mad, by all means seize the unexpected opportunity.

But make a pact with yourself to use it as a temporary energizer. Seek professional career counseling, psychotherapy, or whatever it takes to help you find another job that engages you and adds to your skill bank.

What if you're in a Quadrant III job and an unexpected opportunity surfaces, but you're too traumatized by the prospect of change to act?

The answer depends on whether you're rutted or rooted in Quadrant III.

If you're rutted, you've remained in an unfulfilling job out of habit or circumstance. The idea of moving saps your energy and paralyzes you. Unexpected career opportunities throw you into a panic. You think you'd like to change—until it becomes a real option. Those are the symptoms of being rutted. The causes are myriad: perfectionism, fear of failure, lack of confidence, low self-esteem, feeling this is all you deserve, proving to someone that you can tough it out. The remedy is to forget all unsolicited opportunities and take charge of your career strategy and yourself. It's not going to be easy, but you can do it—slowly and deliberately.

Consciously using ourselves to construct the life work we want and deserve is a continuing challenge. Begin by knowing that you're worth it. Then concentrate on what you need and want. Confront what you are afraid of. Overhaul your career strategy; rethink the skills you need to reach your capstone. If you're at the end of your career rope, find a new capstone. This strategy should focus on Quadrant I and II jobs. Get help from a professional counselor. Sometimes we have become the problem, and our own self-assertions (we're too insecure, too old, too afraid to change; we're not bright enough, educated enough, deserving enough) keep us frozen where we are.

If you are *rooted* in Quadrant III, your situation is different. Your job is like an old, worn hat. Sure it's old, but it's comfortable and you feel at home in it. You feel rooted in this place and this culture and bonded to these people. They're like family. You prefer the known to the unknown. The unexpected opportunity, even if it's a similar Quadrant III job, is a problem. The last thing you want is to be repotted into foreign soil. Change of any kind is unwelcome, even though you're bored with the actual tasks of your job. What can you do? Scrutinize unexpected opportunities for ideas you can use to revitalize your work. Be playful. Tinker with your job duties, adding a few here, delegating a few there. Be more spontaneous. Risk a little, not a lot. *Gently* modify your position. Tell the stranger bearing unexpected opportunity to call back in a year.

When You're in a Quadrant IV Job

You're in trouble and you know it. Any unsolicited offer is welcome. You'll do anything to get out.

Stop! Trading one Quadrant IV job for another is counterproductive. You can't afford it. More is not better. A Quadrant IV change of scenery, with or without higher pay and status, isn't worth it. Like a series of bad love affairs, a series of Quadrant IV jobs will damage your self-esteem and deepen your depression.

The rule here is:

Refuse to see the unexpected opportunity as a rescue. Be your own hero and use this career crisis to get professional help and redirect your future toward Quadrant I development.

You have several alternatives. The best choice is to stay put and face the facts. I know it doesn't feel good, but being an ostrich won't help. Think about what skills you'd enjoy practicing at or outside of work. Make a pact with yourself to change, but take it small step by small step. Take a course; read a book. Regain your sense of personal adequacy through a series of deliberate moves. Slowly but surely, explore new avenues of interest. Don't rush. It took you a while to dig into this spot; it will take you a while to dig out.

A second alternative is to grab any unexpected opportunity as long as it returns you to Quadrant III or is a job you like better than the one you've got. All this will do is give you a temporary reprieve from your mounting sense of personal failure, your feelings of incompetence, and your intense dislike of your job. But there is a saving grace in removing yourself from an aversive work environment where coworkers see your inability to turn your situation around as a permanent and terminal condition. If you grab a Quadrant III unexpected opportunity as part of a salvage strategy, use the new position as a holding maneuver that will allow you to buy the time you need to reconstruct a more meaningful approach to work and life.

Suppose someone offers you a Quadrant I or II job? By all means, consider it. But don't look at it as a panacea. The new job won't fix everything that's gone wrong. Whatever led you into Quadrant IV is probably still lurking out there (or, more accurately, lurking inside you), and you will have to address these issues head on. Find a mentor, career coach, or support group that will assist you in focusing on the problems: false expectations, bad attitude, low self-image, ineffective career strategy, and so on. If you don't do this, you're likely to find yourself back in Quadrant III or IV before you know it.

WHAT TO CONSIDER IN YOURSELF

Sometimes you just can't decide about an unexpected opportunity. It has all the trappings of a dream job, it offers plenty of Quadrant I development, and your friends tell you you'd be crazy to pass it up. Yet you hesitate, wracked by indecision. What should you do?

Respect Your Feelings

Your reluctance to take the job is significant. You may be responding to some subtle but meaningful problem with the job. For starters, assume that if something doesn't feel right, there's something wrong with the job—not you! Take it as a signal to investigate and network. If you're pressured to decide immediately, demand more time. Perhaps they're worried about what your investigation might unearth.

You may be responding to political innuendos that bode trouble or to a gathering storm on the home front should you take this position.

In any case, respect your intuition. Even if you can't put your finger on why you're hesitating, don't assume your worries are groundless.

What if your intuition about the job is positive? Respect it. But follow up with a thorough investigation anyway. It helps to see the facts as friendly allies of intelligent decision-making. If you take a little time to know them better, you won't go wrong.

Timing

As location is to real estate, timing is to unexpected job opportunities.

Timing is a much-overlooked key factor that tells you where

you are in your Doom Loop, in your life, and in relation to various outside events. But given that this is an unexpected opportunity, whoever is providing the opportunity also controls the timing. They have an immediate need. They won't wait months or years until you exit from Quadrant II bliss or get your life in order.

Because you don't control the timing, you're forced to adapt to someone else's perception of where you should be at this point in your career. Unless the opportunity coincides with your desire to bail out of a Quadrant III or IV position, accepting the job offer might not be the logical next step in your career path.

A career decision is not an isolated event. Its timing reflects a complex interplay of life and career issues. It occurs in the context of everything else going on in your life. This career opportunity might be great a year or two from now. But right now it's ill-timed because you still have a lot to learn in your present job; you just got married, had a child, or experienced some other life event that makes you want to stay put; or all of the above and more. Whether you realize it or not, timing is dictating your choice.

Timing issues extend to where you are in your life cycle, which in turn affects how you view a particular unexpected opportunity, regardless of merit. According to researchers such as Daniel Levinson in his book *The Seasons of a Man's Life,* it's normal for people to go through alternating cycles in which they either build and solidify or question what they have been building. It's been my experience that in the building cycle, which can last a decade or more, people are less open to unexpected opportunities that throw them off course. But in the questioning cycle they are ripe for change and susceptible to opportunities that offer quick solutions to difficult life problems.

No matter which quadrant you're in, it's important to ask yourself whether you are in a building or a questioning period. When an unexpected opportunity comes along, realize that this could influence your decision and act accordingly. If you're in a building period you may reject even the best un-

expected opportunity. On the other hand, during a questioning cycle you may grab even a feeble one.

The bottom line here is: don't discount issues of personal
timing.

Consider any unexpected opportunity in view of what else
is going on in your life. If you've just gone through a divorce,
a health crisis, or some other major life trauma involving loss,
proceed with caution. If you're at the edge of your ability to
accommodate another round of uncertainty and change, the
additional stress of adjusting to a new job—even a terrific
one—may be too much right now. Note what you like about
the opportunity, then go after it—if and when the timing is
right—for you. If you just keep breathing, eventually the
timing will be right for you to tackle change.

Know Thyself: Needs and Personal Style

When the unexpected opportunity arrives, determine how
the position fits your own needs, motivations, and values.

Remember: unsatisfied needs motivate us. Anyone who has
ever gone into a supermarket hungry knows how this works.
To the hungry shopper, everything looks good. You end up
buying more than you really want because you didn't pay
sufficient attention to your hunger.

Psychological needs are far less obvious, but they operate
just as forcefully. Your unmet needs for achievement, power,
or security, or a host of other needs, will affect your decision-
making process. If you've been working in a technical job that
downplays power, you might be hooked by the so-so unexpected opportunity that promises to make you a kingpin. If
your job isolates you, you might grab an opportunity that
emphasizes teamwork. Knowing which needs motivate you is
extremely useful. If you can identify the needs at the top of
your list when opportunity knocks, you'll be better able to
evaluate the opportunity objectively.

Personal style plays an important role, too. If you thrive on
spontaneity and risk, the unexpected opportunity will tempt
you to leap before you look. If this is your style, ordinary

precautions such as investigating the company making the offer will seem to require heroic effort. Don't be daunted. Push yourself to make that effort. Refuse to let your personal idiosyncrasies dictate your acceptance or rejection of an opportunity through default.

The secret here isn't transforming yourself into something you're not. Knowing your style simply permits you to gather and analyze information impartially, then make a decision that fits your Doom Loop strategy.

CAVEAT EMPTOR

We all know the clichés—buyer beware, look before you leap, all that glitters is not gold, beware of strangers bearing gifts. Though they may be clichés, they are also valuable warnings for those faced with unexpected career opportunities.

Before buying into the opportunity, take off your blinders and search for the pitfalls. Delay your decision until you've had a chance to play the "Caveat Emptor Game."

The Game

Remember the pictures you used to look at as a kid where you had to find the hidden figures? The pictures looked normal enough, but between the lines and shadings were eighteen jungle animals or the twenty-six letters of the alphabet. Unless you scrutinized the picture closely, you'd miss some of the hidden objects.

Treat the unexpected opportunity like that picture. Your mission is to locate all the hidden problems that will make this seemingly wonderful job your worst nightmare. Use the following questions to expose the flaws.

THE CAVEAT EMPTOR GAME

- What evidence can you find that this is a dead-end job in camouflage?
- Is any part of this organization scheduled for restructuring?
- Is this company a known target for a leveraged buy-out, hostile takeover, or merger?
- Are they looking for someone expendable to nail with an impossible project?
- Is this a job no one else in the company will touch?
- What really happened to the last person who held this job?
- Did they combine two or more job descriptions for this slot?
- Are they hiring you as a token to fill some equal employment opportunity or administrative need?
- Will you be reporting to an impossible boss?
- How much autonomy will you really have?
- What are the politics of this place?
- Are ethical or legal problems brewing here?

To answer these questions, read, research, ask, and listen. Ask "what if" questions that tap into your fears. Look for clues. You may need to be creative in your quest, but do whatever you can to find the answers.

Taking this precautionary approach could save you from being blindsided or even victimized. It will prevent you from taking the job and later complaining, "No one told me it would be this way." Remember, no matter what the facts are, they're friendly. It's what you *don't* know that can hurt you. A decision based on accurate facts will do more for you than one based on assumptions and wishes.

UNFORESEEN COMPLICATIONS

Because they engage our egos, unexpected opportunities leave us vulnerable to significant career complications. Here are some common ones.

Dual Doom Loops—His-and-Hers Careers

Thanks to a number of economic and social shifts, dual-career marriages and partnerships are rapidly becoming the norm, and with them comes a host of complications that unexpected career opportunities can worsen. Two careers mean two voices in any career or relocation decision—a "his" voice and a "hers" voice. Two careers also mean two different Doom Loop trajectories that are randomly in or out of sync—usually more out than in.

In this situation, the unexpected career opportunity typically causes less celebration and more visits to the marriage or couples counselor. The Quadrant III partner who receives the opportunity will jump at it, but the Quadrant I partner will adamantly resist any dislocation. Under these circumstances it is all too easy for dual careers to become "duel" careers.

Conflict is bound to occur because two independent sets of career needs, timing, and interests demand different priorities. In a marriage or partnership, self-interest is expected to yield to partnership interest. But this can be tough.

Where relocation is an issue, feelings of loss come into play. Giving up career gains, losing a supportive network of work friends, feeling uncertain about re-creating Quadrant I or II bliss—these are gut-wrenching problems for the "trailing" partner. It is all too easy for one member of a couple to blame the other, to feel that the partner is selfish, is breaking commitments, and so on.

Compounding the problem are the changing roles of men and women in our society. Both sexes have more latitude today in the roles they assume and the way they choose to balance work and family responsibilities. The old rules have changed. Women can no longer be counted on to assume the role of dutiful spouse and be ready to drop everything for their husbands. Though many men might accept this fact on a theoretical level, they reject it when it becomes a personal reality. Most of us don't realize we're holding onto these old beliefs until they have been violated.

Consider this scenario.

He was the model breadwinner and father for twenty years. He moved up the corporate ladder right into Quadrant III, where he now languishes in a large corner office.

In the meantime she raised the kids, volunteered, worked part-time. Once the kids went to high school, she earned an advanced degree. She now holds a Quadrant I professional job. Sure there's tension. She is happier at work than he is. But given all this, both are coping fairly well.

Then an unexpected career opportunity appears and promises to revive him. It's a Quadrant II position in another state. He wants it; she's livid. From her perspective, it's her turn. From his perspective, she owes him the move.

From an individual perspective, each is right. They both deserve to be happy in their careers. But being in different quadrants of their Doom Loops creates different needs. Exacerbating these differences is the fact that they're also in different stages of their careers. Beyond career issues, each holds old and new sex role expectations that confound their problem-solving efforts even further. Worst of all, without recognizing what's happening, they each begin to take everything personally.

What's the answer? Unfortunately, there's no easy solution. It helps, however, if both people understand their respective Doom Loops and the implications of making an unexpected career change from the vantage point of the partner's quadrant. It also helps to recast the dilemma in terms of changing cultural expectations for men's and women's roles by asking a few questions like: What if the roles were reversed? What options will meet both partners' needs to be in Quadrant I or II jobs and feel good about the relationship?

My advice is: if the outcome threatens the relationship, don't try to tackle this issue by yourself. Get professional help. Too much is riding on the decision, and feelings run far too deep to risk freewheeling blame and adversarial problem-solving.

Younger dual-career couples, because they don't have as much time invested in their careers, often manage the unexpected opportunity much better than their elders. Still, the crisis can be just as intense if they don't take precautions. Specifically, it's wise for younger couples to forge an agreement well before opportunity strikes. For instance, they agree that the woman's career takes precedence over the man's because she is the major breadwinner or because his career will survive dislocation better than hers will. If the self-interest of each partner triumphs over interest in the partnership itself, their careers may thrive, but the relationship itself may be doomed. When unexpected opportunity knocks and she wants to answer because she realizes she is living on borrowed time in her top-of-the-Loop position, but he resists because he is riding Quadrant I success on a fast track into Quadrant II, they must resolve the conflict. The solution is a detailed agreement in advance of the crisis or strong skills in conflict resolution—or both.

In any dual-career decision, understanding your partner's Doom Loop quadrant will help. Understand what your partner sees himself or herself giving up and what your partner thinks he or she needs to feel good about the decision. By refraining from blaming each other and by openly discussing the issues, you enhance the chances of success, both in your careers and in your partnership.

The Prince Charming/Princess Charming Syndrome

You lead a charmed life. You are terrific at a job you enjoy. You have an uncanny knack for being in the right place at the right time. Mentors sprout up around you like weeds. Your career zigzags between tough Quadrant I and II jobs that showcase your skills.

Your problem: you have so many unexpected opportunities that you've never had to define or implement a capstone strategy. You regularly sidestep it, barely remembering what skills you're supposed to acquire. You've never had to look for jobs since they keep falling in your lap. Job searches and informational interviews aren't in your repertoire. You're a golden boy or golden girl par excellence.

For a while, everything will be great. Eventually, however, you'll hit the wall—probably in mid or late career. Despite all your accomplishments, you'll lack direction when no one is pushing you to the next career opportunity. Not being courted is a bitter pill, given your history. You may have nothing more than a perfunctory résumé. Normal job search anxiety and rejection feel anything but normal to you. You take rejection personally and your self-esteem plummets. You barely manage to get through the day. But you get little sympathy for your plight, since by most people's standards you've led a charmed life.

If you've hit the wall—or even if you just anticipate hitting it—here are some tactics. Don't say yes to every unexpected opportunity offered. Take stock of your career mosaic. Reread Chapter 2 on how to select a capstone and think about what you really want to tackle next. Choose a new capstone and design your target mosaic. Plot your target skill acquisition strategy and look for Quadrant I stretch positions. Consider yourself a job search rookie. Go back and read the chapter on the first-job crisis (Chapter 5). Develop up-to-date job search skills. Get out of your workplace cubbyhole and network. And above all else, take your time. Make sure you don't let someone else's agenda keep you from using this opportunity to develop your own.

The One-That-Got-Away Syndrome

You've weathered the crisis of the unforeseen opportunity and decided to stay put. Perhaps the offer was good but the timing wasn't right. Perhaps your spouse wasn't willing to move or you were unwilling to leave a Quadrant II position.

But after a while, something feels terribly wrong. You second-guess your decision. You daydream; you ask, "What if . . . ?" You're suffering from the one-that-got-away syndrome.

Like Greg Denman. Greg was the high-profile director of a prestigious national drug abuse prevention organization in Washington, D.C. He was committed to the cause, the organization, and the job. Both he and his wife enjoyed the perks and social life that went with the territory. The job, issues, and governing board changed so rapidly that Greg had been in the Quadrant I and II corridor of his Doom Loop for nearly five wonderful years.

Then the unexpected career opportunity came along. Greg was recruited for another executive director's position with a large religious fund-raising organization in his hometown in the South. At first, Greg was excited. He enjoyed fund-raising, liked the organization, and had planned on eventually returning to his hometown to retire. He also liked the idea of being a big fish in a small pond.

But the timing was wrong. He wasn't ready to uproot his family, and his wife had just landed a job as a lobbyist. Her career opportunities would be limited if he took the job. Besides, he liked his Quadrant I and II job, and the new one looked as if it might slide into Quadrant III after a year or two.

So Greg said no. It was a well-reasoned decision.

But then a funny thing happened. Greg started to think he had missed a golden opportunity. He talked about his rejected position in glowing terms and downplayed his current successes. He had fallen into idealizing "the one that got away," and it was eating at him.

He found himself enjoying his current job less and thinking about his unexpected opportunity more.

He started blaming: his wife for not being ready to move, himself for not seizing the day. Eventually, he took a job in his hometown as the director of an adolescent drug treatment facility, but he still talked about the one that got away.

The point here is that the unexpected opportunity, even after it's rejected, can still precipitate a crisis. Even though Greg made the "right" decision, the decision itself awakened a new awareness of his own unmet needs—needs for recognition, appreciation, and so on.

How can you avoid this syndrome? First, take a frankly

subjective look at the unexpected career opportunity. Forget impartiality for now. Ask yourself:

- What do I like about the job itself?
- What appeals to me about its context?
- Which of my unmet needs does this job satisfy?
- If I were to say no, what do I think I would be passing up?

Keep a log that documents your changes in perspective during this process. Then examine the opportunity objectively along the lines suggested earlier. Even if the timing is wrong and the Doom Loop advantage isn't there, note any aspects of the job that still appeal to you. Perhaps you need more privacy, or more social interaction, or more public influence than your current job provides.

Obviously, no job is perfect. Idealizing the one that got away tells you that it might have fulfilled some unmet need. But even if it got away, you can get some of it back. Try to incorporate facets of the lost job into your present one. Or search for a new opportunity that gives you what you need.

Unexpected opportunity is one of many potential sparks that can ignite a full-blown career crisis. Some are ignited by personal changes, some by external events. Others have been in the making for a long time and are most likely to surface as you approach midcareer. The next chapter looks at their causes and cures.

CHAPTER 9

∎

Discontent
Before Capstone

I think I need a change.
—Aircraft project manager

I don't know what I want. Maybe something more significant, more valuable. I still like writing, but I've lost my passion. I'm tired of hyping mouthwash and tuna.
—Advertising copywriter

For fifteen years, I was like family. I was slated to be a VP next year. Then they sell out and it's a new ball game. This SWAT team arrives from Boston. If I stay, I'm nothing.
—Director, international marketing

Feeling discontent before reaching your capstone is the career equivalent of going through a midlife crisis. You probably didn't expect it, and no one plans for it. But it's been brewing for a while. You've made a heavy investment in your career only to find yourself blocked or trapped in mid-path. You're no longer a rookie and the stakes are high. You feel frustrated, bored, and ready for a change. But if you're like most people, you don't have a clue as to what to do next.

HOW THE BEST-LAID PLANS GO AWRY

Why do you feel this way? There can be any number of perfectly good reasons. The Doom Loop, for example: your Quadrant I job ossifies over time into a dull Quadrant III routine. Or perhaps the rungs of the corporate ladder have narrowed, resulting in a massive middle-management gridlock that impedes your climb to the top. Or you could be the victim of takeovers, restructurings, or downsizing.

Whatever the situation, you contract a bad case of the midcareer blahs. The symptoms are unmistakable. You used to feel passion for your work, and now you feel nothing. You read the want ads with quiet desperation. You're ready for a midcareer breakout; it's time for a change.

WHAT HAPPENED?

Like a plane crash, this disaster is difficult to ascribe to a single cause. After the fact, any trained investigator can make sense out of the clues. The problem was equipment failure, pilot error, or flight conditions, or the interaction among those problems. Disaster might have been averted if even one variable had been slightly altered. The investigation reveals facts that can prepare us to avoid tragedy the next time. But by the time the investigation takes place, the facts are cast in bronze—a tragic history to be learned from.

So it is with the crisis of discontent before capstone. But midcareer malaise can—and often does—strike more than once. You can avoid it by understanding its causes and cures.

When you're in the midst of this crisis, however, it's hard to do anything at all. You know it's time for a change. But feeling stuck, ambivalent about leaving your job, and indecisive about what to do next is par for the course. A serious sense of loss about who you hoped to become—as well as the prospect of starting all over again—paralyzes you.

This crisis is characterized by many false starts and stops, mounting anxiety, flagging confidence, and frustration. At the same time that you crave change, you fear it. Simple decisions take forever. You become obsessed about making the wrong move. You believe one more career mistake would mean catastrophe.

It won't. Like other career crises, this one can be overcome. Begin by getting a better handle on the various elements of your situation. Take a sheet of paper and draw a line down the middle. One one side, jot down all the driving factors that are pushing you to leave, to change, to bolt for any exit. On the other side, write down all the restraining factors that are holding you in place. Use the career change analysis diagram on this page as a guide.

CAREER CHANGE ANALYSIS DIAGRAM

If you know your desired career change, state it: _____	
Factors Pushing You to Leave	**Factors Compelling You to Stay**

If the list of factors on each side of the line is roughly equal, change is going to take some time. The push factors have to be greater than the factors compelling you to stay or you won't have the impetus to make a move. Look at the nature of the push factors you have listed. Which among them are the most important? The most distressing? Can you resolve some of them without making a complete career change? Look at the pull factors. Which are the most powerful—the ones that you don't think you can do without? With a little ingenuity or negotiation, can you incorporate any of these positive factors into your current work situation?

Gather as much information as you can. The problem, of course, is that you don't yet know whether a change will really solve the crisis. So the trick is not to move quickly; it's to move insightfully.

Ask yourself what you really want from your career and what's possible. Write your answers in a notebook. Wait a week or two and write new answers. Then compare both sets of answers. Are they the same? Different? Discuss your answers with a friend or mentor. Keep in mind your own complexity and hidden needs. Your answers don't have to be terse bullet points on a page. Simplify later.

This is also the time to confront yourself with a second set of critical questions:

- What am I willing to settle for?
- What do I feel I deserve in my career, in life?
- What will I feel like in five years if nothing changes?

Your evolving answers to these questions will begin to shape and define your vision for change. They will also help you identify what you have at stake.

Discontent before capstone is a crisis precipitated by a whole variety of factors. Solving it usually involves much more than avoiding a status-preserving Quadrant III to Quadrant III career shift, or selecting a few Quadrant I skills to enliven your dreary career mosaic. Band-Aid solutions won't do. You may need to rethink and reconstruct how you define yourself through your work.

Capitalize on this crisis. See it as one of life's occasional windows of opportunity. Use it to explore career and life changes that might not have been possible before. Consider it an opportunity to discover what type of work really satisfies you. Perhaps you'll choose an altogether new capstone. Determine how ambitious you are, the trade-offs you're willing to make to achieve your career goals, and whether you can sell your family on a major change in life-style. Ask yourself whether your career discontent serves to mask other distress in your personal relationships or in your self-esteem. Gather as much personal data as you can to identify the sources of your discontent. Perhaps you're rutted in Quadrant III and your expert role. Perhaps you responded to an unexpected opportunity that has put you on the downside of the Doom Loop. Or perhaps you're confusing commitment to your capstone with commitment to a company that takes you for granted. Take as much time as you need to understand your own issues fully. Keep reminding yourself that you're worth it.

Accept that you're temporarily stalled. More important, understand that you can extricate yourself from this crisis with some self-examination and Doom Loop tactics. As unbelievable as it may seem right now, there are life, work, and a satisfying new capstone beyond this crisis.

CAREER DISCONTENT WITH A CAPSTONE

This hurts. When you bang into a wall of discontent before you reach your capstone, you face the bitter truth that you may never achieve your goal. You've been climbing the mountain, confident that your capstone, like the promised land, will eventually come into view. But then it turns out that, like Moses, you may be destined to catch only a fleeting glimpse of your dream. Something is stopping you. It may be something from the outside—organizational restructuring, for instance—or something from within yourself: perhaps you feel too bruised to keep up the pace, or you can no longer tolerate the game-playing or politics necessary to get you where you want to go.

Merely having a capstone puts you in a solid strategic position to analyze what has gone wrong in your career management scheme. You might be moving in the wrong direction, but because you've learned how to use a map and chart a course, you can adjust or change your current capstone with confidence. As you read the following sections, you should be better prepared to pinpoint many of the causes and cures for your discontent and ready to hit the career strategy restart button.

CAREER DISCONTENT WITHOUT A CAPSTONE

This crisis is more troublesome. When you don't have a capstone, you have to begin asking tough questions: What were you actually striving toward that is now so unattainable? What were your expectations about career success, anyway? By what standards are you discontent? And what has changed?

If you're discontent at midcareer and have no capstone, you're not alone. Misery loves company, and you've got plenty.

I suspect that most people don't have a capstone, so don't feel that you're the odd one out. Like most people, you simply chose a profession, and your goal was to progress upward, to get ahead, to earn more money. Without a Doom Loop strategy, you probably didn't realize why you needed a capstone. Perhaps you measured your career success by whether you'd achieved a certain status—kids in private schools, your own home, an upscale car, or whatever.

While there's nothing inherently wrong with any of these ambitions, they lead you to pursue ersatz capstones. This makes it impossible for you to build a well-defined target mosaic and move step by step toward your goal. Without a specific capstone, you'll have trouble measuring your achievements against the numerous, ill-defined standards of success out there. The absence of money, status, and fame can be taken as indicators that you've failed. But then it's always easy to know when you're running on empty. What you're still missing is a standard for knowing when you've reached success.

When midcareer malaise hits a person without a capstone, the situation is exacerbated. Without a capstone, your feelings of professional and personal inadequacy are often magnified. This crisis might be harder for you than for someone with a capstone. But using all the wisdom of hindsight, you still have an invaluable opportunity to grapple with what you truly want for yourself in the years ahead. It's not too late to envision a capstone and enjoy the career benefits it will provide.

Your next step—whether or not you have a capstone—is to understand what is causing this crisis.

THE CAUSES OF YOUR DISCONTENT

Midcareer discontent has many causes. But chances are you're undergoing this crisis because:

- You feel blocked in your progress toward your capstone or some other marker of success.
- You feel trapped in an occupation, a job, or an organization.
- You have undergone some basic change in your beliefs, attitudes, and values that invalidates or transforms your career strategy.

Let's look at what happens when you are blocked, trapped, or transformed at midcareer and at some remedies that can free you.

Blocked

Finding yourself blocked is tied to wanting something better for yourself. No one with a dream is immune. It can happen in any Doom Loop quadrant at any time in your career. The key is to discover what is blocking your path and to decide what to do about it. If you identify the wrong problem, you'll end up with the wrong solution.

Look at the diagnostic checklist that follows and check off all items that apply to your situation. Remember the plane crash analogy—there is usually more than one cause for a mishap.

BLOCKED: A DIAGNOSTIC CHECKLIST

1. _____ Your position (plant, department, staff, budget) is eliminated.
2. _____ Your company is restructured (taken over, merged, downsized, bankrupt).
3. _____ Your industry (the economy) stops expanding (slows down, constricts).
4. _____ Your are plateaued (your opportunities are constricted; the upper rungs of your career ladder are occupied).
5. _____ The competition for the next slot is top-notch and hungry.
6. _____ You differ from company norms (in race, gender, lifestyle, dress, ideas, et cetera).
7. _____ You are taken for granted ("Good old Pat"), passed over, humored.
8. _____ You've been typecast in a certain job (role, grade level).
9. _____ Your boss is hostile (is jealous, has own people, sabotages you).
10. _____ Your personality clashes with that of someone in power.
11. _____ You made political enemies who now block (exclude, bait) you.
12. _____ You hit the "glass ceiling."
13. _____ You are considered too old (too feisty, too fat, too something) to develop or promote.
14. _____ You miss the expected number of promotions for someone at your level.
15. _____ You go from fast track to slow track to dead end.
16. _____ You lack influential friends (sponsors, mentors) in high places.
17. _____ You blew the whistle on someone or something.
18. _____ You innovated a service (product) or acted as an organizational change agent.
19. _____ You made mistakes that now haunt you.
20. _____ You need an advanced degree (new training) to move on.
21. _____ You lack the right skill mix to advance.
22. _____ Your skills and knowledge have become technically obsolete.
23. _____ Your spouse (children) won't relocate.
24. _____ You won't consider a lateral or downward move.
25. _____ Other: _____
26. _____ Other: _____
27. _____ Other: _____

Your answers will tell a story about:

- the characteristics of the work environment you're in
- the current state of that work environment
- the way you've presented yourself in that environment
- the roles you've assumed
- the way people have reacted to you
- the way you've coped with work demands
- the way you've defined your options and other alternatives

These are just assertions about what has happened—they are neither judgments nor excuses. With all this in mind, it's time to unblock yourself.

When the Problem Is in the Environment (Items 1 to 5)

If you're in a shrinking or economically unhealthy work environment, do some research. Is the situation a temporary setback that you can weather or a more permanent state best left behind? Is it a regional or national phenomenon?

In one Midwestern city, three major ad agencies shut down, leaving scores of talented advertising moguls out in the cold. The advertising industry is still healthy, but not in that city.

If you're blocked by a regional occurrence of this type, and you're still in Quadrant I or II of your Doom Loop, move on. It's hard to uproot yourself and your family. But it's also hard to give up a capstone you really want.

If your industry or occupational niche makes the endangered species list, perform a Doom Loop skill analysis of your entire career mosaic. Include your education and experience. Pay attention to your Quadrant I and II skills. Write them down. Look at these skills with fresh eyes. Pretend they constitute a generic job description. Ask a few trusted people in your field to help you brainstorm which jobs, career paths, and occupations might correspond to this set of skills. Don't worry about getting a tight fit right now; look for new ideas. Go out and talk to people in these jobs and in these professions to discover what you have to do to break in. If what you learn appeals to you, take seminars or find an expert to apprentice with, someone who can help ease your entry into the field.

If you're in a work environment that is politically unhealthy, your interests may be best served by moving on. It's easier to acquire political coping skills in a new environment where you don't have a history. Remember, though, that any work environment can create blockage if you lack political skills. So this may be the time to master them. For more on this, see Chapter 11.

When the Problem Lies in How You Present Yourself (Item 6)

Hire someone to critique your appearance, your communication skills, your impact on others, and how you react to them. How we manage ourselves, our moods, and our language is under much closer scrutiny in the workplace than most of us realize. Don't rely solely on advice from your spouse, friends, boss, or subordinates; even if it were unbiased, becoming dependent on their advice might create relationship problems. As you move up the organizational chart, away from Quadrant I positions, you're likely to receive less coaching and far less feedback. Instead of confronting you, people may be more likely to talk about you behind your back or sabotage your projects. They may perceive you altogether differently from the way you perceive yourself, and you won't know it. This can cause serious career problems. It helps to take the attitude that the facts are always friendly. It's what's in your blind spot—what others know about you that you don't—that trips you up.

So if you want to reach your capstone, solicit and cherish old-fashioned feedback from a variety of sources. You need the information it contains. Resist any natural tendency to blame the bearer of bad news. Use feedback to change and monitor how you present yourself. Allow a few months to see whether the changes you have effected are appreciated or whether your situation improves. If not, it might be time to take this personal learning out for a spin in a new work setting.

When the Problem Is that You Are Typecast (Items 7 and 8)

You're typecast in a certain job or role that blocks your progress toward your capstone. You're an accountant who hopes to make a lateral move into training in a Big Eight firm; a secretary who has received an MBA in order to shift toward a capstone in management; an actor who wants to become president of the United States.

The problem you face is not in you. It is in the habitual perceptions of you held by key decision-makers, perceptions grounded in their past experience. Regardless of your current skills and talents, they can't see you in a new way.

Don't get so immersed in your organization's culture that you accept their perceptions as your own! Most people realize how difficult it is for secretaries to break through the walls of their pink-collar ghettos. But few of us realize that professional and staff jobs also become ghettos for those who want to try something new.

The unblocking formula here is "out and up." Seek Quadrant I jobs in environments where you'll start with a clean slate, where your performance will be rated on merit, not on your past lives. Maybe it's hard to leave your company, but consider it their loss. Why waste your effort carrying their old baggage? You'll get much further much faster with a fresh start. If you want to return to the company in a few years as a "familiar stranger," your Quadrant I experience on the outside will make you infinitely more attractive to the decision-makers who are likely to move you toward your capstone.

When the Problem Is Bad Chemistry (Items 9 to 11)

It happens. Personality clashes and bad chemistry block career paths. When someone sees you as difficult, it often means that he or she sees the world in a way that differs radically from your view. Once you identify the problem, it's very solvable. You can remove this blocking factor. How? By altering the self-centered philosophy of the golden rule and by putting yourself in their shoes. In dealing with people whom you see as difficult, or who perceive you as difficult try this. Frame your actions and language so you do unto them as they would have done unto them—not as you would like done unto you. See it their way, speak it their way, present it their way. It may be difficult to do this at first, but generally it will dissolve the communication barrier and subsequent career block quickly and effectively.

It also helps to seek out good chemistry. Take a break from being reactive and look for people in your comfort zone—people who are happy to help you, share information, and coach you. Why make life at the office unnecessarily tough on yourself?

When the Problem Lies in Being Different (Items 12 to 16)

When people respond negatively to your best efforts, it's often because your personality and style are at odds with the organization's norms. Maybe it's because you're over forty-five, you're a woman, or you're a member of a minority. Or maybe it's your life-style, sexual orientation, appearance, or educational background. You're considered "one of them," not "one of us." The result is intended or unintended exclusion from leadership roles. You find yourself underused, over-supervised, and generally left out.

The glass ceiling is a real and frustrating phenomenon. As a workplace token, you're more likely to be highly touted in the beginning in Quadrant I, where you also lack power. By the time you reach Quadrant II you may be languishing without guidance. Your drift into Quadrant III through benign neglect will be taken as further evidence that you never had the right stuff.

It helps if you're aware of the implications of being different. Generally it's a mistake to do anything accentuating that you are different from the mainstream of your organization. Avoid taking on roles and projects where you are the first of your kind to do it. Although it's thrilling to be a pioneer, the career cost of this role is often too high. For example, if you are the first woman engineer to hold your rank, you risk being seen as a representative of your gender, and because of your visibility you may be a target for reactions that have nothing to do with the quality of your performance. Putting out fires related to your "first of your kind" status—whatever it may be—can sap your energy and create massive personal discontent that deflects you from reaching your mature career goals.

Instead, seek organizational cultures that are making a public commitment to developing a diverse work force. Before taking a new Quadrant I or II job, talk to people like you who have been with the organization for a while. Be suspicious of glossy company statistics. Statistics can be deceiving, especially regarding issues like diversity. "Caveat emptor" is a good rule for shopping organizational cultures.

Don't be afraid to think small. Out of necessity, smaller companies tend to use and develop the people they have according to their functional contributions to the organization's success, rather than according to race, gender, personality, and so on. Contrary to what many people think, small companies create many Quadrant I opportunities.

When the Problem Lies in Your Work Conduct (Items 17 to 19)

You can be blocked by your own behavior at work, resulting in premature entry into Quadrants III and IV of the Doom Loop. What kinds of work conduct block your career advancement? Unethical business practices, failure to keep your promises, repeated missed deadlines, an arrogant or uncooperative attitude, and sexual harassment (for the guilty as well as the injured) are typical examples. If any of these is your problem, confront it directly. Recognize that you have a potentially career-stopping problem that will land you in hot water in nearly any organizational culture. Make a commitment to change. Get professional help if necessary to gain insight and control over your detrimental behavior.

Work conduct that blocks career advancement, however, doesn't have to be negative. Sometimes it's even praiseworthy. In some cases you may become a victim of your own high principles. For instance, you blow the whistle on unethical practices within your company, negative publicity results, and you become an instant pariah. Or you innovate and improve company productivity, yet are consistently passed over for promotions.

Current organizational research shows that whistle-blowers, innovators, and change agents pay a steep price for positive contributions. By challenging the status quo, these people set themselves apart. The company views you as too ethical, independent, or innovative. You aren't seen as being one of the gang. People question your trustworthiness, loyalty, or pre-dictability. They block you.

What should you do? You may have been right in your stance, but as a manager of your own career you were inef-fective. Decide what trade-offs affecting your ethics and values you're willing to make to further your career. If you're un-willing to compromise, you should look for an organization where your positive, absolute values are an integral and ap-preciated part of the corporate culture—where they will be assets, not liabilities.

Clearing Away the Obstacles

If you're blocked, what are your options? Consider the case of Ron Hunter.

Ron Hunter's discontent before capstone stunned him. He was wooed and won by an aggressive, smooth-talking head-hunter who convinced him to take a job on the West Coast as associate director of marketing for a privately held cereal company. Ron left his position as a sales manager with a prominent Ohio manufacturer only five months before be-coming fully vested. But Ron was moving from Quadrant III to Quadrant I. He was in hot pursuit of his career capstone in marketing, and the freewheeling California life-style pro-vided a strong secondary draw.

Shortly after Ron's move, his new company went bankrupt. When it went under, Ron went into apoplexy. After all he had risked, he had come up empty. His marketing capstone was blocked.

Ron responded by first consulting his family; they decided they wanted to remain on the West Coast. So Ron made a risky choice. He opted to stay in his job with the bankrupt company. He was betting that it would be at least a year before the company actually went out of business and that in the remaining time he could acquire the necessary Quadrant I marketing, sales, and public relations skills (forged in crisis) that his capstone mandated.

It worked. When the company went out of business, Ron found a top marketing job with another West Coast company. His plan for acquiring target mosaic skills had circumvented his being blocked.

When blocked, you need to identify the obstacle's source and remove, engulf, or find a way around it, moving yourself back into Quadrant I.

It helps if you can harness the anger and outrage generated by the blockage and use it to move on. People do it every day. A woman umpire, a victim of de facto segregation, sues the league. A paraplegic federal employee denied promotion acquires a master's degree in organizational behavior and sets up a consulting firm to design corporate programs for hiring and training disabled workers. In each case, anger over being blocked generated action-producing energy. If you're blocked in Quadrant I or II, you'll have energy to burn. These are the high-energy quadrants (as opposed to the lower-energy Quadrants III and IV). It's easier to take action. If you're blocked in Quadrant III or IV you're more likely to feel immobilized. The power you need to propel the deliberate moves you have to make has dropped out of your survival pack.

The solution is to bolster your confidence and well-being on and off the job in every way that is legal, moral, and ethical. We all face serious obstacles in life; the trick is to fight our natural sense of being victimized and helpless. Take charge of your own attitude. Think of yourself as a problem-solver on the verge of a breakthrough. Focus on the outcomes you want for yourself and on what you and others can do to make them happen. Take a time-out from ruminating over the sorry particulars and do something creative or fun. Look for new sources of energy in yourself and in others. The energy you need can come from friends, family members, coworkers, or professional counselors. Don't slow yourself down by trying to do this alone. A big obstacle lies in your path, and you'll need the strength of others to help you clear the way.

Trapped

You're in a Quadrant III slot in a world awash with Quadrant II expectations. As you move through your Doom Loop trajectory—enduring repeated assaults on your expectations, capstone, and dreams—you lose hope of reaching your goals.

Most often, you feel trapped when you land a Quadrant III position and struggle to avoid the slide into Quadrant IV. Then, as you try to extricate yourself, you encounter your own unexpected resistance to change. Now what's trapping you is you. When the beast wears your own fingerprints, breaking free is a challenge.

All this is different from being blocked. When you're blocked, you run into career barriers that prevent you from reaching your goals. Then, the task is to pinpoint the barriers and find a way around them.

But when you feel trapped at midcareer, you're dealing with ego-crunching paralysis. Logical problem-solving fails to work its usual wonders. The solutions may be obvious, but you don't feel free to take action. You're constrained by expectations, perceptions, and the need to save face—even by your shame at being stuck. The end result is plummeting self-esteem, debilitating anxiety, and fear of failure.

Focus on a time when you felt trapped in your career. What was going on? How did you feel and act? Take a look at the diagnostic checklist on the next page, and see how many of the statements fit your experience.

The statements you've agreed with tell you how you've trapped yourself. They indicate:

- ambivalence about change
- self-doubt
- wishful thinking
- too limited perception of career options

Once you recognize how you've trapped yourself, it's much easier to escape. The paradox is that it takes a lot of energy to keep yourself trapped and surprisingly little to free yourself. It's like getting your fingers stuck in a Chinese finger trap—the kind kids get at carnivals. The harder you struggle to free yourself, the tighter the trap grips your fingers. After the initial panic subsides, kids eventually learn through trial and error that the only way to get their fingers free is to stop struggling and move in a new direction. They shift their movement from pull to push.

TRAPPED: A DIAGNOSTIC CHECKLIST

1. ____ You've been in Quadrant III or IV of your Doom Loop for a year (two years, five years, ten years, or more).
2. ____ You have been in your current position for more than three years (five years, ten years, twenty years).
3. ____ You have no capstone (target mosaic, tactical plan).
4. ____ You dream of doing something else, being somewhere else, being someone else.
5. ____ You compare yourself to anyone who seems more successful (earns more, is happier, has more power) and find yourself lacking.
6. ____ You'd love to start over (with a new degree, occupation, company, identity).
7. ____ You feel sorry for yourself (victimized, out of control).
8. ____ You feel angry (indignant, bitter, cynical) about your plight.
9. ____ You spend a sizable chunk of time rehashing and ruminating over past events.
10. ____ You feel you've devoted yourself to your work (company) only to come up empty.
11. ____ You play the "if only," "why can't they," "they ought to" games.
12. ____ People have told you that you have a defeatist attitude.
13. ____ You believe that getting a promotion is the only way to reestablish your self-worth.
14. ____ You're afraid to leave the security (status, money) of this job, even though you're unhappy.
15. ____ You're afraid that in a new position you will feel like an impostor (fail, be incompetent, look foolish).
16. ____ You consider yourself too old (too politically naive, too lackluster) to develop or promote.
17. ____ You feel incapable of doing (learning, mastering) anything else.
18. ____ You're not sure you really deserve anything better than what you've got.
19. ____ You fear your leaving will let down people close to you.
20. ____ You make disparaging remarks about yourself publicly or in interviews.
21. ____ You sabotage others' efforts to help you get out of this place.
22. ____ You can think of many good reasons for turning down job offers.
23. ____ You secretly hope to be rescued by the company (a recruiter, a competitor).
24. ____ You haven't updated your résumé in the past year.
25. ____ You don't know how to conduct a first-class job search.
26. ____ You don't network on a regular basis.
27. ____ You feel depressed, hopeless, or lethargic about your future.
28. ____ Other: _____

This also is an excellent strategy for extricating yourself from all kinds of midcareer traps.

When the Trap Is Your Ambivalence About Change

You get anxious when you think about doing something new. Although you want to leave, you worry about trading known pitfalls for unknown ones. After a while, your Quadrant III or IV position actually starts to look attractive. You think of a hundred and one reasons to stay put. So you decide to stick it out. But as soon as you do, you reexperience the panic and shame of being trapped. The cycle repeats itself ad nauseam. Unless you're fired or your spouse threatens to leave you, you're likely to remain ambivalent and stuck.

To get unstuck, try something new. Redirect your focus from thinking about your current situation to taking any actions that move you in the direction of Quadrant I. The more actions you take, the more opportunities you create to break free. Even small actions are good, as long as they represent some change in direction. In fact, the smaller the better. That's because small actions are manageable, not overwhelming. They require no heroics, and they don't call adverse attention to what you are doing. When you tell people about a small win almost no one will be threatened, so you will encounter little external resistance to the changes you set in motion. This gives you a free field. And as coworkers and family members sense your growing control of the situation they are more likely to become your allies.

Set a three- or four-month limit on the first round of action you define. Also, don't bet everything on one spin of the wheel. Instead, play a variety of numbers and make small bets. Obtain continuing-education catalogs and highlight courses that appeal to you. Look for Quadrant I content (subjects you like but as yet are not good at). Enroll in a lunchtime seminar or two. Browse through the career section at the library. Take out books on Quadrant I or II careers that attract you. Hire someone to redesign your résumé. Have lunch with one person per week who can tell you about a job or field that sounds interesting. Volunteer for a Quadrant I or II position outside work. Join a new business or professional association.

In other words, shift your focus from the status quo to gradual involvement in opportunity-creating activities. The more opportunities you create, the less likely you are to feel trapped. Take a chance or two. Be playful. As the unfamiliar becomes familiar, you'll acquire the enthusiasm and momentum necessary to leave your current situation without looking back. With less ambivalence about change and just a few modest successes, you'll be able to escape your trap.

When the Trap Is Self-Doubt

Self-doubt at midcareer is a relentless villain. It can easily trap you in Quadrant III. If you've chosen a competitive fast track, you're used to comparing yourself with the best and brightest to keep your edge. But no matter how terrific you are, the supply of people to fill CEO, VP, and other prestigious slots exceeds the demand. Approximately 75 percent of the people competing for these top positions in today's flattened organizations will find themselves locked out. Even though you're well aware of these statistical realities, self-doubt can easily creep up on you, whispering that you're not as good as you thought you were.

Self-doubt can lead to self-defeating behavior that immobilizes you on the backslope of the Doom Loop. It de-energizes you, encouraging you to settle for a no-risk, no-growth Quadrant III job or capstone. When this happens you find yourself comparing your intelligence, skills, and savvy with those of others—and all too often you find yourself lacking. The result? Your self-esteem plummets.

The antidote is simple. When you are feeling vulnerable, refuse to compare your lot with that of others. Realize that everyone at every level has many of these doubts. Instead of letting them trap you, take a hard look at your skills. Focus on developing new Quadrant I challenges that build on the skills in your career mosaic. Branch out and generate a series of alternative career paths. There are many capstones that will fit who you are as well as or better than your current one.

You have many choices. Begin to build a qualified skill profile that can be transferred in whole or in part to an exciting new capstone.

When the Trap Is Wishful Thinking

Being trapped puts you in a state of red alert. It grabs your attention. You can't take your mind off it. Instead of doing something constructive, you're spending your time bogged down in plain old wishful thinking. Were you to log your thoughts, you'd probably find that many of them focus on being rescued or wanting your current situation to be different.

What's wrong with this? Plenty. You're like a prisoner in a cell staring through the window at a tiny patch of blue sky, wishing you were somewhere else, wishing you could see the grass and trees. You curse your imprisonment. You wait for the warden to let you out. You hope your good behavior will earn you an early parole.

It won't. But if you simply get up and try the door, chances are you'll find it isn't and never has been locked.

Action changes situations; wishful thinking doesn't. It's an energy waster that only offers you a false sense of control over events you don't like. Eventually this wishful thinking trans-forms you into a victim.

The trick here is to realize that although you genuinely feel trapped, you're usually much freer than you believe. Even when you feel trapped in a Quadrant III or IV slot there are actually many open doors that can lead you back to an exciting capstone and to Quadrant I and II involvement. To find them you must be willing to do something new. Remember the Chinese finger trap. Stop struggling. Shift from pull to push. Switch career paths; rethink your capstone; jump to a new Quadrant I or II slot in a new company.

You're not going to be able to do these things unless you stop ruminating over the wrongs of your current situation. Whatever change is to occur has to begin right now. So stop trying to control or rewrite the past. Forget it, at least for now. You may feel that this is harsh advice, but it's not. Take a chance. Talk to your boss about wanting new challenges, new leads. Redesign one part of your job to your own specifications and implement them. Go after a Quadrant I skill group. Network with friends. Don't wait for the company, a recruiter, or someone else to unlock the door to your future. It's already open.

When the Trap Is Limited Career Options

We often design our own career traps. Tunnel vision, losing track of what's happening in the organization, fear of risk—each does a nice job of limiting our career options. So do addictions to moving up, misplaced company loyalties, and poor career management skills.

By viewing traditional advancement in grade, rank, and salary as your only acceptable options, you greatly accelerate your probability of plateauing. If you're blind to lateral, downward, and outside career options, you'll probably end up in Quadrant III. If you're risk-shy, you become dependent on the goodwill of others—for promotions and everything else. For better or worse, this makes you vulnerable to their agendas. By resisting growth options like going back to school, taking lateral or downward moves, becoming a member of work teams where functions are shared and traded, or leaving your current employer for a Quadrant I job, you get yourself stuck.

How do you broaden your career options? First, get comfortable taking small risks that create new responsibility, opportunity, and learning. Take a course that builds a new skill group on your target mosaic. If you don't have a capstone, brainstorm a list of possible ones. Relax and have fun with all this. You're not making any major commitments at this point.

Tinker with your job description to squeeze out at least one new capstone skill within the next sixty days. Tell your boss exactly what (not why) you want to learn.

Study position listings within your company to learn the lateral moves that give you maximum skill-building payoff. Be low-key in this process. Remember, you're just window-shopping, not buying. See what makes your pulse race. Would you be more interested in a lateral move if it were accompanied by a pay increase? If so, try negotiating that increase.

Once management realizes you want a developmental challenge, they may be willing to work with you.

Conduct a "barrier analysis." This is how high achievers solve problems. Write down the two or three most appealing options. For each option, list all the reasons you couldn't possibly do it. Let 'em rip. Next, take one "I can't" at a time. View it as a simple barrier that's blocking your path. Your job is to create a detour around it. Find alternate paths. Talk to people you respect and see whether they can help you get around the toughest barriers. Then write a step-by-step plan for getting around each one.

Finally, implement your plan—step by step—and test the options that will help you escape your trap. Evaluate your progress at each step. It's your plan; you can change it at will. And say good-bye to being trapped.

Trapped on the Backslope of the Doom Loop

Rhonda Timmons was trapped in Quadrant IV. Her first job after high school was with the phone company. Two degrees and twenty-three years later, she was still there, manacled by "velvet handcuffs" to telecommunications work she no longer liked or was good at. Rhonda was suffering from "dustout"—the severe stress of being underutilized in the workplace. She was trapped by her own need for security, a high salary, and very limited transferable skills. It didn't help that middle-aged Rhonda also thought she was past her prime. Even though she was making it through each day on automatic pilot, she was in more danger of being fossilized than axed. But despite her Quadrant IV misery, she couldn't break free.

Most people trapped at midcareer are in Quadrant III or IV. They are the ones who stayed too long, who chose security over risk, who let others determine their future for them, who slid over the top of the Doom Loop. Even though everyone may know they have plateaued, plateauing tells only part of the story.

Faulty thinking, not plateauing, is what usually traps people. If Rhonda could look at her situation from a fresh perspective, she'd have a better chance of escaping her trap. The key for people who are trapped like Rhonda is to get back to Quadrant I or II. Here are some tactics for cycling back:

- Restore your vitality and energy by putting your own needs on a front burner—both on and off the job. See yourself as worthy and capable.
- Combat your own faulty and option-limiting thinking by talking over your situation with a career management professional or a senior member of your field. Read two or three good self-help books and pinpoint how your thinking differs from the approaches they suggest.
- Recognize certain old learning and attitudes as villains that can rob you of your future career satisfaction.
- Study your target mosaic; look for skill sets that still hook your enthusiasm.
- Do something new that promotes Quadrant I learning—like taking on a new work project or volunteering for a task force or work team.
- Follow and expand your Quadrant I and II interests both in and out of work.
- Get involved with all manner of new things, people, and activities.
- Network with people who love to think about new ideas and possibilities.
- Join a professional or personal support group.
- Brainstorm a new capstone, skill set, or work environment.

For Rhonda, joining a working parents' neighborhood support group was an effective tactic. Even though she couldn't hear how defeated she sounded, strangers could. They urged her to find something she wanted to do and get involved. She volunteered to teach English as a second language to new immigrants. She wasn't overjoyed by the task at first, but it was a Quadrant I activity. Using her old Quadrant III and IV telecommunications and computer skills, she designed learning programs and developed several prototypes for software featuring self-directed learning. The challenge of designing new programs reenergized her. She began talking about innovation, not boredom. "Dustout" became a thing of the past. Rhonda used her spare time at work (and there was a lot of it) to perfect her designs. A year later, she landed a Quadrant I job as a product development manager for a small telecommunications company.

It takes courage to risk change, particularly when you feel trapped. Challenge your own ambivalence and self-doubt by taking any reasonable action that leads to greater involvement and new experience.

Transformed

"I'm not the same person I used to be."

Like the hero of Kafka's story "The Metamorphosis," you wake up one morning to find yourself transformed. Although you know it didn't happen all at once, such personal change is still unsettling. For better or worse, you have a compelling new perspective that won't go away. No matter what quadrant you happen to be in, you have entered a Quadrant III zone that extends well beyond work life. The old career capstone, not to mention the old life-style, just won't do.

Transformation doesn't occur simply because you're getting older. It piggybacks on all kinds of other life crises—job elimination, downsizing, the birth of a child, the loss of an important love relationship, divorce, an empty nest, illness, and other factors. Transformations are personal reactions to the stark realities of life teamed with the basic human need to find a meaningful, whole, and balanced life-style.

As you can see from the checklist on the next page, transformations yield new beliefs, yearnings, limits, and options.

Take a minute and make a list of the statements you've checked. Your list describes more than the symptoms of your discontent. It defines the beginnings of a generic action plan for managing your future growth. It's likely to contain the following transformational themes:

TRANSFORMED: A DIAGNOSTIC CHECKLIST

1. _____ You find yourself questioning your old values (life-style, achievements).
2. _____ You've recently gone through a life crisis (divorce, illness, loss of a family member, loss of job).
3. _____ Promotions don't mean as much to you as they used to.
4. _____ You no longer feel as compelled to prove yourself to anyone.
5. _____ Holding a job you enjoy is more important than high pay or status.
6. _____ You want to express who you are in your life work.
7. _____ You don't want to waste any more time working on trivial projects.
8. _____ You want to use your capacities to make an impact.
9. _____ You find you're no longer willing to put up with office politics (personalities, games).
10. _____ Your priorities have shifted.
11. _____ You feel burned out.
12. _____ More than ever, you want to lead a balanced life.
13. _____ You long to spend more time involved with your family (spouse, children, friends).
14. _____ You are concerned with making a contribution to society (humanity, science).
15. _____ You want to express your individuality (creativity, ideas).
16. _____ Having more private time for yourself is important.
17. _____ You want to donate more time to community service (boards, volunteer work, the arts, the environment).
18. _____ Taking better care of yourself (fitness, diet, meditation, travel) is a priority.
19. _____ You have the urge to improve your mind (with reading, courses, a new degree).
20. _____ Spirituality (religion) has become more central to you.
21. _____ You want to put more fun in your life (play more, develop a hobby).
22. _____ You would like to mentor, teach, coach others.
23. _____ You want to try something altogether new and different.
24. _____ Your focus has shifted to how many years you have left to accomplish something, and you feel a sense of time urgency.
25. _____ You're excited about the future, but afraid to change.
26. _____ Other: _____

- a diminished passion for traditional achievement
- a shift of emphasis to balancing career and personal life
- a reevaluation of what's really worth doing

These themes often surface at midcareer. When you've just left school, you're driven by the need to prove yourself. You're consumed with learning the rules of the game, achieving, and getting ahead. This leaves you little time for quiet reflection on the meaning of things. These years are rich and productive as well as turbulent. Tough situations test your limits, develop your sensitivity, and force you to establish personal boundaries. As time passes, you learn what you're made of, what you're willing to put up with. And as you face your own failures—your trustworthiness, your loyalties, your likes and dislikes become clear.

Finally, this readies you for transformation. You're still learning about yourself—learning things above and beyond the dictates of a particular boss or workplace. This process may be stressful, but it helps you realign your career strategy with your changing perception of yourself.

Using Transformation to Reset Your Strategy

Whenever you alter your core beliefs or values, you see the world with fresh eyes for a time—however brief. You've broken out of the mold. You may no longer like what your company, your job, or your way of life stands for. From the perspective of your values, you find yourself deep in the pit of Quadrant IV. You may feel angry, disillusioned or burned out. Eventually, you resist maintaining the charade. The path to your capstone—even if it's short—no longer seems worth pursuing. Something in you is saying, "Okay, I've experienced life one way; now it's time to experience it another way."

Let's look at a few of the discontents that are part and parcel of being transformed and how you can use them to reset your midcareer strategy.

Diminished Passion for Traditional Achievement

By midlife, or as a result of some critical life experience, your emphasis begins to shift. Getting your career ticket punched the right way isn't the only game in town. After the latest corporate restructuring and body count, you wonder, "Is this all there is?"

The struggle to reach your capstone no longer seems worth all the sacrifice. You've lost your passion for work and question the trade-offs. You begin to magnify trivial career blocks. Suddenly, your hobbies and long-ignored outside interests seem more important and more compelling than your job. It would be nice to spend more time with your kids, the community, your lawn. It's as if the less developed parts of yourself are breaking through and clamoring for recognition.

Don't be over-critical of yourself. You need a new way to evaluate yourself that keeps pace with the person you are becoming. Try seeing yourself as becoming balanced, not soft. Pay attention to your new interests. They're valuable clues. When your appetite for achievement begins to flag, one re-energizing strategy is:

- **Shift gears and embark on a search for Quadrant I interests, skills, and experiences not directly related to your job.**

Even though these kinds of interests are emerging not from work, but from your personal development—they are significant. Consider ways to incorporate these values in Quadrant I or II of your work life. Seek a few challenging new work projects that won't adversely affect your standing in the office. If you fail at a project, don't stop trying. Look outside work for ways to explore your new interests. Try professional and community boards. Resist the urge to downplay these interests. Remember, they might point the way to a new, more satisfying capstone.

One top financial officer became involved in teaching disabled children. Ultimately, this experience led him to a new degree and a career in human resource training. There are many ways to achieve; you may be entering a new realm.

A Shift to Balancing Career and Personal Life

Most high achievers don't lead particularly balanced lives. They make trade-offs, and one is saying good-bye to personal time with friends and family. Marathon work hours, airport leapfrog, and taking your briefcase to bed do little to enhance the quality of family life.

For years, professional women have struggled to balance it all. During the late 1970s and early 1980s, I used to conduct workshops on this theme. My audiences were mobs of exhausted women searching for clues on how to excel as executives, parents, and wives while keeping fit and doing Book-of-the-Month Club. I told them to forget it. There aren't enough hours in the day. You have to set priorities and live by them.

What's different today is that both professional men and women are confronting these issues, and at every stage of their careers. Young people complain about the egregious demands their companies place on them; they want more time for their families, to work out, to sit and meditate, to play with the dog.

For most people, the issue of balance becomes crucial at midcareer. Maybe you're downsized out of a job or you receive a long-sought-after promotion and find it's not what you expected or that it's too lonely at the top. At this point, you realize you are much more than your career. A Los Angeles public official deciding against reelection declared that his job was "not as much fun as other things these days. . . . Simply put, my priorities have changed. Quite frankly, over the past few weeks, I have been more interested in the birth of my grandchild rather than . . . reelection" (*Los Angeles Times*, March 13, 1990).

Successful midcareer women may face another agenda. If proving themselves in the world had been an all-encompassing priority, they may now crave time to build a personal life. As one top accountant tersely remarked about her personal life: "I want one."

Transformation requires honoring these shifts in priorities and figuring out how to implement them. It requires commitment and tenacity. Old habits die hard. Assign scheduled time for friends and family. Do the same with intimacy. Eschew or delegate obligations that keep you at the office late into the evening or otherwise interfere with your new priorities.

Gain balance by seeking new arenas beyond your career. Make a list of skills you rarely use in your job but might enjoy, and target them for development. If your job consists of a boring routine, use personal time to involve yourself in conceptual thinking, creativity, spontaneity—take a writing course or start to travel. If you work with things, participate in activities that give you high-intensity interaction with people—join lively social groups or volunteer to serve on a board.

The strategy for achieving balance is:

- **Earmark balance as a personal capstone and develop a target mosaic that specifies the skills you need to achieve it.**

At midcareer, allowing your job to be the sole definition of yourself is a costly strategic error.

Questioning Old Values: What Is Worth Doing?

You used to be one of the gang. You cared about being visible, playing office politics, increasing the company's productivity—all the good things. No more. All these things have lost their meaning.

Your sudden lack of interest might be the result of a specific precipitating event: a friend has been fired, you've gotten caught in political crossfire, your company has been raided. Or there might be a nonspecific cause: accumulated events or amalgams of personal growth and professional experience can catalyze a crisis of values.

Whatever the cause, you can experience serious discontent before your capstone even if you have a capstone that fits your skill preferences. It can happen even if you have the ideal Quadrant II job!

The lesson here is:

If the content of your work has lost meaning, you might as well be in Quadrant IV.

Any line of inquiry that helps clarify what's important for you will help redirect your career back on a satisfactory track. Ask yourself value-focused questions, such as:

- Who are my personal heroes?
- What do I admire most about these people?

Your answers will provide clues to what's meaningful to you. Read biographies and carefully note your reactions to the accomplishments and values of their subjects. Consider how you can incorporate some of these values into your career. General values—courage, vision, compassion—suggest that you tinker with your behavior rather than your job description. Content-centered values—like working with handicapped children or saving the environment—will probably require you to go back to the drawing board for a new capstone.

Another method of clarifying what's worth doing involves writing ten statements on ten index cards. Each statement should describe what you want to accomplish in life during the next five to ten years. Next, take a second set of ten cards and write a statement on each describing what you want to accomplish in your career during that same period.

Discuss both sets of cards with a friend or someone you trust. Look for patterns and similarities. Rank each group according to what is most important for you to achieve. Identify the core values that correspond to each achievement. The strategy for dealing with value shifts, therefore, is:

• **Identify your emerging life values and incorporate them into a newly recast career capstone.**

Incorporating values into capstones isn't as difficult as you might imagine. There are many shortcuts. A top salesperson, whose transformation included a desire to help people with AIDS, made a job shift from regional sales manager in computers to regional sales manager of a pharmaceutical firm experimenting with a new drug for AIDS. This integrated his emerging shift in values with his career development and gave both legitimacy. As a result, he's remotivated and back to Quadrant I.

Your values can become integral to your capstone in many ways. Switching a capstone from a profit to a nonprofit arena sometimes achieves this goal. Under other circumstances, realignment will require more arduous or dramatic measures, such as new Quadrant I education and retraining related to a new field or new capstone.

In either instance, when your new capstone captures your quest for meaning and balance, you will have used your transformation to stem the crisis of discontent before capstone.

Aligning Work with Transformation

Jody Greenberg had always been a high achiever. Only thirty-nine years old, she was marketing director for a major jewelry house. Jody was single-minded in her pursuit of a capstone: president of a jewelry or accessories division. But she began questioning the trade-offs she had made along with the values and life-style she had bought into. She was constantly on the road, and even her outrageous phone bills had failed to salvage her last three love relationships. Jody enjoyed travel, but she was beginning to wonder if what she was doing was worth the cost. Although she ascribed her chronic backaches to the strain of carrying her computer and sample cases, her physician blamed her spate of minor health problems on work-related stress. Despite her high business profile, Jody felt isolated and alone in her work and in her life. While Jody was charging around the country like a lone ranger, her old college buddies had settled into tried-and-true patterns of community or family life. No one called her; room service and CNN gave structure and continuity to Jody's weeknights. Despite her imminent promotion, Jody was wearing out. At the same time, she felt intellectually understimulated by the industry. She wondered whether her efforts really mattered. And she longed for a circle of peers outside work.

Jody's midcareer malaise derived from her personal transformation. And it was this transformation—not the lack of learning and challenge in her job—that pushed her over the top of the Doom Loop into Quadrant III.

Jody was discontent in that quadrant, and the only way to return to the Doom Loop's friendly side was to align new work challenges with her emerging values and personal growth. Tactics useful to someone in Jody's position are:

- Focus on what is important to you; be clear about what is and is not worth doing.
- Take time to reflect on who you are and what you want in life: read, consult professionals, hire a psychologist to conduct a personality assessment.
- Look for new ways to increase your self-awareness.
- Analyze your capstone to see how it still fits your values.
- Adapt your skills and knowledge to work compatible with your values.
- Find new ways to contribute to your organization, community, family.
- Seek Quadrant I learning through courses and volunteer work.
- Take steps to realign who you have become with what you do for a living.

Jody decided that her lack of intellectual stimulation and dwindling circle of friends were key sources of discontent.

Rather than quit her job, she enrolled in an executive MBA program—a relatively low-risk, low-profile move designed not to attract her employer's attention. She now had more reason to limit her travel and remain in town. This gave her a chance to develop a few university friends. Though many of the courses were old hat, one course in cultural diversity intrigued Jody. She liked the idea of managing cultural differences in a business setting and using her business skills in a rapidly changing global economy. Prospects looked good enough for her to switch to a master's degree program in international business with an emphasis on cultural diversity. This shift provided Jody with a career direction more compatible with her values—her desire to challenge her mind with new ideas, to develop a circle of peers, to make a contribution beyond the bottom line, to tackle larger global issues, and to work with more diverse people. Jody was back in a Quadrant I career track with a redefined capstone when she took a job as president of an international marketing division.

To head back to Quadrant I, first identify what your personal transformation is about. Then realize that Quadrant I comes in many packages. Consider all kinds of available options like job trading, opportunities for cross-training, serving on task forces, and taking on temporary projects, as well as more radical career shifts. If you can think of no way to bring your job into alignment with your personal transformation and you are unable or unwilling to make a career switch right now, develop new relationships, interests, and experiences outside work that stretch your perspectives in ways compatible with your values.

BACK TO THE FUTURE: TURNING PRE-CAPSTONE DOOM INTO ZOOM

Are you blocked, trapped, or transformed?

Once you pinpoint your pre-capstone category, you'll still need to find your way back to Quadrant I challenges. This requires that you:

- decide whether or not to redefine your capstone
- get yourself back into Quadrants I and II

Let's examine these two steps. Then I'll give you the final strategy: using career accelerators that will speed you away from your discontent before a capstone crisis hits.

CAPSTONE DIAGNOSTICS: TO REDEFINE OR NOT TO REDEFINE?

You're probably itching to trash your capstone. Why not? You're unhappy, exasperated, desperate. But before you do anything dramatic, take a deep breath and think it through. Don't be impulsive. Your Quadrant III status combined with other life crises may be distorting your perspective.

Therefore, be methodical. Conduct a thorough diagnosis of what is wrong with your capstone. Matrix map, then analyze your current capstone skills—the ones you already possess that are relevant to your capstone—by Doom Loop quadrant. Then do the same for the skills you still need to reach your capstone, the ones in your target mosaic.

Analyzing Your Current Capstone Skills

List the skills you've already acquired in pursuit of your capstone. Then assess these skills. How do they rate according to your own current preferences and performance?

CAPSTONE SKILLS YOU ALREADY HAVE

Skills	Good At	Not Good At	Like	Don't Like
1.				
2.				
3.				
4.				
5.				
6.				
7.				
8.				
9.				

Once you've rated your skills, plot your ratings on the Doom Loop grid. Where do most of your skills fall?

What If Your Skills Cluster in Quadrant II?

Sometimes this type of capstone skill analysis yields surprises. Even though your acquired skills fall in Quadrant II, which should make you feel happy and satisfied, your work is bereft of personal meaning. You feel lukewarm about your capstone. You're tempted to hit the restart button. Wait a minute. Resist this impulse, at least at the outset.

Instead, try a more playful approach. List your Quadrant II capstone skills. Brainstorm about how to apply them to a job that will be more personally satisfying, more in line with your values or mission. The goal is a lofty one: to identify what is really worth doing in life. It's easy to get so caught up in other people's shoulds and oughts that you overlook what's meaningful to you.

Use this vital knowledge to tinker with your capstone until you get a match that feels right. Depending on the issues, switching industries, organizational cultures or seeking counseling may be a smarter solution than tossing out your old capstone. It's important to identify the causes of your Quadrant II discontent so that you don't reinvent the same problem in a brand-new capstone. Because new capstones aren't always the panaceas we hope for, you may well find yourself in the same crisis a few years down the road.

What If Your Skills Cluster in Quadrants II and III?

If your capstone-related skills cluster in Quadrants II and III, congratulate yourself. That's where they should be. At this point they should be your old new skills. The competence you've developed in these skills should keep them from falling into either Quadrant I or Quadrant IV. You'll be in a good position to tackle the remaining Quadrant I learning you'll need to qualify for your capstone.

But what if you're still miserable? Then look further. Examine the capstone skills you've placed in Quadrants III and IV. Do some of those skills repulse you? For some people, even a few rotten apples spoil the whole bunch—and a few hated skills far outweigh all the positive ones.

If this is the case, don't automatically abandon your capstone. Maybe there's a way to minimize the skills you deplore. Rather than more dedication, consider more delegation. Or restructure your job in a way that shifts the priorities away from these troublesome skills. Consider hiring an assistant or learning how a computer or other advanced technologies might help. Or talk to people in other work settings or industries to see whether you can find an environment where those hated Quadrant III and IV skills aren't as important.

What If Your Skills Cluster in Quadrants III and IV?

When most of the capstone skills you've mastered turn out to be wholly owned subsidiaries of III and IV, it may be a fine time for trading capstones. No matter how good you are at what you do, you can't stand doing it. It's time for a change. But before you pack your bags and head for the nearest new capstone, take some time to analyze the remaining skills in your target mosaic to ascertain what you still need to acquire.

WHAT'S LEFT TO LEARN: ANALYZING YOUR TARGET MOSAIC

Take a look at the target mosaic for your capstone. Whatever your quadrant of the Doom Loop, these are the skills that will determine what you will be learning and how you will be feeling in the months or years ahead. So don't make any final decision about a capstone until you've analyzed the skills you've yet to master.

CAPSTONE SKILLS YOU STILL NEED

Target Mosaic Skills	Good At	Not Good At	Like	Don't Like
1.				
2.				
3.				
4.				
5.				
6.				
7.				
8.				
9.				

The Skills You Need Are in Quadrant I

If the remaining skills in your target mosaic are in Quadrant I—rejoice! You still have plenty of learning and challenge ahead.

But what if you're apathetic about the prospect of mastering these remaining skills? If you're close to achieving your capstone, you might be experiencing the end-of-the-journey blues. Reaching a capstone is like finding the pot of gold at the end of the rainbow. And yet, as you approach your target, it's natural to resist giving up the quest, the old dream. Why? Because your daily progress toward your capstone has given structure and meaning to your life. It's kept you focused, even sane. What will you do without it after you arrive at your capstone? As people near their goals, progress often becomes slower and more strained. Paradoxically they encounter more, not less, resistance. Anticipating the end of what you started so long ago can be bittersweet. You may wonder: What's left for me? Am I too old to start something new?

If this fits you, confront your fears head on. Talk them through with a professional or a good friend. Then, if it feels right, push on through your fears toward your capstone. Once you achieve your capstone, your fears might dissipate. If not, you'll still have an undeniable feeling of accomplishment, and a new capstone could be in the offing. The next chapter will help with that.

The Skills You Need Are in Quadrant IV

No wonder you want to bail out. If the skills you've already acquired cluster in Quadrants II and III, it looks as if you've saved the worst for last. If so, prepare yourself to tackle them one at a time. Break the remaining skills down into small, manageable chunks. Try to pick up these skills through out-of-town seminars in pleasant places and through short-term projects. A winning tactic is to team these Quadrant IV skills, whenever possible, with Quadrant II skills; a spoonful of sugar helps the medicine go down. If you can integrate the inevitable Quadrant IV skill acquisition that comes with any complex capstone in your overall plan, you'll overcome the last obstacle that stands between you and your goal.

All the Skill Sets Are in Quadrants III and IV

If most of the skills you already have or need to acquire reside in Quadrants III and IV, you have undeniable evidence that it's time for a change. Go back to the drawing board. Redefine your capstone by analyzing your current pattern of preferences, values, and motivators. What are you excited about doing? Go back and read the chapter on capstone power. If your career satisfaction matters, take your time and choose wisely and well.

HITTING THE MID-CAREER ACCELERATORS

When you're discontent before capstone, you try to disengage from your current work by slamming on your career brakes to control the damage. Midcareer accelerators provide an alternative—they are high-energy tactics that turn doom into zoom.

Such accelerators are critical. Blocked, trapped, or transformed, you need a new way of seeing yourself, a fresh perspective to catalyze Quadrant I action and energy. Let's look at two key accelerators.

Career Accelerator 1: A Free-Agent Stance

The law of diminishing returns reigns at midcareer. It seems unfair. You've gained so much experience and wisdom, yet you merely seem to be trading less upward mobility for more and more responsibility. This doesn't mean there are no more golden opportunities—just that fewer exist at this stage and no one can be counted on to lead you to them. There's no guardian angel hovering at the top of the Loop to stop you from plateauing in Quadrant III or dropping into the abyss of Quadrant IV. You're on your own, and the sooner you acknowledge that fact, the faster you'll be able to capitalize on it.

Taking a free-agent stance means taking responsibility for your fate. As a free agent, you're a self-managing career unit. You must consciously use your own resources and ingenuity to create the right future. This requires you to become investigative, adaptive, and self-reliant. Free-agent skills are nomadic skills that travel well; they're no-nonsense survival skills. But as important as these skills are, they're no more important than the following attitudes of a free agent:

- You see yourself as the entrepreneur or designer of your own career. Your primary mission is successfully managing your own career progress.
- You commit yourself to zigzagging between companies or industries to find new, challenging Quadrant I positions leading to your capstone.
- You stay alert to hidden career opportunities and are willing to take risks to reach them.
- You believe you deserve to succeed.
- You are comfortable with promoting yourself.

Since this approach calls for you to market and sell yourself, you will need to be proficient in a number of self-promotional skills essential at midcareer. These include:

- **Investigative skills**—These skills are integral to promoting your own success. They require that you thoroughly research the facts, the players, and their various personalities, so that you grasp who has what at stake in which outcomes. If you haven't done your investigative homework, your other efforts are likely to fall short of the mark.
- **Advertising skills**—The idea here is that you are your only product, and you need to position your accomplishments to gain product and brand recognition for yourself. This requires learning how to maintain visibility in targeted markets without being seen as a braggart or egoist.
- **Marketing skills**—Your task is to determine the needs of various organizations or people through focused and skillful interviewing, and to figure out how to align their needs with your own.
- **Self-presentation skills**—The challenge here is to empower yourself by controlling as much as is yours to control in any human interaction. This requires that you be exquisitely aware of the impact of how you look and sound, as well as of what you say to others. Learn to pinpoint areas of similarity quickly and connect with people in the first five minutes.
- **Sales skills**—Think of sales skills as the fine art of developing long-term relationships, rather than as hit-and-run contacts. Train yourself to be a good listener, so that you can persuade people that what you have to offer fits their needs, and to have the discipline and structure to close the sale.
- **Networking skills**—These skills allow you to contact many people in diverse social and business settings to ask them for help in exploring your career options. It's true that networking has a strong component of "I'll scratch your back if you'll scratch mine," but it also has high payoff. And it's predicated on goodwill and altruism be-

tween strangers. But when you network, you open the door to reciprocal requests—so be prepared.

Once you get comfortable with these and other free-agent skills, you're likely to find them very useful.

Career Accelerator 2: Building Midcareer Megaskills

When you're first starting out, it makes sense to acquire basic career advancement skills like interpersonal, communication, analytic, production, and political skills. Along with specific technical and professional skills, this mix helps you get ahead early in your career when you're intent on proving yourself.

Now things have changed. Many of your old familiar skills have tumbled over the top of the Loop into Quadrants III and IV. Advancement and technical skills have landed you in your midcareer slot, but they're no longer enough. Confronted with massive cutbacks and middle-management shrinkage, you're likely to face new challenges requiring new abilities to adapt and to cope.

You're expected to take on leadership and entrepreneurial tasks that go well beyond your training and technical competence. As you reach out and try your hand at innovation, negotiation, and coaching, odds are you feel skill-deficient. You face a choice between the challenge of developing your abilities as a senior-level decision-maker and stagnation. You may be called on to resolve complex human problems, take on mentoring functions, empower new work teams, and make other significant contributions to your organization.

This is a tall order for anyone. At midcareer you are a seasoned veteran who knows the world of work. People look to you for advice on new trends and developments. But having spent many years in your job is no guarantee that you will have developed the right kinds of higher-level skills—"megaskills"—to manage these complex midcareer demands. And your company may be of little help. Many organizations fail to recognize that developing these skills in their midcareer employees is just as vital to operational success as training newcomers.

If you're in this position—and especially if you're discontent before capstone—it's time to acquire these midcareer mega-skills. Such skills are high-energy Quadrant I career boosters. Your midcareer success will increasingly depend on your mastery of change-centered megaskills that help you adapt to an unpredictable and turbulent workplace.

No matter what you decide about your capstone—to redefine it or to stick with it—developing megaskills has a high payoff: more meaningful participation in your work.

Look at the following list of the megaskills I've developed in the course of corporate consulting and use it as a guide for deciding which ones you want to target:

QUADRANT I ACCELERATORS: MIDCAREER MEGASKILLS

- **Change management skills**—managing uncertainty with openness and vision
  - *Transition management skills*—helping people create bridges across situations involving loss and change
  - *Crisis management skills*—bringing reason and direction to chaotic change
  - *Team-building skills*—transforming individuals with disparate self-interests into a unified, goal-directed team
- **Adaptability skills**—overcoming old learning to achieve situational flexibility
  - *Reframing skills*—redefining situations in ways that break old patterns of seeing things
  - *Learning skills*—viewing every situation as an opportunity to gain new insight and skill
- **Trouble-shooting skills**—identifying problems and marshaling resources to find new resolutions

—*Problem-solving skills*—gathering data, making and testing hypotheses, reviewing options, choosing and implementing action

—*Conflict-resolution skills*—finding common underlying interests among opposing positions or factions and moving to defined agreement

—*Set-breaking skills*—seeing things in openended, creative, or unusual ways

—*Consulting skills*—acting as a facilitator, enabling individuals and groups to identify problems and work toward agreed-upon resolutions

- **Esprit de corps skills**—building ownership and participation with key others

  —*Leadership skills*—conveying a vision and influencing others

  —*Collaborative skills*—moving from individualistic competition to cooperative problem-solving

  —*Mentoring and coaching skills*—teaching and training Quadrant I colleagues

  —*Feedback skills*—giving and receiving specific information about performance

- **Transcultural skills**—moving beyond ethnocentric boundaries to accept differences

  —*Multicultural skills*—respecting differing cultures, norms, and people reflecting variant values, attitudes, customs, and ways of doing things

  —*Diversity skills*—adapting to a changing workplace with diverse people, norms, roles, behaviors, beliefs, and attitudes differing in key aspects from your own ethnocentric expectations

  —*Adaptability skills*—being sufficiently in command of yourself to achieve situational flexibility without abandoning your core values

Think about your own professional development in terms of these megaskills. Which would be particularly helpful to you to develop at this point in your career, given your particular organization and job? After targeting one or more sets of megaskills, commit your time and effort to building them. They're not instant skills. They take time, experience, and practice. Mastering them might require significant shifts in attitudes and behavior.

Courses, seminars, and books on leadership, organizational development, teamwork, conflict negotiation, creative problem-solving, and cultural diversity are all good starting points. Look for learning experiences that have a strong interactive component, where you can try out what you're learning and get straight feedback from others. Seek out leadership roles on voluntary boards that attract all kinds of people. You won't master midcareer megaskills sitting in a corporate boardroom with a bunch of well-socialized clones intent on maintaining the status quo. Take on assignments involving change and risk. I believe the best places for a novice to master many of the midcareer megaskills are professional associations and community action groups or committees where people are united by a common purpose, and where taking an unpopular or experimental stance won't cost you your job. You may also want to involve yourself in personal growth seminars, retreats, and training that foster new insight and awareness in group settings. Force yourself to spend time with people substantially different from yourself in terms of their political views, nationality, race, sexual orientation. Analyze and learn from your own reactions to these different perspectives. Unpack whatever old baggage you've been carrying that prevents you from hearing the other person's point of view. Stay open. Treat everything that happens as a rich source of data you can learn from.

To become more adaptive you will need the best feedback you can find on how you affect others and on how you are perceived in groups. If you are serious about mastering these midcareer megaskills, hire a career coach or enlist the help of a seasoned mentor. There's no single way to gain these skills, but they are among the most valuable you can learn.

Remember: megaskills are a powerful antidote to discontent before capstone. As you add megaskills to your profile, you'll create new opportunities for meaningful Quadrant I learning. The depth and flexibility these skills foster could make your midcareer blues a distant memory.

■

CHAPTER 10

Doomed at Capstone

I can get all my work done in three hours. Then what? Schmooze for another five? What the hell do I do with the rest of my time?
—President, construction company

It's hard for people to understand how I feel about my job. They envy me. But I'm sick and tired of letting my career define who I am.
—Local TV news reporter

I felt like a fish out of water from the beginning. I never fit this industry. But I toughed it out right to the top. My fantasy? Don't laugh! To be a gardener!
—Plant manager, aeronautics industry

Yesterday someone asked me what I looked forward to. I said 'death.' I want a job where I have control over my life, where I don't have to be a fire fighter. I want a reason to get up in the morning.
—Principal, urban high school

When doom happens at capstone, it's a prime-time career shocker. It seems like a contradiction in terms. How can you possess the prize you've coveted and still feel bad?

The irony of being doomed at capstone is that your best-laid plans have not gone awry. Quite the contrary. You've achieved what you aimed for—a career bull's-eye. That's what makes your predicament all the more inexplicable. The paradox of being doomed at capstone stuns most people. You wonder how you could have struggled so hard for so long to reach your destination, only to find that you've bought a piece of swampland. The road's been long and hard, and you're bitterly disappointed. Whatever happened to happy endings?

To a disinterested onlooker, being "doomed at capstone" may seem an enviable crisis. But for people in the thick of it, these are indeed difficult times. Even though they've achieved their capstones, they suffer a sense of loss and letdown. When no one gives them sympathy for their dilemma, they feel even worse.

Naturally, none of this helps those who are doomed at capstone. Feeling isolated and misunderstood, they respond by leading lives of quiet desperation, defensively stuffing their feelings, buttoning their lips, and secretly dreaming of escape.

If you are in the midst of this crisis, this chapter brings hope. No one has to remain doomed at capstone. Doomed at capstone does not have to mean the end of your journey. An unhappy ending often leads to surprisingly happy new beginnings.

First, however, prevent history from repeating itself by understanding what went wrong. Recognizing the early symptoms of this crisis gives you an edge. Second, be assured that you can retread, not just retreat. Even if you can't make your current capstone work, you can redesign it or find a new one. Third, you can apply a Doom Loop approach to turn this crisis around by infusing your capstone with new Quadrant I skill-building that involves learning and growth. Finally, you may want to take a more radical approach: to move beyond your job description to actively foster more global Quadrant I skill-building in and beyond your organization.

294 THE DOOM LOOP SYSTEM

WHEN THE TOP OF
THE MOUNTAIN ISN'T ENOUGH

People feel doomed at capstone for many reasons—choosing the wrong capstone, arriving too late at an overripe top-of-the-Loop capstone, failing to track their own critical shifts in priorities, encountering unanticipated economic conditions or technological shifts, and so on.

But sometimes the culprit is your own ambition. The top of the mountain just isn't enough. For high achievers, in particular, getting there is more than half the fun. They love the climb. The struggle to reach the next peak imparts direction, structure, and meaning.

If this describes you, consider the implications. Like a mountain climber, you'll enjoy the view for a only brief time before repacking your gear and moving on. Your sights will always be set on the next peak. For you, life at the top is more of a chore than a challenge.

So when you find yourself doomed at capstone, the problem isn't necessarily that you've gone after the wrong capstone or become mired in Quadrant III. It may be that you haven't taken your career strategy far enough. When you fail to plan for a challenging post-capstone work life, you inadvertently doom yourself at capstone.

If learning and challenge are central to who you are, you have two basic alternatives:

- **The standard blue sky option**—moving onward and upward to the next bigger and better capstone.
- **The terra firma option**—staying put and redesigning your current capstone to provide maximum long-term challenge, control, diversity, and learning.

If you're motivated by challenge but unwilling to be a "capstone jumper" the rule is:

When the top of the mountain isn't enough, change the mountain.

The new challenge is to transform your capstone into a personalized learning environment. Look for all kinds of new functions, tasks, roles, and training that interest you. Don't become a victim of work that is too narrowly defined. Fight back. Mount a frontal assault on the natural bent toward career stasis.

Stretch your capstone into a satisfying long-term position by applying the lessons of the Loop:

- See yourself as a free agent responsible for designing your own skill acquisition package.
- Keep your attention focused on what counts: Quadrant I and II learning.
- Target new Quadrant I skills that increase the breadth and depth of your performance and adaptability.
- Target and master higher-level midcareer megaskills.

Remember, reaching your career capstone is no reason to stop acquiring new skills and knowledge. Quite the contrary! To maintain your post-capstone motivation, you will need more Quadrant I and II growth, not less.

What if your organization fails to create opportunities for developing its top-level people? In this kind of culture, doom at capstone becomes a sure thing. High achievers and other ambitious types will go over the top of the Loop into Quadrant III or move on in record time. This has negative implications for everyone.

If this describes your organization and you can't figure out a way to buck the system or enhance your capstone, move on. It's basic self-preservation. But before trashing your current capstone, try it again in a new organization that has a stronger commitment to challenging its work force.

THE DAWNING OF DOOM

Can you be doomed at capstone and not know it? Yes and no. In this crisis you may feel unhappy without entitlement, without legitimate cause. It's a little like being bored in a marriage. It's not a good situation and you know it, but you're also not sure it's a good idea to confront the situation. You worry that your known misery may be preferable to an unknown misery. When you're doomed at capstone you're caught up in an unexpected and nameless life event. That makes it easier to deny the problem. But denying it doesn't make the problem go away.

THE "AGAINST ALL ODDS" PRINCIPLE

Although you're not married to your capstone, you might as well be. The more you've invested in reaching it, the harder it is to face your doom objectively and move on. You've played the Horatio Alger role, only no one's written the sequel. This is when the "against all odds" principle comes into play:

The more uphill your struggle and the more time and education you invested, the greater is your resistance to recognizing that you're doomed in the job you lusted after.

This makes the dawning of doom a slow, painful awakening. Some typical "against all odds" contenders include:

- **Crossovers**—mainly blue- and pink-collar workers who, often at great personal cost, have crossed over into white-collar and professional occupations.
- **Ground-breakers**—mainly women who have gained entry into traditionally male occupations and industries, or

anyone else who is the first of his or her type in a given
field.
* **Minorities**—those who have fought rejection and prej-
udice to pry open doors and gain access to career paths
that were formerly off limits.

Because members of these groups have invested a good
deal of effort as well as their sense of personal identity in
achieving career success—often with little external support—
the stakes for hanging onto their capstones are excruciatingly
high. And, as you might guess, this makes doom at capstone
particularly painful. But the consequences of doom at capstone extend well beyond personal failure for many "against
all odds" types. As role models for those who are inspired by
their successes, they are in a "damned if you do, damned if
you don't" double bind. If they hang onto their acquired status
even though they are doomed, they're likely to be unhappy.
But if they let go and move on they may be seen as quitters.
Or their leaving may be taken as evidence that people of their
kind simply lack the right stuff to manage success. Regardless
of the outcome, their plight attracts unwelcome attention,
both from those who have stuck their necks out to help them
arrive and from the next set of contenders who are hoping
for a storybook ending that will make their own journey easier.
If they respond to their own doom at capstone by taking care
of themselves, these dissatisfied "against all odds" types often
feel they're letting the people down who count on them.
    The "against all odds" category applies to many others be-
sides crossovers, ground-breakers, and minorities. If you've
spent your career struggling against adversity, you may feel
at home in this group. Some people take on the mantle of
the underdog even though they're not in the groups described
above. Like warriors, they may be so used to fighting to survive
that they learn to ignore the pain of their own injuries.
    Being in the "against all odds" category can prolong the
dawning of doom. And the longer the prolonging, the more
time it will take to resolve your plight. Even worse, the longer
you languish, the more likely you are to be mired in a Quadrant III slot where you lack the wherewithal to turn the sit-

uation around. The bottom line for doomed "against all odds" capstone contenders is that it is very painful for them to let go of their capstones and move on.

To put all this in perspective, consider the evolution, dawning, and resolution of Bob Fuller's doom.

THE EVOLUTION

In many ways Bob Fuller seems an unlikely "against all odds" contender. He grew up in a white, middle-class Maryland suburb during the 1940s. His parents wanted him to study medicine, but on the recommendation of his college debating team adviser, he chose law. No one was surprised when he made law review and earned a law degree from a top Eastern school.

But law school was a Quadrant III experience for Bob. Even though he felt trapped, he stuck with it because everyone said it would get better, because he owed $30,000 in loans, because he performed well, and because he was at a loss as to what else he might do.

After graduation, however, Bob's anxiety about his future in his new profession soared so high he felt immobilized. To everyone's amazement, he didn't take the bar exam. Bob was hurting in ways his family couldn't understand. Whenever he thought of going to work, he suffered dizziness, chest pain, and abject panic. With great effort and the help of a supportive friend, Bob got himself into a holding pattern of sorts. He clerked for a judge in a job he termed "the most menial imaginable." Professionally and socially he felt like a pariah; his self-esteem plunged. After spending more than $35,000 on psychotherapy over the course of three years and doing a great deal of soul-searching, he took the bar exam and passed. He pragmatically decided to go into transactional business law in order to restore his family's faith in his abilities to function and earn a respectable living. His capstone was to become a partner in a corporate firm by age thirty-two.

Bob did well. He reached his capstone at age thirty-one. Though he had forfeited his social life during his climb to partner, the status, money, and family approval seemed adequate compensation. Bob felt good about the fact that he was doing what he had originally set out to do. He had made lemonade from lemons and was proud of it.

THE DAWNING AND DENIAL OF DOOM

Bob's expertise in corporate taxes brought him cases that were narrowly defined. His success as a specialist propelled him from Quadrant II to III within four years after making partner.

But it took him eight more years to do anything about it. Bob had paid a high psychological price to reach his capstone. He felt he had too much at stake in his career to change it and that he had no viable alternatives. Everyone was so proud of how well he was doing. He handled the problem by working harder and drinking more.

Bob then entered another phase. He questioned his own judgment. "Why wasn't he happy now?" he asked his therapist. When the therapist suggested that he didn't like his work, Bob gave this knee-jerk response: "That's absurd. I'm good at it. I worked hard to get here. It's what I wanted. Why wouldn't I like it?"

Though Bob hid his desperation from his partners, he had begun to isolate himself. He ceased attending local bar association functions and delegated mountains of work to associates. Eventually the senior partners noticed the change in him.

One partner accurately assessed that Bob was a victim of his specialization and tried to involve him in different cases. Though Bob resisted at first, he finally agreed to do some legwork on a juvenile drug charge as a courtesy to a client. Bob approached it as a Quadrant IV task. But once he got involved, he realized he enjoyed learning something new. As he started to take seminars and courses outside his area, Bob realized there was something better out there. His search for alternatives had begun to breathe life back into him.

Bob decided to pursue public-interest law. But right after

he made this decision, he got cold feet. He went into such a panic over the thought of change that he returned to his specialty.

Bob was miserable. Finally he sat down with a senior partner and talked about his fear of change. At the next partners' meeting, they kicked the issue around and determined that Bob's focus on public-interest law could be a plus for the firm. They encouraged Bob to pursue this field.

But even with this official dispensation for tinkering with his capstone, Bob balked at change.

THE RESOLUTION

What Bob still didn't realize was that public-interest law was not the ultimate solution. It was merely a bridge, allowing him to pass from Quadrant III back to Quadrant I. Without giving up his old capstone or his "against all odds" stance, Bob could tap into what he liked doing and create a new pathway. Intermediate skill-building in public-interest law would open many doors. Finally, Bob took some transitional steps. He began to network with environmental leaders, went to public-policy meetings, and, most important, recouped his energy and involvement in work.

Bob used public-interest law to squelch his doom at capstone. He realized that he enjoyed environmental law but also understood he wanted more hands-on interaction. After researching various career paths, Bob identified a new capstone —director of a wilderness preservation or similar environmental foundation. Although his decision disappointed those who had invested in maintaining Bob's status quo, this capstone would build on his knowledge of law and his analytic skills. It would also provide him with Quadrant I skills and knowledge in management, finance, public relations, and group dynamics. He could use his current capstone position as a springboard to his new capstone. It didn't take long for Bob to resolve his crisis.

DIAGNOSING DOOM

Why spend more time trying to figure out what went wrong? Like most people who accept that they're doomed at capstone, all you're looking for is a quick way out—and soon. Why not just change jobs or choose a new capstone? Why beat a dead horse by diagnosing your doom?

Because you need to get a handle on what led you into this predicament. If you don't identify the problem, you won't know what to fix. If you identify the wrong problem, you'll fix what ain't broke and risk repeating history by making the same mistake over again.

When you're doomed at capstone, there are two probable causes:

- Something is wrong with your capstone.
- You've gone over the top of the Loop into Quadrant III or IV.

Although these problems can intertwine like a double helix, each requires a different remedy. Let's take a few moments to sort out and identify the hallmarks of your doom at capstone.

CAPSTONES THAT DOOM YOU

You're not just doomed in your job; you're doomed in your capstone. To understand how this happened, review the list of capstone problems on the next page and mark the ones that apply to you.

Your Capstone Is Wrong (Items 1 to 4)

You bought a ticket to the wrong destination. Now you're there, and you have to figure out what to do next. If you can determine why you chose the wrong capstone—lack of self-knowledge, limited real-world experience, satisfying other

TYPICAL CAPSTONE PROBLEMS

1. ____ You chose the wrong career capstone.
2. ____ You allowed yourself to be chosen for the wrong career capstone.
3. ____ You let the organization groom you according to its needs, not your own.
4. ____ You confused your occupation or professional identity with a capstone.
5. ____ You chose a near-term, top-of-the-Loop capstone.
6. ____ You disregarded challenge and chose a Quadrant III capstone.
7. ____ You disregarded your preferences and chose a Quadrant IV capstone.
8. ____ You stayed too long in your capstone.
9. ____ You outgrew your capstone.
10. ____ You put your efforts into Quadrant III maintenance, not growth.
11. ____ You failed to deliberately enrich your capstone.
12. ____ You forgot to design a new post-capstone capstone.
13. ____ Other: _____
14. ____ Other: _____

people's expectations, taking the most expedient route—then you'll know what to avoid the next time.

It may be that you didn't choose the wrong capstone, but that someone else chose the wrong one for you. It could have been a parent, a teacher, a spouse, a mentor, or a company. Although many companies develop their employees, the way a given company does this may not be right for you. If you allow yourself to be shaped by others' agendas, you can wake up one morning to find yourself in the wrong capstone.

If you're a professional, you may have confused your capstone (a prosecuting attorney) with your professional identity (a lawyer). As a result, professional identity becomes an ersatz capstone that creates further confusion, since you may have landed in the wrong job within the right profession. The solution may be not to switch fields but to identify your real capstone.

What helps? In all these situations, the key is to be aware

of your own needs and to resist other people's gratuitous advice. Their counsel is more likely to reflect their needs than yours. Place a priority on knowing your own personality, preferences, interests, motivations, and values. The right capstone should fit you like a glove. It should let you express who you are through your work. If you're doomed at your capstone, assess how that capstone fits these priorities. If it doesn't fit, refuse to prolong the agony—find a capstone that does.

Analyzing the needs your current capstone doesn't satisfy can be a shortcut to understanding what your next capstone should offer. The following checklist shows needs that, if unmet, can speed doom at capstone.

Decide which unmet needs are most important to you. Analyze this information and use it to design a more fulfilling capstone and as a standard for evaluating your next capstone choices.

UNMET NEEDS ASSOCIATED WITH DOOM AT CAPSTONE

1. ___ Achievement	11. ___ Persuading	21. ___ Stability
2. ___ Caretaking	12. ___ Analyzing	22. ___ Camaraderie
3. ___ Competing	13. ___ Helping	23. ___ Stimulation
4. ___ Order	14. ___ Belonging	24. ___ Meaning
5. ___ Connectedness	15. ___ Learning	25. ___ Leadership
6. ___ Contributing	16. ___ Coaching	26. ___ Compensation
7. ___ Collaborating	17. ___ Adventure	27. ___ Security
8. ___ Controlling self	18. ___ Organizing	28. ___ Privacy
9. ___ Controlling others	19. ___ Recognition	29. ___ Autonomy
10. ___ Innovating	20. ___ Predictability	30. ___ Status

Other unmet needs: _____
_____
_____

Your Capstone Is in the Wrong Quadrant (Items 5 to 7)

No career capstone should last forever. But the right capstone should contain sufficient Quadrant I challenge and

Quadrant II satisfaction to keep you happy and satisfied for years to come.

A common problem leading to early doom at capstone is choosing a low-risk, short-stretch capstone incestuously close to your current level of expertise. If a top-of-the-Loop job is your capstone, doom is right around the corner. Sometimes this happens when you're blocked on your way to a high-challenge capstone. You end up in a holding pattern of various Quadrant II jobs that are satisfying and sufficiently related to your capstone to keep you content in the short run. Unfortunately, by the time you finally succeed in reaching your capstone with its long-awaited panoply of power and status, it's too little too late. You're overqualified and bored in Quadrant III.

Whatever the reasons, choosing a Quadrant III capstone leads to near certain doom, but many people choose it anyway. If you're more concerned about security, pay, or factors other than challenge and satisfaction, the Quadrant III capstone might tempt you. It's a safe harbor for those unwilling to take risks or make mistakes. Although this strategy lowers your anxiety for the time being, you eventually pay a high price for taking this kind of position—failure to fulfill your potential, inability to use all your skills and talents, and first-degree doom at capstone.

What about Quadrant IV capstones? Surprisingly, lots of people actually choose them. Workaholics and high achievers are likely candidates. If you're more interested in proving yourself than in being happy or satisfied in your work, Quadrant IV capstones offer you a chance to be a masochistic learner—as you master skills you neither like nor are good at.

You may choose a Quadrant IV capstone for other reasons, too. For example:

- You progressed into Quadrant IV by staying in your capstone too long.
- You have little expectation that your work should be satisfying.
- You feel incompetent.

- You have a history of paying too little attention to your own needs.
- You feel this is all you deserve.
- You can't see any other options.

If you landed in a Quadrant IV capstone because of poor career strategy teamed with low self-confidence, it's unlikely you'll be able to marshal the energy you need to bail out on your own. To get free, you may need to lean on others and get support until your confidence rises. Although you're still in charge of yourself, going it alone is a serious error right now.

Here are a few remedies for being doomed at the top of the Loop, or in Quadrant III and IV capstones:

- **Enrich the capstone**—Use whatever means possible to innovate and integrate Quadrant I and II learning and activities into your daily work.
- **Develop yourself**—Look beyond your career capstone; formulate educational and personal capstones grounded in Quadrant I learning. Seek whatever coaching and counseling you need to gain important insights into the ways you have developed and changed.
- **Choose a new capstone(s)**—Seek Quadrant I and II capstones that are sufficiently complex and challenging to sustain your needs for growth and adaptability over a period of years. Weigh how important what you are doing is to who you are and what you value in life. Ask yourself hard questions like, "How will I feel fifteen years from now about having spent so much of my life in this type of work?"

Capstone Fever (Items 8 to 10)

You stayed too long and outgrew your original preferences. Now you have a bad case of capstone fever. You're itching to try something, anything, new. Your need to change is counterbalanced by a lingering mixture of constraints holding you

306 | THE DOOM LOOP SYSTEM

in place. You may still hope the situation will get better, or think leaving is an admission of failure, or simply feel unable to muster the momentum to get going. In other words, you're stuck.

Or the fever's course may simply follow Doom Loop dynamics. With the passage of time and the gaining of experience, your Quadrant II capstone has become a Quadrant III capstone. As you go over the top of the Loop, you shift your attention from proving yourself to holding your ground—you guard against slipping into Quadrant IV.

What to do? Move in the direction of what you want yet fear—change. No magic wand will appear to make things better. Instigating positive change takes will and motivation, and you're likely to be uncomfortable with the change at first. Serious growth-producing change is rarely easy.

Realize this and do it anyway. Force yourself to explore new opportunities and challenges. I've talked about the need to make changes in small, manageable steps, and that certainly applies here. Don't expect your colleagues or family to be of much help. They may be more resistant to change than you are! Depending on the severity of your capstone fever, hire a consultant or a therapist, or find a friend or peer who has weathered a similar bout and can help you through yours.

Post-Capstone Paralysis (Items 11 and 12)

Once you've reached your capstone, you may become so immersed in the daily grind that you forget to keep planning for your future. Whether you plan for it or not, the future is waiting for you. By failing to plan, you've discovered a dangerous shortcut to being doomed at capstone. Forget happy endings. Once you've reached your capstone, you must continue to reach even further. Arriving at a coveted capstone feels good, but it's hardly the end of the road. Things change; people change; you change. If you haven't examined your "what next" options and taken appropriate action, you could contract a bad case of post-capstone paralysis.

The antidote is a solid post-capstone plan. Try enriching

your Quadrant I and II skills and developing new interim or long-term capstones that you can work toward right now.

AN OUNCE OF PREVENTION: AVOIDING THE CAPSTONE BUSTERS

Some career settings are more likely to trigger doom at capstone than others. If you're in one of these situations, forewarned is forearmed. Let's look at three relatively common ones: the family business, the entrepreneurial venture, and the professional position.

Groomed and Doomed: The Family Business

You have a guaranteed job and you instinctively know the ropes. You've been watching how the business operates all your life. They're not likely to fire you, and there's usually a clear-cut capstone agreed upon in advance: heir to the throne.

When Danny Peters joined his father and grandfather in a multistate auto parts business right after obtaining his business degree, he started out doing inventory and odd jobs, working his way up through sales and finance before taking root in the firm with his promotion to general sales manager. At age thirty-six, Danny became the company's vice president. When his dad retired four years later, Danny became head of the company.

All appearances to the contrary, Danny was doomed at capstone.

What went wrong? As Danny put it to me, "How much time do you have?" For one thing, Danny's grandfather still showed up at work every day and was a vocal critic of the changes Danny instituted, including computerized inventory control, extensive trade advertising, and the hiring of outside consultants. Danny's father also expressed his displeasure with his son's newfangled management style.

Danny learned the hard way that the family business breeds

accountability without authority. It's tough for older family members to hand younger ones the reins.

Without functional autonomy, you never learn to become your own person. You feel more like a child trying to please Mommy or Daddy than an independent businessperson. Someone's always looking over your shoulder. What's going on is the *real* family business:

- hand-to-hand combat over roles and turf
- resistance to passing the torch to the next generation
- difficulty in seeing the heir apparent as an adult, rather than as a recalcitrant child
- ongoing struggles for power and control
- business- and family-splitting feuds
- raw feelings grounded in unresolved family conflicts
- doubts about the heir's ability to protect and defend the family fortune

Familiarity is an Achilles' heel. As you struggle to prove yourself, you overreact to criticism and lack of appreciation. No matter how sophisticated you are in dealing with strangers, relatives tap into the old reptilian part of your brain, evoking unbridled rage.

You take a predictable journey over the top of the Doom Loop. Since you've been groomed for the job from the time you could walk, daily challenges turn into dull Quadrant III or IV tasks.

Extricating yourself from the hold of a family business is hardly kid stuff. Besides losing the perks and status associated with any capstone, deciding to bail out brings you face to face with:

- your family's reactions to the news
- charges of desertion and ingratitude
- real issues regarding the survival of the business
- the difficulty of trying to extricate your identity from the business
- your own limited work experience outside the business

What should you do? Don't clean out your desk and leave. Instead, give yourself some breathing space. How? Figure out what you want to happen next. Part I was theirs; Part II is yours. Develop a succession plan for the business. Look for Quadrant I skills to add to your broadened multipurpose skill profile. Acquire strong outside business contacts that promise new opportunity. Find a mentor in a different line of work. Pump up your educational credentials through seminars, courses, or a new degree.

Then make a decision. Either reshape your capstone within the business and return to Quadrants I and II, or exit to seek new challenges and job satisfaction elsewhere. If you leave, this may represent something far more significant than a job or capstone change. For the first time you go head to head with the major life challenge of independently defining who you are and what you want. Take your time in this process. Keep a journal; pay attention to your thoughts and feelings. And don't make the mistake of thinking you have to isolate yourself from the goodwill and interest of others to attain your independence.

Doomed by Your Own Hand: Entrepreneurship

Entrepreneurs are a feisty lot, willing to put their egos on the line for a chance to run their own show. The act of entrepreneurship propels independent businesspeople into high-risk, high-challenge Quadrant I learning. The problem is that the same traits that drive entrepreneurs to succeed on their own—high ego investment, self-reliance, autonomy, risk-taking, and relentless dedication to success—can also doom them to doing it all by themselves.

Kim Schwartz fell victim to this syndrome. While still working for a major publisher, Kim dreamed of running her own public relations firm. A gutsy and self-empowered go-getter, she was willing to bet the ranch on doing a better job—her way.

"Failure just isn't in my vocabulary," she maintained. While Kim's headstrong "can do" attitude permitted her to take risks, it also caused her to downplay them. Although she had acquired considerable Quadrant II and III skills in the publishing industry, starting her own public relations firm put her at the bottom of the Doom Loop (for both Quadrant I and IV skills). The facts were that she had no management, finance, or business acumen.

But Kim was undaunted. Like many high achievers, she thrived on high-velocity challenge. Operating on a shoestring, she did everything herself. In her first year, she managed to attract a few solid clients. During her second year in business, she hired a staff to help out. And that's when the problems surfaced.

Like many entrepreneurs, Kim relished control. She didn't feel comfortable hiring mistake-prone Quadrant I and II employees. She didn't want to take any chances on hiring people who would give her less than a perfect performance. So she hired reliable drones—Quadrant III old-timers—who didn't add value to her business.

This problem was compounded by Kim's toxic management style, consisting of one part oversupervision and two parts underdelegation. The mixture drove her stifled employees into a Quadrant IV tizzy. Predictably, quality slipped, deadlines were missed, clients complained, and people quit in droves. In her fourth year of business, Kim's firm was in trouble.

Kim had always been obsessive about details. Nothing was too small for her personal attention. Faced with unmotivated Quadrant IV employees, she took her obsession with details to an extreme, burying herself under a landslide of Quadrant III and IV chores. There weren't enough hours in the day to handle both the details and the major issues. Kim burned out in the capstone she loved.

Kim also overlooked the need to acquire management and motivational skills. She forgot that developing her employees and keeping them challenged in Quadrants I and II of their Doom Loops were critical to the business bottom line. And her overcontrolling style drove her into Quadrant III and IV maintenance rather than Quadrant I and II challenge.

But there was more. Kim couldn't abide failure. A plus

when she was starting her PR firm, this rapidly turned into a minus when things began to go wrong. Kim's standard pattern of denial teamed with a propensity to work harder became a liability. She had become so self-reliant that she inadvertently discounted the kinds of upward feedback and dialogue that keep any business functional. Rather than sitting down with her employees and getting their input on what was happening and on how to solve problems, Kim let her own addiction to work and self-reliance take over. Without confronting the right problems, she couldn't resolve them. Without enlisting the help and expertise of others, she burned out. Doomed at her capstone, Kim eventually shut the firm down.

If you are an entrepreneur, what can you do to prevent doom at capstone? For starters:

- Refuse to become obsessed with details; don't do it all yourself; involve and develop your employees.
- Make a commitment to fostering your people's skills by deliberately pushing them into Quadrant I and II challenges.
- Risk hiring Quadrant I and II people, and remember it's okay for them to make mistakes, too. That's the way most of us learn.
- Do a periodic quadrant analysis of your own skills and theirs. Sit down with your employees and discuss which quadrants they are in and why. Then work together to develop a plan with them for getting them back into Quadrants I and II.
- Prune your own job description: delegate your routine Quadrant III or IV business maintenance skills to people who genuinely like them.
- Look for new Quadrant I and II skills to keep yourself challenged and motivated.
- Be open to seeing failure as an expensive but valuable opportunity to learn something startlingly new.

When your capstone involves being an entrepreneur, first Doom Loop the skills required for both business start-up and maintenance. The skills for each are likely to be different.

Make it your business to acquire expertise in the kinds of business maintenance skills you need well before a crisis hits. Use this hiring principle:

Hire people whose Quadrant I and II skills dovetail with your own Quadrant III and IV skills. That will keep them learning and make everybody happy.

Your people will have the same opportunities for autonomy, control, and learning that you need. It helps to remember that you're not the only one who benefits from being in Quadrant I.

The Professional: Doomed by the Mantle of Professional Expertise

They certainly don't warn you about it in graduate school. Like most important facts of life, you have to figure it out for yourself. Your professional role has hidden liabilities that can unleash unanticipated doom at capstone.

People enter professions for many reasons—interest in a certain field, the allure of high status or pay, the mobility afforded by a professional degree, the need to prove themselves, the desire to please a parent, and so on. Ironically, many people enter a professional occupation to avoid winding up like their parents—tied to a boring "no think" job.

For a while, it looks as if your investment has paid off. Even if there are no bells and whistles, you advance in your profession, enjoying the pay, status, and recognition. As the years pass, you move up and eventually reach your capstone.

Then one day it hits: the staggering realization that you can't stand your job. Your professional identity has become a powerful vise that crushes the free and idiosyncratic parts of yourself. No matter how you try to deny it, you're face to face with a disconcerting conflict. Take a look at these episodes from the lives of people doomed by their professional roles:

- A top-ranking executive of a public utility feels obligated to wear a business suit to do her grocery shopping because her image reflects her company. She rightly laments, "I have no private life."
- A bookish, introspective head nurse insists that in her twenty years on the job, "I never really felt like myself."
- An electrical engineer one day announces, "This job just isn't me," and takes a night job as a bartender.
- A hospital pharmacist feels so trapped that he writes, "If I stay in this job any longer, it will be a battle just to keep myself alive."

These are powerful statements of acute doom in professional capstones. When someone at a cocktail party asks what you do and you lie or change the subject, your career has become an active problem that requires immediate attention. If you respond to this conflict by turning your personal life upside down—starting an affair, drinking heavily, having a child, for example—it's time to tackle your career anxiety head on.

What precipitates doom at capstone among professionals? Here are some possibilities:

- Your professional code of behavior transcends your occupation and sticks to you—no matter where you are or how you see yourself. Consider the entertainer who has to look the part and be ready to dispense autographs on demand the physician who maintains an authoritative manner, ready for any emergency even on the tennis court; the psychologist who keeps all matters confidential inside and outside the office to avoid any information leakage. These codes can keep you wound so tightly that you forget what it's like to loosen up and be yourself.
- Other people's expectations and stereotypes of how you should look, act, and talk—lawyers are confrontational,

social workers are empathic, bankers are stuffy—begin to box you in.

- Your realize that your true personality is masked by your professional identity, which you've been hiding behind or conforming to for years. You discover that you have traded off or given up cherished parts of yourself and that these parts clamor for their day in the sun.
- The tyranny of being an expert makes it nearly impossible for you to recycle at will into Quadrant I learning or risk admitting, "I don't know."

If any of these describe your current situation, what should you do? When you have merged yourself with your work, the hunt to find yourself again may take time. Begin by sorting out and reassessing who you are, as opposed to what your professional identity is. This personal knowledge can lead you to a capstone within your profession that is compatible with your values—and, in turn, help you construct a more balanced life-style.

Try not to be an expert all the time. Get comfortable saying, "I'm not sure," or, "I'll have to think more about that." Free yourself to be more creative, to be more of a learner, or to be whoever you are. In nonwork situations, experiment with not taking yourself so seriously. Within reasonable bounds, purposely confound other people's expectations of how a journalist, an accountant, or whatever you are is supposed to act. See what happens. All these approaches, combined with taking on new Quadrant I challenges, are excellent anti-doom tactics.

AVOIDING ORGANIZATIONS THAT FOSTER DOOM

Doom at capstone doesn't always come because of the capstone. Sometimes the culprit is the organization. And some organizations are more deleterious to your capstone health than others. The trick is to get the right fit between you and the organizational culture and beware of organizations and organizational cultures that put you in doom's way.

Getting the Right Fit

Like a foreign country, every organization has a culture. When the organization's style of conducting business matches your own way of doing things, you're in a comfort zone. You have the freedom to explore new Quadrant I niches without undue worry.

For instance, you like chitchat; the organization values communication. You like to work your tail off; the organization rewards top producers. You want recognition; the company has an employee incentive plan. It's the fit that counts.

Like being with a close-knit group of friends, being in an organization that fits gives you confidence. Because you're in step, you paradoxically have more freedom to risk nonconformity while expanding your Quadrant I and II skill repertoire.

While this fit is important throughout your career, it's especially important after you've arrived at your capstone and may be inclined to let things coast a bit. Feeling at home in an organizational culture gives you the freedom to continue your own growth. This will help ensure that there will be life after capstone.

Conversely, certain kinds of organizations foster doom at capstone. Only the timing of the crisis is in question. View as suspect any organization that heavily solicits your allegiance with perks, salary, or status, or that has a mission and operating style running counter to your own values and beliefs. Watch out for organizational climates that foster doom by style, design, or definition. Beware of these doom-bearing organizations:

• **The disempowering organization**—Over and over again, it fails to appreciate and reward your efforts. You achieve an "empty" capstone—empty of the motivation you need to sustain learning and challenge. The result is a clear shot into Quadrant IV.

• **The top-down organization**—If you're at a middle level, it excludes you from important decision-making and transforms you into a Quadrant III pawn. You have no sense of ownership or participation. You're isolated in your capstone.

• **The highly politicized organization**—It deflects your focus from the tasks at hand toward basic self-protection and territorial infighting. Your capstone becomes an elective office, and this leaves little time for anything but getting reelected.

• **The people-redundant organization**—It underutilizes your talents and abilities, burying you instead under mountains of busywork. The payroll is heavy with kindred spirits. Shell-shocked, you move into dustout and intellectual lassitude in Quadrant III, where you have lots of company.

• **The bureaucratic organization**—It traps you in rules, regulations, and routines. It discourages Quadrant I movement and training, except through elaborately choreographed ritual. If you stay put, your work identity starts to fade and you seek fulfillment in other parts of your life.

• **The restructuring or downsizing organization**—The once-normal workplace is transformed into an unpredictable rumor mill that chews up job security. Cutbacks and outplacement are the norm. Bailout and doom are the order of the day.

• **The high-output organization**—It overloads its best and brightest, propelling them into warp-speed burnout. Forget vacations, forget having a family—the company is your life. Even though the rewards are high, you feel doomed in a position you formerly cherished.

This shopping list of dooming organizations is by no means complete. Companies come up with all sorts of ways to doom you at capstone or earlier. Determine whether your organization is one of these and if so, be prepared to move on.

AVOIDING ATTITUDES AND MYTHS
THAT ACCELERATE DOOM AT CAPSTONE

By this time in your career you should know better, but these old saws can cut you to the quick. These are the myths that put you on automatic pilot and hurt your career when you're not looking. Even though they're endemic to our culture, the ones you hold are your own responsibility. Beware of the following:

"The Company Should Take Care of Me"

Regardless of rank and title, we all have compelling needs to belong somewhere, to be taken care of, not to be abandoned. And we drag these very real needs with us into our work lives. It's natural to see workplaces as surrogate parents or families. Most of us grew up in families that fostered an elaborate set of expectations along these lines. Perhaps American companies were once closer to the family model, but in this age of downsizing and streamlining, the model no longer works. The people you are working with are not beholden to you in any way—other than ways they choose. So don't mistake someone who is not on your side, except in the most perfunctory or self-serving way, for a warm and caring surrogate parent. Even if the organization's heart is in the right place, other complex issues make taking care of you a secondary priority.

So don't get complacent. A good operating dictum is:

Rely on no one else to look after your needs, security, and professional development.

No matter where you are in the organization, believing that the company will take care of you sets you up for major career disappointment and Quadrant III doom. The higher the level of your capstone, the more likely this belief will violate others' expectations that you should be taking care of them, not they of you. Your demands to have your own needs satisfied may ignite new workplace discontent, both in you and among your colleagues. So no matter what your position or capstone, don't put your career's fate in someone else's hands.

The "Happily-Ever-After" Capstone

You've arrived. It's been a long, hard climb and you plan to stay for the millennium. Unlikely. Remember, capstones aren't forever. Either outside forces—a downturned economy, a takeover, baby boomer demographics, or politics—are likely to push you out, or the Doom Loop's dynamics will turn that ideal Quadrant I job into a lackluster Quadrant III or IV position. Change is the unavoidable order of the day.

The cradle-to-grave capstone has become a rare beast indeed, and if you resist growing and learning, you'll be inviting doom. It pays to monitor yourself regularly in your capstone. Be vigilant. Check your career health; take your psychological pulse from time to time. Because things are always changing, you should be alert to these changes. See your career as requiring continual reconstruction. Most of the building-block skills and opportunities for your next, more satisfying capstone are already available, awaiting your attention.

"The Glass Is Half Empty"

Do you view your career pessimistically? If so, you may be creating a self-fulfilling prophecy that hastens your doom at capstone. When your perspective is consistently negative, you accelerate your passage into Quadrants III and IV. Certainly there are times when pessimism is justified. Confronting the downside of a situation is a survival tactic that prepares you to take remedial action. But when it comes to enriching their capstone, pessimists only know what to avoid—not what to aim for.

If this describes your perspective, redirect your attention.

Concentrate on the upbeat. Consider strategies for expanding your capstone or focus on constructing your next one. Any bright person can find endless reasons for avoiding change, but the bottom line is to avoid being stuck in a Quadrant IV job. If your attitude is the residual problem, try taking a more upbeat approach and see what happens.

"You Can't Teach an Old Dog New Tricks"

Psychological research shows that old dogs can and do learn new tricks—it just takes them longer. That's primarily because old dogs know a lot more than young dogs, and old learning sometimes gets in the way of new learning. When you think you know the answers, it's easy to become complacent instead of curious. This is counterproductive, since:

Old dogs who learn new tricks *keep* learning new tricks.

The payoff is exponential. People who learn to recycle into Quadrant I throughout their careers will do this not only before they reach their capstones, but after they have reached them as well. This creates obvious advantages: you become more effective, adaptable, and marketable—in other words, less expendable.

Often when you reach your capstone, your roles and relationships with others tend to change. Because you have more authority or status, people react differently to you. This means you must develop new power strategies and greater situational adaptability. Your potential for Quadrant I learning, paired with your old experience, could be your most valuable asset. Remember: old dogs need to keep learning new tricks to prepare for their next capstone.

"My Company Do or Die"

This misguided belief comes from another age. Just because your parents or grandparents stayed in one place forever doesn't mean you should.

The advantage of staying with one company is that it simplifies your choices and shelters you from confusion, anxiety, and risk (read growth). When you've been in one place long enough, life is predictable, though boring. Quadrant III becomes a safe harbor. As you watch the days of your life go by, you feel secure and miserable.

Why do people remain with one company if they are unhappy? Sometimes it's because other people's opinions of us matter more than our own unhappiness.

You worry that if you leave the company after twenty years, people might think you're disloyal, a failure, or—heaven forbid—a job hopper. You fear you'll lose your professional credibility and good reputation.

It's generally a mistake to plan your career around what other people think. You can't control their thoughts. It's hard enough for most of us to control our own. But you can control much about your career. Besides, when you leave a company where you've been dissatisfied, most people will envy your ability to take charge.

If you stay in your organization too long, you may pass the point of no return—you'll be looked upon as a single-company person who lacks the diversity to fit easily into another organization's culture. In today's competitive job market, twenty or more years with one company is much more likely to be seen as a liability than an asset.

Sometimes taking the same capstone in another company reenergizes you, providing the burst of challenge and learning that your current company fails to offer. If in doubt, keep reminding yourself that there's nothing noble about being taken for granted or suffering in a capstone or a company you no longer love.

THE DOOM BUSTERS

Once you're doomed, then what? First, confront the fact that even though change is hard, its absence is harder. Since either option creates discomfort, pragmatism dictates that you opt for the outcome that gives you the best chance of a fresh start. Framed this way, change is the only promising pathway.

Capturing the Teachable Moment

When you're doomed at capstone, you've inadvertently backed into a teachable moment. You're acutely aware that your old ways of doing things have failed you. In a teachable moment, you're not concerned with defending the old order; you're open to seeing what else is out there. This shift allows you to enter a "search and find" mode where you can try out new behaviors and gain new insight from your experience.

Below are some suggestions to help you seize this teachable moment:

* **Keep an attitude notebook or a journal.** Carry it around like a security blanket. Every day jot down your responses to feelings about and attitudes toward your work. Devote one section to tracking your likes. Forget your dislikes for the time being. Chances are you already know them by heart. Note your preferences and values.
* **Focus on who you are, not what you do.** To let your career guide your identity is to let the tail wag the dog. Be introspective, tackle self-discovery. What's missing in your life? How do you want to develop yourself over the next ten years? What are the sources of your discontent, your pain? Sometimes people lose track of themselves over the years. Try giving yourself some attention. See who it is you've been overlooking.
* **Identify your mission.** Start with what's important to you, what's worth accomplishing. For every driving passion there's a career capstone waiting in the wings. Whether you want to improve the quality of health care or make people laugh,

there's a capstone for it. Let the passion define your mission; then let your mission define your capstone.

• **Restore fun to your career equation.** Seeing work and fun as polar opposites will transform any capstone into a Quadrant III bore. So ask yourself what's fun, and brainstorm novel ways to combine fun and work. Conduct a fun audit; do a personal history of what's been fun for you from your earliest recollection onward. Look for patterns. If traveling is fun, look for work that involves new places and cultures; if socializing is fun, add more PR functions to your capstone, and so on.

• **Resist early shutdown.** A teachable moment wreaks havoc with old ways of thinking as it pries open your curiosity. You may feel as if you've unlocked Pandora's box. It's natural to want to make quick decisions, nail down the lid, and go back to the way things were. But this is usually an error. Ironically, at the time when you most want to shut down and push on, you're often on the verge of a major insight. Just remind yourself that you can always shut down later; it's staying open to ambiguous and confusing data that's difficult. Try giving yourself a limited extension before actually closing off your options.

LIFE AFTER DOOM

Let's assume you haven't been able to avoid doom at capstone. When doom happens, you feel like there's not going to be any afterlife. But there will be. Every capstone is a transition from one place to the next, not a culmination of your entire career. As a strategy, your capstone has given you an opportunity to build a qualified skill profile driven by your own preferences. If you value ongoing challenge, you'll always be on your way to somewhere else. Seen this way, a capstone is just a special case of a Quadrant II job.

The problem is that you may not have another capstone waiting in the wings. Without a new capstone, you may be uncertain about how to proceed. Since clinging to your current capstone is a losing proposition, it's important to break out of the status quo by examining your "what next" possibilities. Don't panic. Do consider the following post-capstone do's and don't's:

THE POST-CAPSTONE DOS

- Keep up appearances; opportunity can strike any time, anywhere.
- Tell people you trust that you're thinking about a change.
- Act upbeat about the possibility of change.
- Set a strategy for networking, then implement it relentlessly.
- Solicit feedback from friends, family, and professional colleagues about where else you might fit outside your current workplace.
- Use professional association meetings and publications for new ideas.

THE POST-CAPSTONE DON'TS

- Don't conduct your job or capstone search all by yourself.
- Don't veto other people's ideas for you without investigating them.
- Don't disqualify yourself for any reason; let others do the disqualifying.
- Don't settle on something before exploring what is really possible.
- Don't fall for the first "pretty" face that comes along.
- Don't take something just because you're tired of looking.
- Don't become a lame duck by announcing your intention to leave.
- Don't damage yourself politically by wearing your discontent on your sleeve.

FOUR POST-CAPSTONE ERRORS TO AVOID

It's wise to think long and hard about your next steps and to stay alert to the dangers of four all-too-prevalent post-capstone errors. If your "what next" decision-making process includes any of the following errors, you could be heading for post-capstone doom:

- the do nothing, steady at the helm fallacy
- the more is better fallacy
- the throw out the baby with the bathwater fallacy
- the trendy job fallacy

The Do Nothing, Steady at the Helm Fallacy

Do something! If you opt for on-the-job retirement—reacting to doom by riding out your job on automatic pilot—then you can expect to reside in Quadrant IV for the remainder of your work life. Ask yourself if this is an acceptable trade-off. What, if anything, do you gain with this strategy? If your worth is tied up in your work, the "do nothing" option could result in a serious blow to your self-esteem.

There are exceptions—for example, perhaps you plan on retiring soon and just need to hold on a bit longer. If you insist on making this error, try using either of the following two tactics to keep doom at bay:

- **Compress the time necessary to do your job and channel your energies into Quadrant I activities in or outside the workplace that are genuinely important to you.**
- **Maintain a sufficiently rich inner life to sustain you through the drab years ahead.**

The More Is Better Fallacy

This is the classic top-of-the-Loop Quadrant III error. "More is better" can be a dangerous misjudgment when it means more of Quadrant III. It ignores the Doom Loop dictum for satisfying Quadrant I challenge and growth. After doom hits you in your capstone, you may become the ultimate career cynic: if you can't have career satisfaction you'll go for more pay, more power, and more perks. You'll show them. In my experience, this is the most common and costly trade-off that people make in this crisis. The "more is better" fallacy solves none of the real issues that are creating discontent.

The Throw Out the Baby with the Bathwater Fallacy

This is a drastic, black-and-white solution to capstone doom. It calls for you to start over again with a blank slate. When your career capstone is really a dreadful mismatch with your needs and values, this can be a good thing to do. The hotel manager with a love for classical languages who went after a Ph.D. and became a university professor is one example. But more often people use this approach because they feel frustrated, fed up, and angry.

They become so upset with where they are in their careers that they want to discard everything they've accomplished and set off into the golden glow of a brand-new, stress-free life. It's no use telling them that change doesn't have to be dramatic or total to be satisfying. In any career there is usually a lot worth salvaging and building on. It's just hard to see in the heat of the moment.

Using skills you already have to edge toward a new capstone gives you a greater chance of success and involves much less risk than starting from scratch. When your need for change involves denying your strengths as well as your weaknesses, you risk being doomed at capstone in perpetuity.

The Trendy Job Fallacy

You respond to capstone doom by looking for rescue in the form of a trendy new position, working for one of the hundred best companies or in one of the twenty-five hottest jobs for the 1990s. This makes you feel like you've got something special, but what's "in" for others might not hit the spot for you. Think preferences, challenge, values, and staying power before junking your career as a social worker to go into bankruptcy law.

POST-CAPSTONE STRATEGIES

When you're sick of your job, it's natural to think you're sick of your company, your field, your spouse, and everything else. Resist the temptation to run. Instead, explore the terrain inside and outside the organization.

Are you sequestering yourself in your office behind closed doors? When you don't feel up to office banter it's natural to move into a more introverted mode. The problem is that this puts people, ideas, and information at a distance. People sense that you're disengaging. This makes it easy for them to unplug you from Information Central. You're cut off from the mainstream just when you need it most.

Now let's get specific. How do you devise a viable post-capstone strategy?

Opportunity Shopping Inside the Company

Your immediate post-capstone strategy is to reverse your process of disengagement. As the major stakeholder in the outcome, you need to break out of your private world, stop staring out the window, and go exploring.

Take a fresh look at your organization. Go opportunity shopping inside the company. Find out which career moves are possible inside this organization. Learn what they want that also coincides with what you want. Even though this is a last-ditch effort, relax and have some fun. Talk yourself into taking a playful stance. Ask yourself: If you were from another planet, who would you talk to in order to find out what's really going on here? To discover new trends? To locate the cutting edge? How would you learn about new opportunities here?

Here are some methods of exploration:

Reconnect with People

Pry yourself out of your office and go talk to people—all kinds. Let people know you exist. Networking can radically alter the course of events. Build relationships and gather information. People will be surprisingly helpful. Find out what they're doing. Explain that you're taking some time to become better informed about opportunities that exist within the company. Word will spread that you're available, and if you respond and follow up your initial efforts, these people will connect you to other opportunities.

Gain More Visibility

Don't tell people you're doomed, depressed, or thinking of leaving. If they hear you whine, they'll recede into outer space. Instead, be your own PR agent. Embark on an aggressive impression-management program. Construct a positive public image. Present yourself in an upbeat way commensurate with your position and ambition. Look and act the part. Treat every contact as a mini-job interview. Work your extroverted side by making small talk and exchanging information. The more outgoing you are, the more you'll be perceived as an attractive candidate for other positions in the company. Never subvert a career opportunity before it gels. You can always turn it down—after they make you an offer.

Plunge Back into the Information Stream

Read your organization's propaganda—annual reports, news releases, newsletters, memos, job listings, brochures. Ask simple "who, what, why, when, where, and how" questions. Use this information to track down projects, trends, political developments, seminars, opportunities, and people. Keep asking yourself pointed questions like: What interests you? What gets you excited? Follow up on your leads.

Learn What the Possibilities Are

Your organization may still have a lot left to offer you. Look for new position listings, specially created positions, job trading, cross-training, task forces, cross-functional teams, special projects, formal mentoring systems, professional networks, in-house training, educational benefits, and so on. Analyze each possibility in terms of your own needs and Quadrant I opportunities. Look at lateral or downward moves as potential springboards to higher-level capstones. See your next position as a challenging pass-through position rather than a final resting place. If you've been in Quadrant IV too long, look for any move that better aligns your own interests with those of the company.

See Yourself in New Roles

View your own interests as a template that you place over everything you've learned to see what matches, what engages you. Let yourself consider any bona fide opportunity, no matter how silly or risky it may seem at the moment. Assume a "try-on mentality" that permits you to see yourself in new roles, assignments, and jobs without committing yourself to them.

You'll want the specs for your next capstone to synchronize with your preferences and personality. Your natural psychological set points define your personal comfort zone. If you're doomed at capstone, you may be struggling with a job that's at odds with who you really are. Find Quadrant I challenges that are in your psychological comfort zone. Beware of "opportunities" for which you already possess the requisite skills. Take one of these and you'll be back in Quadrant III in record time. Remember that too much mastery creates doom.

Distinguish Between Your Company and Yourself

Have you ever been so overidentified with your organization that you couldn't distinguish between your own needs and those of the organization? Perhaps for a time, they were compatible. But then something happened—perhaps a restructuring or a change in management—and your needs diverged. The resulting dissonance mimics doom at capstone.

For instance, a doomed news commentator became outraged over a cutback in national news coverage in favor of local events. By the end of the week he felt wiped out and ready to switch fields.

What to do? Get some distance from the situation. Take some time to analyze the company's values and rewards. Then scrutinize your own needs and values—what motivates you, what's worth doing? Ask yourself which skills you still want to develop.

When the newscaster realized that he and the station management were at loggerheads, it became clear to him that he was not doomed in his capstone—just in that particular work environment. He moved on to a better fit with another station.

You may eventually do the same if your needs and the organization's are out of alignment.

Bury Your Dead Capstone, Not Yourself

Your capstone is dead and you're going nowhere. You've spent months agonizing about your doomed job, hating yourself and your inertia but feeling unable to move. Rigor mortis is setting in and you blame yourself.

Stop. It's time to get your priorities straight. You're more important than this job. Much more. And if you're not going to change it, stop replaying its horrors. Instead, turn your efforts back to yourself, where they belong.

You can do a number of things to extricate yourself from a moribund capstone. Begin by analyzing your own career mosaic. Select a few skill groups you want to expand or gain additional mastery in. Browse through the list of midcareer megaskills in the previous chapter for ideas. Consider developing some dormant aspect of your interests. Use your current position as a base of operations for acquiring at least one exciting new skill or taking one new seminar.

A doomed vice president of operations developed his writing, presentation, and training skills by bidding on projects that required these skills and by taking advantage of two in-house seminars. Eighteen months later he took a lateral transfer to a job in corporate communications, on his way to a PR capstone.

Like him, you may find that these new skills give birth to a new capstone. Or perhaps they simply add to your skill repertoire. In any case, you're alive and growing again.

Get a New Hat for an Old Head

The kids are in college, your spouse is between jobs, and you're going to be vested in two years. You need security much more than change. But because you're stuck, you're also doomed.

Even if you don't move on, you can inject new life into your capstone by taking on new roles, degrees, or projects. A doomed software designer took advantage of her company's generous educational benefits by studying for a master's degree in public health, knowing it would allow her to pursue another capstone in the future.

Just because you're stuck right now doesn't mean you won't ever break free. To make the interim palatable, don't just hang in there. Use this down time to acquire new skills and credentials you can use later on.

Consider Working on a Special Project

Special projects can breathe new life into an otherwise dead capstone. Become part of a ground-up project that requires you to take on many roles and gain new expertise.

By joining a newly formed task force on wellness in the workplace, a burned-out personnel supervisor rescued herself from near Quadrant IV oblivion and eventually gained a new capstone, administering wellness programs for an independent vendor.

Volunteer to head a work team where everyone learns and shares each other's functions. A research chemist alleviated his Quadrant III capstone blues by joining a cross-functional work team focused on quality of work life. Quadrant I learning and teamwork restored his zest for work, even though he remained unhappy with his capstone.

Some organizations offer a variety of intrepreneurial options through which you can develop independent profit centers or take an idea and transform it into a freestanding unit. Tackle an existing project or initiate one of your own in a way that takes you back to Quadrant I learning. Look for cutting-edge activities that let you become part of a developing esprit de corps. A doomed manufacturing engineer joined a prestigious corporate task force on globalization that led her to an altogether new capstone in international operations. Any project that gives you new skills and knowledge is worth investigating.

Opportunity-Shopping Outside the Company

The payoff can be high when you look for opportunities to revitalize outside your company. But don't wait until you've exhausted opportunities inside the organization. Begin immediately. Searching on the outside is easier to do because you don't have to worry as much about office grapevines and political fallout.

Here are a few tactics to consider:

Network on the Outside

What's required here is deliberate effort and persistence, but the results are well worth it. The people you'll meet outside your company will become part of your personal sales force—agents who will throw your name into the hopper as they serendipitously encounter situations that dovetail with your needs. Network with everyone—old colleagues, former coworkers, bosses and mentors, old friends, college and graduate school buddies. Even if you haven't talked to them in decades, they'll probably be glad to catch up with you.

Even though networking on the outside takes more planning than popping into a colleague's office down the hall, initiate communications with as many new contacts as possible. Talk to people who hold positions similar to your own in different locations or related industries. Share ideas and brainstorm possibilities and mutual contacts. Encourage people who hold capstones you want to pursue to provide you with specific information, leads, and contacts.

But when you network, do more than make contact. Tell the other person who you are and what you need so that he or she can help in a focused way that creates the right opportunities.

The more people you plug into your network, the greater your chance of finding something that interests you.

Discover Job Opportunities on the Outside

Try the library, professional and business journals, and even the classifieds. These storehouses of information live up to their promise. They are rich veins of knowledge about new career directions, trends, and capstones. Mine them as much for ideas and knowledge as for actual jobs.

If this seems like a humbling experience—something you'd expect to do in college, not now—remember that you have the credentials, skills, and experience to interpret this information in sophisticated ways you couldn't have dreamed of then.

Right now, the key to your success is to go fishing with a big enough net to catch whatever is swimming around and then sort out what interests you.

Scan back issues of local business journals. If you're in a profession, browse through the professional journals and association newsletters in your field. Use your intuition to locate what appeals to you. Once you've pegged an area, take notes on jobs, industries, professions, places, people, and contacts. Then follow up interesting leads with calls and visits to the organizations, as well as targeted networking and informational interviews.

Don't neglect the classified section of newspapers, business and professional journals, and association newsletters. Their "want lists" can provide capstone ideas and alternatives, as well as real leads. Even ad hype gives early clues to deciphering specific organizational cultures. You'll also see which companies have large personnel needs because of rampant growth or turnover.

Such research efforts have potentially high payoffs. You'll be able to use this information to make more informed career decisions.

Exercise Your Retread Options

Starting over again isn't for everyone, but it could be right for you. If you're willing to peel away even a small part of your acquired security and status, to return to Quadrant I and once again climb up through the ranks in a new field, here are three retread options.

Go for an Advanced Degree

By entering a part-time program that hooks your excitement you can nip capstone doom in the bud. Your job stays the same but you don't. Because you can see the light at the end of the tunnel, your current work situation becomes bearable. Consider a full-time program if you can swing it financially. You'll enter your new field at a higher level and with greater pay than you would have with experience alone. This can put you closer to Quadrant II on entry, or on a faster track to your capstone.

Be a Volunteer

Using volunteer and board experience to retread is another alternative. What such experience lacks in legitimacy and professional credentials is offset by the contacts and opportunities you encounter. For example: a doomed-at-capstone CPA serving on a hospital board became an expert in health care finance and made a successful transition over time to a new capstone as a chief financial officer in a teaching hospital. The contacts helped.

Build on a Hobby

Sometimes an interest or hobby paves the way to a new capstone. Another example: an unhappy city planner used his longstanding interest in city architecture and culture to write a guide to the history and architecture of local neighborhoods in the Southeastern town where he grew up. This led him to a new capstone of director of a foundation concerned with historic preservation—a capstone that combined his interests in architectural restoration and educating the public.

Shopping for Alternative Life-Styles

When you're doomed at capstone, the antidote may be a radical change of work context. Sometimes it's the nine-to-five, married-to-the-company routine that's wearisome. If you're ready for an alternative, there are plenty—in and out of the mainstream. These are just the tip of the iceberg:

- the American dream—owning your own business
- job sharing or part-time or flex-time positions
- independent consulting
- telecommuting
- cottage industry—working at home
- mission- or cause-driven work (e.g., environmental reclamation)
- house spouse/homemaking
- a scaled-down life-style requiring less income
- early retirement

To find out which alternative might be right for you, first identify what's missing in your life. When you've constructed a life that is seriously skewed toward one thing—power, money, work, or achievement, for example—your lack of balance may be what's dooming you.

Your desire for an alternative life-style may be a clue that you want to feel more integrated. Pay more attention to ignored parts of yourself—whether they are artistic, spiritual, or emotional. When you lock away critical aspects of yourself, they eventually break out and demand attention.

The crisis of being doomed at capstone is an extraordinary opportunity for real choice, a chance to consciously make life significantly better in the years ahead. If you've been a single-minded achiever, it's a chance to develop new friendships, to become more nurturing, to pay attention to community and family.

Use the listed alternative work styles as a springboard for

generating even more alternatives for yourself. Look for one that promises to give your life the type of balance it needs. You may not require a new capstone. You may just crave a new work style that provides you with an environment more appropriate for the person you've become—or the one you long to become.

LET YOUR VALUES BE YOUR GUIDE

Forget the quick-fix post-capstone job. At this point, you're likely to be in a mature stage of your life and career, where even the ideal Quadrant I career capstone may not be enough. Your next capstone should engage your values—your personal sense of what's worth doing.

Ed was a senior manager in a nationally respected engineering firm who was doomed at the director level. When a few of his friends offered him a chance to run their manufacturing plant, at nearly double the pay and half the distance from his house, Ed grabbed the opportunity. He reorganized the plant, did time and motion studies, put in a performance appraisal system, and still managed to finish his work in six hours. He liked the people, and the stockholders sang his praises. But after two years of recognition, challenge, status, and money, Ed realized that he had slipped into Quadrant IV. He deemed what he did for a living trivial.

The new job's heavy Quadrant I orientation had obscured the fact that this position and its higher salary merely upped the ante on Ed's perception that his work was meaningless.

To counteract such a situation and increase your post-capstone staying power:

Find a post-capstone position that fits your idea of what is worth doing in life. View a preponderance of Quadrant I skills as a necessary but insufficient condition for constructing a meaningful career path.

Ed took a hard look at his situation. He bought a small manufacturing business that used his existing skills along with Quadrant I entrepreneurial skills. His goal was to be his own person, expand the business, and become an active force in the community. By engaging his values as well as his need for challenge, Ed chose a post-capstone capstone with staying power.

CHOOSE A POST-CAPSTONE CAPSTONE THAT LETS YOU CONTRIBUTE

For post-capstone decision-makers in their thirties, forties, and fifties, the desire to make a contribution may become paramount. They want their work to matter, not just to be a source of personal income. Values count.

You don't have to win a Nobel Prize or find a cure for cancer to feel this way, either. A stockbroker turned landscaper said he believed his contribution was to make cities more beautiful; a teacher turned hairdresser said she liked helping people feel better about their appearance.

Or your values may swing in the opposite direction. A nurse devoted to helping others for years may suddenly realize that it's time to apply her well-honed interpersonal skills to a job in business, to reap greater financial rewards for herself and her family.

Tap into the values you want to focus on. You and only you have responsibility for charting your course and taking care of yourself in your career. Become aware of what your personal needs and values dictate, then factor these into choosing your next capstone.

FUTURE CRISIS, FUTURE MASTERY

When you have successfully navigated the crisis of doom at capstone, you will have restored passion and commitment to your work life. You will have taken charge of your career, opting for challenging Quadrant I and II skills that fit your preferences and values and let you express who you are in your work. This process takes courage and perseverance. It reaffirms your capacity to adapt and find future capstones that work for you.

But don't expect this to be your last career crisis. If you have the capacity to learn, grow, and change, you may face doom at capstone again. And your experience in overcoming this crisis once will serve you well when you need to overcome it again.

Having read the past six chapters, do you feel better prepared to avoid or master these typical career crises? I hope your answer is yes. But before you can say you're truly prepared, there's one critical set of skills you'll need to master, one that can make all the difference between career success and failure.

That's organizational politics—the focus of the next chapter.

CHAPTER 11

■

Politics:
The Don't Go Anywhere
Without It Skill

Politics. I'm not good at them, I don't like them, and I'm not going to play.
—New MBA, marketing

I hate the massive egos, the backbiting, wondering who's trying to get my job.
—Burned-out senior editor, publishing

It's a constant battle of one-upmanship. You worry all day about doing something wrong. I've learned you're either in control or you're the victim.
—Executive director, trade association

After the CEO who hired me left, they poisoned the well! They blocked my projects, reassigned my staff, even had me report to a manager I had trained.
—Demoted director, corporate fund-raising

At this point you've mastered the Doom Loop—selecting capstones, managing career crises, setting career strategies, and implementing tactics that move you toward your goals. You've tapped into your likes and values to choose the right capstone. You've been using Doom Loop principles to recycle yourself into Quadrants I and II. High-paying, low-satisfaction jobs in Quadrants III and IV no longer turn your head. With your target mosaic in hand, you're busy transforming yourself, skill by skill, into a qualified contender for your next capstone.

Even the six career crises we've discussed shouldn't knock you off course for long. They're predictable transitions with a positive side of helping you reset your course. With effort and just a little luck, success should be around the corner.

But if this is to happen, there's one more topic to cover.

Even the best-conceived career management plan can topple like a house of cards without one critical skill set—politics. And even a demon Doom Looper can be derailed by organizational politics.

Having a strategy and the necessary tactics for reaching your capstone is important, but it is not enough to ensure success. You still have to implement your plan in a competitive, dog-eat-dog, people-intensive work environment where self-interest is the rule, not the exception. Whether or not politics are in your job description, there's no way to avoid them. If your job involves people, you dare not leave organizational politics out of your skill portfolio. Political skills are survival skills essential for managing your success in social pecking orders where hard work and achievement take a backseat to power, control, and group dynamics.

For most people, politics are a Quadrant IV skill set—one they don't like and aren't good at, yet can't avoid. This creates mammoth problems. Fortunately, with a little coaching, most of them are solvable.

ORGANIZATIONAL POLITICS: A WELL-KEPT SECRET

Organizational politics upset a lot of people. Rightly so. Caught off guard by factors they deem wholly peripheral to their work, they feel demeaned, devalued, and traumatized. What, they wonder, does any of this gratuitous backbiting have to do with work? When politics rob you of the recognition and status you believe you deserve, it's normal to feel resentful and angry. But most people know little about political self-defense. They don't know how to decipher the intricate unwritten rules that govern success and failure in most organizations. Most don't even know what hit them until well after they've emptied their desks and are visiting their outplacement counselors.

This gives politics a bad reputation. Politics are so distasteful to many hardworking types that they despair of ever getting past them. When you're politically vulnerable it's easy to think politics are dirty business—dishonest scheming to give undeserving characters advantages they couldn't otherwise achieve. This leads many people to feel they're above "playing" organizational politics. But as much as people malign politics, they're still an unavoidable fact of daily life in any workplace with more than one worker.

Yet when it comes to getting help in understanding them, they're one of the best-kept secrets of modern organizational life.

Finding out how to handle politics is a lot like finding out how to use birth control was for a teenager in the 1950s. You know there is something you ought to be doing, but you can't find anyone who will tell you what or how.

You thought it was hard to get good coaching in managing your career? Well, try your luck at getting someone to coach you in politics. If you're like most people, nobody ever coached you in political one-upmanship when you got your first job or at any time thereafter. You're on your own. Looking back at my own career, it seems to me that my mentors knew less about organizational politics than I did—and that certainly wasn't much. Nor can you rely on business school or graduate school professors to give you basic survival training in organizational politics; most business and graduate school courses quickly gloss over politics, if they mention them at all. Even the library colludes in keeping politics a secret; look up politics in popular management books and you'll find the gurus strangely silent.

All this silence makes it easy for you to plunge into your career with built-in vulnerability to dangerous political undertows. Compounding the problem is a set of time-honored cultural assumptions—like the one that says hard work pays off or the one about openness promoting trust—that leave you unprepared for managing the informal, often invisible, power structures that govern your success.

But stick around. Power politics are indigenous to the dynamics of any group. Before long, you'll confront the P-word face to face, bigger than life—infiltrating your meetings, projects, and relationships, and influencing outcome after outcome. Even though your sights are set on your capstone, politics creep up to wreak havoc with your plans. Unless you enjoy watching your pet projects, staff, and job security buffeted by subtle but cataclysmic forces that have nothing to do with the tasks at hand, you have to be prepared in advance. You can't afford to ignore the political crosswinds for long if you want to hold onto what you've got.

When the impact of politics first dawns on you, it can take the wind out of your sails. This unsettling feeling of being blindsided often marks the beginning of your induction into a lifelong high-stakes on-the-job training course. Some people take this instruction well; some people fight it. But, like it or not, eventually everyone gets the message:

Without a mastery of organizational politics, professional competence and a career management strategy like the Doom Loop are necessary, but insufficient, conditions for career success.

Although this has probably always been true, in today's lean-and-mean corporate environments, rife with justifiable insecurity and radically shifting power bases, you will need every bit of political moxie you can muster. The newly restructured organizations of the 1990s are competitive playing fields without referees, cluttered with confusing ambiguities and competing factions. The resulting double messages about teamwork, loyalty, and security place more responsibility on you for managing your own career. Although the responsibility is greater, you'll find fewer guidelines for decoding what it actually takes to succeed. And the increasingly diverse work force of the past few years has made the few remaining rules obsolete. It's hard for most of us to know what's expected anymore. All this calls for greater ability to read between the lines. Survivors can expect to negotiate treacherous hidden agendas and mixed messages throughout their careers.

If you don't activate your political horse sense, you might as well park your career plan in a time capsule.

Political skills channel your attention to the murky gray areas of corporate cultures where alliances are forged, where information is exchanged, where stakeholders in various outcomes fight to preserve their own interests. You must become an expert at interpreting innuendo in social situations, at figuring out who has what at stake where and when, and at distinguishing who actually controls resources versus who merely appears to. It's these competing patterns of personal and professional self-interest that make organizational power politics hum. And as they play out against the stark backdrop of what your organization rewards and punishes, you will be well advised to protect your own turf.

Sure it sounds overwhelming. But the only thing that will truly overwhelm you is putting your head in the sand. It's too late to argue that you don't like politics or that you're not going to play. That's a rookie's mentality that will push you right out the door.

THE DANGERS OF
IGNORING ORGANIZATIONAL POLITICS

My advice here is simple and succinct: don't. Lots of people have hoped that if they ignored them, politics would go away. Mostly the people went away. There's the marketing director who was passed over for promotion after ten years of productive work in her company, the corporate vice president who lost a mentor and the right to be heard by key decision-makers, the bank officer who was fired after righteous whistle-blowing on a colleague, and the widely published professor who lost his second battle for tenure.

Each of these bright, hardworking people ignored, misread, or was caught unaware by organizational politics. As a result, each faced painful career derailment and gut-wrenching angst. They addressed the wrong issues—and not so surprisingly came up with the wrong solutions.

The marketing director addressed a political problem, her boss's patently unfair positioning of two junior coworkers for a promotion she knew she deserved, by working even harder to prove how good she was. But all she did was wear herself out and speed her fall from grace.

The whistle-blowing bank officer fought for what he believed was right in the face of strong, unified opposition. Although he did the right thing, it failed to solve the problem, win him kudos, or pay his children's private school tuition. It did, however, give him an opportunity to learn, the old-fashioned way, that martyrdom is a career-stopping liability.

Sometimes people try to ignore politics by leaving a volatile work setting for altogether new vistas. Although this sometimes works, a change of scenery can plunge you into an unknown setting with an even less friendly bunch of dragons where history is likely to repeat itself. The professor who was twice denied tenure lost to two different, but equally outrageous, clutches of political dragons.

When politics halt you in your tracks or keep you from being effective, it's natural to feel discouraged and paranoid, or to construe politics as evil. After all, you're just trying to do your job, whereas someone else is purposely trying to make you look bad. You just want to slink off to lick your wounds and recover.

But whether you see politics as the use or abuse of power usually depends on which side you're on. The problem is that when you ignore politics altogether, you may not even realize there are sides. And you emerge from difficult situations sadder, but no wiser.

Organizational politics, like mountains, cannot be ignored. They command your attention just because they're there, and because there are few easy ways to get around them. No matter which quadrant of your Doom Loop you're in or where you are in your career, you're never too old, too rich, or too smart to get a better handle on organizational politics.

THE DOOM LOOP AND POLITICS

This is where the rubber meets the road. If you intend to get the mileage you need from your Doom Loop strategy, plan on topping off your personal career mosaic with high-octane political savvy. Don't misunderstand. I'm not suggesting that you trade your capstone, your target mosaic, or your commitment to professional excellence for Machiavellian tactics. But it helps to be on a first-name basis with the positive side of power politics.

Let's look at how the Doom Loop strategy interacts with political awareness to yield four strategic career positions that affect your work life.

FOUR STRATEGIC CAREER POSITIONS

	Politically Naive	Politically Savvy
Non-Doom Looper (Unintentional)	Rudderless	Machiavellian
Doom Looper (Intentional)	Blindsided	Concordant

This is an altogether different matrix from the Doom Loop matrix, so don't confuse them. All I have done is combine the question of whether or not you are using an intentional career management system with whether you are politically naive or savvy. The matrix shows four different strategic career positions:

- **Blindsided**—Although you're an intentional career manager, politically you're a novice. You don't even realize you're a sitting duck.
- **Rudderless**—You're neither an intentional career manager nor a political ball of fire. You're unprepared to do anything but drift.
- **Machiavellian**—Without a career management plan, but with plenty of political horse sense, you're like an opportunistic virus seeking a host.
- **Concordant**—You're an intentional career manager who is tuned in to the power dynamics of your workplace. All bets are on you.

Which combination best describes you? Each one leads to different approaches that affect your career success. Let's look at each strategic career position and how it plays out.

Blindsided

Doom Loopers who ignore all but the most blatant organizational politics are at high risk for being hit broadside. If blindsided describes your approach, you may be paying too much attention to the tasks at hand and not enough attention to people, contexts, and politics. Unfortunately, this will land you in Quadrant III's organizational backwaters.

That's what happened to Hal Franchetti. Hal was a high-achieving, no-nonsense sales manager who carefully constructed an A+ target mosaic for his capstone of district manager, only to be dismissed before he arrived there. Despite his high performance, Hal was blindsided because he ignored a few too many obvious political realities—an inbred clique of old college buddies, a high premium on off-the-job socializing, and a tacit "don't rock the boat" rule.

Hal was a typical high achiever—impatient, brimming with ideas, hooked on challenge and unswervingly goal-oriented. His autonomous, workaholic style set him apart from the rest of the sales force. Eventually all his innovative ideas were implemented by his company—without Hal at the helm. He just didn't fit. And he made matters worse by not looking up from what he was doing long enough to realize it. When Hal was fired he belatedly got the picture, and it hurt.

Like Hal, many nonpolitical, highly driven professionals are blindsided. From their perspective, they're doing a great job; it's their coworkers and supervisors who create chaos. And maybe they're right. Too bad that being right doesn't get them what they want.

Who is most likely to be blindsided? High achievers, task-oriented workaholics, productivity addicts who hate to schmooze, lone rangers who operate outside the "buddy" news network, independent creative types, and goal-driven career managers who can't see the forest for the trees. New entries to the work force and people who work in independent areas like research and development are also likely candidates. Even old-timers who fail to keep up with new organizational dictates like self-managing work groups and team decision-making can be blindsided by the changing order. When you are blindsided, you have your eyes on the twin balls of competence and career progression, but you miss the fact that there are three balls up there. When the third one lands it can knock you off your feet. You need to know how to juggle all three.

The lesson to be learned here is that if you are a serious Doom Looper you can't afford to ignore or misread organizational power bases, changes in the organizational climate, or the personality mix of the key players. If you do, expect to be blindsided, sandbagged, or worse. It's important to see political skills for what they are—basic survival skills. Without a crash course in them, you'll be the one to crash.

Rudderless

This position is one to shun. For all practical purposes it is a Quadrant IV look-alike. With neither political nor career management know-how, the rudderless person is reduced to following other people's agendas—taking orders and moving through a series of jobs that get him or her nowhere. Such people are career flotsam, aimlessly bobbing wherever the tide pulls them. Shirley Dubin could write a book about being adrift in a career. She got her nursing degree right after high school and became a night nurse to support her husband's medical school education. She hated the work, but the money was steady, so she stayed. Twenty-five years and two husbands later, Shirley is appalled that she's still in nursing. She says, "Every single day I'm reminded I don't want to be there— ninety percent of my job consists of what I don't like." What's worse is her steady stream of complaints about the power politics of her hospital: the doctors have to be treated like gods. The orderlies sleep on the job, so she has more to do. She is given all the bad shifts and the toughest floors. The head nurse makes her a scapegoat. Et cetera.

All this is a given for Shirley. She accepts it and feels beaten down, because she has no defenses against either career doom or political mistreatment. By relinquishing her control to others, she has embraced the victim's role. She is rudderless on all counts. No one is taking care of Shirley's career, least of all Shirley, and she has acquired no organizational savvy or clout. Like many people with no career plan and no political horse sense, Shirley drifted into her career—then helplessly watched the scenario play out. Like other rudderless souls, she has been in Quadrant IV so long she's not sure she's capable of managing anything else. She doesn't realize she should be scanning the organizational horizon, taking a self-protective stance, taking care of herself. Instead she feels trapped, a pawn who exercises little control over her life.

Who is likely to be rudderless? You'll discover some unlikely bedfellows in this group. The usual occupants are people in their first jobs who haven't yet learned the ropes and lifers who are stuck in low-control, high-stress pink- and blue-collar ghettos without easy exit. But in pared-down organizational structures, many traditional managers have been cut adrift, and suddenly find themselves rudderless. In restructured and decentralized organizations you'll find many managers who haven't yet recovered their bearings. They've lost the traditional vertical pecking order they know and trust, as well as their mentors and power bases. For the time being they lack their old career direction and political know-how.

If rudderless describes your career management position,

realize this is a common problem. Your first task is to see that you still have many choices and that you deserve much better than this in your career. Exercise your personal power by taking one step at a time to extricate yourself and regain a sense of direction; there's a lot to learn.

The primary lesson to be learned here is that no one will take care of you in your career but you. When you abdicate responsibility for your own direction and ignore organizational power plays and operating systems, you're doomed to drift.

Machiavellian

When people think about workplace politics at their worst, it's the Machiavellian types that come to mind. These are the highly self-interested, politically glib glad-handers whose main career strategy rests on being in the right place at the right time or hitching their own wagons to someone else's rising star. Like roulette, when this strategy works, the payoff is high. But since the wheel is fickle, their career success depends on external forces they don't control.

Lenny Terrill was a classic Machiavellian type. He had a simple "it's not what you do, it's who you know" formula for getting ahead in advertising. He lunched in the right places, hobnobbed with the right people, appeared in the right gossip columns. Networking is a euphemism for Lenny's entrenchment in the grapevine. "They can't fire me," he laughed, "I've got too much on everyone." He exploited his contacts and successfully positioned himself for opportunities before they became public. For a long time, this approach worked well for Lenny. Then Lenny's mentor became involved in his own legal and ethical morass and was deposed. Considerably tarnished by association, and without his mentor to protect him, Lenny rapidly fell from grace and became the agency pariah. Although Lenny was no slouch, he hadn't built a skill-based, qualified career profile, either. This limited his options. His career progress, for all its stylish bravado, was largely dependent on serendipity. Lenny was on his way out.

Who is likely to use the Machiavellian approach? All kinds of people looking for quick career fixes and shortcuts. Some are convinced it's the way the world turns. At some point, power brokering becomes highly addictive. Bright, ambitious types in cutthroat industries may bet on politics to give them the needed edge. Sometimes Machiavellis lack credentials, confidence, or both. Power politics help them camouflage their deficiencies. But personality can also be a factor. If you are motivated by the need to control people and resources, influence events and outcomes, and cut back-room deals, organizational politics offer you quite a nice bailiwick for your natural preferences!

The worst of the Machiavellian types are pathological game players who have little empathy for other people's positions. These relentlessly self-centered parasites take what is yours and what is theirs. They make little distinction. They are the ones who run roughshod over others and give politics their nightmare reputation.

Just remember, this is different in kind and degree from ordinary self-interest. There is nothing wrong with self-interest in and of itself; self-interest motivates. In fact, it is essential for anyone who wants to achieve career success.

Issues of self-interest aside, there are still serious problems in using a Machiavellian strategy. Pragmatically speaking, success rests too heavily on unpredictable factors and too little on your own skills and abilities. Ironically, in fast-changing organizational environments, this approach gives all but the very talented political strategist far too little control.

The lesson to be learned here is that Machiavellis often risk their career success with every unforeseen shift in organizational leadership and structure. As competitive pressures destabilize and downsize organizations, Machiavellis are hard-pressed to figure out just where to hitch their wagons. This may lead them to take larger risks and make serious errors. It could be time for the Machiavellis to switch their strategy to the concordant style discussed next. This is the best tactic for regaining control during changing times.

Concordant

This is the ideal style—that of the intentional career manager who has acquired considerable aplomb in heeding and reading organizational environments. Jenny Davis is a good example. She is the highest-ranking female executive in a large financial institution. After college she worked her way up from a clerical position in the pension division. She formulated her capstone—a bank CEO—about five years ago, and most of the pension division's power brokers concur that she is on her way. She has developed relevant skills and credentials with the single-minded focus of a kid playing a video game. Whenever Jenny approaches the top of the Loop and moves toward Quadrant III, she deploys her favorite work credo: "If the job doesn't change, change the job." But Jenny never does it alone. Jenny is a master networker who has the support of mentors, allies, and plenty of fans, inside and outside the company. Her political skills are impressive. She holds standard pre-meeting meetings before raising new issues. She carefully positions her accomplishments inside the company with key people, avid supporters, and witty memos that command attention. She maintains high visibility in the community by serving on prestigious voluntary boards.

People like Jenny have learned to read the organizational norms and align them with their own professional needs. They have decoded what the organization really rewards. They understand the informal power structure. This enables them to unobtrusively position their daily achievements with decision-makers, gaining the visibility they need for success.

When your career and political goals are concordant, there's a good fit between your personal career strategies and the context of the particular position. Jenny is an excellent example of this. She has aligned her personal career strategies with the particular context of her position, making her career and political goals concordant.

The lesson to be learned here is that mastering political survival skills like reading norms, networking, quiet diplomacy, marketing, empowerment tactics, positioning projects, and resolving conflict, along with your Doom Loop strategy and tactics, will enable you to reach your capstone—intact.

WHAT ARE ORGANIZATIONAL POLITICS, ANYWAY?

What do politics mean to you? Your answer depends largely on your experience. Politics mean many things to many people—mostly negative things, I might add. Everyone complains about them; nearly everyone recognizes them (even if it's too late), but few can say exactly what they are. But even when they can't say what politics are, most people will say they don't like them.

This creates a double-edged problem. If you're going to add a set of skills to your target mosaic to help you maneuver through troubled political waters, you ought to know just what you're dealing with. And if you're going to stay motivated to learn this set of skills, you'd better not be repulsed.

Try asking a group of people to describe organizational politics, and you'll get as many answers as people. There's no common definition, but the trend line is unmistakable. For different people politics are:

- empire building
- the use and abuse of power
- hidden agendas and alliances
- playing people off against each other
- infighting over power and control
- selling your soul to people you don't like
- one-upmanship, putdowns, and sabotage
- being rewarded and punished for things other than performance
- personality clashes and bad will

What links these descriptions is a pervasive sense of disenchantment, distrust, and disempowerment. Politics are seen as nasty business. No wonder people avoid them.

Let's agree to deviate from that path. Let's take a more

upbeat approach that lets you use politics to your own advantage in your career. Politics have three components that affect your career progress:

- clashing needs and interests
- hidden alliances among stakeholders
- insider-outsider people sorting

Understanding these components will help you recast politics in a more positive light. As a Quadrant I student of politics, you'll find that keeping an open mind will serve you well.

Clashing Needs and Interests

Everyone has self-interest, including you. But because no two people are alike, neither are any two sets of self-interest. This translates into a real-life drama of power plays and continuing clashes over control of resources. Conflict in organizations is not dirty; it's simply evidence that everyone is still breathing.

Once you see politics as motivations and behaviors that serve basic self-interest, it's easy to see how power and control crawl out of the woodwork wherever people relate to each other. That's why you can't duck politics. They're everywhere —at work, in the PTA, at neighborhood association meetings, and in the family. Once you begin to think like this, politics get less irritating. If politics are simply normal friction caused by competing self-interest among people and groups, then why should politics be distasteful? Why not see them as just another skill to be mastered?

People who make a holy war out of avoiding organizational politics see politics as a repulsive Quadrant IV skill set. This keeps them from investing the time and energy they need to become politically literate. They couldn't play politics if they wanted to! As a result, no one is minding their interests.

Hidden Alliances Among Stakeholders

Webster's New World Dictionary (Second College Edition, 1984) defines politics, in part, as "factional scheming for power." Although you may find scheming for power objectionable, it's actually quite normal for people who have something at stake to get together to protect their interests. If the state tried to take your property through eminent domain, you bet you and your neighbors would meet to discuss how to act together to protect your homes. There is nothing inherently evil about wanting to protect your own interests. The problem is that different groups of stakeholders have different sets of interests. And the interests of each group are not always obvious. So you had better ferret out what various stakeholders are up to. But don't count on anyone giving you a play-by-play account.

Contrary to popular opinion, most people's scheming and collusion are strictly kid stuff. Even seasoned political pros rarely orchestrate their plans in majestic detail. Much of what happens takes place in the heat of the moment. There's no master blueprint. Because political scheming is dicey, you'll need to protect yourself, well before all the facts are in. Techniques won't help you as much as general principles. Since your adversaries will probably be shooting from the hip, you'll have to make sense of events by understanding the nature of political alliances. These alliances usually:

- concentrate power in a few trusted hands
- help some stakeholders meet their needs at the expense of others
- allow entrenched power brokers to maintain the status quo
- get things done quickly through nonstandard channels
- speed critical information to key decision-makers
- stop threats to the old order through rituals, policies, and so on
- slow down the overall rate of change and cut losses

- determine how newcomers are hazed and otherwise persuaded to accept established ways of doing things
- keep out people who are too different or who will escalate change

So when you look at some political action, ask yourself how it serves these purposes. Which stakeholders get what payoffs? Your job is to figure out what's going on, and to get the situation to work for you rather than against you.

For better or worse, politics are a tool with many uses that serves many masters. By learning to read a group's power dynamics, you gain an edge. You don't have to hurt anyone or do anything unethical. Understanding is power. The goal is to manage yourself with less vulnerability and more control. This improves your chances of reaching your capstone intact.

Insider-Outsider People Sorting

Go anywhere in the world, and you'll see that people constantly sort each other into two basic camps—"us" and "them." It's simple. If you're "one of us," you're a trusted insider. If you're "one of them," forget it. No matter how good your work is, if you're an outsider you'll have a harder time getting recognized. This puts you at a big disadvantage. It takes much more effort for you to be effective. You get more criticism and less support for your accomplishments. As one outsider put it, "When I do good work I get no feedback. That's how I know I'm doing well."

As an outsider you feel far less appreciated because you *are* less appreciated. You're locked out of lunch meetings where insiders swap information. You're not invited to the tribal premeeting meetings where insiders set each other up for success. When you're an outsider, you're all dressed up with nowhere to go. You're taken for granted until you do something wrong; then you may be vilified. No wonder you're so astounded and angry when someone who does mediocre work wins accolades from the group in power.

Despite this widespread "us" versus "them" trend, most people cling to the idea that they should be judged solely on the quality of their work. But quality of work is just one blip on the large screen when insiders judge you. For many hard-working types this whole approach is an outrage. They react with anguish and upset. They say things like, "I'm so angry I'd like to take a month off to go beat some rugs somewhere," or, "I don't get any support around here," or, "I've gotten to the point where I don't enjoy going to work anymore." They don't need a big push to blame office politics.

In fact, it will help make you a better career manager if you mentally separate your job performance from the context of your job. Then you can think of politics as anything besides job performance that involves other people at work and that adversely affects your ability to be effective and get rewards. Note the word "adversely." It's interesting that people rarely complain about cliques, alliances, and social banter that they enjoy or that work in their favor. When you're "one of us," rather than "one of them," it's odd how politics lose much of their sting.

THE BIG CHALLENGE:
ACHIEVING POLITICAL LITERACY

It's never too late to wage a full-scale war on your own political illiteracy. You may be a Ph.D. who can't read the unwritten codes for behavior, can't decipher the hidden agendas that create havoc in meetings, and can't understand the power alliances that govern decisions. You may be a top manager who is so task-oriented that you forget all about maintaining good relations with your people. In either case, your political illiteracy sets you up for predictable failure. The more you see politics as personally repugnant, the less likely you are to invest in learning them. So it's in your best interest to change this perception and see politics as an essential skill to master. The challenge is to become politically literate without damaging your integrity.

Actually this is easier than most political illiterates believe. Political skills are like any other skills, with a few exceptions.

First, you won't see these skills listed in most job descriptions. Second, they are mandatory protective gear for nearly any job. Political skills are group survival skills. They require you to focus on the human side—the relational and motivational side of the workplace. They help you avoid the predictable pitfalls that keep you from reaching your capstone. They reduce the restraints that hold you back from success. It's tough to attain your capstone without them. Achieving political literacy helps you reach concordance and avoid being blindsided.

Look over the political skills literacy checklist on the next page and identify the skills you still need to master. Then decide in which quadrant of your Doom Loop the ones you have checked fall. Add any other political skills you believe are important but not included in this list.

Take out some paper and list the Quadrant I political skills you have checked; then list the Quadrant IV political skills you still need to acquire. These two subsets outline the skills that belong on your master target mosaic list. They require your immediate attention. Your task will be to learn each one without requiring damage control. Start with your Quadrant I skills to get you moving, since these skills are ones you like but are not yet good at.

But first a word of caution. Whenever you're learning Quadrant I and IV skills, by definition you're a novice. You can expect to make mistakes. That's the evidence that you're learning something. But when you're learning political skills, you're dealing with volatile, sometimes hidden issues that could affect many stakeholders in your organization and determine your future.

So your safest bet as a novice is learning your new political skills outside the workplace. Try voluntary professional and local groups. They are usually rich fiefdoms of power dynamics where you'll learn everything you ever needed to know about politics and more. Or hire a consultant. Look for an experienced career coach or an old salt in your field who has spent a lifetime observing political infighting. Another good choice is someone who has recently retired from your line of work. Ask to buy his or her services as a personal consultant on a short-term basis.

POLITICAL SKILLS LITERACY CHECKLIST

Mastery Status
(Yes or No)

Doom Loop Quadrant Status
(I, II, III or IV)

1. Yes — I — You recognize which family, professional, and cultural myths (eg., hard work will be rewarded) you have been using to guide you.

2. Yes — I — You know what your own personal and professional needs are.

3. Yes — III — You can "read" an organizational culture's unwritten rules.

4. Yes — III — You know what makes a person an "us" versus a "them" in your organization.

5. No — II — You look and dress the part of someone successful in this group.

6. No — IV — You play the part of someone who fits your organization's culture.

7. Yes — II — You pace your style and tempo to the group's (in terms of work rate and quality, social amenities, and so on).

8. Yes — II — You know how to identify and attract a mentor in new situations.

9. Yes — II — You routinely get help from key people on your projects and problems—whether you need it or not.

10. Yes — II — You periodically analyze the organization's informal information network to learn how information gets around—where channels are open, blocked, and dead-ended and by whom.

11. Yes — I — You know how to use information channels to promote yourself and your projects.

12. Yes — III — You can identify the stakeholders in any project and note their special interests and alliances.

13. No — I — You know who the gatekeepers in the organization are and how to get past them.

14. Yes — II — You like people without confusing this with trust.

15. Yes — II — Your emphasis is on being effective, rather than on being right.

16. _Yes_ _II_ ___ You pay close attention to what people do, as opposed to what they say.

17. _Yes_ _II_ ___ You learn who has which hidden agendas and why.

18. _Yes_ _II_ ___ You observe what's really rewarded in this place, not what they say is rewarded.

19. _Yes_ _II_ ___ You observe what leaders and key players are doing—including alliances, shifts, and detours.

20. _No_ _I_ ___ You align your own needs with what the organization actually rewards.

21. _Yes_ _II_ ___ You develop relationships with key stakeholders, gatekeepers, and power brokers that foster common interests.

22. _Yes_ _II_ ___ You form working alliances with stakeholders and power brokers that protect your interests.

23. _Yes_ _II_ ___ You deliberately promote your accomplishments with top stakeholders and decisionmakers.

24. _Yes_ _III_ ___ You cultivate an extensive network, including some unlikely allies.

25. _Yes_ _II_ ___ You consistently take good care of coworkers and support staff.

26. _Yes_ _II_ ___ You earn your stripes in both the task and relational aspects of your job.

27. _Yes_ _II_ ___ You use a small-wins strategy to keep yourself and your successes visible in ways that don't threaten anyone.

28. _Yes_ _II_ ___ You use conflict resolution skills to acknowledge others' viewpoints, listen to their stories, and learn their interests.

29. _Yes_ _II_ ___ You adopt protective camouflage, moving with the flow of group thinking, not against it, blending with norms to get breathing space.

30. _Yes_ _II_ ___ You have sufficient people skills to manage the difficult people who work with you and still gain their support.

31. _Yes_ _II_ ___ You deliberately network and form alliances outside the organization.

32. _No_ _IV_ ___ You know when to cut your losses and move on.

Keep in mind that political skills are sophisticated ones that spiral and build on themselves and on experience. So wherever you are in your career, you'll always be able to find new levels of political challenge requiring new levels of political skill mastery.

POLITICAL SKILLS AND
YOUR DOOM LOOP QUADRANT

As you looked over the political skills literacy checklist you may have noticed that the skills begin with your own self-awareness. Then they shift—first to organizational awareness, then to issues of effective positioning, trust, and self-protection. This progression gives you a strong political operating base that you can use for development as you move through the quadrants of the Doom Loop.

Each of the political skills on the political skills literacy checklist applies to all quadrants. But some are more critical to one quadrant than another. Let's look at the quadrants and see how these political skills play out.

Political Tactics for Quadrant I (Primarily Items 1 Through 11)

In Quadrant I jobs political skills are vital to your career success. They are essential to success in the other quadrants too, but in Quadrant I they are trickiest. They can make or break your success before you gain a toehold. You are most vulnerable to being blindsided in Quadrant I where skill-building—not working with the nuances of people, places, and personalities—steals your attention. Whenever you enter a Quadrant I culture or tackle Quadrant I projects you face subtle political challenges to:

- rethink your own personal and professional beliefs
- learn the new culture's mythology

- fit the new mythology and become "one of us," not "one of them"
- know how information makes the rounds
- find a mentor

Rethink Your Beliefs

You don't enter an organization as a blank slate. You come in with your own values, assumptions, and expectations. Some will work for you; some won't. To keep politics from derailing you, it's important to recognize and rethink these personal and professional myths.

Sometimes this hurts. Personal mythologies have a sacred quality, especially the ones you got from your parents or the ones that are part of the American dream. These feel integral to who you are. Professional mythologies are no different. Even though we get them later, we pay a high price for them—years spent in the socialization vats of professional schools, internships, and apprenticeships.

But when you're operating on assumptions that turn out to be wrong, you're shooting yourself in the foot, and politics aren't to blame. You put the wrong key in the lock. Go over this list of personal and professional mythologies that trip up the best and brightest. Then add your own favorites.

PERSONAL AND PROFESSIONAL MYTHS THAT CREATE POLITICAL VULNERABILITY

- Hard work pays off.
- Proving competence is what counts.
- Top performance will be rewarded.
- I can't make any mistakes.
- When things go wrong, work harder.
- The company will take care of me.
- A professional identity gives credibility.
- Independence is what wins respect.
- Everyone values objectivity.
- Openness promotes trust and acceptance.

- Everyone should be my friend.
- If I like someone, I can trust him or her.
- If I don't hurt anyone, no one will hurt me.
- Expertise is what it takes to succeed.

When your own myths don't match your organization's realities, what should you do? You can let go of your mismatched myths for the time being (just ice them, don't trash them) or find a new organizational culture that's a better match. Either choice is better than operating under inappropriate assumptions that are sure to disappoint.

What about professional myths? These are more subtle but no less treacherous. There are at least two that you need to be aware of:

- Your professional values will be respected in any workplace.
- Your excellent performance will be rewarded.

When you decided to be a professional you got much more than an education. You got indoctrination in professional values. And many, like individual achievement, autonomy, and independent problem-solving, are admirable—unless they are at odds with your work culture. In the flatter, less layered organizational cultures of recent years, the group—not the individual—takes priority. The lone ranger, expert posture you adopted in college or graduate school could target you for jealousy or disdain in a team-centered work environment. This leads to unwelcome problems that require considerable political mop-up.

Consider the case of Carl Grenell. As a new human resources specialist in a *Fortune* 500 company, he used his computer science expertise to design a system for instantly tracking flex benefits that was a real tour de force. Carl had been an academic whiz kid who earned praise for his single-minded focus and ability to solve problems in record time. But his new work group responded differently from his professors. Even though Carl wasn't known for his sensitivity, he was freezing in the chill of the group.

What Carl failed to realize was that the team had been working on flex benefits for more than six months and had just put a working plan in place. Since Carl was still operating out of an expert achievement model, he didn't reveal his system to the group until he had all the bugs out and it was a *fait accompli*. The group felt no ownership in Carl's technical triumph. To the contrary, they felt he had preempted and one-upped them. Carl had become a threat. Carl, on the other hand, felt unappreciated and excluded. The rift between them widened and worsened until management finally hired an external consultant to clear the air.

How could Carl have avoided this career-stopping confrontation? By taking time to gather information about the work values and operating style of the team before stepping in with his standard "I'll fix the problem" approach. This information would have shown him that he needed to de-emphasize the value he placed on individual achievement and show good faith by sharing his expertise and insights through the team process already in place.

To avoid such damaging political backlash when you are new to a group, you must be willing to identify and then emphasize those parts of your own values that align with your current situation. If the workplace is team-oriented, don't insist on being the little red hen and doing it all yourself. Try putting more collaboration and teamwork into your operating system.

Old expectations and habits can wreak career havoc when your situation changes. If your training or last job emphasized open communication, you may encounter political aftershocks in Quadrant I, where, as a novice, you don't know who you can and can't trust. What you say in good faith to someone you like can be used against you by people playing their own agendas. This often feels like betrayal.

Even achieving excellence can throw you into deep political trouble as a Quadrant I newcomer. Maybe high productivity is more important to you than hobnobbing with the gang after work. But when it comes to achieving success in political climates, doing your personal best isn't everything. Sometimes pursuing excellence just transforms you into the professional equivalent of a blue-collar rate buster. Anything that gives you visibility and negative press before people get to know you dooms you to being an outsider.

When Marianne Kantor stayed late at work to get an edge on organizing her next day's agenda, she missed the office's standing Thursday-night happy hour. When she spent her Saturdays catching up on her expense reports, she missed the office baseball games. Marianne's relentless pursuit of excellence led to high performance payoff. She became the top performer in the sales group within a year of being hired. Too bad that no one greeted her in the corridors, that co-workers interrupted her well-planned presentations, that her boss loaded more and more work on her without an increase in pay or status. Marianne blamed it all on politics. But her relentless dedication to work, and her failure to understand the importance of off-worksite bonding were costly contributing factors.

In Quadrant I, it pays to collect detailed data about performance standards *before* taking off like a wildcat. No matter how anxious you are to prove yourself, it is politically advantageous to match—not exceed—prevailing standards.

Learn the New Culture's Mythology

This is your top political mission. When you take a Quadrant I job, your overriding concern is showing everyone that you have the right stuff. But from a political viewpoint, this is rarely what proving yourself is about. Proving yourself has more to do with your ability to:

- decipher the workplace culture's unwritten rules (everyone eats in the company cafeteria; fast-trackers work on Saturday)
- understand the myths people use to create an identity (we're party animals; we put in long hours; we're a team)
- match what people in the culture look and act like (wire-framed glasses; athletic builds; sports; no family talk; no brown suits)
- figure out what is important in this culture (don't question

authority; never trust Personnel; be loyal to your coworkers; do whatever it takes; test newcomers)

When you enter a new job or organization you're a stranger
in a strange land. The landscape only looks familiar. To fit
in and survive, you're going to have to pass as a native. The
standards you will be judged by may have little to do with
your values, the quality of your work, or your worth. But you
can count on one thing. What you don't know *will* hurt you.

Whatever you do, don't let your guard down too fast. Don't
assume that just because your coworkers dress like you or
have similar ambitions they also share your innermost values.
They only look like clones. Apparent sameness is their protective camouflage. Underestimating differences in the workplace has a high career cost. You may relax only to find
yourself being sabotaged by that friendly "boy or girl next
door" coworker.

From the first day you step into a Quadrant I work environment, see yourself as a cultural exchange student whose
mission is to learn the host country's customs. This makes it
easier for you to use one of the most effective and simplest
political tactics for newcomers—getting help. Asking for help
early, whether you need it or not, decreases your chances of
error and makes you more accessible. You instantly become
part of the group. People have a chance to get to know you
and identify with you. By networking and building relationships before you even get a computer password, you encourage your coworkers to experience ownership in your projects.
They're less likely to sabotage someone they have helped and
are getting to know.

Keep getting their advice. What works in Quadrant I works
in Quadrants II and III as well. Let them take some credit
for your success. By empowering them, you stand a better
chance of making them allies—not enemies.

Become an Insider—*"One of Us"*
Fitting the culture helps your coworkers sort you into the
"us" rather than the "them" stack. Insisting on doing things
your way or establishing your unique individuality often back-

fires in Quadrant I. That is what people do when they don't understand politics. They don't yet realize that being seen as special isn't necessarily what getting ahead at work is about. Behavior that deviates merely hammers home the point that you're different—"not one of us." So no matter how many jobs you've held, your first political task is to discern the unwritten rules that specify "the way we do things around here" and match them.

The principle, simply put, is:

In Quadrant I, clones do better than mavericks— much better.

In Quadrant I, where you are still an unknown commodity, this principle affects your success. So identify every commonality you can find between yourself and your coworkers. Then expand on them. No matter how good you are, you won't be effective unless you're seen as "one of us."

All this conformity makes some people chafe. They believe that looking and acting the part is phony, that they're selling their souls to the company store, that they can't be themselves. But a lot depends on your perspective. American culture has always stressed individualism. This is terrific, but timing is important, too. And Quadrant I is the wrong time to establish your individualism. In Quadrant I it can be a liability. In Quadrant I you earn trust by showing you belong.

You have many choices about how you present yourself. The more your style, behavior, and performance match the norms, the more receptive people will be to you and your work. In Quadrant I, no one yet knows the magnitude or brilliance of your performance. By selectively choosing the parts of yourself you want to make public, you gain control —an edge. Until you are a proven commodity, the closer the perceived fit the more likely you are to be seen as an insider.

Some cultures fit you better than others. When the fit is

good, mastering organizational politics will feel more natural and less Machiavellian. When the fit is poor, you'll feel like the proverbial square peg in a round hole. When the gap between your style and theirs is too great, it's often better to cut your losses early and move on. So assess and choose your environment as carefully as your capstone.

Know How Information Makes the Rounds

You may feel like a sneak and a sleuth, but knowing how information makes the rounds and where it gets blocked, distorted, or amplified gives you real power. The two things you want to avoid are:

- being locked out of the information pipeline
- not knowing how to get your own information into the pipeline

In any new situation, do a communication analysis as soon as you know everyone's name and function. Diagram on a sheet of paper who talks to whom about what under which circumstances. This will take time. Observe who gets copied on memos. Figure out who are the town criers, the gatekeepers, the protectors of the crown, the bottlenecks, the dead ends, the distorters. They'll give you plenty of clues. Don't do anything illegal, immoral, or unethical. Just be a good detective.

Town criers tell all. Once you know who they are you can broadcast news at will. Gatekeepers are more selective: they permit or deny a message's access to organizational rainmakers. You'll want to take some time getting to know them. Protectors of the crown distort information to make top authority look good, so be forewarned. And bottlenecks block or delay news, whereas dead ends prefer to bury it. Since distorters will scramble your messages with incredible skill before gently putting them back into the pipeline, there's high payoff in putting them at the bottom of your communication hierarchy.

Enter your own unique piece of information into the pipeline, then test to see if and when it arrives at all the checkpoints you have identified. When you're in Quadrant I, this exercise is basic to grasping the politics of your work group. As you get a better grasp of the social pecking order, you can use this knowledge of the network better to position your own projects and conduct your own public relations campaign.

Find a Mentor

Mentors may be overrated, but they provide valuable short-cuts to learning the political ropes in Quadrant I. You can master power politics and personalities without a mentor; it just takes longer. But in your search for a mentor, be careful who you pick or allow to pick you. Don't fall for a technically competent recluse or someone sitting at the bottom of the information chain. Search for a guru with political moxie who is willing to share his or her insights. Then proceed with caution. Guard against becoming too closely bonded or identified with your mentor, unless you want your mentor's political fate, for better or worse, to be your own.

Political Tactics for Quadrant II (Primarily Items 12 Through 23)

Once you've made it into Quadrant II, your hidden agenda should be to stay there awhile. As in Quadrant I, there's more to track in Quadrant II than performance. Although you're delighted to be there doing a good job, other people are watching you carefully. Whether you realize it or not, the power and control you gain in a Quadrant II job cause subtle shifts in your roles and relationships. Competition and jealousy may be brewing as close as the office coffeepot. Even though you're one happy camper, you'd better stay alert and protect your turf. While you're plunging full steam ahead, so are your adversaries.

Let's assume you have been able to effect a pretty nice match between your own style and needs and the culture you are working in. You're considered part of the group—an insider. You use the informal information network like broadcast news and can recite the place's unwritten rules in your sleep. Even so, there's more to Quadrant II politics. You'll need to stretch to the next level of Quadrant II mastery by:

- distinguishing what's real from how things appear (What is really rewarded versus what they say is rewarded? What hidden agendas power those pre-meeting meetings? Who is for you and who isn't? Who is trustworthy and who isn't?)
- identifying stakeholders whose interests in your projects coincide or conflict with your own
- developing relationships with gatekeepers, decision-makers, power brokers, and rainmakers, and forming strong alliances
- realigning your own needs to fit the changing needs of the organization

Distinguish What's Real from How Things Appear

This is a lifelong, often painful educational process. There are no quick remedies for our natural propensity to blindly trust the appearance of things. From a psychological viewpoint, trust is healthy—but only when appropriate to the situation. From a political perspective, hidden agendas and outright deception make unexamined trust a costly liability. In Quadrant II, when your career is on track and you are accruing power, you can't afford to be fooled by pretty mirages. Wishing and hoping won't protect you.

Organizations can be misleading about what they reward. If you trust false information, you'll squander your efforts doing the wrong things—which won't help your career. So avoid taking corporate propaganda as gospel. Find the most successful people in the workplace and find out exactly what behavior and accomplishments they were rewarded for. Don't waste time being a good boy or girl doing what management says it wants if no one gets rewarded for doing that. For example, in a Western college, the dean told a newly hired assistant professor that teaching was what counted. But, despite becoming a teaching superstar, the assistant professor was axed when he came up for tenure. The official reason

POLITICS | 369

was that his publication record was below par. In fact, however, his meager number of publications would have presented no problem had he been more visible in the community and local media, had he participated in annual fund-raising, and had he served on more college committees. By taking the dean at his word, this young professor made a classic political error: he failed to research what behaviors the college really did reward with tenure.

Recognize that unless there is a perceived need for your favorite contributions, your work is likely to go unsung. Talk to people who know the ropes and get feedback about the value of your contributions and how to position them. Enlisting their help can convert them into potential allies.

Hidden agendas also make it hard to decipher what's real. They're a dime a dozen, but hard to spot. Smoke them out. Take the approach that everyone has them and that what you don't know will be lethal to your Quadrant II tenure. When people with competing hidden agendas clash, the result is politics at their worst. You could be hurt in the crossfire. So make it your business to discover exactly what these hidden agendas are. Gather evidence unobtrusively. It may not be easy; if these agendas were obvious, they wouldn't be called "hidden." For example, Charlie says he's backing you in your bid for promotion, but the truth is that his lukewarm memo to his boss tells a very different story. The reason? Charlie wants to keep you right where you are, doing his work. Don't let yourself be fooled. Be persistent and perceptive. Unless the stakes are very high, most people leave trails. Hidden agendas can't trip you up too badly when you know when and where to expect them. That lets you plan and protect yourself. It's the unexpected that hurts.

It also helps to be able to distinguish your friends from your enemies. You might think this would be an easy distinction, but where people compete over scarce resources like money, power, and status, it's no small feat. Ask any divorce lawyer. When you mistake an enemy for a friend you feel a profound sense of betrayal. This issue lies at the heart of most people's distrust of politics.

Over and over again, I have found that the most common

and devastating political mistake that my clients make in Quadrants I and II is confusing liking with trust. Remember:

Liking, in and of itself, is an insufficient reason to trust someone.

It helps to think of liking and trust as two separate dimensions. Liking is a reaction you have to being treated pleasantly, being complimented, having favors done for you. Trust, on the other hand, is a serious judgment you make about a person's reliability and honorable intentions based on consistent data and experience gained in the thick of battle. A good rule is:

In all phases of your career, like many more people than you trust.

If you trust as many people as you like, get ready to dodge political bullets. Until people have earned your trust, keep privileged information to yourself or find a confidant outside your workplace who can do you no harm.

Identify Key Stakeholders

Stakeholders by definition are not disinterested, unbiased parties. Stakeholders have a vested interest in controlling outcomes. They have a stake in what happens. Depending on the particular situation, they can be allies or adversaries. In either case, it's usually situational, not personal.

It helps to remember that every project you tackle comes with its own unique set of stakeholders. The trick is to identify them and learn exactly what they have at stake before committing yourself to a course of action. Some stakeholders will want to help you simply because their objectives match yours. Others will oppose you—even if they genuinely like you—because their interests conflict with yours. People with nothing at stake are less likely to get involved in the fray, so trying to persuade them to pitch in and help is often a waste of time.

Once you figure out which stakeholders' interests differ from yours, don't sit back and wait for the inevitable conflicts to surface. Head them off early. Contact your allies, figure out who will help you, and develop a strategy for dealing with those stakeholders most likely to stand in your way. You're going to have to spend time, either at the front or back end of projects, negotiating with people whose self-interests run counter to your own. In the long run, negotiating on the front end is a time-saver. Find people who are comfortable with particular stakeholders, who can put forth your viewpoint in a persuasive way. Where it's not too risky, involve stakeholders in planning. Develop solid skills in conflict resolution. With goodwill, you can usually find a way to satisfy stakeholders' underlying interests and needs as well as your own. By getting them involved in decision-making from the ground up, you also reduce their opposition to your projects. This slows down your burnout rate and keeps you in Quadrant II longer.

Develop Power Relationships

This is a never-ending process that wins you enough support to hang onto your Quadrant II position as long as possible. It's not enough to identify gatekeepers, power brokers, and rainmakers; you need to cultivate them and form alliances. They need to know who you are, see you in a positive way, and buy into the importance of your ideas and projects. There are no secrets to developing relationships with those in power. All it takes is good communication, stressing common interests, being intentional about what you are doing, and getting their input early on. It helps to develop alliances with people who have a broad range of interests, and to include people who work behind the scenes or who can mobilize resources quickly. When it comes to alliances, don't put all your eggs in one basket.

Realign Your Self-Interest

When your self-interest is well served and matches the needs of your employer, you have a built-in buffer against the political undertows of competing interest groups. Management is on your side. People tone down their questioning of your pet projects or motivations. You get encouragement and kudos for doing what you enjoy and are competent at. Good alignment makes good political and career sense.

The problem is that in Quadrant II it's tempting to get so involved in the nitty gritty of daily work life that you begin to drift off course—both with regard to your capstone and with regard to periodically aligning your needs and goals with the organization's. My caveat is: don't get careless. Just because you are in Quadrant II, don't assume you're immune to the political vicissitudes of the workplace. Situations change quickly, and if you're not tracking what's happening you could end up a Quadrant II casualty.

To avoid a political push into Quadrant III, take stock of what you want from your work life and see how that stacks up against your organization's goals and mission. Inventory your career needs (e.g., building new skills, taking a leadership role, gaining more community visibility). See how these align with current workplace values. Let's take a quick look at what you might find.

Suppose you find that neither your own self-interests nor your organization's are being met? Then even though you enjoy your work and are good at it, you have no staying power. Forget about a long tenure in Quadrant II. In the next restructuring you're likely to be out the door. Political enemies will see you as expendable—Quadrant II deadwood. If you can't find a way to realign your interests for a better fit, you have a sure-fire formula for hurtling over the top of the Loop into Quadrant III.

Suppose the organization's interests are met but yours are not? Whether you realize it or not, you've put yourself in a one-down position. Politically speaking, you've given away your power. Although you're still in Quadrant II, you're likely to begin to feel unappreciated and taken advantage of. Other people notice this. They discount you. This undermines your peaceful enjoyment of Quadrant II. If you can't establish a better alignment soon, you might want to cut your losses and move on. Otherwise, Quadrants III and IV are waiting.

What if you're meeting your own needs at the organization's expense? You are an opportunist, a free agent who isn't likely to win the congeniality award for teamwork from your colleagues. But this can be a reasonable situation for you anyway, so long as you keep building target mosaic skills that move you toward your capstone, and remember to watch your back. You have put yourself in a potentially hostile political situation in which enemies could make it hard for you to maintain your gains.

The ideal situation is where your self-interest aligns with your organization's like a solar eclipse. You are on an automatic fast track. Your work and efforts are more likely to be appreciated, and you will attract a bevy of natural allies and supporters. Your politically savvy colleagues will find it expedient to jump on your bandwagon. This is the ideal political Quadrant II position and the only one that makes solid political and career sense.

If you're in a situation in which there are no good alignments, and the trade-offs for fitting this organizational culture are unacceptable to you, it's probably wise to move on even though you are in Quadrant II.

Political Tactics for Quadrants III and IV (Primarily Items 24 Through 32)

These quadrants often call for damage-control tactics. Both Quadrant III and Quadrant IV jobs put you in a weakened, at-risk position. Not enjoying your work and feeling trapped in your job set you up as a tempting target for organizational housecleaning and political power plays. Whether or not you intend to, you flash your disenchantment to the world. Career crises simply intensify all this. What your adversaries are counting on is your having neither the collegial support nor the resilience to fight back. And they're often right.

But sometimes Quadrant III and IV people pursue recreational politics to offset the ennui of their jobs, and they play with a vengeance. For some of them, politics are the only game in town. These burned-out Quadrant III and IV employees become crusty opponents everyone else has to contend with.

Whatever your political predilection, the trick in Quadrants III and IV is to get maximum mileage out of whatever you've already got going for yourself—friends, allies, outstanding political debts, skills, and accomplishments. In the absence of commitment and enthusiasm, use these protective skills as a springboard for setting a strategy that helps you contain damage and regain energy:

- small-wins skills to position your accomplishments
- conflict management skills
- camouflage skills
- people management skills
- networking skills
- transitioning skills

Small-Wins Skills

In any organizational setting it's important to position yourself, to call attention to your accomplishments so that people know what you're doing and how very good you are. Unless you have a press agent or an adoring parent or boss, you have to do most of this positioning yourself, without appearing to be an egotistical braggart. The Quadrant III and IV dilemma is that the less you achieve, the less you have to position. And the worse you feel about your work, the less you feel like positioning anything anyway.

One simple remedy requires that you break down any project you're working on into very small, manageable parts—the smaller and more trivial the better. Then, every time you finish one part, you make a point of matter-of-factly telling your coworkers what you've done. This keeps you visible in an upbeat way. It's politically savvy because it threatens no one while telling everyone you're still breathing and still a real player. Yet, since what you are positioning is such a small accomplishment, no one is likely to take a potshot at you. The benefit to you is that it raises your self-esteem—bit by bit.

Fred Harris was a Quadrant IV insurance agent whose organizational credibility had been dropping all year. No wonder; he spent most of his time hiding in his office avoiding contact with clients and coworkers alike. Using a small-wins approach, Fred broke down the project of finding new leads into a couple of simple first steps—finding out when and where local organizations were meeting, and scouting the newspaper for individual leads. Whenever he found something promising he made a point of stepping outside his office and telling someone that he was following a hot new lead. Even though Fred still wasn't producing any business, his small-wins strategy worked. He became less isolated. Coworkers noticed Fred in a positive way. They began showing an interest in his situation, sharing information and office gossip with him. As he felt more included, he gained energy to follow up on leads. Even though a major career change still loomed in Fred's future, he had recovered considerable political viability.

Conflict Management Skills

These are important political skills for any quadrant, but they're a career saver on the backside of the Doom Loop, when winning is decidedly not everything or the only thing. What you want is support, not adversaries. This subset of skills allows you to hear and acknowledge other people's side of things and reach a common understanding without being unduly bruised or bruising. When your personal power is nil, this basic survival skill helps defang ugly political beasties and gives you breathing space. You won't regret reading a book or taking a course in conflict management.

Camouflage Skills

Sometimes when you're in a Quadrant III or IV position the best tactic is to hide or to duck until you regain the resilience to bail out or fight. Stay out of harm's way by keeping a low profile. For example, stop whining about how bad things are. Forget about being rescued; your complaints merely cause people to note your plight and move away from you.

Try conforming to the unwritten rules and style of your organization until you blend. Avoid letting your appearance or behavior deviate enough to call undue attention to your Quadrant III or IV travail. It also helps if you refuse to make excuses or to be defensive. Because you feel beaten, you may be overreacting to criticism you would shrug off during happier Quadrant II times. Fade until you have regained the energy to make your comeback.

People Management Skills

When it rains it pours. The worse things get in Quadrant III or IV, the greater the synchronicity between bad politics and irascible personalities. Even if you don't have the right stuff to manage political scheming, it helps to fall back on your people management skills to help you cope with difficult personalities. Take a refresher course or read a book on assertiveness. Set limits; let people know you still have self-respect. Not getting hooked by the other person's barbs helps. So does a history of taking care of coworkers and support staff, who often will be glad to watch after your interests when you're down. Having allies in unexpected places at various levels of the organization helps, too. Don't be afraid to ask your allies for their ideas and support.

Networking Skills

When you don't enjoy your work, networking skills may have appeal. Networking can get you out of the office and occasionally out of your situation into a brand-new job. Be visible and accessible: attend organizational events, professional meetings, seminars, and so on. The trick is to network and form new alliances in other parts of your organization and outside it. This gives you support, a political buffer, and a channel for opportunity. It's another form of job protection.

Transitioning Skills

The job is bad and the politics are bad. Not only are you in Quadrant III or IV of the Doom Loop, you are in the strategic career position we called rudderless earlier in this chapter. Why stay? Your best bet may be the ultimate political skill of knowing when to pull up stakes and move on. Transitioning requires a blend of exiting, job search, and self-management skills. Exiting skills involve more than saying good-bye. They may involve negotiating a severance package and outplacement services, arranging for part-time work or office space during your transition, training your replacement, getting solid references from people you trust, and putting an outside support network in place before leaving. It's always a good idea to have an up-to-date résumé and a well-planned job search strategy in advance of leaving. And self-management skills, like managing time and priorities and keeping your spirits up, are essential to a successful transition. But before you leave your Quadrant III or IV job, be sure to do a Doom Loop Quadrant Analysis and read the next section.

WHEN YOU LOVE YOUR
WORK AND HATE YOUR JOB

Christine Wozniak was ready for a career change. She had complained about her job for most of our hour together.

> I hate my job. I want to be rewarded for my efforts, not just results. I can't stand another day of their 'what have you done for me lately' attitude. I don't get any support for my projects. Everyone constantly tells me to slow down. I'm a professional, but I might as well be in a union job. My boss has an ego the size of Texas. The people in the office drive me crazy. They can't do anything by themselves! Everything that happens is based on power struggles I have nothing to do with. I deserve better than this. I want a new career.

She certainly sounded unhappy, but I was unconvinced. I hadn't heard her say anything about being bored or frustrated with her work in speechwriting and public relations. So I asked. We listed the skills her high-power job demanded. She loved writing, liked interviewing her clients, enjoyed investigating the facts, couldn't wait to see a finished publicity piece. Was she good at these skills? Her face brightened and she glowed with pride. "Let me bring you my portfolio next time."

As it turned out, Christine and public relations were a match made in heaven. Christine and her workplace were not. Christine's independent professional style rankled her boss and her coworkers. She didn't socialize, network, or ask for help. She didn't care about office gossip. What she cared about was doing her best and getting recognition for it.

From a subjective viewpoint, Christine felt as if she was in Quadrant IV of the Doom Loop. She felt depressed about work and her self-esteem was plummeting. But a Doom Loop Quadrant Analysis revealed that she was in Quadrant II.

The problem was that Christine's needs and style weren't aligned with those of her workplace. The fit was all wrong, and the already adverse politics of the place were being further agitated by this lack of compatibility. All this made Christine miserable in her Quadrant II job.

Where politics and alignment misfire, your feelings about your work can be deceptive. So before you chuck your job and head for the hills, take this precaution:

• **Do a Doom Loop Quadrant Analysis of the skills and tasks involved in your work. Plot the skills in all their appropriate quadrants and see whether the results reflect your feelings.**

If the results show that you're unhappy in a Quadrant I or II job, think about the context of your work, the people, the personalities, the politics. If you enjoy the skills of your job, if you're becoming more competent, and if the work is meaningful, the context of your workplace is probably what's giving you heartburn.

The remedy is to aggressively seek and find a Quadrant II work environment that gives you a hand-in-glove fit with your self-interest and style, and where the politics are manageable. Remember, the closer the alignment is, the less repugnant the politics will be.

JUGGLING ALL THE BALLS

There are literally no two ways about it. Succeeding in your career means juggling a lot of balls. If you want to keep them all in the air, you can't forget which balls are up there at any given moment. The minute you put your eye on the wrong ball or forget which ones are airborne, gravity guarantees a crash. So it is with careers. Even yours and mine.

The mistake most of us make is in thinking we're tracking only one ball—the ball of performance. Companies collude in perpetuating this myth. But most of us eventually learn that competence alone, or the lack of it, rarely derails careers.

In this book I have stressed the importance of making your own preferences and values central to your career equation. Still, beyond performance and preferences, career success requires your ability and willingness to wend your way through competitive political environments that mix and mismatch personalities, power, and hidden agendas. Unfortunately, many people shun developing political literacy—"the don't go anywhere without it" skill set—and this puts them at a disadvantage.

Taken alone, neither political astuteness, nor competence, nor preference, nor the Doom Loop constitutes the answer. It's their synergy that propels and sustains your success.

The challenge is to keep your attention focused on all these balls without dropping any. This isn't easy, but it is necessary if you want to reach your capstone feeling good about yourself and your work.

You need an easy way to remember to keep yourself focused on what counts in your career. I like the well-known drawing of the chalice and the faces that you see on the next page. This comes from the work of the Gestalt psychologists of the 1940s and has many uses.

When you first look at the drawing you see only the chalice (performance) or only the faces (the contextual factors—politics, preferences, and values). The paradox is that to see both, you must keep shifting your attention back and forth.

That's the lesson, pure and simple. To keep all your "career balls" in focus and in the air, you need to continually switch

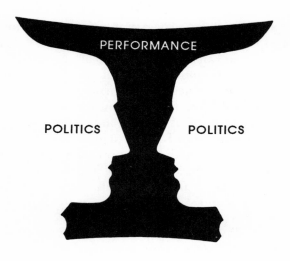

your attention back and forth from chalice to faces, or from performance alone to politics, preferences, and values. If you fix your gaze on only one, you ignore the others and put yourself in jeopardy.

So to take care of yourself in your career, remember:

> • Keep shifting your focus back and forth to inte-
> grate job performance, preferences, and politics
> into your vision of what is important to your ca-
> reer success.

You can't afford to take your eye off any one of them for long. The more you practice, the easier it gets. And the more you'll take control of your career success.

CHAPTER 12

The Doom Loop
in Perspective

> I'm tired of living out my dad's life—stuck in a job
> to bring home a paycheck.
>   —Outplaced executive
>
> I got my MBA to keep my brain engaged. Now how
> do I get someone to use it?
>   —Frustrated technical support adviser
>
> I feel like a good seed that's been planted in bad
> soil. I've never been in situations where I can flour-
> ish.   —Bored flight service manager

People want more from their work lives than a drab nine-
to-five grind. They want to feel engaged in work that has
personal meaning. They want to be recognized, to be a part
of things. Just about everyone would rather have a Quadrant
II than a Quadrant III job.

But if you have pinned your hopes and dreams on succeeding in your career, you need more than just those hopes
and dreams.

You're going to face difficult personal realities. It's hard to
give up a big paycheck even when the big-paycheck job engages only twenty percent of your brainpower. People tell you
to hang onto your dull job because it's safe, the economy is
bad, and good jobs are hard to find. Your family thinks you're
crazy because you're a successful professional and you want
to do something different and risky.

Chances are you'll also have to deal with such distressing workplace issues as hostile takeovers, layoffs, organizational restructuring, the nightmare boss, cutthroat office politics, and other events that diminish your motivation and discourage your personal involvement in your work.

These circumstances often lead bright, capable people to feel disappointed about their careers and themselves. Not only are they disappointed but they also hate the trade-offs they make, the ones that leave them employed but miserable.

If you feel this way, you can take some comfort in being part of a larger trend. Men and women from all walks of life want more than their jobs are offering them. They want more than money and status. They even want more than competence and productivity.

They want to feel good about themselves and their work. They want to balance their careers with family life. They want to wake up and look forward to going to work each morning. In short, they want work that lets them express, not suppress, who they are.

This is a big change from the past. It is, in fact, a workplace revolution. How do you fit into these massive changes that have turned the workplace upside down?

MANAGING THE BRAVE NEW WORLD

Planning a career in the midst of change is tricky business. Simply mastering change's growing vocabulary is a job in itself. Globalization, the mommy track, deployment, telecommuting . . . these new words signify important shifts in the way we see and do things, shifts that require our continuing adaptation and growth.

Change affects everyone's career. Global competition, for instance, is putting new pressure on organizations to abandon their traditional ethnocentricity and accommodate foreign cultures they don't fully understand. This puts the business community in Quadrant I (or IV) as it scrambles to pick up the new skills required to survive in expanding international markets.

On the home front, we're dealing with a progressively diverse work force increasingly made up of the new majority: women, minorities, and foreign-born workers. This rapid demographic change has transformed nearly everyone into a learner. Even the corporate white male has become a stranger in a strange land. Suddenly everyone needs coaching in change-intensive midcareer megaskills.

People's values are shifting, too. They want balance as well as success in their careers. They want fun and happiness in their lives. They want to spend more time with their families, friends, and special interests. Growing emphasis on parent-child relationships is affecting organizational life, giving birth to innovative work forms such as telecommuting, flex-time, and job sharing. These new work forms require new levels of sophisticated skills in self-management and negotiation. The focus is increasingly on Quadrant I learning as you go.

To survive in this topsy-turvy world requires a lifelong commitment to learning and new skill-building. Technological breakthroughs alone require continual skill updating to avoid obsolescence. People are living longer and demanding richer, fuller careers.

It's hard to stay in one place long enough to acquire all the necessary new skills. Job security has all but vanished. With downsizing, takeovers, and early retirement packages as givens, it's time to throw traditional career strategies to the winds.

A single career that lasts a lifetime is history. So are the days of single-minded devotion to a company that would take care of you forever. Finding a job you're good at and rising through the ranks to the top of one company is a career strategy that belongs in a glass case at the Smithsonian.

As organizations struggle with fewer layers of management and greater uncertainty, they're turning to new work structures with decentralized management styles and to more teamwork and self-managing work groups. This means you have to let go of your old ways of seeing things and learn brand-new rules.

And even though the old rules aren't working, it's still hard to know which of the new ones to follow. When it comes to managing our own careers in this period of change, we are in an evolutionary time warp, at the mercy of misleading anachronisms. A lot of career advice springs from past eras —the days of the gold retirement watch or the 1940s postwar expanding economy. So people do what they've always done. They turn to each other for advice, only to find that their friends and relatives know even less than they do.

All this is frustrating. But it doesn't have to be.

THE DOOM LOOP: A PRINCIPLE, NOT A TECHNIQUE

The Doom Loop is a method for the times. It is a user-friendly career management tool that fits the new challenges of the 1990s. It's much more than a matrix with a cute little half-loop showing what will happen if you don't watch out. The Doom Loop is a principle. It's a way to believe in yourself and take responsibility for your own career. It offers you a series of tactics to help you achieve your goals.

It is a change-based, learning-centered method for gaining control of your own career in a world where you're the only one tending the store. The Doom Loop helps you figure out what's important to you. It shows you how to implement your plan in a way that gets you closer and closer to your capstone, regardless of whether or not your company is bought or sold, your mentor falls from grace, you are male or female, or you belong to a minority.

The Doom Loop helps you become a free agent. It encourages you to manage your career as a sensible, entrepreneurial business venture.

The Doom Loop reminds you to respect and prioritize your own preferences and values. You don't have to give up who you are for a paycheck. The Doom Loop helps you combine strategy and tactics with the heart and soul of your own personal mission. This combination enables you to withstand the inevitable daily stress of work life and stay with your plan. Your capstone and target mosaic hold you on track and fit your values and your preferences, not just your abilities.

When you choose a Quadrant I challenge that falls in your

personal comfort zone, change is far less risky and far more satisfying. Growth and challenge that go with the grain of your preferences provoke far less debilitating anxiety than Quadrant IV growth and challenge that run counter to your preferences.

You are in charge of yourself. You don't have to wait to be discovered by some friendly mentor or ideal corporation that will tell you how to live and what to learn. You make the decisions; no one else does. You are a free agent with responsibility for staying informed, believing in your own worth, and taking an active and affirmative stance. You can empower yourself.

You know how to do it. What's left is implementing your plan.

BUT WHAT WILL THEY THINK OF ME?

Careers don't play out in a vacuum. You'll be implementing your Doom Loop strategy in many different workplaces. What will your employers think of your Doom Loop tactics? Will they bristle at your self-directed career management style? Will they view you as an opportunistic job hopper?

I think not.

The leaner, meaner companies of the 1990s need to keep their best and brightest employees. They need to keep them in the company and keep them happy, learning, and growing. They've already eliminated many of their less productive employees through downsizing, golden parachutes, and early retirement. Now the trick is to hang on to who's left.

Traditionally, organizations have done very little to develop their employees according to Doom Loop principles of continual learning and recognizing personal preferences. Instead they have relied on a collective "what have you done for me lately" stance. They rarely promote their people to Quadrant I. They are more likely to promote you based on Quadrant III ability than on Quadrant I potential for learning what *you* want to learn.

But it is becoming clearer that organizations have to be good gardeners. They need to grow their people, provide good soil for good seeds, and periodically transplant workers to new, nutrient-rich soil that gives them exactly what they need to thrive.

Some organizations try—they move their people around via lateral transfers and cross-training. This beats retiring workers in place but still misses the mark.

Management too often waits for good performers to hit Quadrant III or IV. Then they move good old Harry to a new Quadrant IV spot and call it renewal. If Harry perks up, it's not for long. By Doom Loop standards that's not development: it's Chinese water torture. Embracing movement for movement's sake doesn't do a thing for the organization or the employees. No matter how you cut it, you're doing people no favors by transferring them from Quadrant III to Quadrant IV.

But the light is dawning. Managers are beginning to realize that the Peter Principle (moving competent people to a new level at which they will prove themselves incompetent) is not such a good idea. They're starting to understand that the principle behind the Doom Loop—developing people by tapping into their Quadrant I preferences and their capstones —makes better sense.

The sudden "aha" of the 1990s is that the old management cliché "people are our most valuable asset" deserves more than lip service. It deserves action.

Corporations need Doom Loopers.

They need people who are self-starters, motivated by their own career needs, and able and willing to adapt to change. Doom Loopers are exactly what leaner, more decentralized organizations would have invented had they only thought of it.

BECOMING CAREER PARTNERS

Organizations have an implied mandate to become better career partners with their people. This isn't for altruism's sake but for survival in a fast-paced environment. They want—or should want—highly motivated Quadrant I players. You want—or should want—Quadrant I learning that will move you toward your capstone.

It could be a match made in heaven.

Human resources departments have the awesome charge of making this match happen. How do they motivate a work force to achieve more—with fewer resources, less job security, and less opportunity for promotion? It's not easy, especially if their organizations still rely on the old carrot-and-stick approach. But I've found that an increasing number of organizations are embracing career planning and career coaching for their employees, helping people find and achieve what they want for themselves.

Good career partners make it their business to learn their employees' likes and dislikes. If you're a manager, you can use the Doom Loop to help your subordinates become enthusiastic self-starters.

This means sitting down with workers and talking over their hopes, their dreams, their capstones, and their current Doom Loop quadrants. This approach is particularly helpful as the diversity of the work force increases. Organizations that embrace this approach can easily reframe the Doom Loop into employee motivation and competence:

A DOOM LOOP CAREER PARTNERSHIP

	Motivated LIKE	Not Motivated DON'T LIKE
Competent GOOD AT	Satisfied QUADRANT II	Bored QUADRANT III
Not Competent NOT GOOD AT	Challenged QUADRANT I	Miserable QUADRANT IV

- **Quadrant I employees are challenged**—motivated and striving toward competence.
- **Quadrant II employees are satisfied**—both motivated and competent.
- **Quadrant III employees are bored**—competent, but not motivated.
- **Quadrant IV employees are miserable**—neither motivated nor competent.

The Doom Loop provides a framework for organizational responsibility to employees. Organizations need deliberate, well-structured programs to help their people stay on the upside of the Doom Loop. They need to frame and build a Quadrant I-centered culture. When they work closely with their employees to find the right organizational paths for building their Quadrant I target mosaic skills that lead employees to their private capstones, they create a win-win partnership.

And when you become a Doom Looper who is acquiring skills to qualify you for your own private capstone, your motivation and enthusiasm also become an asset to your company.

THE LESSONS OF THE LOOP

Before you put this book back on the shelf, take a few minutes to think over what you've learned that can help you become a better manager of your own career. Grab a sheet of paper. Think over the lessons of the Doom Loop and jot them down.

Everyone will have his or her own list. I'm going to give you mine, a distillation of what the Doom Loop has offered me and my clients:

- Know yourself. Even better, like yourself. You do good things for people you like. Why not include you?
- Refuse to let your career or your life happen to you. You can't change the past, but you can be the chief architect of what happens next.

- Take a free-agent stance. Stay informed, believe in yourself, and take an active and affirmative role on your own behalf.
- See yourself as an entrepreneur whose life savings are on the line. Your business is managing your own career, and your bottom line is Quadrant II capstone success.
- Make lifelong learning a number-one priority. There's a big payoff.
- Even if you don't use it, having a plan helps—so set a five- or eight-year capstone. Or set two.
- Strategy and tactics are useful tools, but to hold your interest over the long haul, integrate the heart and soul of your mission into your strategy.
- Your capstone sets your direction, so if you lose interest in your capstone, change it. The only person who can truly box you into a career you hate is the person you see in the mirror.
- Fight locking into something too early; let yourself be uncomfortable while you gather more data.
- Pay attention to your intuition. When you're unhappy, take time to figure out what's really going on. Tackle politics, tackle Quadrant I. Risk leaving; risk taking action.
- Respect and value your own preferences, not other people's dictates. And don't think your preferences are written in stone. As you are exposed to diverse experiences, you will change. And so will the people you come in contact with.
- Risk leading from your preferences, rather than your proven Quadrant II and III abilities. Sure it's scary, sure you'll feel anxious. But once you begin, it's also fun and satisfying.
- Keep on building skills for your development, even if you aren't sure of your capstone.
- Get used to thinking and dreaming beyond your next capstone.
- Realize that everything you do and have done counts and contributes to your ability to cope. Even if a skill or value isn't in your target mosaic, you've lost nothing by gaining it.

- Don't see longevity in a job as a mark of honor—it's often the mark of a fossil.
- Be aware of and prepared for politics, personality conflicts, and power plays.
- Tune in to the context of your job and what your organization's culture demands.
- Recognize and learn to negotiate the predictable career crises that touch your life.
- Achieve and maintain balance, find a mission, keep fun on a front burner, and stay in Quadrants I and II.

If you agree with the tenets of this book, you need to enlist the aid of the one person who can make all the good things happen—you. Get to know your likes and dislikes, your hopes and dreams, the fears that hold you back. Use this knowledge to select or redefine your capstone. Then, carefully and deliberately, develop your target mosaic. Find jobs, tasks, training, and seminars that corral as many Quadrant I skills as you can learn that lead you toward your capstone. Look for an organization that fits your values and encourages you to learn and develop new skills.

Remember:

You deserve to be in a career that involves and challenges you.

THE REST IS UP TO YOU

For me, writing this book was a Quadrant I job. Like most Quadrant I skill-building, it took a little courage to try something new—even though this was something I wanted to do. It was challenging, overwhelming, scary, confusing, exhilarating, esteem-building, liberating, anxiety-producing. Eventually I got better at most of the required skills. The experience has made me more confident that my next book will be a Quadrant II job.

The action you take is up to you. My advice is to start small and to stay with it.

I'm confident that you'll be able to make a similar jump from Quadrant I to II for the skill sets you want to master. You'll find yourself able to stay on the upside of the Doom Loop, to choose, to learn, to enjoy developing competence in whatever areas make your pulse race. So do it. Begin today.

I've given you a simple two-by-two matrix and all it implies. The rest is up to you.

INDEX

observing contexts of, 148
in quadrant I vs. quadrant IV,
139–42
quadrants and, 120, 122, 127, 131,
134–37, 139–43, 145, 149
and respecting past, 147–48
self-management and, 146–47
setting time limit on stays in, 136–
137
skills and, 126, 128, 132, 134–44,
149
and staying balanced, 145–46
strategy for getting started at,
128–29
what next tactics for, 142–44
first-job selection, 120–27
avoiding common mistakes in,
121–24
classifieds in, 122
college placement offices in, 123
giving in to convenience in, 123
personal approaches to, 123
using competencies in, 120–21,
145
Franchetti, Hal, 345–46
free-agent skills, 285–87
Fuller, Bob, 298–300

Greenberg, Jody, 277–79
Grenell, Carl, 361–62
ground-breakers, 296–97

Harris, Fred, 375
Hunter, Ron, 260

interpersonal skills, 46, 49, 138
intuition, 389
in capstone selection, 33, 49–51
matrix mapping vs., 94–95
in skill evaluation, 88–95
unexpected opportunities and, 236
investigative skills, 286

Jett, Charles, 2–8, 11–12
job skill profiles, 76

Kantor, Marianne, 363
Keefer, Richard, 5–8

Lange, Mindy, 41–43
learning:
being fired and, 188, 191, 202, 206
capstone selection and, 21, 135
and discontent before capstone,

267, 269–70, 272, 278, 282–84,
290–91
and doom at capstone, 294–95,
304–5, 311, 314, 316, 319–20,
328, 330
in Doom Loop dynamics, 95–97,
113
first-career disappointment and,
156, 167, 175–76, 179–81
first jobs and, 127–29, 132, 134–
136, 142, 144, 146
focussing of, 135–36
political skills and, 348, 351, 355–
356, 363–64
in quadrant I job opportunities,
103
target mosaics and, 75–76
unexpected opportunities and,
221–22, 226, 230–33
to use Doom Loop, 11–14
Licata, John, 50–51

management consulting jobs, 2–5
management skills, 46
marketing skills, 286
matrix mapping:
in career change, 6–8
in Doom Looping, 93–95, 106–7
in evaluating job opportunities,
106–7, 116, 214
first-career disappointment and,
170, 181
intuition vs., 94–95
plotting skills in, 3–5, 90–94,
106–7
political skills and, 344–45
preference/performance, 85–90,
95–96
quadrants in, *see* quadrants
Medden, Martha, 185–88
megaskills:
and discontent before capstone,
287–91
and doom at capstone, 295, 329
mentors:
being fired and, 185–88, 198,
201–4, 206, 210, 212
capstone selection and, 40
and discontent before capstone,
290
first-career disappointment and,
165, 175–76
political skills and, 347–48, 367
unexpected opportunities and,
230, 235, 243

If you would like further information on career management seminars, organizational consulting services or training products related to the Doom Loop, please call:

1-800-925-9675

or write to:

**New Options, Inc.
501 North Lindbergh Boulevard
St. Louis, Missouri 63141**